image comics presents

THE WALKING DEAD
™

ROBERT KIRKMAN
CREATOR, WRITER

CHARLIE ADLARD
PENCILER, INKER

CLIFF RATHBURN
GRAY TONES

RUS WOOTON
LETTERER

CHARLIE ADLARD
&
CLIFF RATHBURN
COVER

SKYBOUND

For SKYBOUND ENTERTAINMENT

Robert Kirkman - CEO
J.J. Didde - President
Sina Grace - Editorial Director
Shawn Kirkham - Director of Business Development
Tim Daniel - Digital Content Manager
Chad Manion - Assistant to Mr. Grace
Sydney Pennington - Assistant to Mr. Kirkham
Feldman Public Relations LA - Public Relations

FOR INTERNATIONAL RIGHTS INQUIRIES,
PLEASE CONTACT SK@SKYBOUND.COM
WWW.SKYBOUND.COM

image

IMAGE COMICS, INC.
Robert Kirkman - chief operating officer
Erik Larsen - chief financial officer
Todd McFarlane - president
Marc Silvestri - chief executive officer
Jim Valentino - vice-president

Eric Stephenson - publisher
Todd Martinez - sales & licensing coordinator
Jennifer de Guzman - pr & marketing director
Branwyn Bigglestone - accounts manager
Emily Miller - administrative assistant
Jamie Parreno - marketing assistant
Sarah deLaine - events coordinator
Kevin Yuen - digital rights coordinator
Tyler Shainline - production manager
Drew Gill - art director
Jonathan Chan - senior production artist
Monica Garcia - production artist
Vincent Kukua - production artist
Jana Cook - production artist
www.imagecomics.com

THE WALKING DEAD, VOL. 6: THIS SORROWFUL LIFE. Fifth Printing. Published by Image Comics, Inc.
Office of publication: 2134 Allston Way, 2nd Floor, Berkeley, California 94704. Copyright © 2012 Robert Kirkman,
LLC. All rights reserved. Originally published in single magazine format as THE WALKING DEAD #31-36.
THE WALKING DEAD™ (including all prominent characters featured in this issue), its logo and all character
likenesses are trademarks of Robert Kirkman, LLC, unless otherwise noted. Image Comics® is a trademark of
Image Comics, Inc. All rights reserved. No part of this publication may be reproduced or transmitted, in any form
or by any means (except for short excerpts for review purposes) without the express written permission of Image
Comics, Inc. All names, characters, events and locales in this publication are entirely fictional. Any resemblance
to actual persons (living and/or dead), events or places, without satiric intent, is coincidental. For information
regarding the CPSIA on this printed material call: 203-595-3636 and provide reference # RICH – 433829

PRINTED IN USA

ISBN: 978-1-58240-684-8

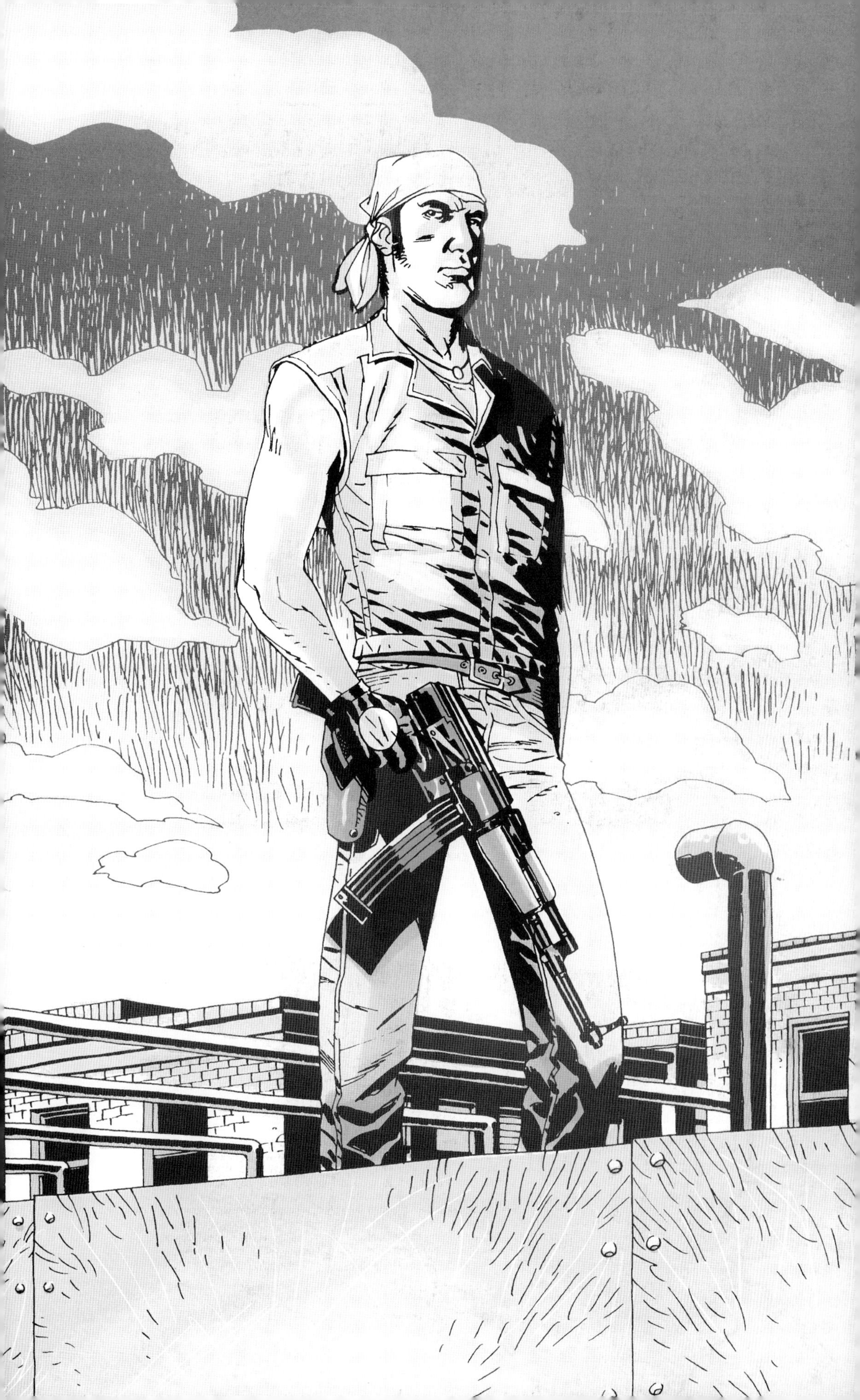

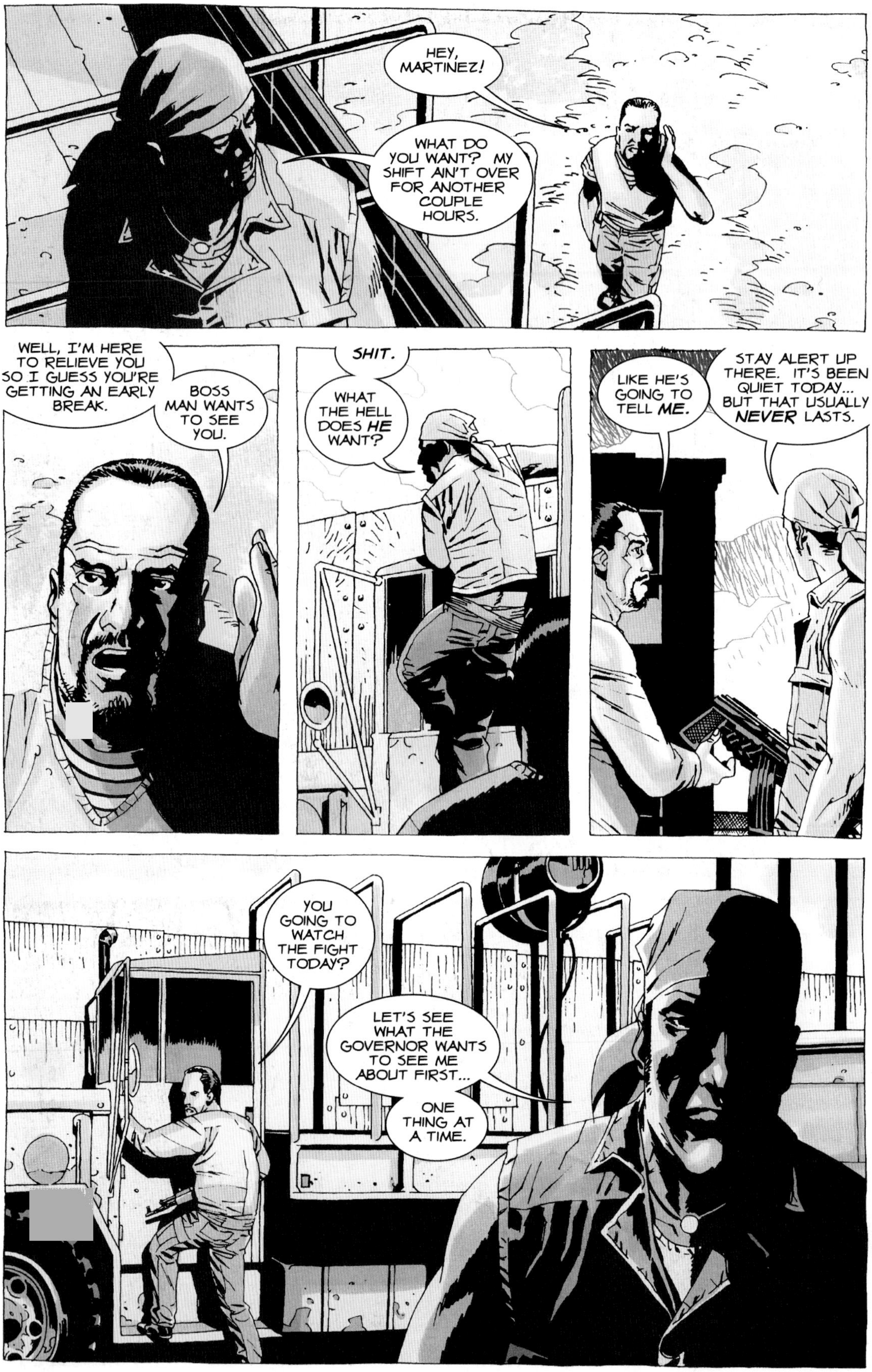
HEY, MARTINEZ!
WHAT DO YOU WANT? MY SHIFT AIN'T OVER FOR ANOTHER COUPLE HOURS.
WELL, I'M HERE TO RELIEVE YOU SO I GUESS YOU'RE GETTING AN EARLY BREAK.
BOSS MAN WANTS TO SEE YOU.
SHIT.
WHAT THE HELL DOES HE WANT?
LIKE HE'S GOING TO TELL ME.
STAY ALERT UP THERE. IT'S BEEN QUIET TODAY... BUT THAT USUALLY NEVER LASTS.
YOU GOING TO WATCH THE FIGHT TODAY?
LET'S SEE WHAT THE GOVERNOR WANTS TO SEE ME ABOUT FIRST...
ONE THING AT A TIME.

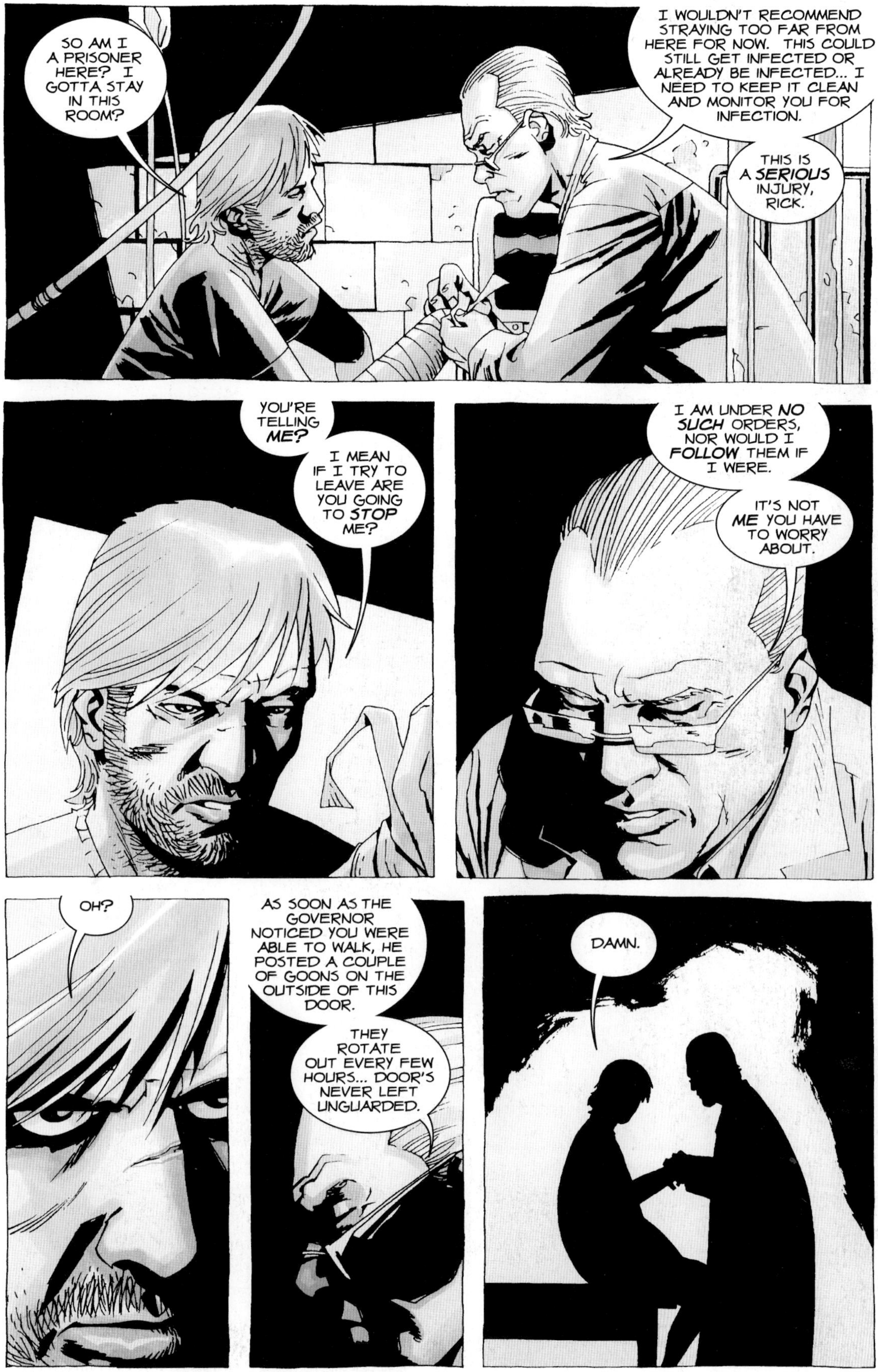
SO AM I A PRISONER HERE? I GOTTA STAY IN THIS ROOM?
I WOULDN'T RECOMMEND STRAYING TOO FAR FROM HERE FOR NOW. THIS COULD STILL GET INFECTED OR ALREADY BE INFECTED... I NEED TO KEEP IT CLEAN AND MONITOR YOU FOR INFECTION.
THIS IS A SERIOUS INJURY, RICK.
YOU'RE TELLING ME?
I MEAN IF I TRY TO LEAVE ARE YOU GOING TO STOP ME?
I AM UNDER NO SUCH ORDERS, NOR WOULD I FOLLOW THEM IF I WERE.
IT'S NOT ME YOU HAVE TO WORRY ABOUT.
OH?
AS SOON AS THE GOVERNOR NOTICED YOU WERE ABLE TO WALK, HE POSTED A COUPLE OF GOONS ON THE OUTSIDE OF THIS DOOR.
THEY ROTATE OUT EVERY FEW HOURS... DOOR'S NEVER LEFT UNGUARDED.
DAMN.

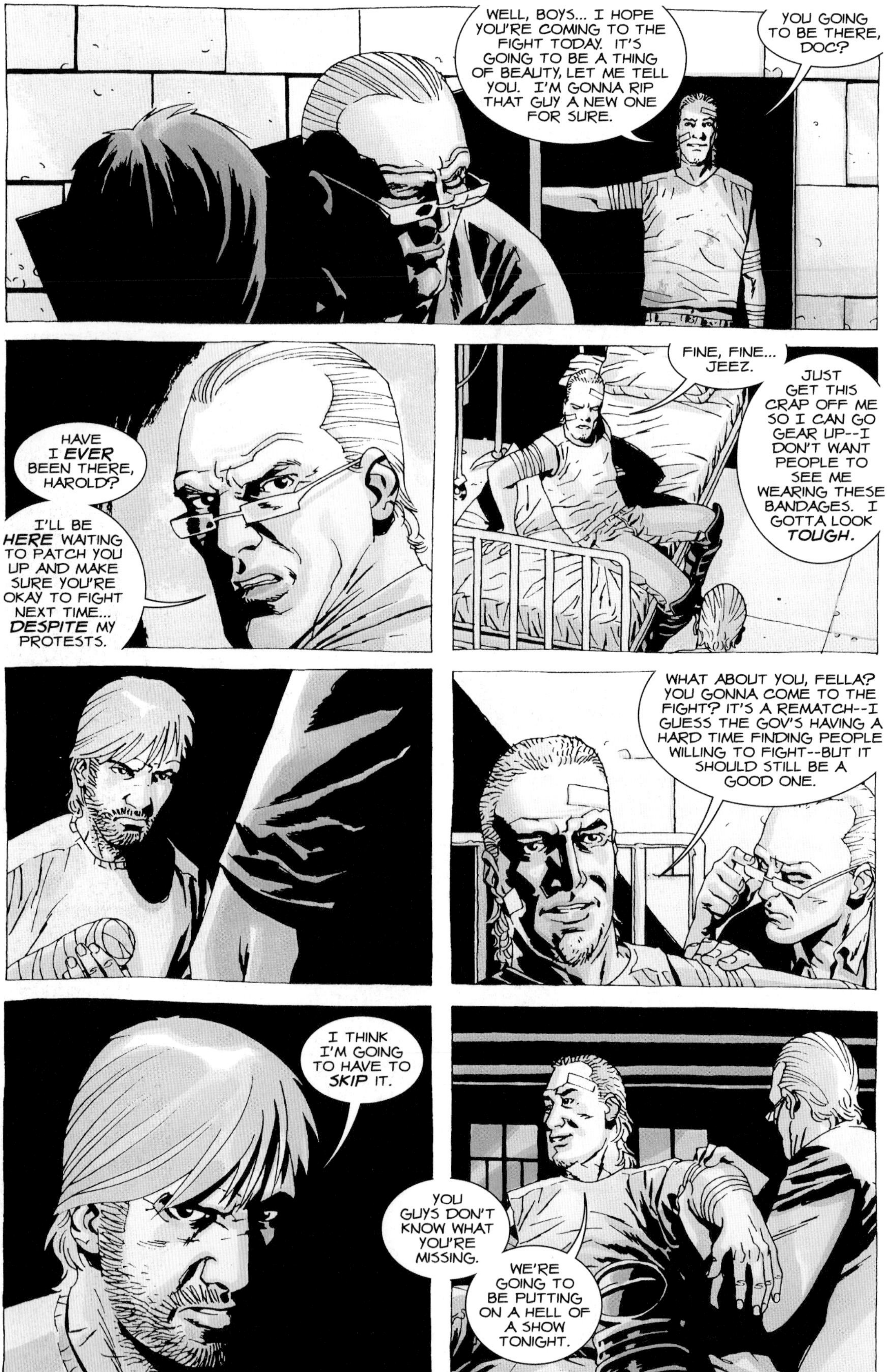
WELL, BOYS... I HOPE YOU'RE COMING TO THE FIGHT TODAY. IT'S GOING TO BE A THING OF BEAUTY, LET ME TELL YOU. I'M GONNA RIP THAT GUY A NEW ONE FOR SURE.
YOU GOING TO BE THERE, DOC?
HAVE I EVER BEEN THERE, HAROLD?
I'LL BE HERE WAITING TO PATCH YOU UP AND MAKE SURE YOU'RE OKAY TO FIGHT NEXT TIME... DESPITE MY PROTESTS.
FINE, FINE... JEEZ.
JUST GET THIS CRAP OFF ME SO I CAN GO GEAR UP--I DON'T WANT PEOPLE TO SEE ME WEARING THESE BANDAGES. I GOTTA LOOK TOUGH.
WHAT ABOUT YOU, FELLA? YOU GONNA COME TO THE FIGHT? IT'S A REMATCH--I GUESS THE GOV'S HAVING A HARD TIME FINDING PEOPLE WILLING TO FIGHT--BUT IT SHOULD STILL BE A GOOD ONE.
I THINK I'M GOING TO HAVE TO SKIP IT.
YOU GUYS DON'T KNOW WHAT YOU'RE MISSING.
WE'RE GOING TO BE PUTTING ON A HELL OF A SHOW TONIGHT.

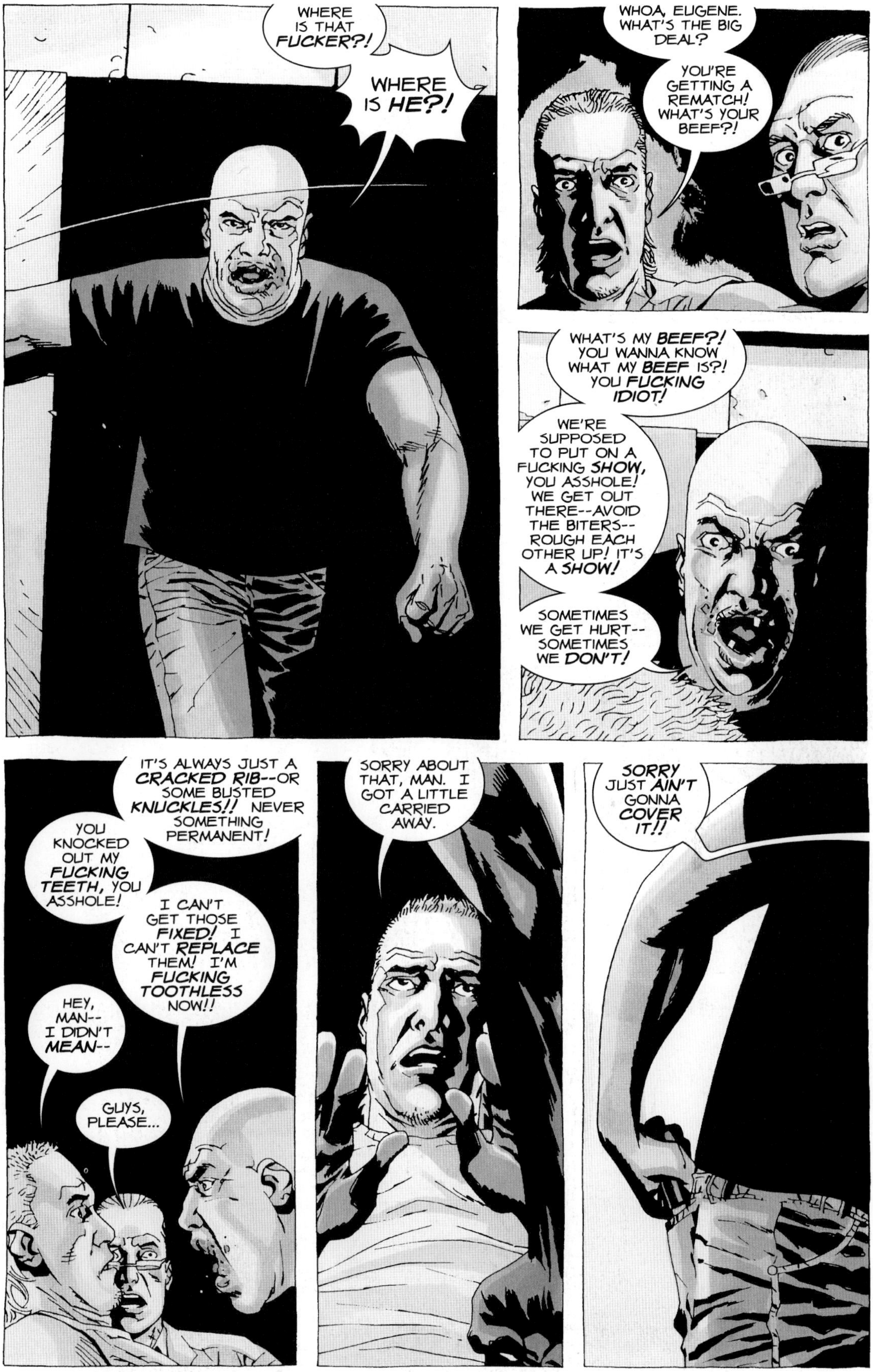
WHERE IS THAT FUCKER?!
WHERE IS HE?!
WHOA, EUGENE. WHAT'S THE BIG DEAL?
YOU'RE GETTING A REMATCH! WHAT'S YOUR BEEF?!
WHAT'S MY BEEF?! YOU WANNA KNOW WHAT MY BEEF IS?! YOU FUCKING IDIOT!
WE'RE SUPPOSED TO PUT ON A FUCKING SHOW, YOU ASSHOLE! WE GET OUT THERE--AVOID THE BITERS--ROUGH EACH OTHER UP! IT'S A SHOW!
SOMETIMES WE GET HURT--SOMETIMES WE DON'T!
IT'S ALWAYS JUST A CRACKED RIB--OR SOME BUSTED KNUCKLES!! NEVER SOMETHING PERMANENT!
YOU KNOCKED OUT MY FUCKING TEETH, YOU ASSHOLE!
I CAN'T GET THOSE FIXED! I CAN'T REPLACE THEM! I'M FUCKING TOOTHLESS NOW!!
HEY, MAN-- I DIDN'T MEAN--
GUYS, PLEASE...
SORRY ABOUT THAT, MAN. I GOT A LITTLE CARRIED AWAY.
SORRY JUST AIN'T GONNA COVER IT!!

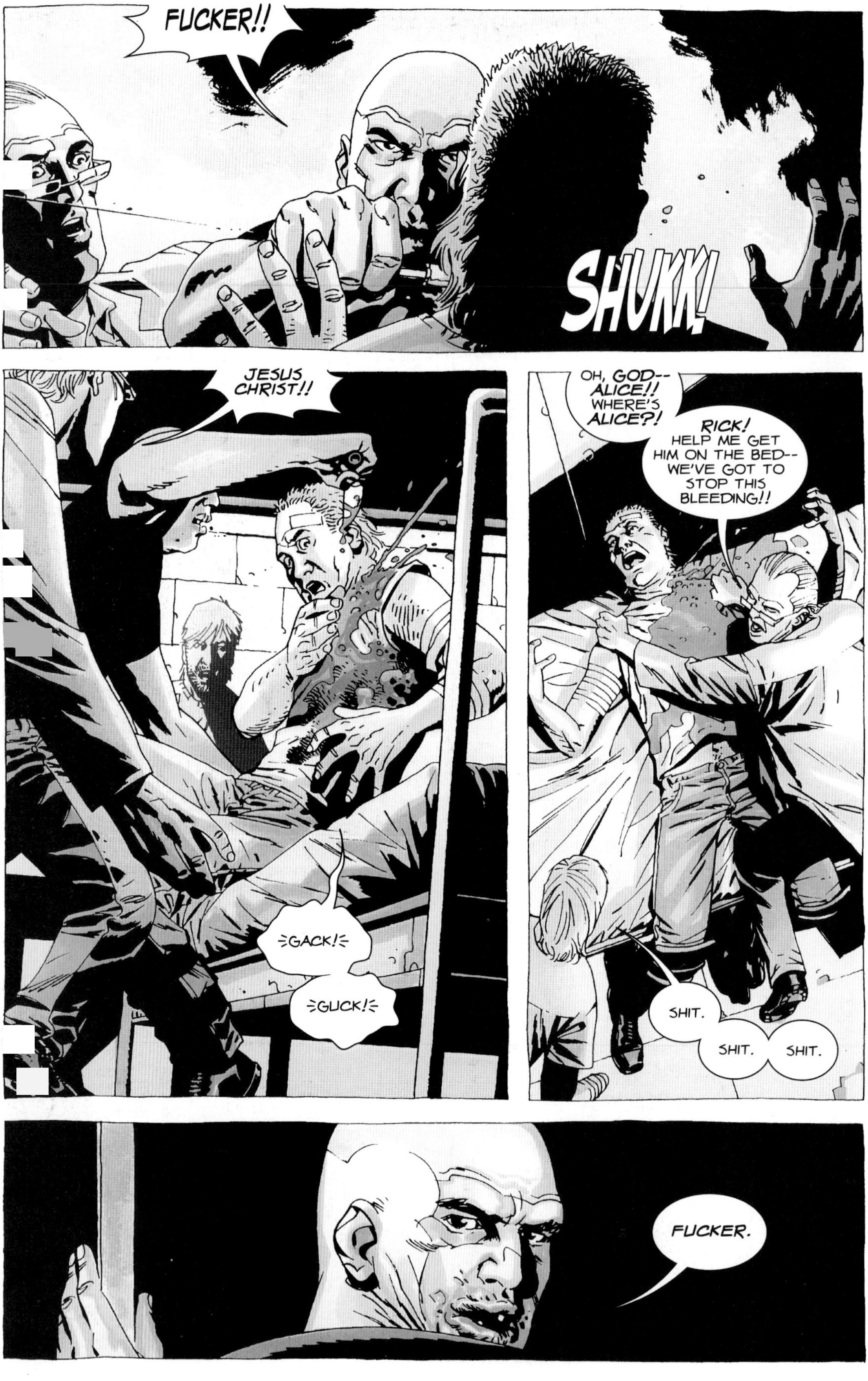
FUCKER!!
SHUKK!
JESUS CHRIST!!
GACK!
GUCK!
OH, GOD-- ALICE!! WHERE'S ALICE?!
RICK! HELP ME GET HIM ON THE BED-- WE'VE GOT TO STOP THIS BLEEDING!!
SHIT.
SHIT.
SHIT.
FUCKER.

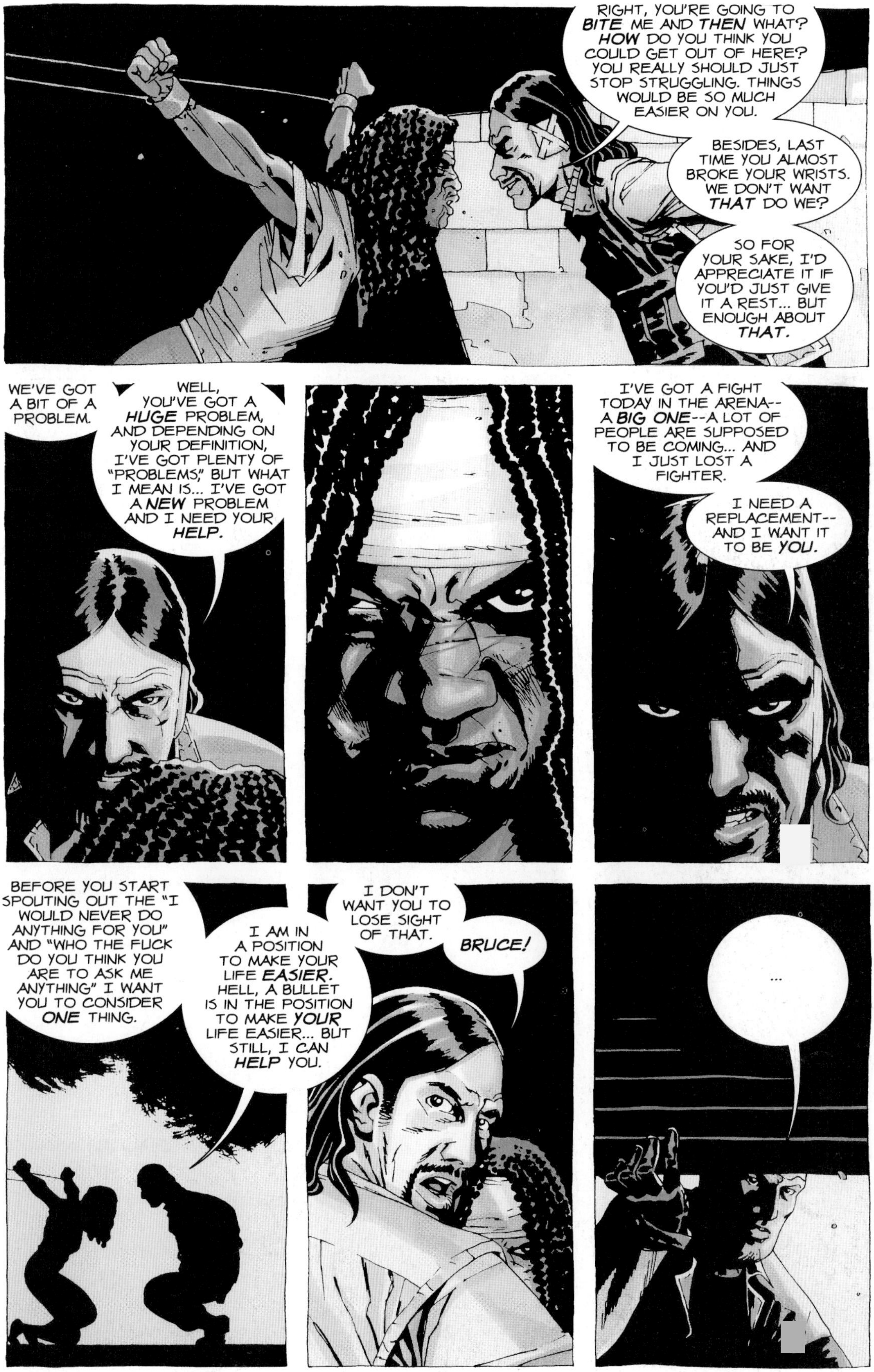
RIGHT, YOU'RE GOING TO BITE ME AND THEN WHAT? HOW DO YOU THINK YOU COULD GET OUT OF HERE? YOU REALLY SHOULD JUST STOP STRUGGLING. THINGS WOULD BE SO MUCH EASIER ON YOU.
BESIDES, LAST TIME YOU ALMOST BROKE YOUR WRISTS. WE DON'T WANT THAT DO WE?
SO FOR YOUR SAKE, I'D APPRECIATE IT IF YOU'D JUST GIVE IT A REST... BUT ENOUGH ABOUT THAT.
WE'VE GOT A BIT OF A PROBLEM.
WELL, YOU'VE GOT A HUGE PROBLEM, AND DEPENDING ON YOUR DEFINITION, I'VE GOT PLENTY OF "PROBLEMS," BUT WHAT I MEAN IS... I'VE GOT A NEW PROBLEM AND I NEED YOUR HELP.
I'VE GOT A FIGHT TODAY IN THE ARENA-- A BIG ONE--A LOT OF PEOPLE ARE SUPPOSED TO BE COMING... AND I JUST LOST A FIGHTER.
I NEED A REPLACEMENT-- AND I WANT IT TO BE YOU.
BEFORE YOU START SPOUTING OUT THE "I WOULD NEVER DO ANYTHING FOR YOU" AND "WHO THE FUCK DO YOU THINK YOU ARE TO ASK ME ANYTHING" I WANT YOU TO CONSIDER ONE THING.
I AM IN A POSITION TO MAKE YOUR LIFE EASIER. HELL, A BULLET IS IN THE POSITION TO MAKE YOUR LIFE EASIER... BUT STILL, I CAN HELP YOU.
I DON'T WANT YOU TO LOSE SIGHT OF THAT.
BRUCE!
...

I WOULD LIKE TO GIVE *THIS* TO YOU. I'M SURE YOU'D LIKE TO HAVE THIS ALSO.

YOU'RE GOING TO BE FIGHTING A MAN, TO THE CROWD, WELL, YOU'RE GOING TO NEED TO APPEAR TO HAVE THE *ADVANTAGE*. PEOPLE DON'T LIKE WATCHING GUYS BEAT THE SHIT OUT OF GIRLS.

I KNOW. I DON'T REALLY GET IT EITHER.

IF YOU'RE COMING AT HIM WITH A *SWORD*, IT'LL BE OKAY FOR HIM TO CLIP YOU A GOOD ONE WITH A BASEBALL BAT.

IN RETURN, YOU GET A FULL WEEK OF REST, AND FOOD, AND MAYBE EVEN A CHAIR OR A BED, I'LL HAVE TO LOOK INTO IT.

TO BE HONEST, OUR LITTLE RELATIONSHIP HAS BEEN PRETTY EXHAUSTING. I *NEED* A BREAK.

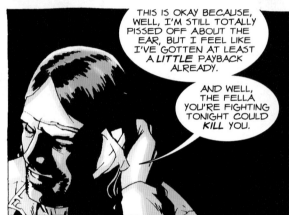

THIS IS OKAY BECAUSE, WELL, I'M STILL TOTALLY PISSED OFF ABOUT THE EAR, BUT I FEEL LIKE I'VE GOTTEN AT LEAST A *LITTLE* PAYBACK ALREADY.

AND WELL, THE FELLA YOU'RE FIGHTING TONIGHT COULD *KILL* YOU.

OH, AND I *DON'T* WANT YOU TO KILL THIS GUY. THAT'S THE SECRET WE DON'T REALLY TELL PEOPLE... OUR LITTLE ARENA FIGHTS ARE MORE THAN A LITTLE STAGED. THE DANGER WITH THE *BITERS* IS THERE-- SURE, BUT YOU'RE REALLY NOT *SUPPOSED* TO HURT YOUR OPPONENT *TOO* MUCH.

A FEW GASHES HERE AND THERE, SURE, WE CAN HANDLE THAT... BUT NOTHING MORE...

OR THE DEAL IS OFF.

YOU DON'T HAVE TO DECIDE NOW.

YOU'VE GOT *TWENTY* MINUTES.

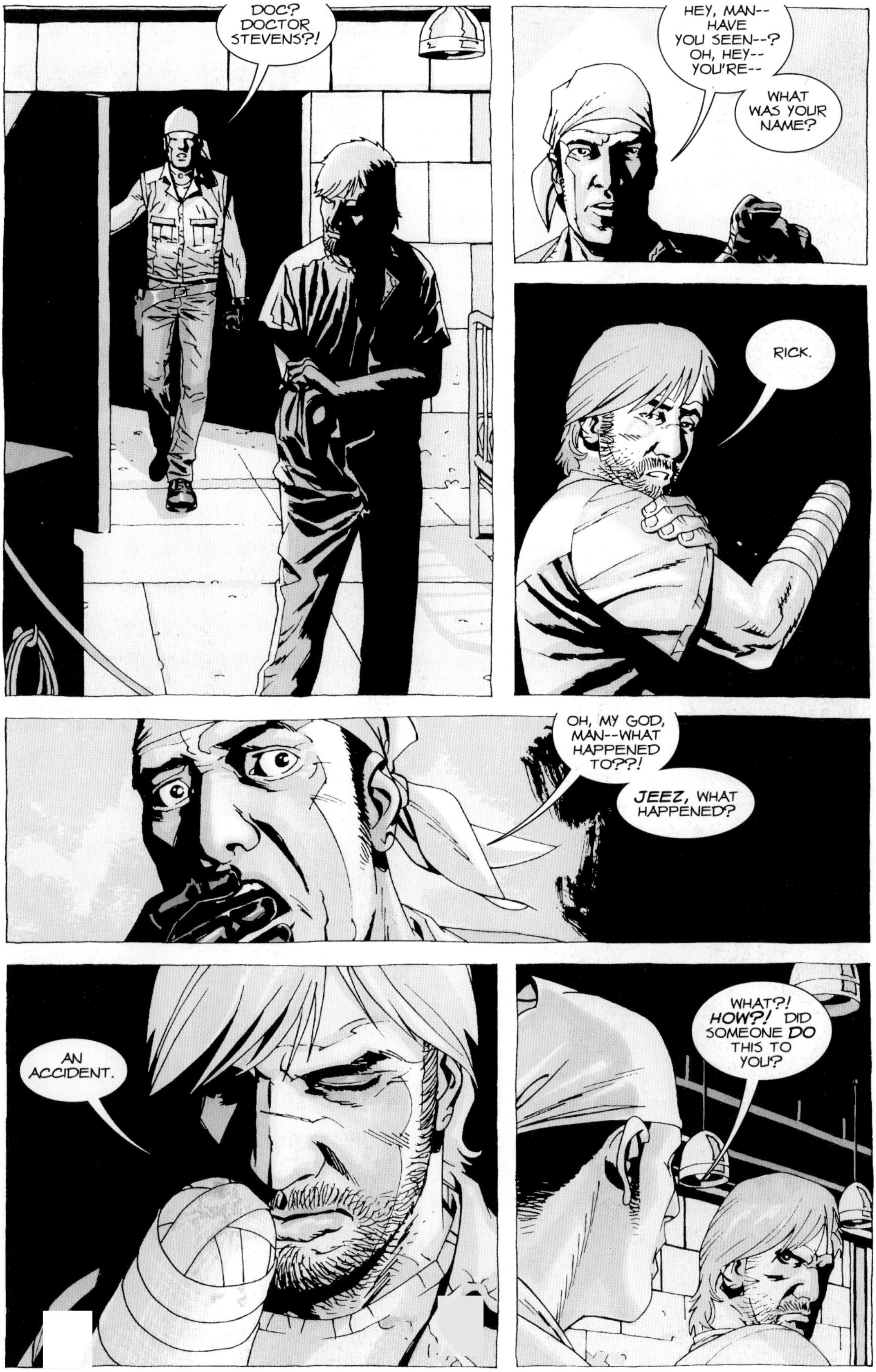
DOC? DOCTOR STEVENS?!
HEY, MAN-- HAVE YOU SEEN--? OH, HEY-- YOU'RE--
WHAT WAS YOUR NAME?
RICK.
OH, MY GOD, MAN--WHAT HAPPENED TO??!
JEEZ, WHAT HAPPENED?
AN ACCIDENT.
WHAT?! HOW?! DID SOMEONE DO THIS TO YOU?

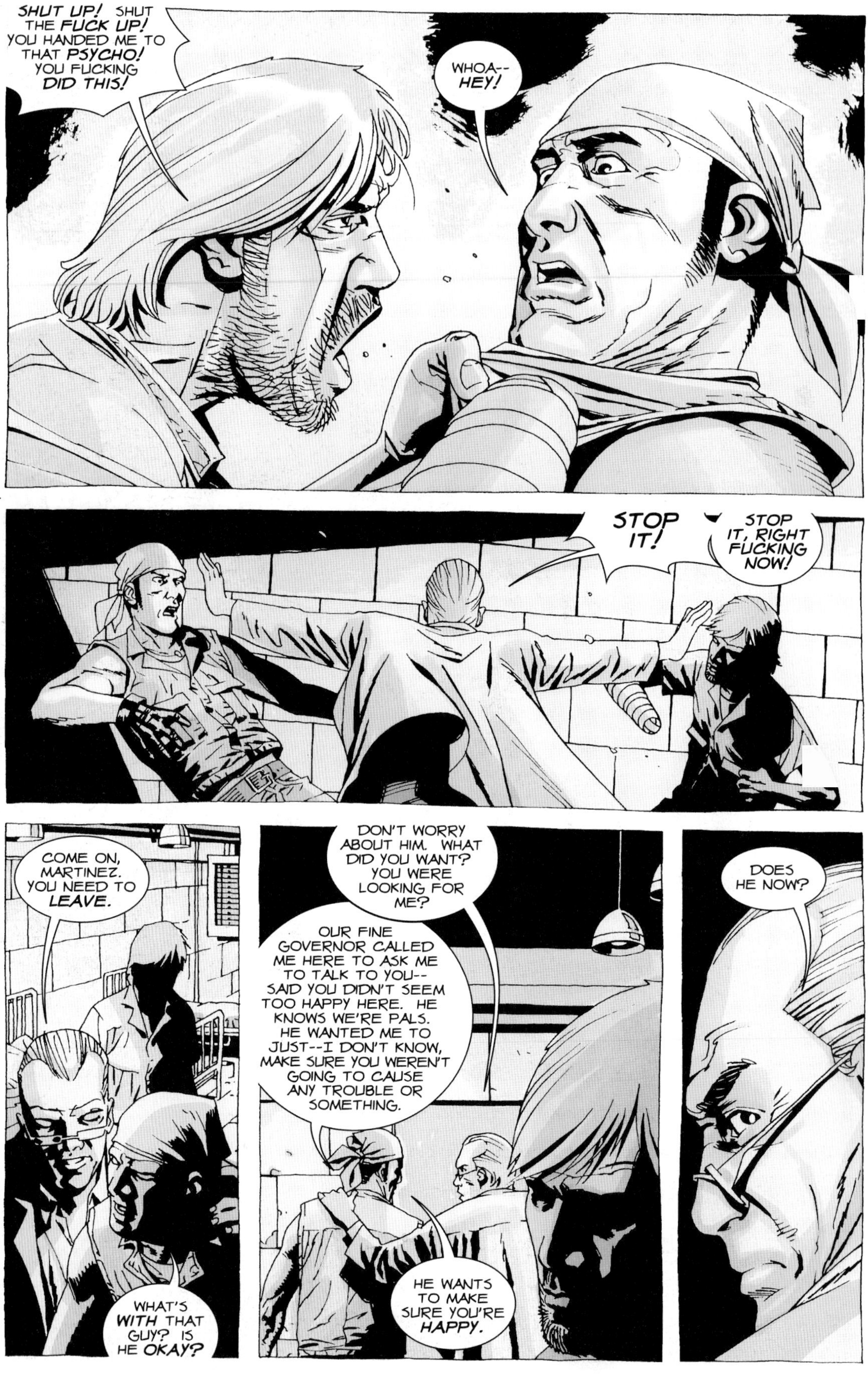
SHUT UP! SHUT THE FUCK UP! YOU HANDED ME TO THAT PSYCHO! YOU FUCKING DID THIS!
WHOA-- HEY!
STOP IT!
STOP IT, RIGHT FUCKING NOW!
COME ON, MARTINEZ. YOU NEED TO LEAVE.
WHAT'S WITH THAT GUY? IS HE OKAY?
DON'T WORRY ABOUT HIM. WHAT DID YOU WANT? YOU WERE LOOKING FOR ME?
OUR FINE GOVERNOR CALLED ME HERE TO ASK ME TO TALK TO YOU-- SAID YOU DIDN'T SEEM TOO HAPPY HERE. HE KNOWS WE'RE PALS. HE WANTED ME TO JUST--I DON'T KNOW, MAKE SURE YOU WEREN'T GOING TO CAUSE ANY TROUBLE OR SOMETHING.
HE WANTS TO MAKE SURE YOU'RE HAPPY.
DOES HE NOW?

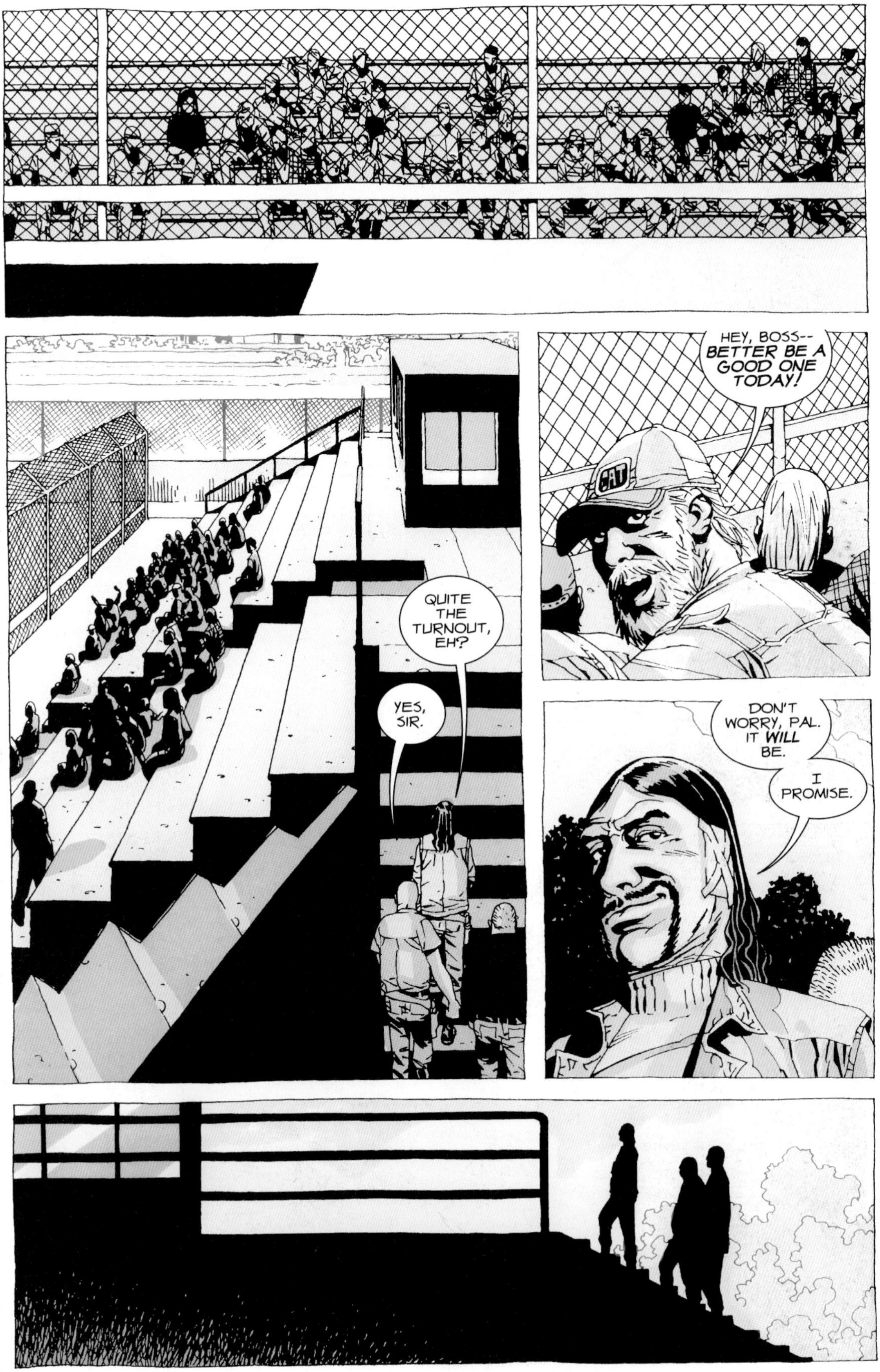
QUITE THE TURNOUT, EH?
YES, SIR.
HEY, BOSS-- BETTER BE A GOOD ONE TODAY!
DON'T WORRY, PAL. IT WILL BE.
I PROMISE.

YOU SURE ABOUT THIS, BOSS?

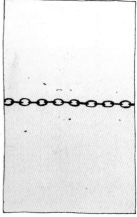

THIS IS GOING TO BE GOOD.

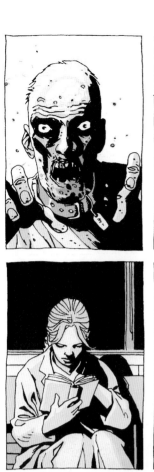

THE CHANCE TO SEE THIS BITCH TAKE A BEATING WITHOUT *ME* BREAKING A SWEAT?

YEAH-- I THINK IT'S A GOOD MOVE.

HERE WE GO.

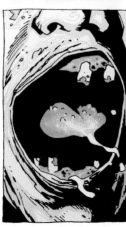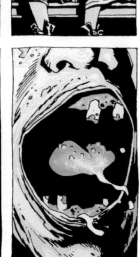

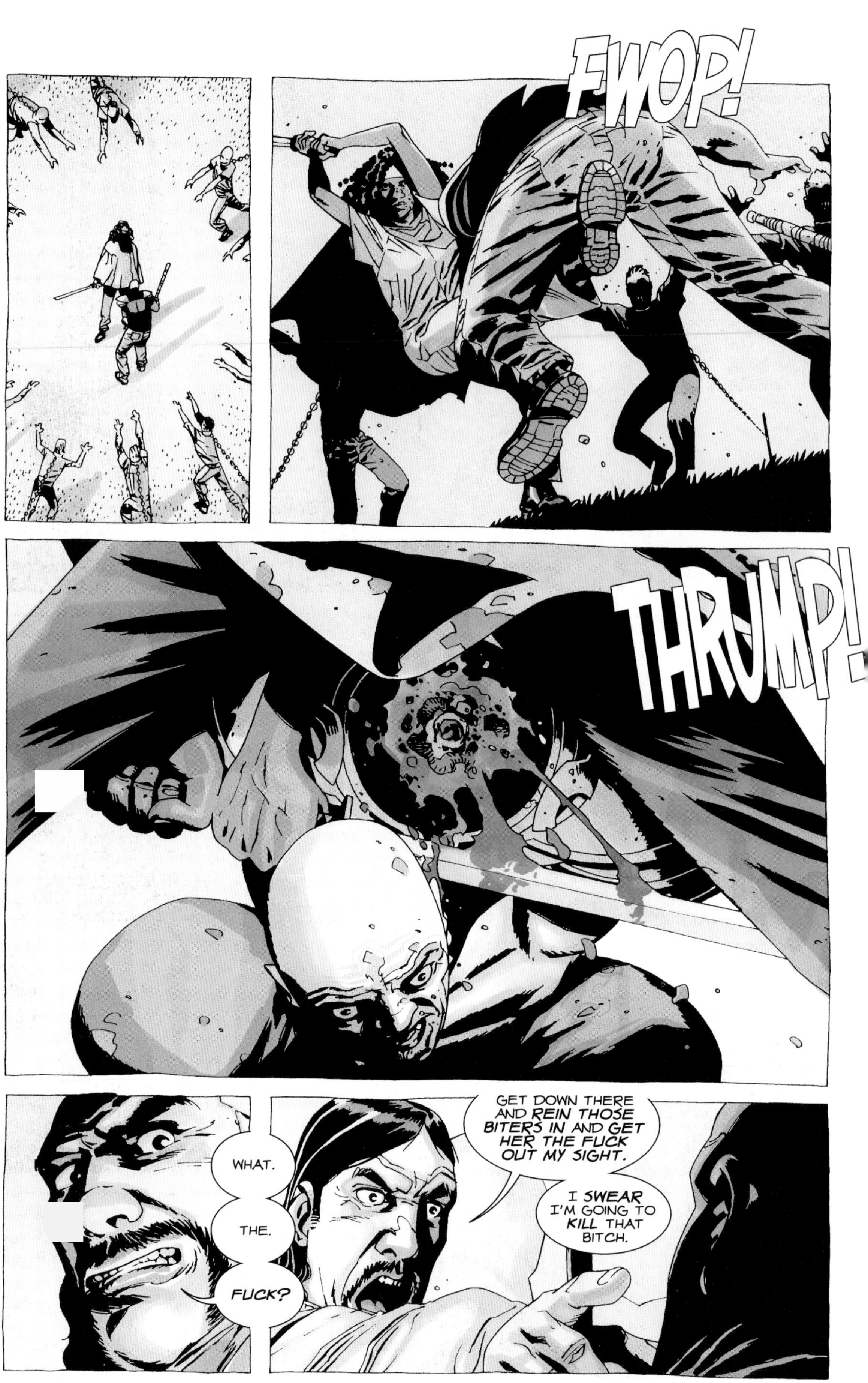

FWOP!
THRUMP!
WHAT.
THE.
FUCK?
GET DOWN THERE AND REIN THOSE BITERS IN AND GET HER THE FUCK OUT MY SIGHT.
I SWEAR I'M GOING TO KILL THAT BITCH.

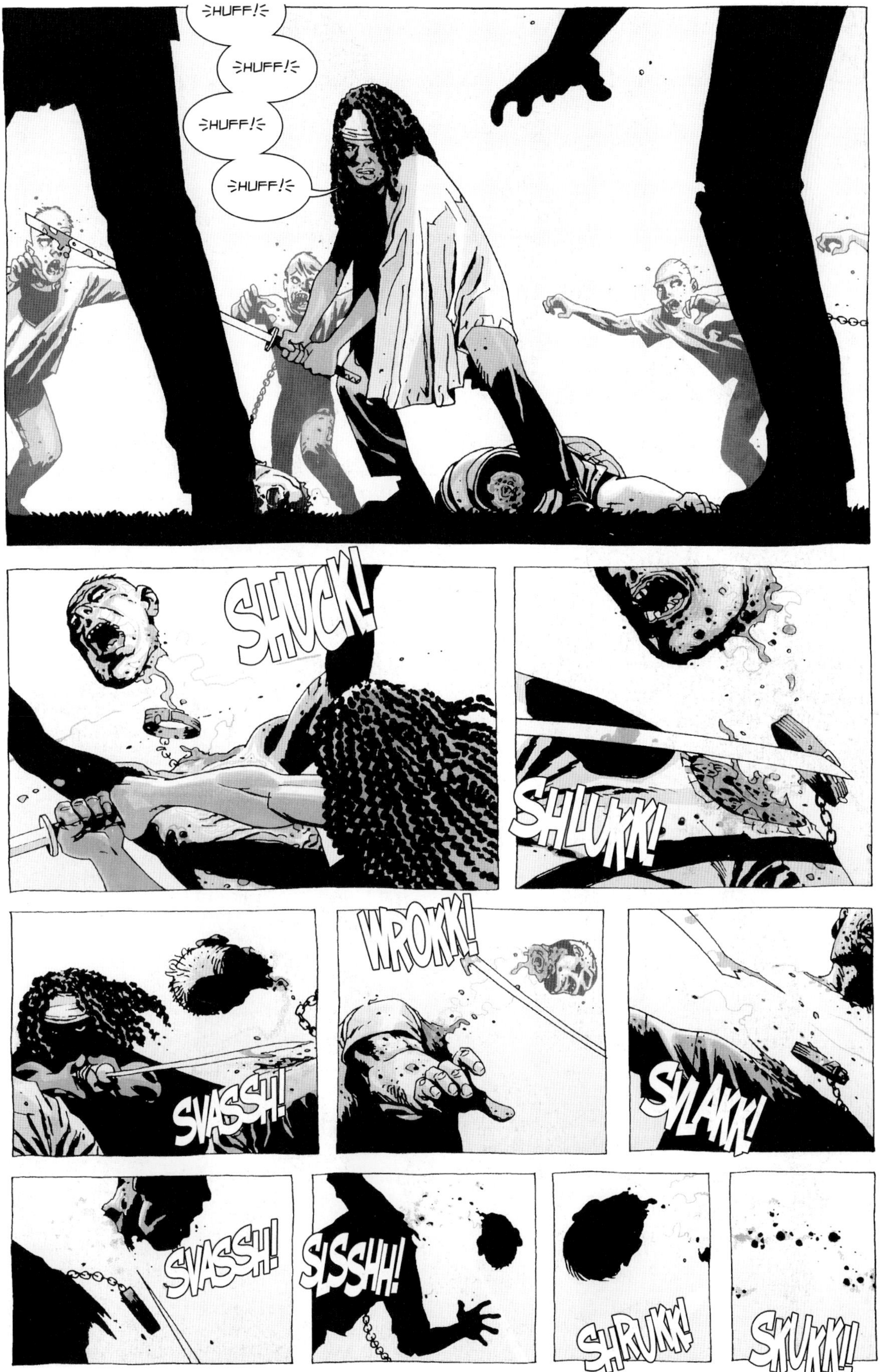

HUFF!
HUFF!
HUFF!
HUFF!
SHUCK!
SHLUKK!
SVASSH!
WROKK!
SVLAKK!
SVASSH!
SLSSHH!
SHRUKK!
SKUKK!!

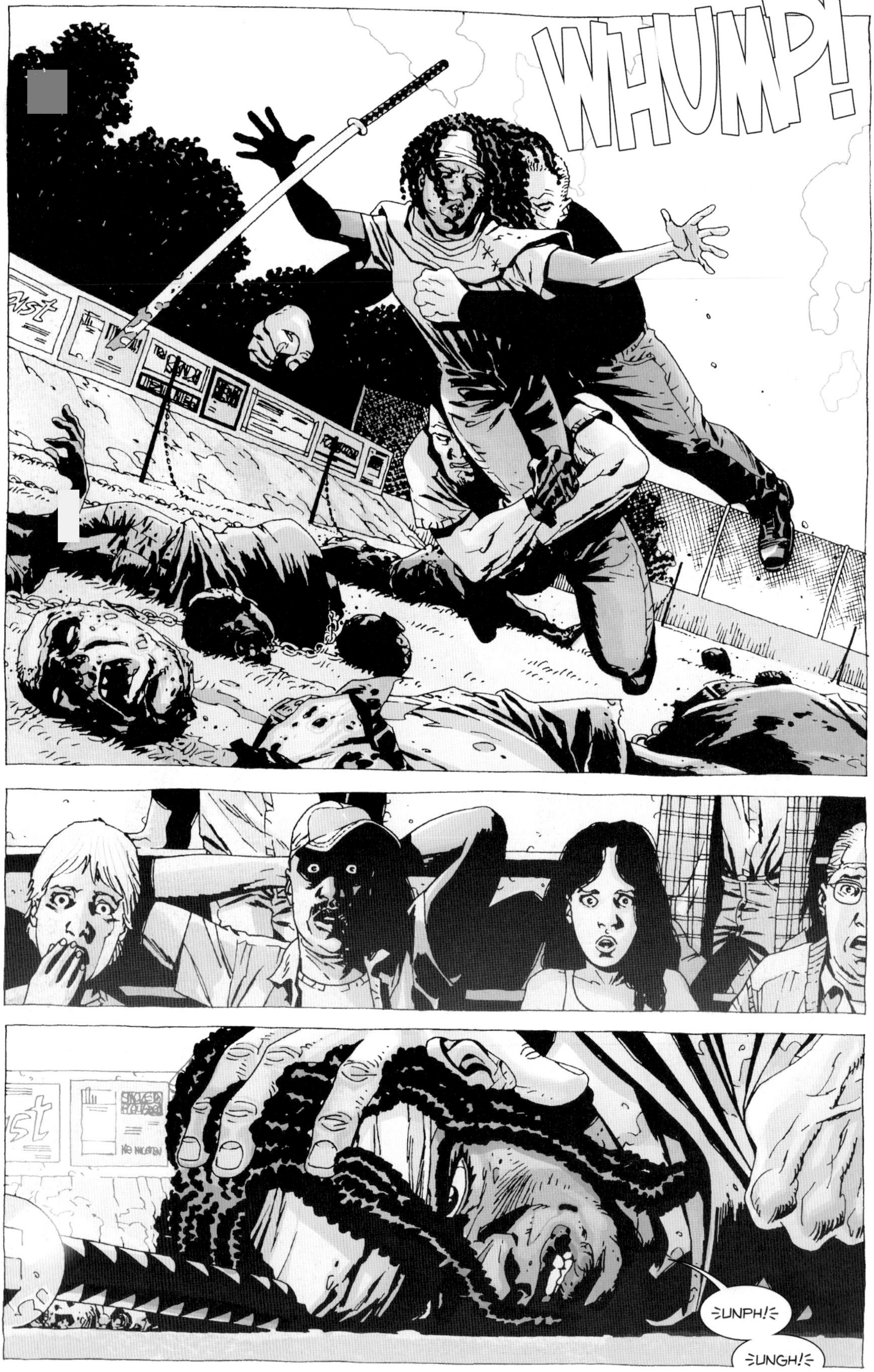
WHUMP!
UNPH!
UNGH!

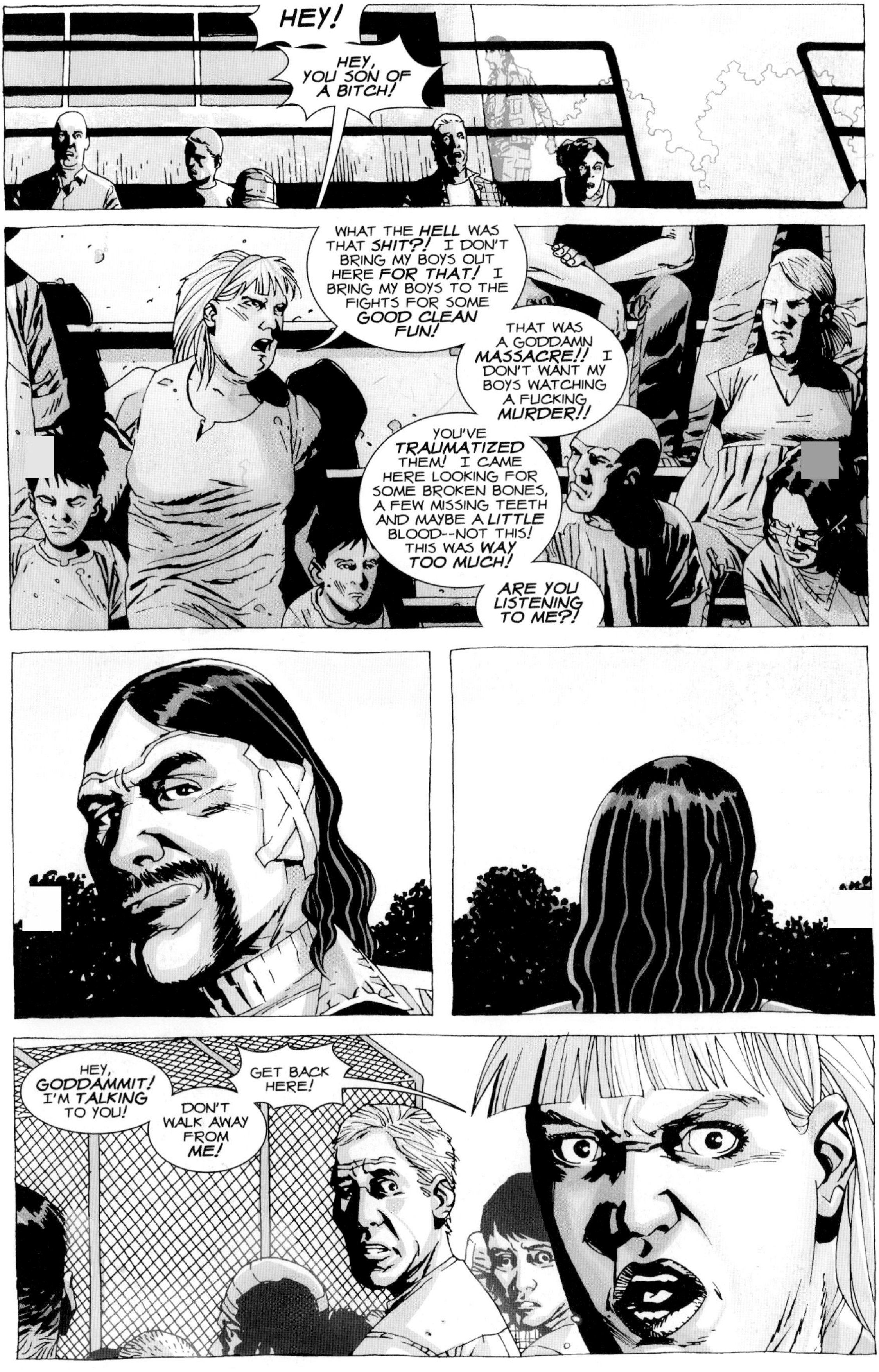
HEY!
HEY, YOU SON OF A BITCH!
WHAT THE HELL WAS THAT SHIT?! I DON'T BRING MY BOYS OUT HERE FOR THAT! I BRING MY BOYS TO THE FIGHTS FOR SOME GOOD CLEAN FUN!
THAT WAS A GODDAMN MASSACRE!! I DON'T WANT MY BOYS WATCHING A FUCKING MURDER!!
YOU'VE TRAUMATIZED THEM! I CAME HERE LOOKING FOR SOME BROKEN BONES, A FEW MISSING TEETH AND MAYBE A LITTLE BLOOD--NOT THIS! THIS WAS WAY TOO MUCH!
ARE YOU LISTENING TO ME?!
HEY, GODDAMMIT! I'M TALKING TO YOU!
GET BACK HERE!
DON'T WALK AWAY FROM ME!

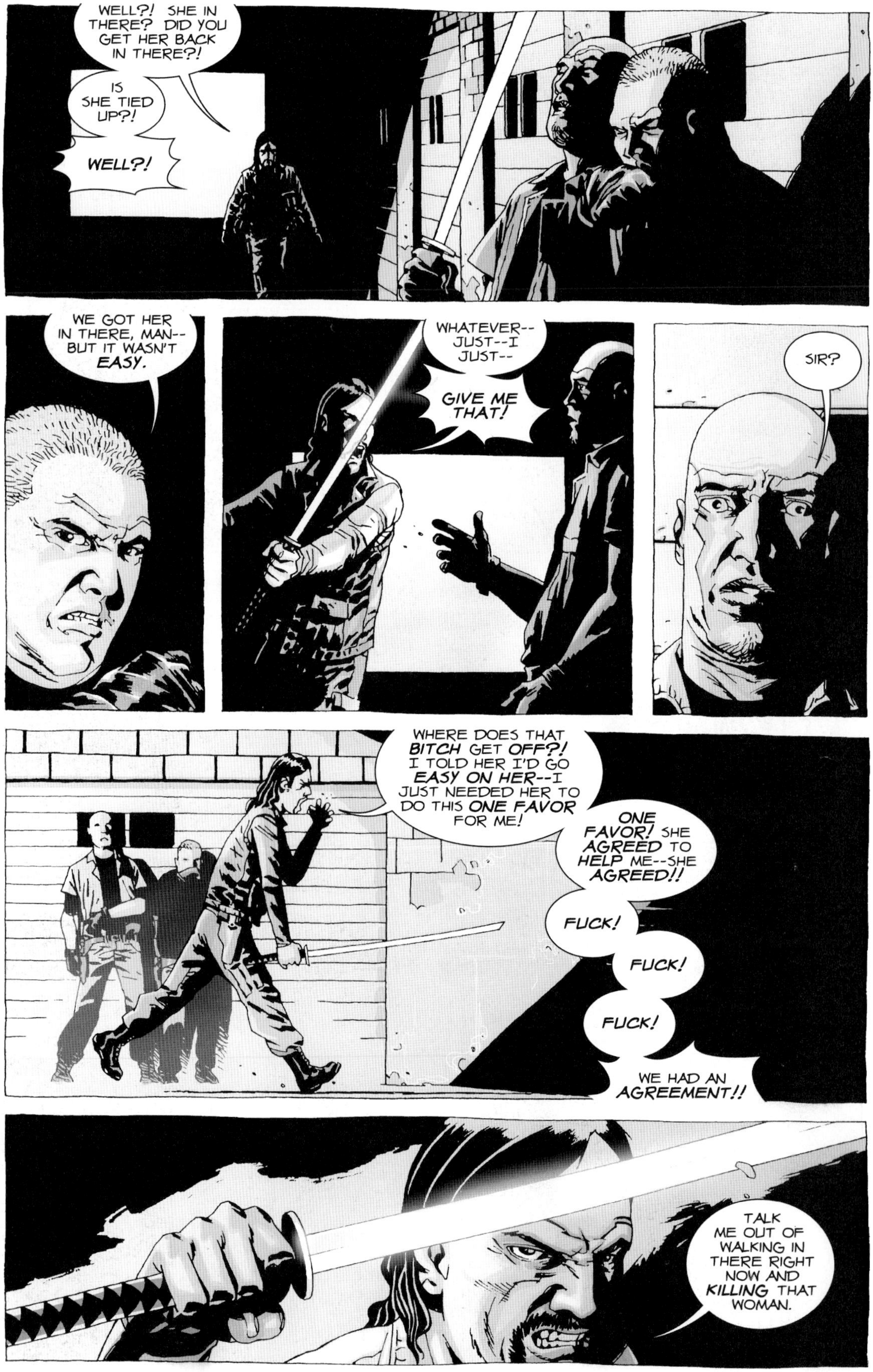
WELL?! SHE IN THERE? DID YOU GET HER BACK IN THERE?!
IS SHE TIED UP?!
WELL?!
WE GOT HER IN THERE, MAN-- BUT IT WASN'T EASY.
WHATEVER-- JUST--I JUST--
GIVE ME THAT!
SIR?
WHERE DOES THAT BITCH GET OFF?! I TOLD HER I'D GO EASY ON HER--I JUST NEEDED HER TO DO THIS ONE FAVOR FOR ME!
ONE FAVOR! SHE AGREED TO HELP ME--SHE AGREED!!
FUCK!
FUCK!
FUCK!
WE HAD AN AGREEMENT!!
TALK ME OUT OF WALKING IN THERE RIGHT NOW AND KILLING THAT WOMAN.

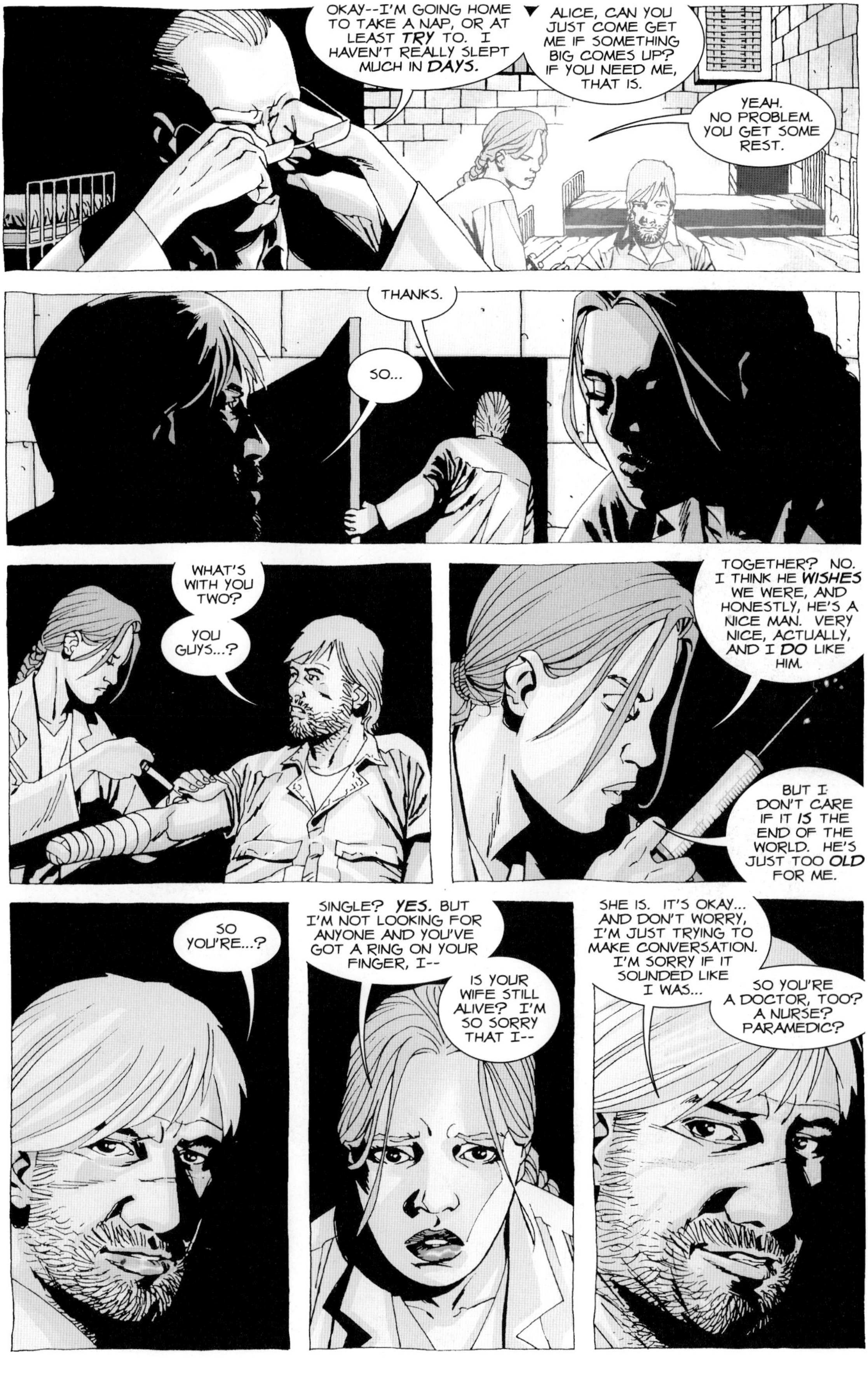
OKAY--I'M GOING HOME TO TAKE A NAP, OR AT LEAST TRY TO. I HAVEN'T REALLY SLEPT MUCH IN DAYS.
ALICE, CAN YOU JUST COME GET ME IF SOMETHING BIG COMES UP? IF YOU NEED ME, THAT IS.
YEAH. NO PROBLEM. YOU GET SOME REST.
THANKS.
SO...
WHAT'S WITH YOU TWO?
YOU GUYS...?
TOGETHER? NO. I THINK HE WISHES WE WERE, AND HONESTLY, HE'S A NICE MAN. VERY NICE, ACTUALLY, AND I DO LIKE HIM.
BUT I DON'T CARE IF IT IS THE END OF THE WORLD. HE'S JUST TOO OLD FOR ME.
SO YOU'RE...?
SINGLE? YES. BUT I'M NOT LOOKING FOR ANYONE AND YOU'VE GOT A RING ON YOUR FINGER, I--
IS YOUR WIFE STILL ALIVE? I'M SO SORRY THAT I--
SHE IS. IT'S OKAY... AND DON'T WORRY, I'M JUST TRYING TO MAKE CONVERSATION. I'M SORRY IF IT SOUNDED LIKE I WAS...
SO YOU'RE A DOCTOR, TOO? A NURSE? PARAMEDIC?

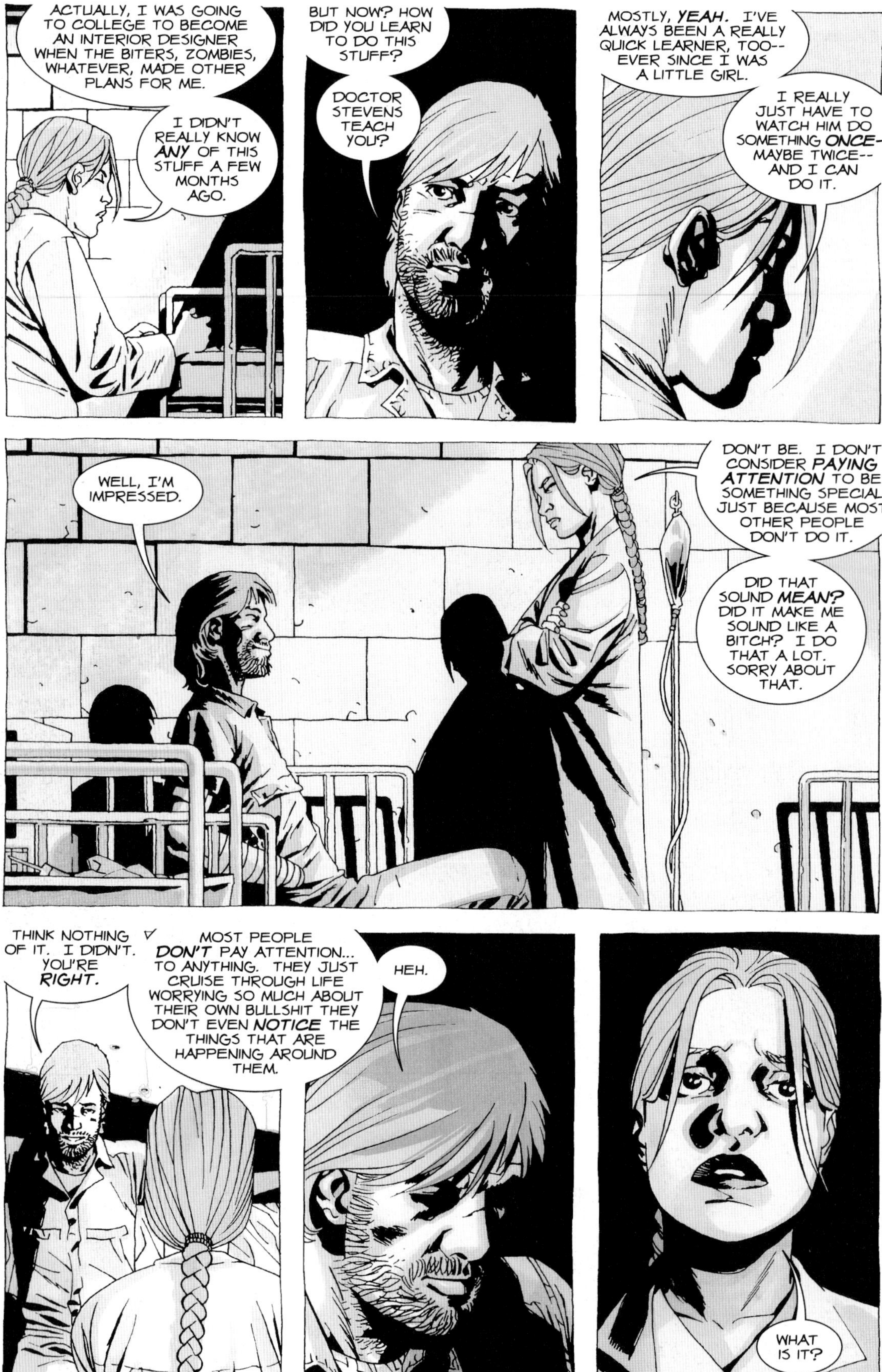
ACTUALLY, I WAS GOING TO COLLEGE TO BECOME AN INTERIOR DESIGNER WHEN THE BITERS, ZOMBIES, WHATEVER, MADE OTHER PLANS FOR ME.
I DIDN'T REALLY KNOW ANY OF THIS STUFF A FEW MONTHS AGO.
BUT NOW? HOW DID YOU LEARN TO DO THIS STUFF?
DOCTOR STEVENS TEACH YOU?
MOSTLY, YEAH. I'VE ALWAYS BEEN A REALLY QUICK LEARNER, TOO-- EVER SINCE I WAS A LITTLE GIRL.
I REALLY JUST HAVE TO WATCH HIM DO SOMETHING ONCE-- MAYBE TWICE-- AND I CAN DO IT.
WELL, I'M IMPRESSED.
DON'T BE. I DON'T CONSIDER PAYING ATTENTION TO BE SOMETHING SPECIAL JUST BECAUSE MOST OTHER PEOPLE DON'T DO IT.
DID THAT SOUND MEAN? DID IT MAKE ME SOUND LIKE A BITCH? I DO THAT A LOT. SORRY ABOUT THAT.
THINK NOTHING OF IT. I DIDN'T. YOU'RE RIGHT.
MOST PEOPLE DON'T PAY ATTENTION... TO ANYTHING. THEY JUST CRUISE THROUGH LIFE WORRYING SO MUCH ABOUT THEIR OWN BULLSHIT THEY DON'T EVEN NOTICE THE THINGS THAT ARE HAPPENING AROUND THEM.
HEH.
WHAT IS IT?

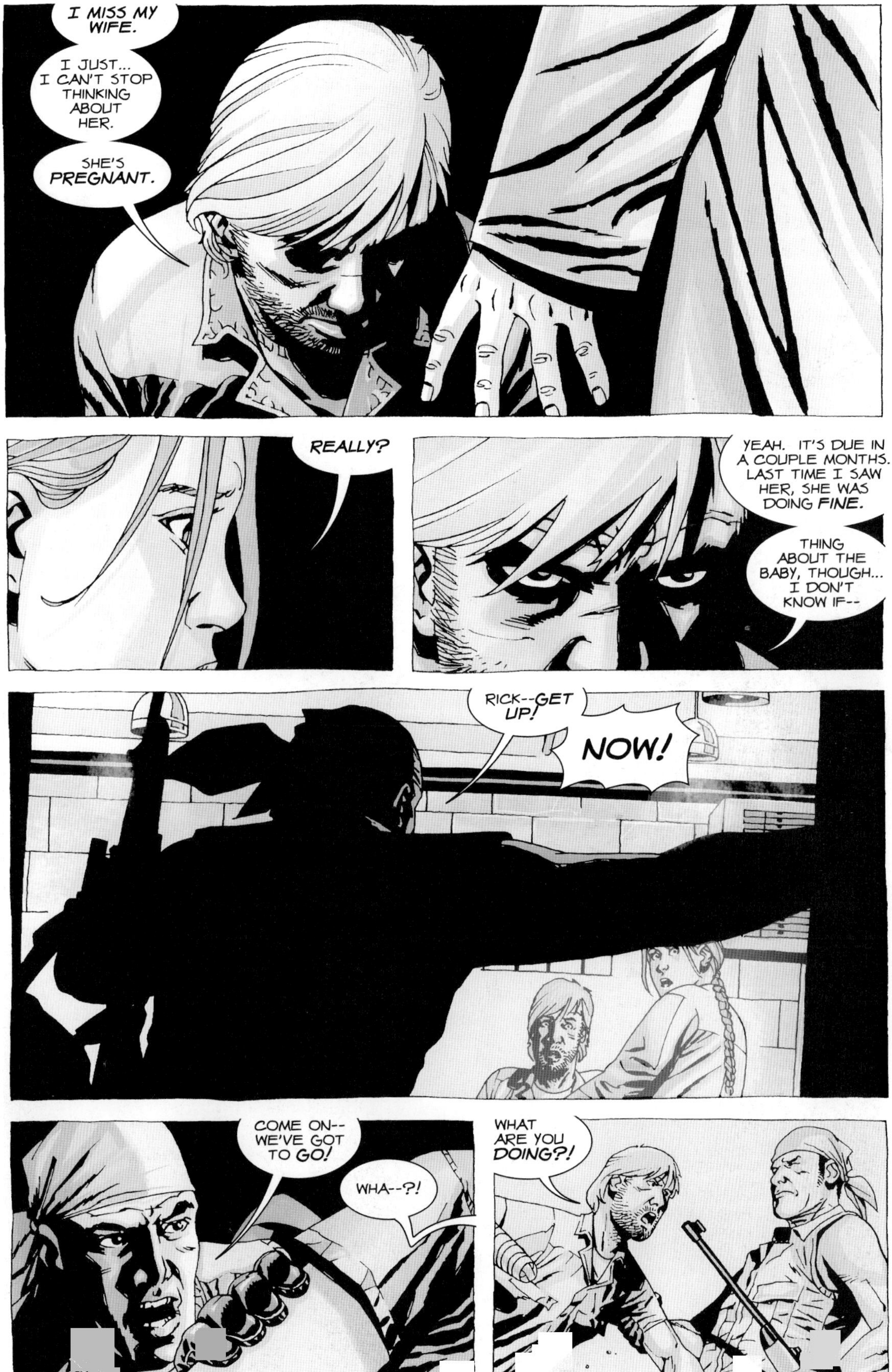
I MISS MY WIFE.
I JUST... I CAN'T STOP THINKING ABOUT HER.
SHE'S PREGNANT.
REALLY?
YEAH. IT'S DUE IN A COUPLE MONTHS. LAST TIME I SAW HER, SHE WAS DOING FINE.
THING ABOUT THE BABY, THOUGH... I DON'T KNOW IF--
RICK--GET UP!
NOW!
COME ON-- WE'VE GOT TO GO!
WHA--?!
WHAT ARE YOU DOING?!

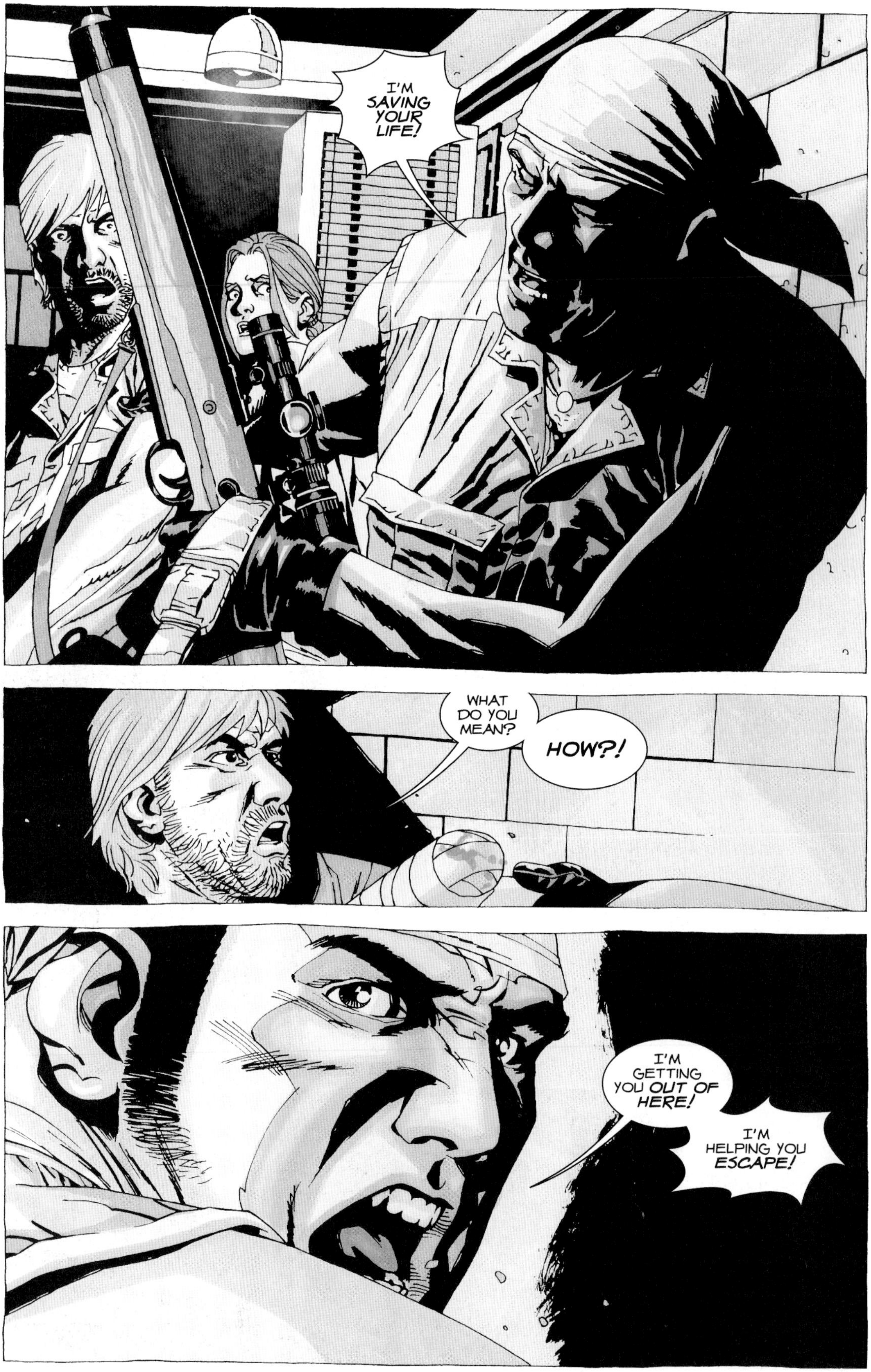I'M SAVING YOUR LIFE!
WHAT DO YOU MEAN?
HOW?!
I'M GETTING YOU OUT OF HERE!
I'M HELPING YOU ESCAPE!

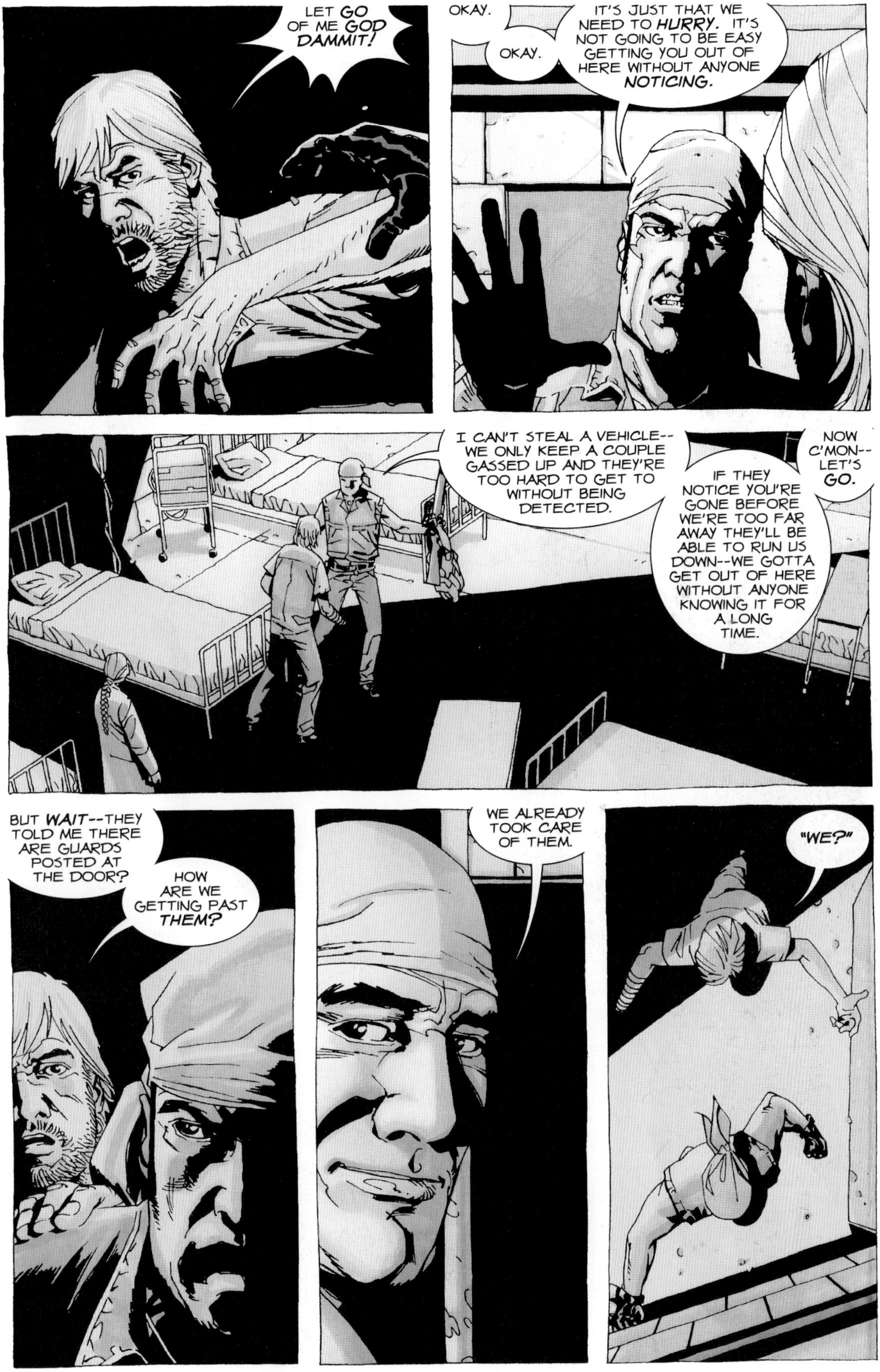

LET GO OF ME GOD DAMMIT!
OKAY.
OKAY.
IT'S JUST THAT WE NEED TO HURRY. IT'S NOT GOING TO BE EASY GETTING YOU OUT OF HERE WITHOUT ANYONE NOTICING.
I CAN'T STEAL A VEHICLE--WE ONLY KEEP A COUPLE GASSED UP AND THEY'RE TOO HARD TO GET TO WITHOUT BEING DETECTED.
IF THEY NOTICE YOU'RE GONE BEFORE WE'RE TOO FAR AWAY THEY'LL BE ABLE TO RUN US DOWN--WE GOTTA GET OUT OF HERE WITHOUT ANYONE KNOWING IT FOR A LONG TIME.
NOW C'MON--LET'S GO.
BUT WAIT--THEY TOLD ME THERE ARE GUARDS POSTED AT THE DOOR?
HOW ARE WE GETTING PAST THEM?
WE ALREADY TOOK CARE OF THEM.
"WE?"

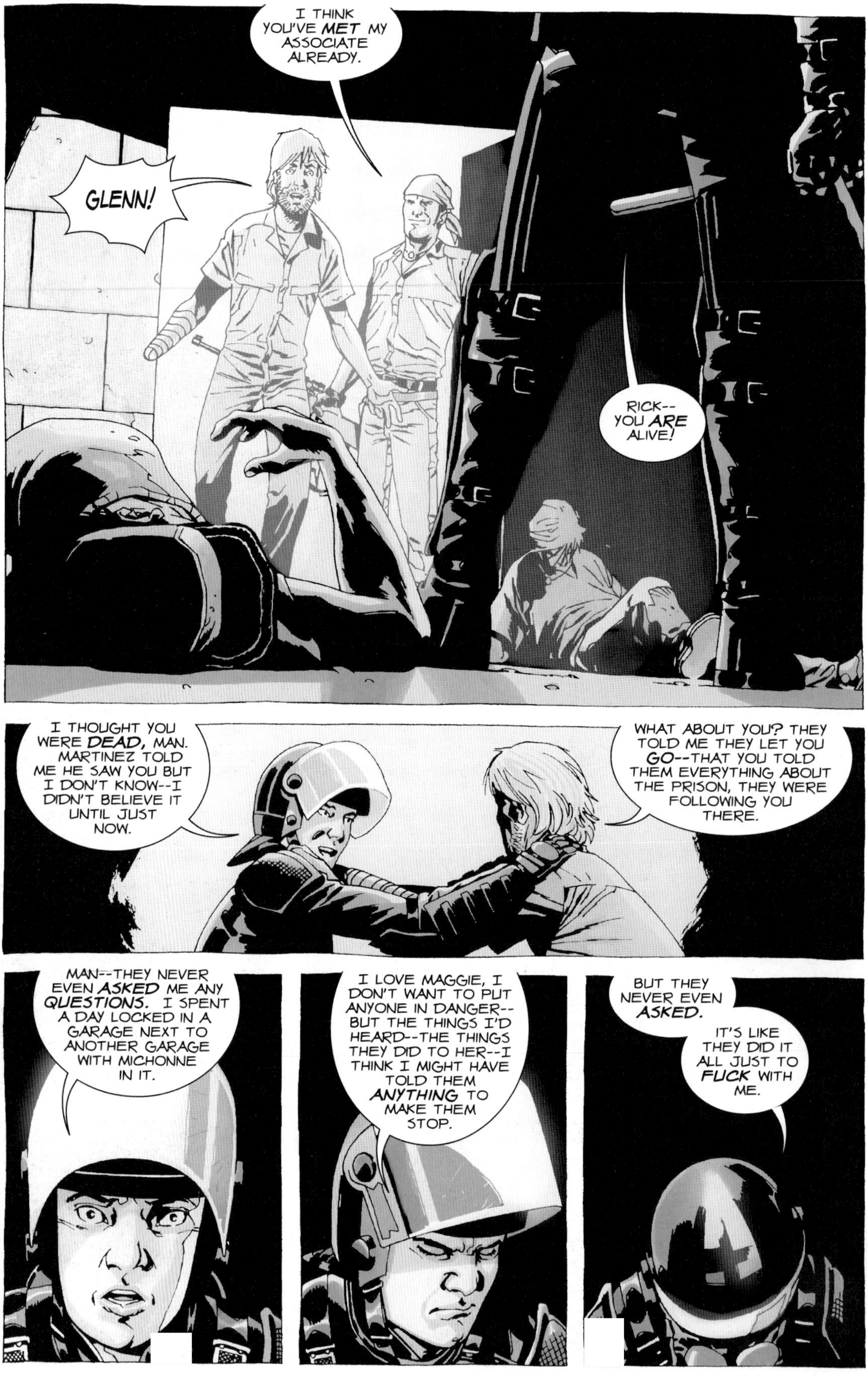
I THINK YOU'VE MET MY ASSOCIATE ALREADY.
GLENN!
RICK-- YOU ARE ALIVE!
I THOUGHT YOU WERE DEAD, MAN. MARTINEZ TOLD ME HE SAW YOU BUT I DON'T KNOW--I DIDN'T BELIEVE IT UNTIL JUST NOW.
WHAT ABOUT YOU? THEY TOLD ME THEY LET YOU GO--THAT YOU TOLD THEM EVERYTHING ABOUT THE PRISON, THEY WERE FOLLOWING YOU THERE.
MAN--THEY NEVER EVEN ASKED ME ANY QUESTIONS. I SPENT A DAY LOCKED IN A GARAGE NEXT TO ANOTHER GARAGE WITH MICHONNE IN IT.
I LOVE MAGGIE, I DON'T WANT TO PUT ANYONE IN DANGER--BUT THE THINGS I'D HEARD--THE THINGS THEY DID TO HER--I THINK I MIGHT HAVE TOLD THEM ANYTHING TO MAKE THEM STOP.
BUT THEY NEVER EVEN ASKED.
IT'S LIKE THEY DID IT ALL JUST TO FUCK WITH ME.

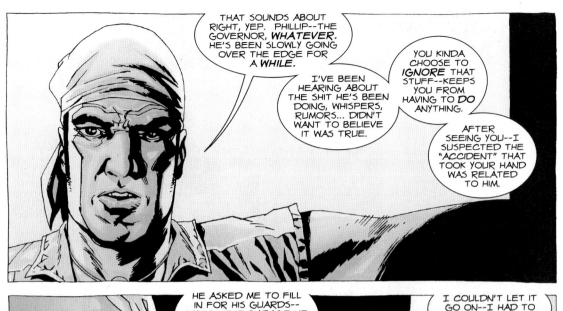

THAT SOUNDS ABOUT RIGHT, YEP. PHILLIP--THE GOVERNOR, *WHATEVER.* HE'S BEEN SLOWLY GOING OVER THE EDGE FOR A *WHILE.*

I'VE BEEN HEARING ABOUT THE SHIT HE'S BEEN DOING, WHISPERS, RUMORS... DIDN'T WANT TO BELIEVE IT WAS TRUE.

YOU KINDA CHOOSE TO *IGNORE* THAT STUFF--KEEPS YOU FROM HAVING TO *DO* ANYTHING.

AFTER SEEING YOU--I SUSPECTED THE "ACCIDENT" THAT TOOK YOUR HAND WAS RELATED TO HIM.

HE ASKED ME TO FILL IN FOR HIS GUARDS-- WATCH THE GARAGE HE WAS KEEPING GLENN IN. I DIDN'T KNOW HE WAS KEEPING *PRISONERS* IN HERE.

I MOSTLY WORKED SECURITY-- ALL MY TIME WAS SPENT ON THE *FENCES.*

I COULDN'T LET IT GO ON--I HAD TO HELP PUT A STOP TO THIS MADNESS.

WE'RE STILL *HUMAN,* GODDAMN IT.

MY *GODDAMN CLOTHES.* WE WERE WEARING *RIOT GEAR* AND WHEN THE DOCTOR WAS WORKING ON ME SOMEONE *HAD* TO SEE MY PRISON JUMPSUIT.

CHRIST.

WHAT DO YOU MEAN?

THAT'S HOW HE KNEW ABOUT THE PRISON.

HOW COULD I BE SO *STUPID?*

COME ON-- WE'VE *GOT* TO GET OUT OF HERE.

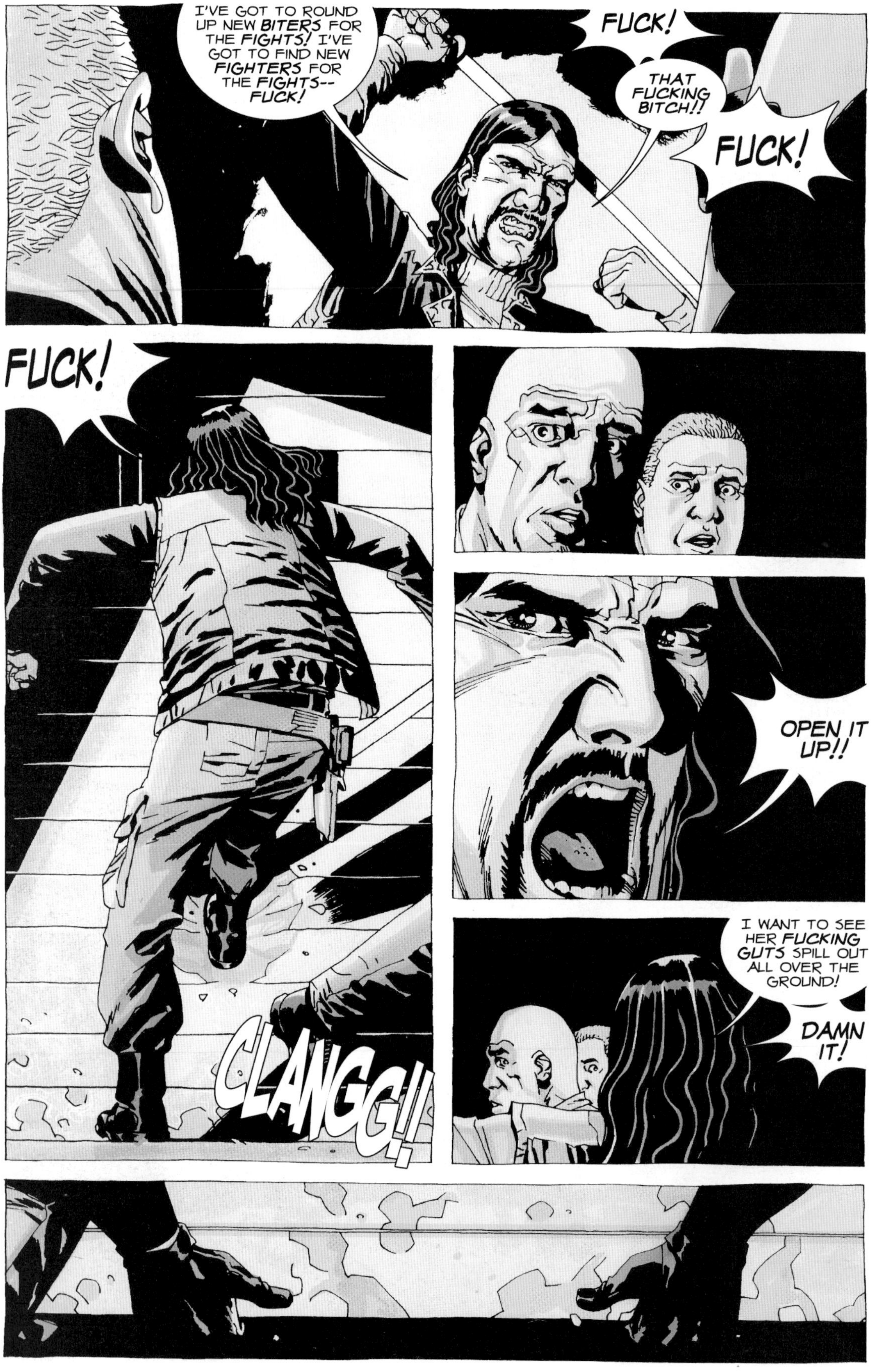
I'VE GOT TO ROUND UP NEW BITERS FOR THE FIGHTS! I'VE GOT TO FIND NEW FIGHTERS FOR THE FIGHTS-- FUCK!
FUCK!
THAT FUCKING BITCH!!
FUCK!
FUCK!
OPEN IT UP!!
CLANGG!!
I WANT TO SEE HER FUCKING GUTS SPILL OUT ALL OVER THE GROUND!
DAMN IT!

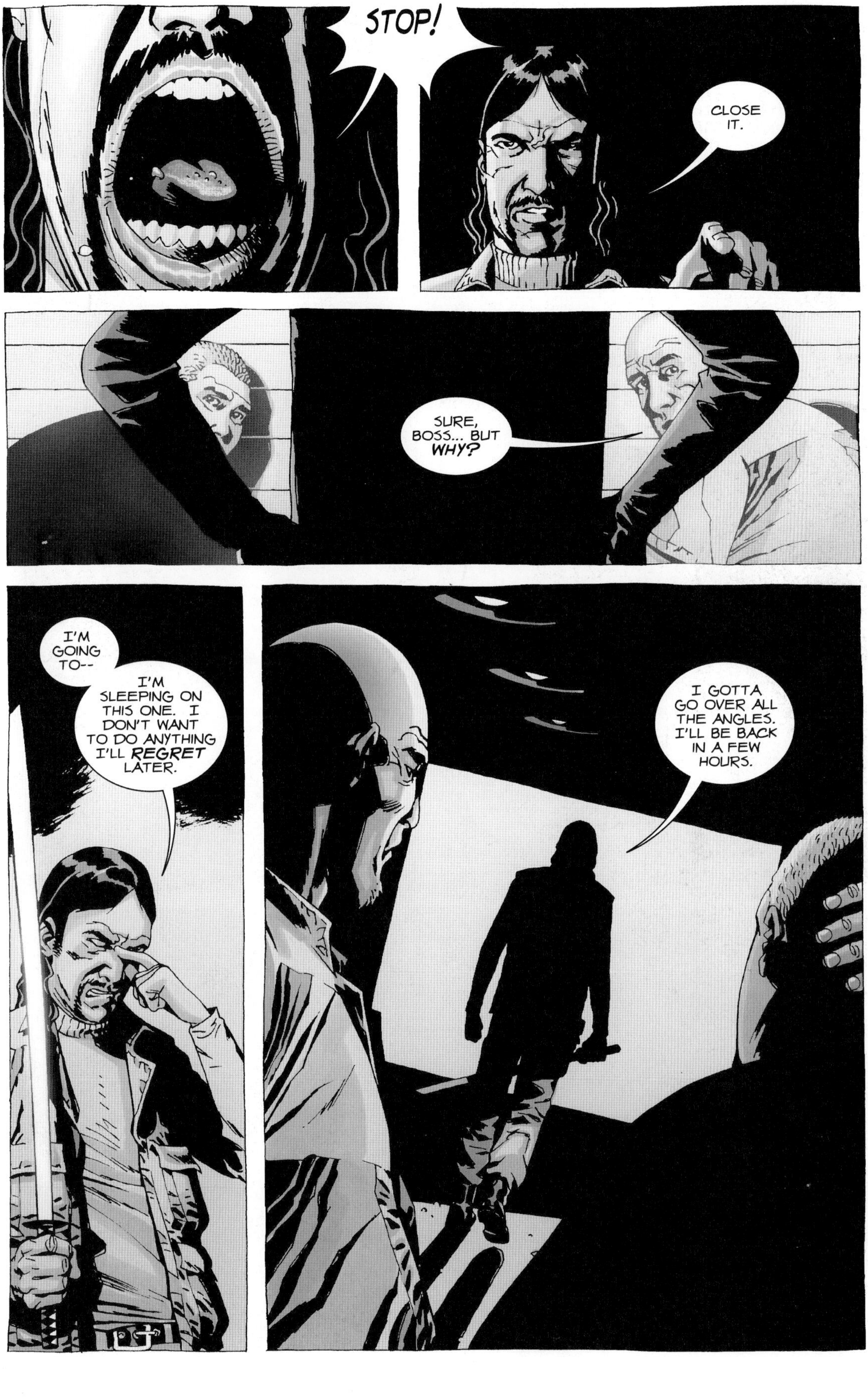
STOP!
CLOSE IT.
SURE, BOSS... BUT WHY?
I'M GOING TO--
I'M SLEEPING ON THIS ONE. I DON'T WANT TO DO ANYTHING I'LL REGRET LATER.
I GOTTA GO OVER ALL THE ANGLES. I'LL BE BACK IN A FEW HOURS.

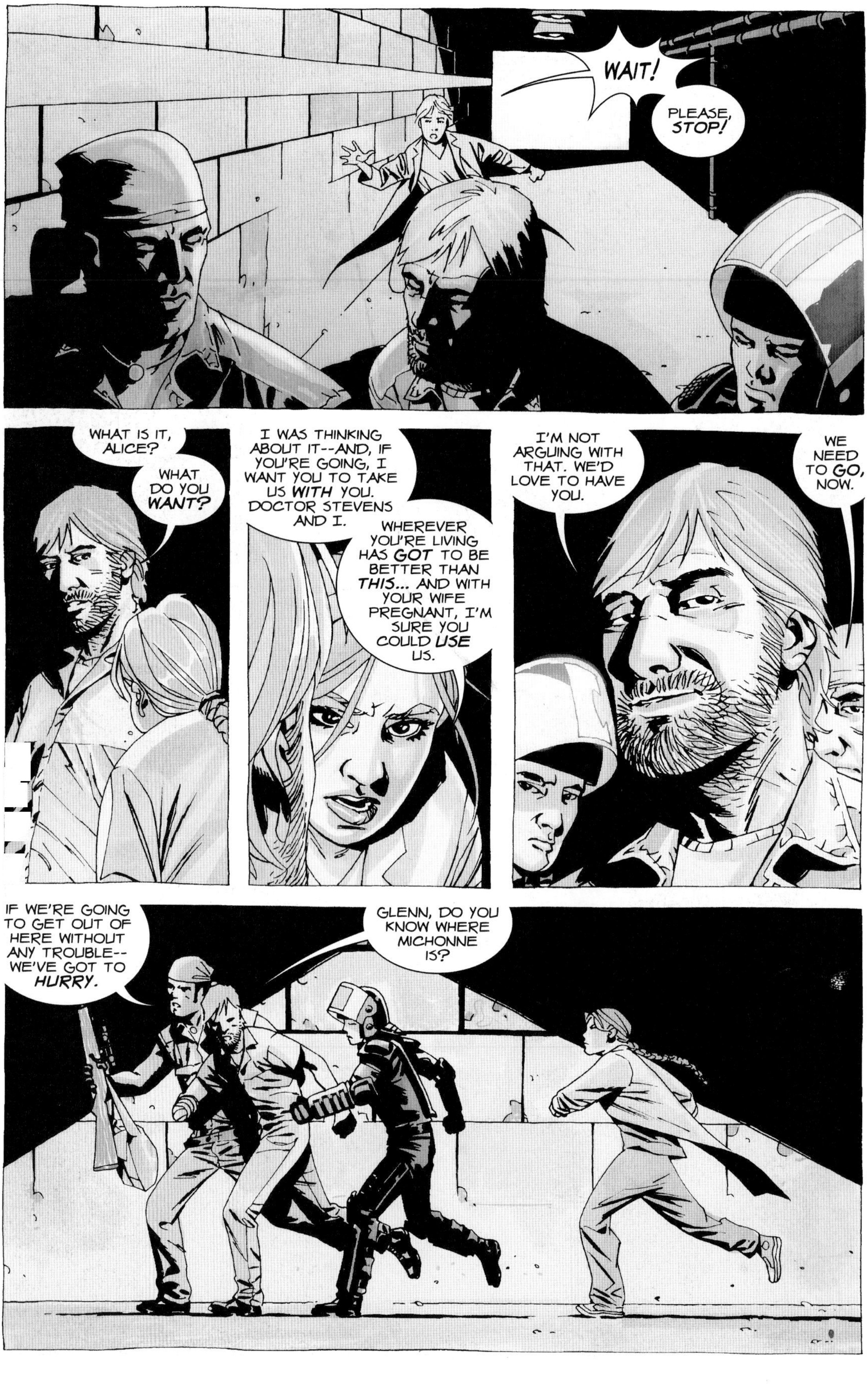
WAIT!
PLEASE, STOP!
WHAT IS IT, ALICE?
WHAT DO YOU WANT?
I WAS THINKING ABOUT IT--AND, IF YOU'RE GOING, I WANT YOU TO TAKE US WITH YOU. DOCTOR STEVENS AND I.
WHEREVER YOU'RE LIVING HAS GOT TO BE BETTER THAN THIS... AND WITH YOUR WIFE PREGNANT, I'M SURE YOU COULD USE US.
I'M NOT ARGUING WITH THAT. WE'D LOVE TO HAVE YOU.
WE NEED TO GO, NOW.
IF WE'RE GOING TO GET OUT OF HERE WITHOUT ANY TROUBLE-- WE'VE GOT TO HURRY.
GLENN, DO YOU KNOW WHERE MICHONNE IS?

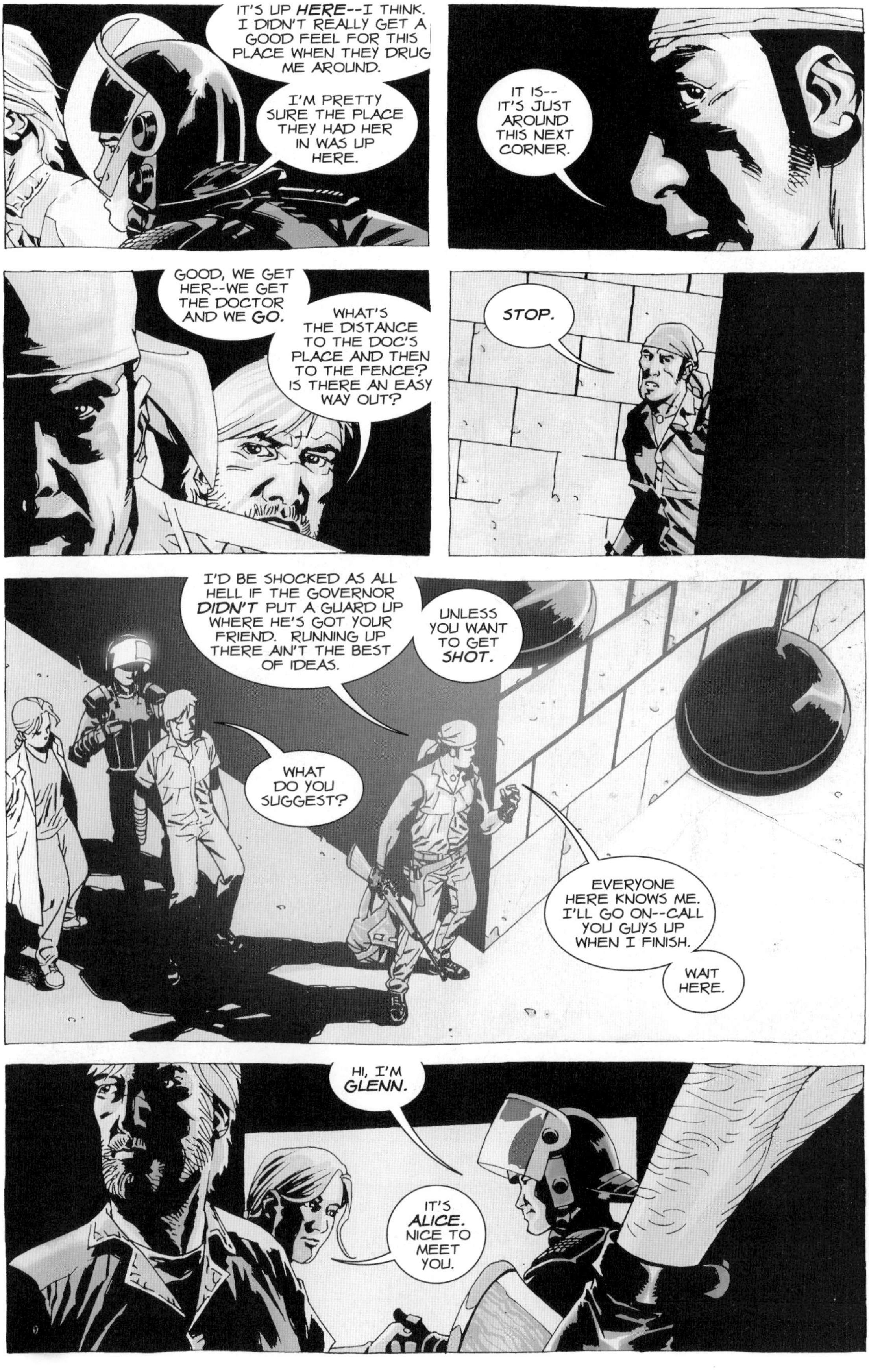

IT'S UP HERE--I THINK. I DIDN'T REALLY GET A GOOD FEEL FOR THIS PLACE WHEN THEY DRUG ME AROUND.
I'M PRETTY SURE THE PLACE THEY HAD HER IN WAS UP HERE.
IT IS-- IT'S JUST AROUND THIS NEXT CORNER.
GOOD, WE GET HER--WE GET THE DOCTOR AND WE GO.
WHAT'S THE DISTANCE TO THE DOC'S PLACE AND THEN TO THE FENCE? IS THERE AN EASY WAY OUT?
STOP.
I'D BE SHOCKED AS ALL HELL IF THE GOVERNOR DIDN'T PUT A GUARD UP WHERE HE'S GOT YOUR FRIEND. RUNNING UP THERE AIN'T THE BEST OF IDEAS.
UNLESS YOU WANT TO GET SHOT.
WHAT DO YOU SUGGEST?
EVERYONE HERE KNOWS ME. I'LL GO ON--CALL YOU GUYS UP WHEN I FINISH.
WAIT HERE.
HI, I'M GLENN.
IT'S ALICE. NICE TO MEET YOU.

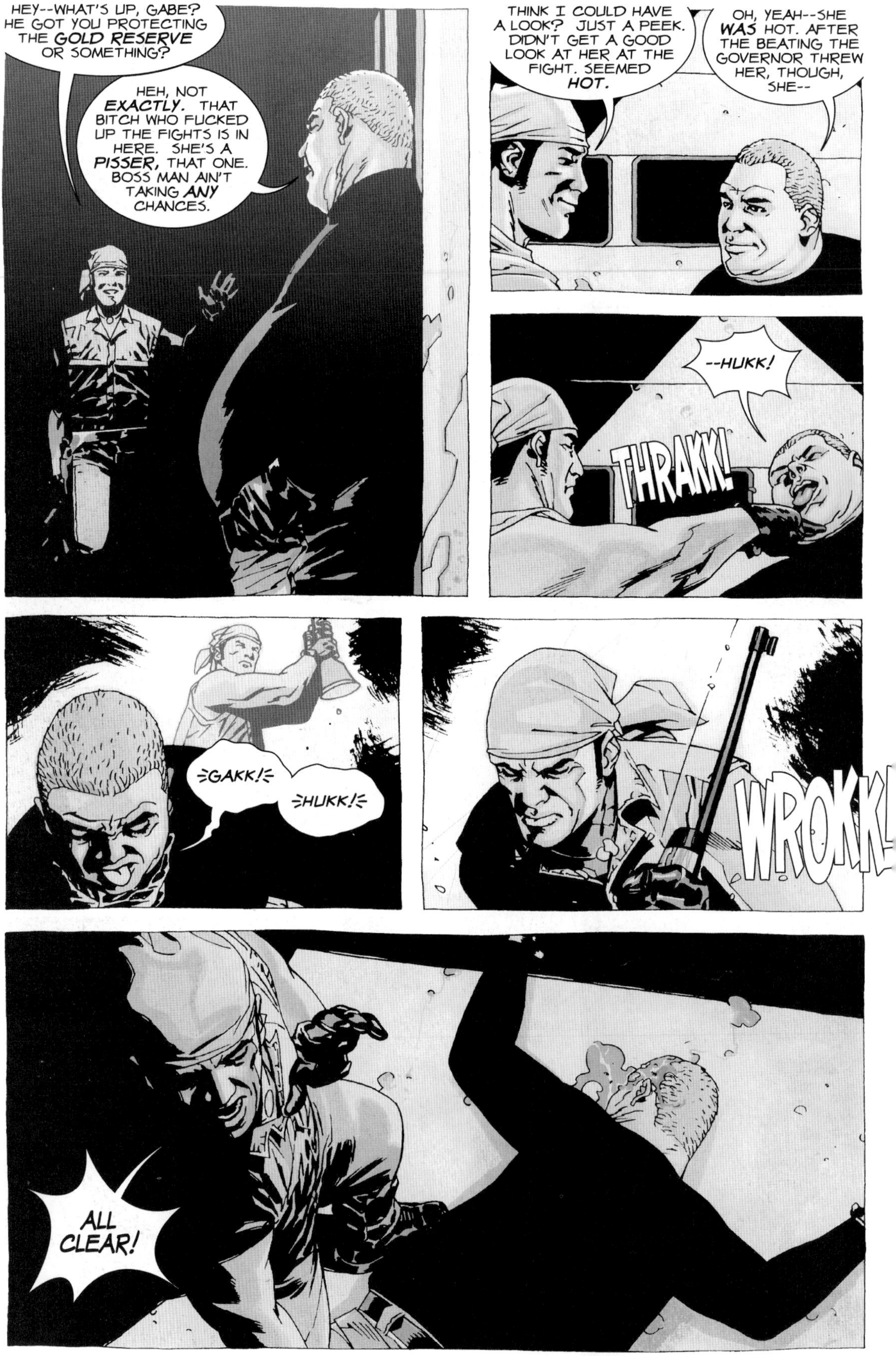
HEY--WHAT'S UP, GABE? HE GOT YOU PROTECTING THE GOLD RESERVE OR SOMETHING?
HEH, NOT EXACTLY. THAT BITCH WHO FUCKED UP THE FIGHTS IS IN HERE. SHE'S A PISSER, THAT ONE. BOSS MAN AIN'T TAKING ANY CHANCES.
THINK I COULD HAVE A LOOK? JUST A PEEK. DIDN'T GET A GOOD LOOK AT HER AT THE FIGHT. SEEMED HOT.
OH, YEAH--SHE WAS HOT. AFTER THE BEATING THE GOVERNOR THREW HER, THOUGH, SHE--
--HUKK!
THRAKK!
GAKK!
HUKK!
WROKK!
ALL CLEAR!

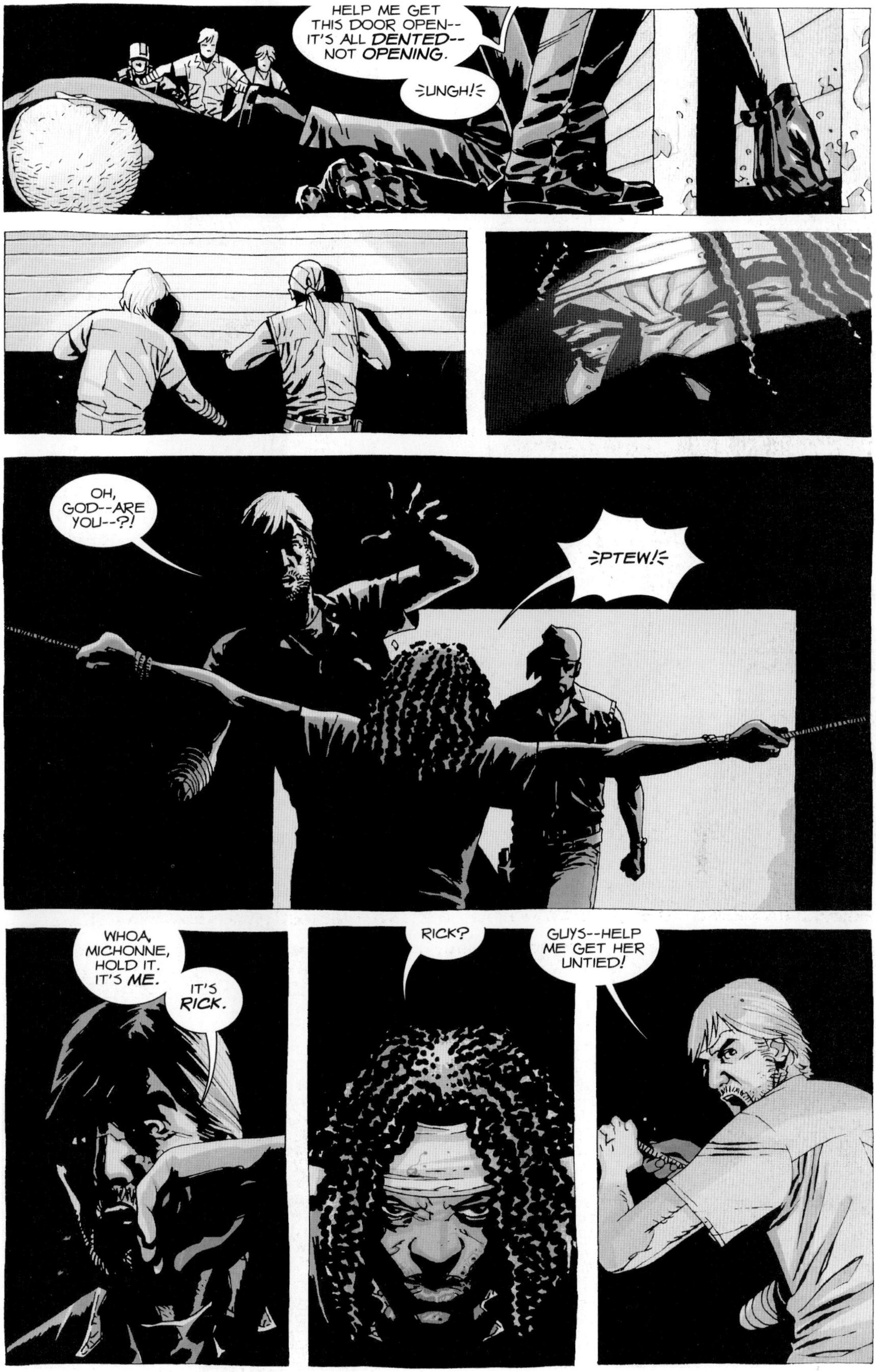
HELP ME GET THIS DOOR OPEN-- IT'S ALL DENTED-- NOT OPENING.
UNGH!
OH, GOD--ARE YOU--?!
PTEW!
WHOA, MICHONNE, HOLD IT. IT'S ME.
IT'S RICK.
RICK?
GUYS--HELP ME GET HER UNTIED!

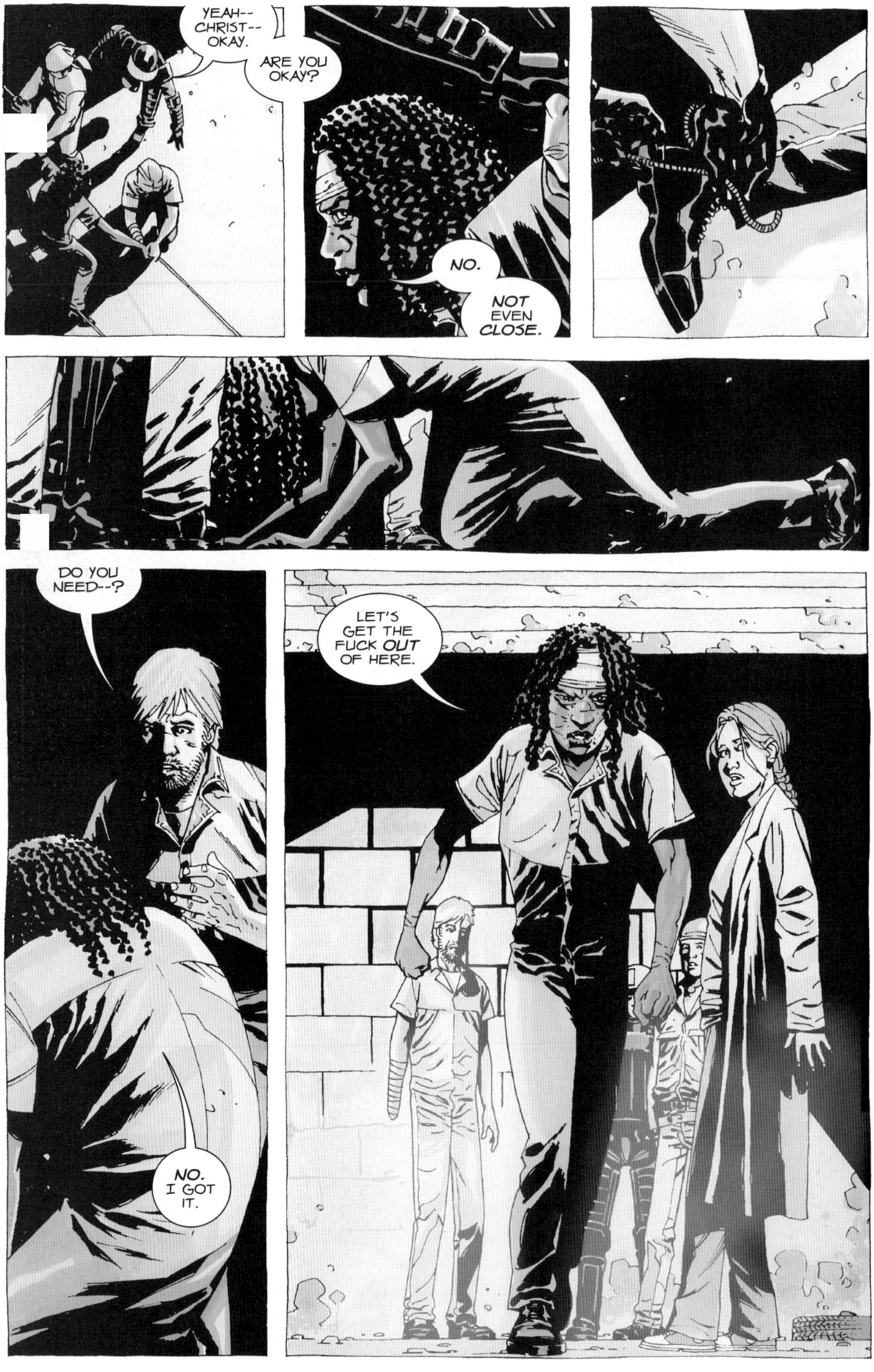

YEAH-- CHRIST-- OKAY.
ARE YOU OKAY?
NO.
NOT EVEN CLOSE.
DO YOU NEED--?
NO. I GOT IT.
LET'S GET THE FUCK OUT OF HERE.

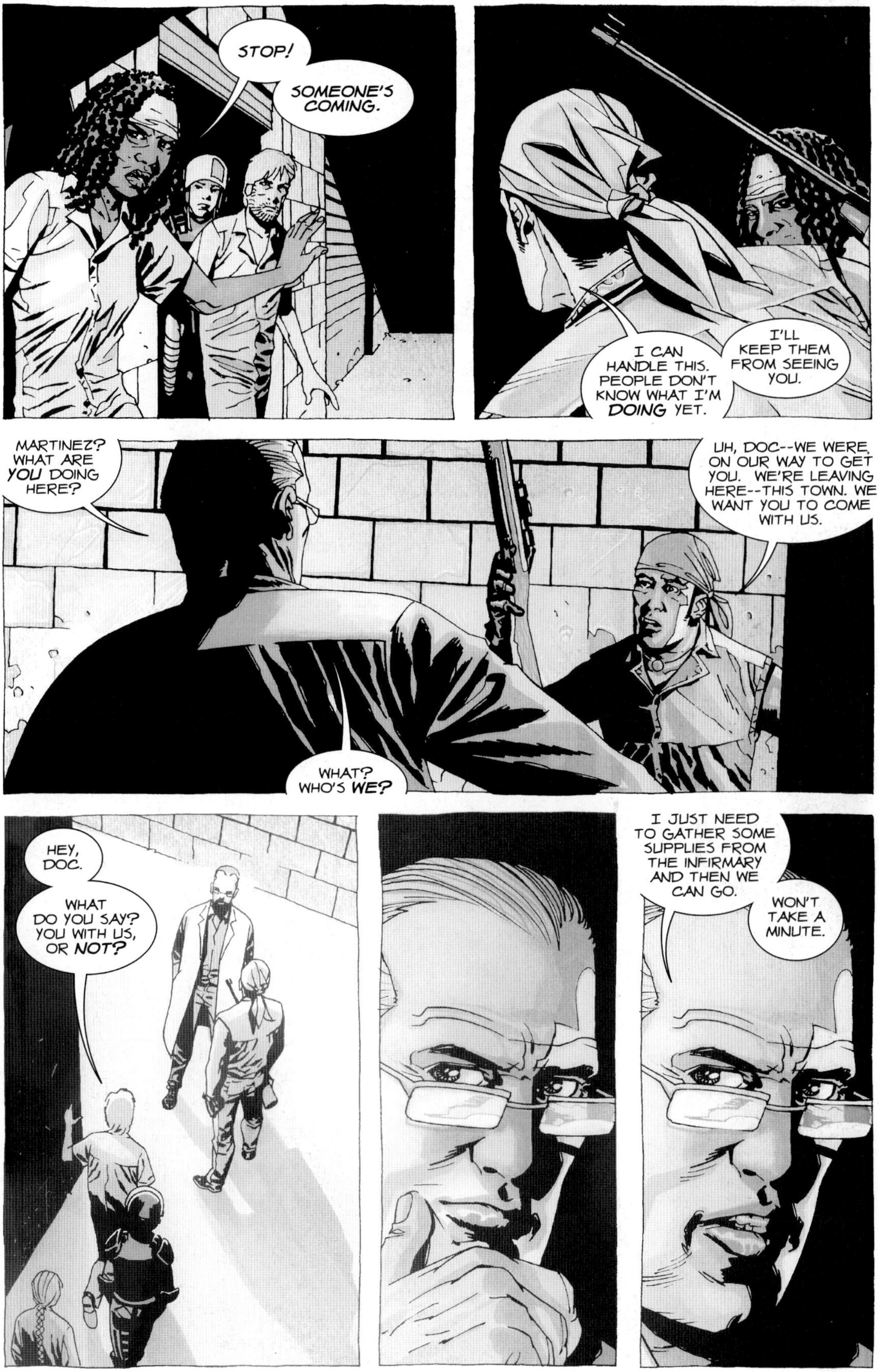
STOP!
SOMEONE'S COMING.
I CAN HANDLE THIS. PEOPLE DON'T KNOW WHAT I'M DOING YET.
I'LL KEEP THEM FROM SEEING YOU.
MARTINEZ? WHAT ARE YOU DOING HERE?
UH, DOC--WE WERE ON OUR WAY TO GET YOU. WE'RE LEAVING HERE--THIS TOWN. WE WANT YOU TO COME WITH US.
WHAT? WHO'S WE?
HEY, DOC.
WHAT DO YOU SAY? YOU WITH US, OR NOT?
I JUST NEED TO GATHER SOME SUPPLIES FROM THE INFIRMARY AND THEN WE CAN GO.
WON'T TAKE A MINUTE.

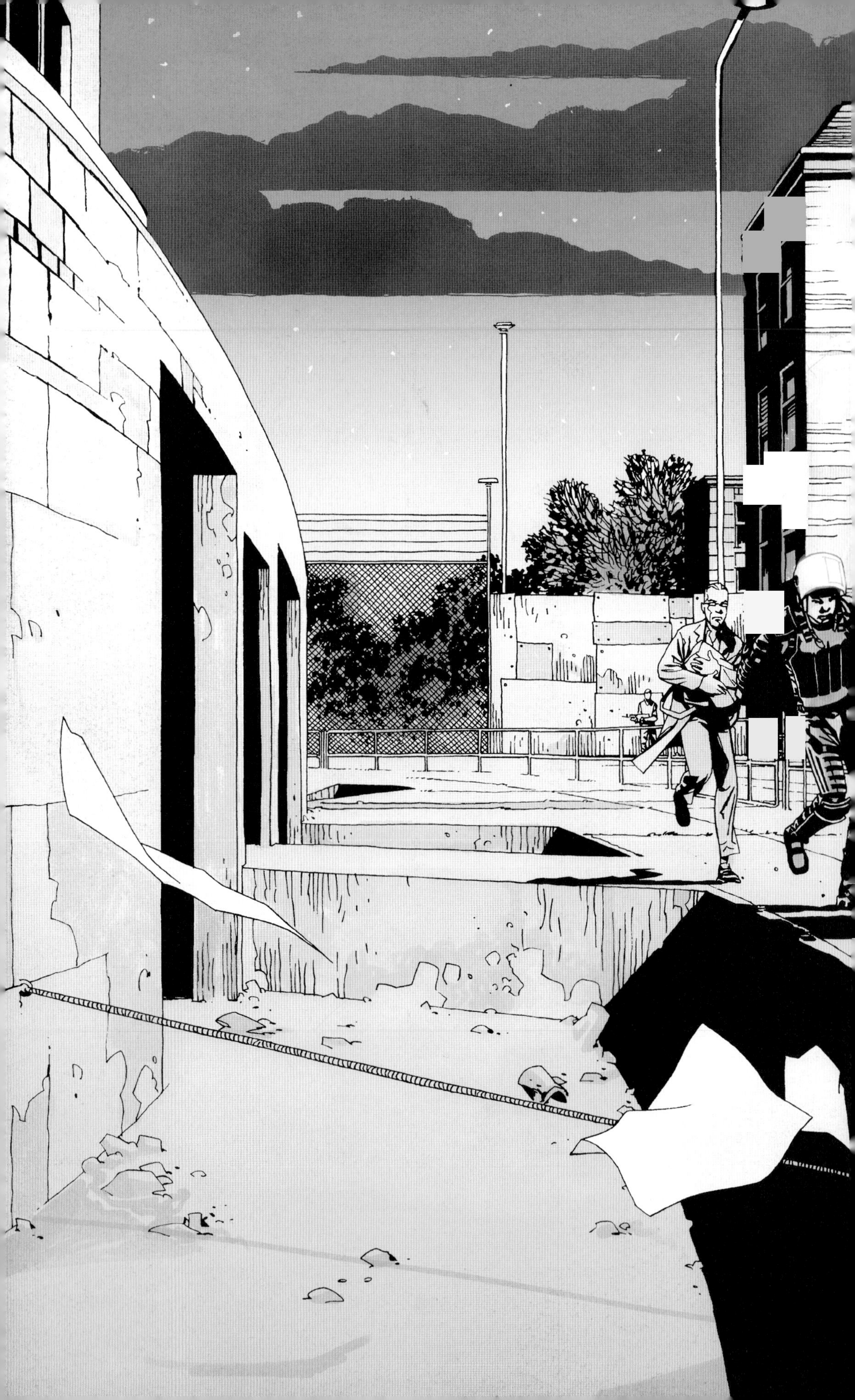

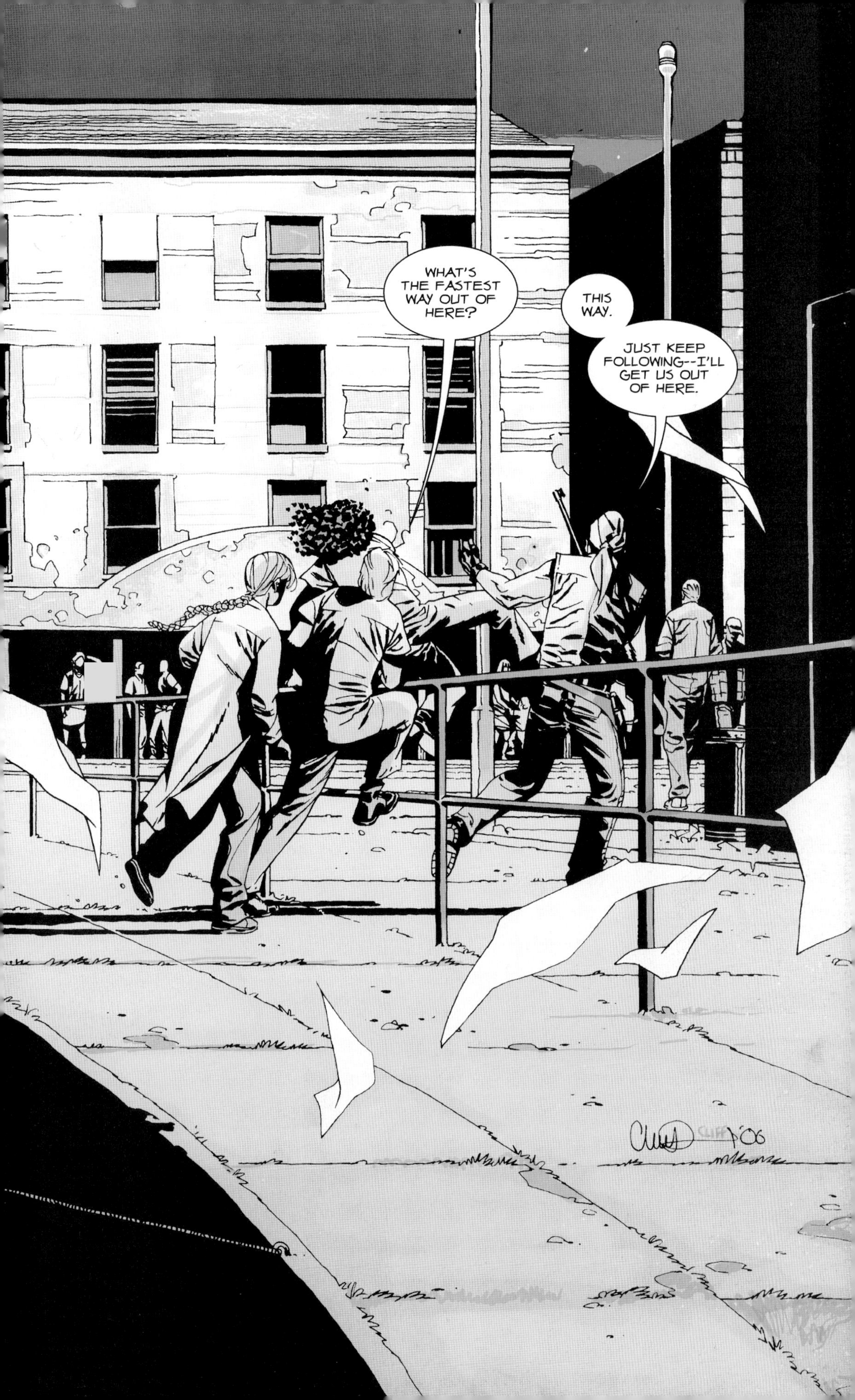
WHAT'S THE FASTEST WAY OUT OF HERE?
THIS WAY.
JUST KEEP FOLLOWING--I'LL GET US OUT OF HERE.

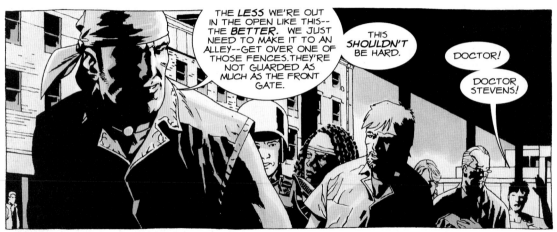

THE *LESS* WE'RE OUT IN THE OPEN LIKE THIS-- THE *BETTER*. WE JUST NEED TO MAKE IT TO AN ALLEY--GET OVER ONE OF THOSE FENCES. THEY'RE NOT GUARDED AS MUCH AS THE FRONT GATE.

THIS *SHOULDN'T* BE HARD.

DOCTOR!

DOCTOR STEVENS!

OH, HELLO MISS WILLIAMS.

UM... WHAT CAN I DO FOR YOU?

I'M SORRY TO BOTHER YOU LIKE THIS BUT MY SON, MATTHEW, HE'S GOT A SLIGHT *FEVER*. I'M SURE IT'S NOTHING BUT I DON'T WANT TO TAKE ANY CHANCES.

DO YOU HAVE ANY TIME LATER TODAY?

OF COURSE. I--I JUST...

JUST BRING HIM BY MY OFFICE LATER TODAY. IF YOU COULD--

I'LL SEE HIM *THEN*. I'LL BE--I'LL MAKE SURE I FIT HIM IN.

SURE, I'LL-- ARE YOU OKAY DOCTOR STEVENS?

YOU SEEM UPSET.

I'M *FINE*-- *REALLY*. I'M JUST--I'M IN THE MIDDLE OF SOMETHING RIGHT NOW.

I DON'T MEAN TO BE RUDE BUT I *MUST* BE GOING.

I'M *SORRY*.

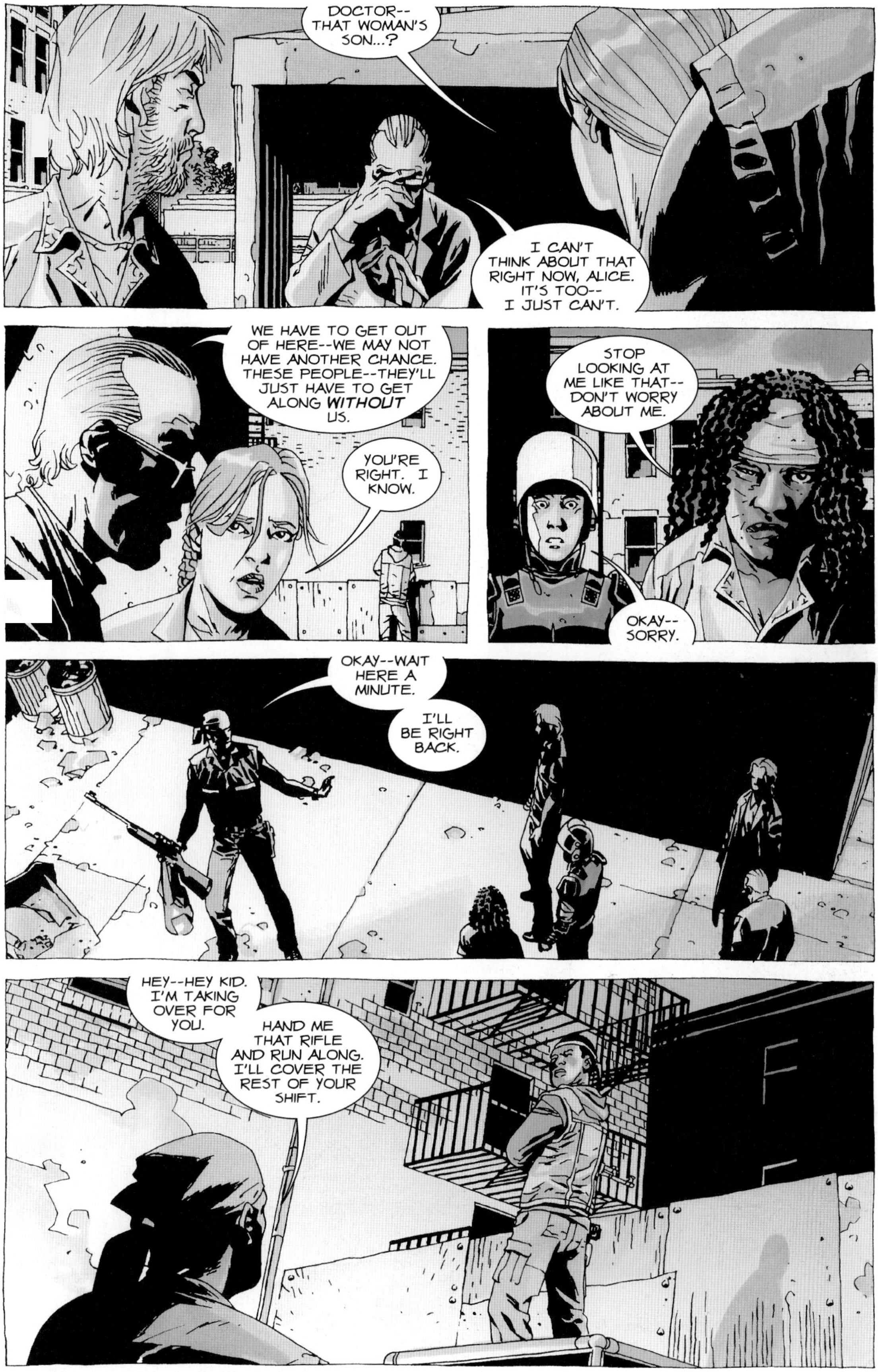
DOCTOR-- THAT WOMAN'S SON...?
I CAN'T THINK ABOUT THAT RIGHT NOW, ALICE. IT'S TOO-- I JUST CAN'T.
WE HAVE TO GET OUT OF HERE--WE MAY NOT HAVE ANOTHER CHANCE. THESE PEOPLE--THEY'LL JUST HAVE TO GET ALONG **WITHOUT** US.
YOU'RE RIGHT. I KNOW.
STOP LOOKING AT ME LIKE THAT-- DON'T WORRY ABOUT ME.
OKAY-- SORRY.
OKAY--WAIT HERE A MINUTE.
I'LL BE RIGHT BACK.
HEY--HEY KID. I'M TAKING OVER FOR YOU.
HAND ME THAT RIFLE AND RUN ALONG. I'LL COVER THE REST OF YOUR SHIFT.

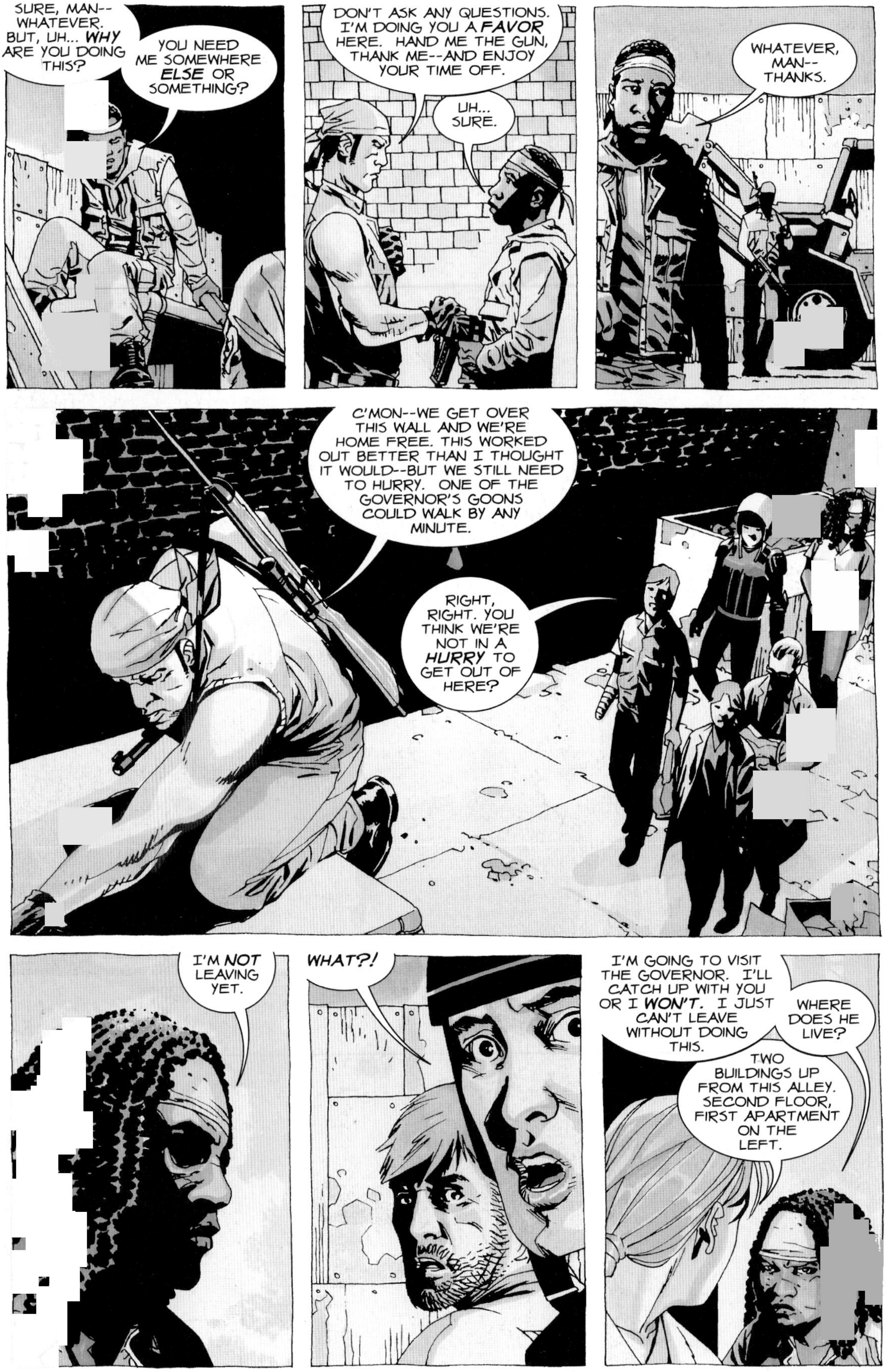

SURE, MAN--WHATEVER. BUT, UH... WHY ARE YOU DOING THIS?
YOU NEED ME SOMEWHERE ELSE OR SOMETHING?
DON'T ASK ANY QUESTIONS. I'M DOING YOU A FAVOR HERE. HAND ME THE GUN, THANK ME--AND ENJOY YOUR TIME OFF.
UH... SURE.
WHATEVER, MAN--THANKS.
C'MON--WE GET OVER THIS WALL AND WE'RE HOME FREE. THIS WORKED OUT BETTER THAN I THOUGHT IT WOULD--BUT WE STILL NEED TO HURRY. ONE OF THE GOVERNOR'S GOONS COULD WALK BY ANY MINUTE.
RIGHT, RIGHT. YOU THINK WE'RE NOT IN A HURRY TO GET OUT OF HERE?
I'M NOT LEAVING YET.
WHAT?!
I'M GOING TO VISIT THE GOVERNOR. I'LL CATCH UP WITH YOU OR I WON'T. I JUST CAN'T LEAVE WITHOUT DOING THIS.
WHERE DOES HE LIVE?
TWO BUILDINGS UP FROM THIS ALLEY. SECOND FLOOR, FIRST APARTMENT ON THE LEFT.

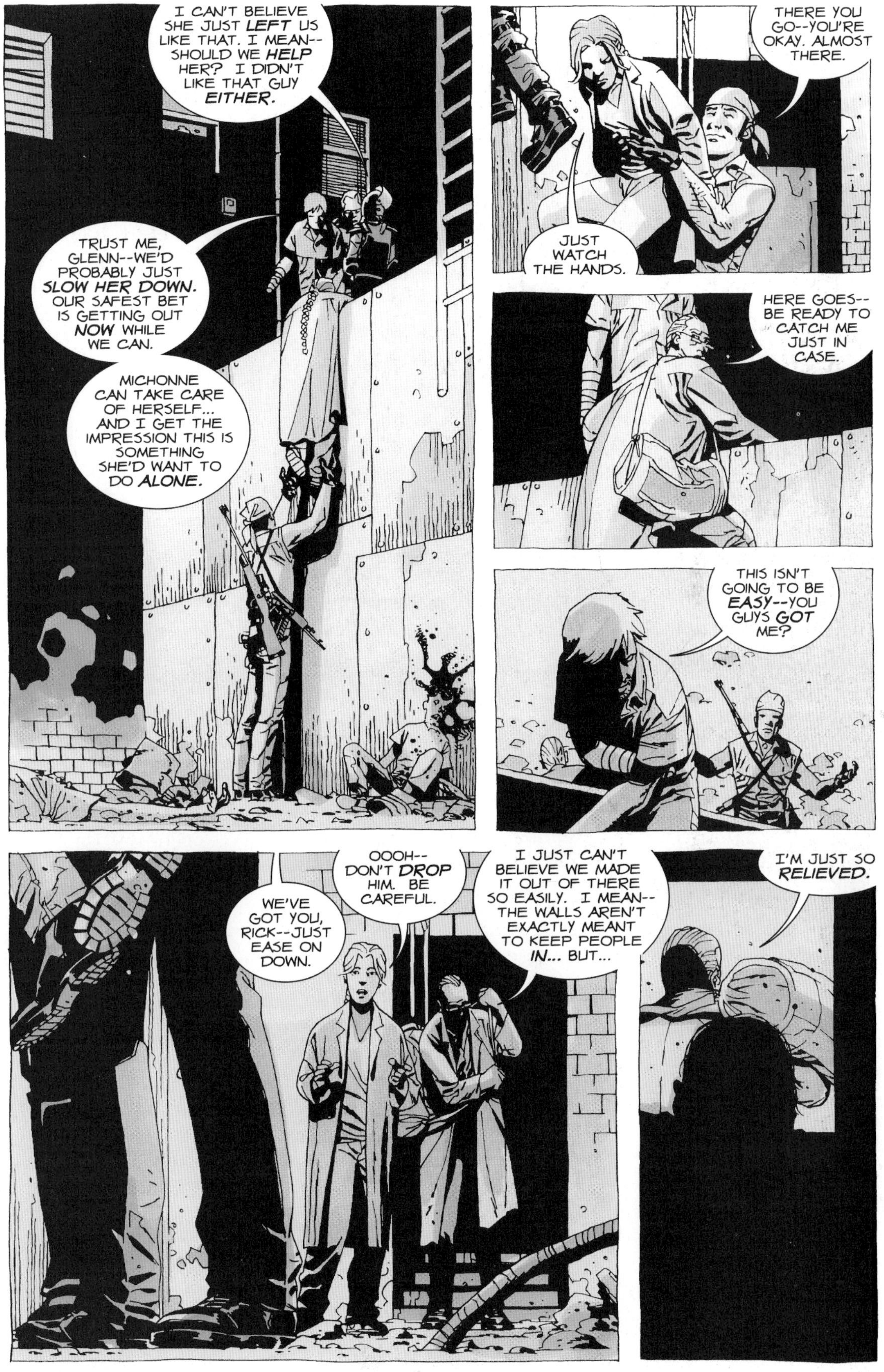

I CAN'T BELIEVE SHE JUST LEFT US LIKE THAT. I MEAN--SHOULD WE HELP HER? I DIDN'T LIKE THAT GUY EITHER.
TRUST ME, GLENN--WE'D PROBABLY JUST SLOW HER DOWN. OUR SAFEST BET IS GETTING OUT NOW WHILE WE CAN.
MICHONNE CAN TAKE CARE OF HERSELF... AND I GET THE IMPRESSION THIS IS SOMETHING SHE'D WANT TO DO ALONE.
THERE YOU GO--YOU'RE OKAY. ALMOST THERE.
JUST WATCH THE HANDS.
HERE GOES--BE READY TO CATCH ME JUST IN CASE.
THIS ISN'T GOING TO BE EASY--YOU GUYS GOT ME?
WE'VE GOT YOU, RICK--JUST EASE ON DOWN.
OOOH--DON'T DROP HIM. BE CAREFUL.
I JUST CAN'T BELIEVE WE MADE IT OUT OF THERE SO EASILY. I MEAN--THE WALLS AREN'T EXACTLY MEANT TO KEEP PEOPLE IN... BUT...
I'M JUST SO RELIEVED.

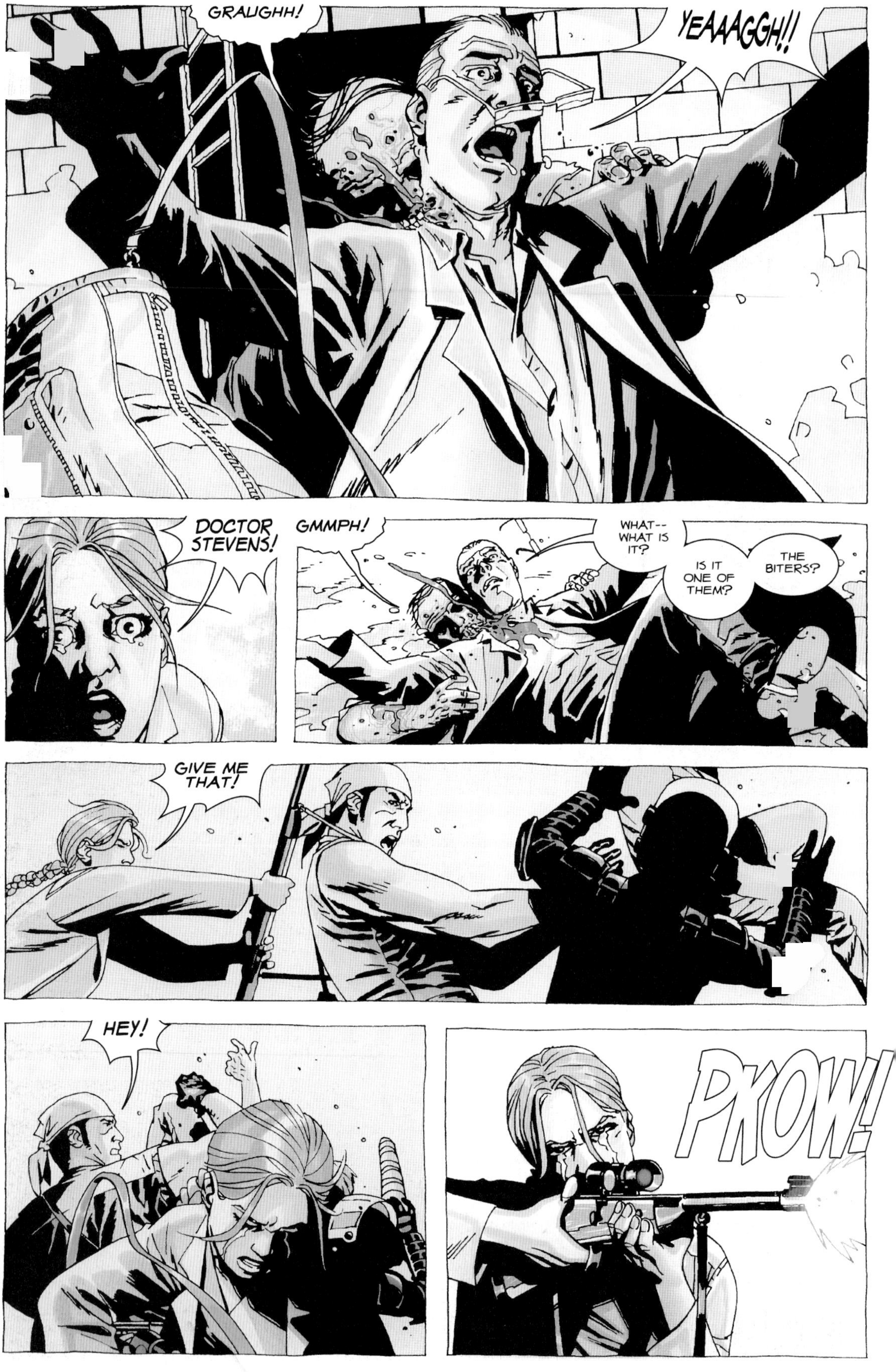
GRAUGHH!
YEAAAGGH!!
DOCTOR STEVENS!
GMMPH!
WHAT-- WHAT IS IT?
IS IT ONE OF THEM?
THE BITERS?
GIVE ME THAT!
HEY!
PKOW!

IT'S OKAY...

IT'S *OKAY*, ALICE...

I'M NOT *DYING*... THINK OF IT... *SCIENTIFICALLY*... I'M JUST...

EVOLVING... INTO A DIFFERENT-- *WORSE* LIFE FORM. I'LL STILL EXIST... IN *SOME* WAY.

TAKE THE SUPPLIES... YOU'LL NEED THEM TO TAKE *CARE* OF THESE PEOPLE.

USE WHAT I TAUGHT YOU.

GO.

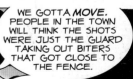

WE GOTTA *MOVE*. PEOPLE IN THE TOWN WILL THINK THE SHOTS WERE JUST THE GUARD TAKING OUT BITERS THAT GOT CLOSE TO THE FENCE.

BUT THE SOUND WILL ATTRACT ANY BITERS CLOSE BY TO THIS AREA-- WE NEED TO BE *GONE* WHEN THEY GET HERE.

I--HE WAS A GOOD FRIEND--I'LL MISS HIM, *TOO*.

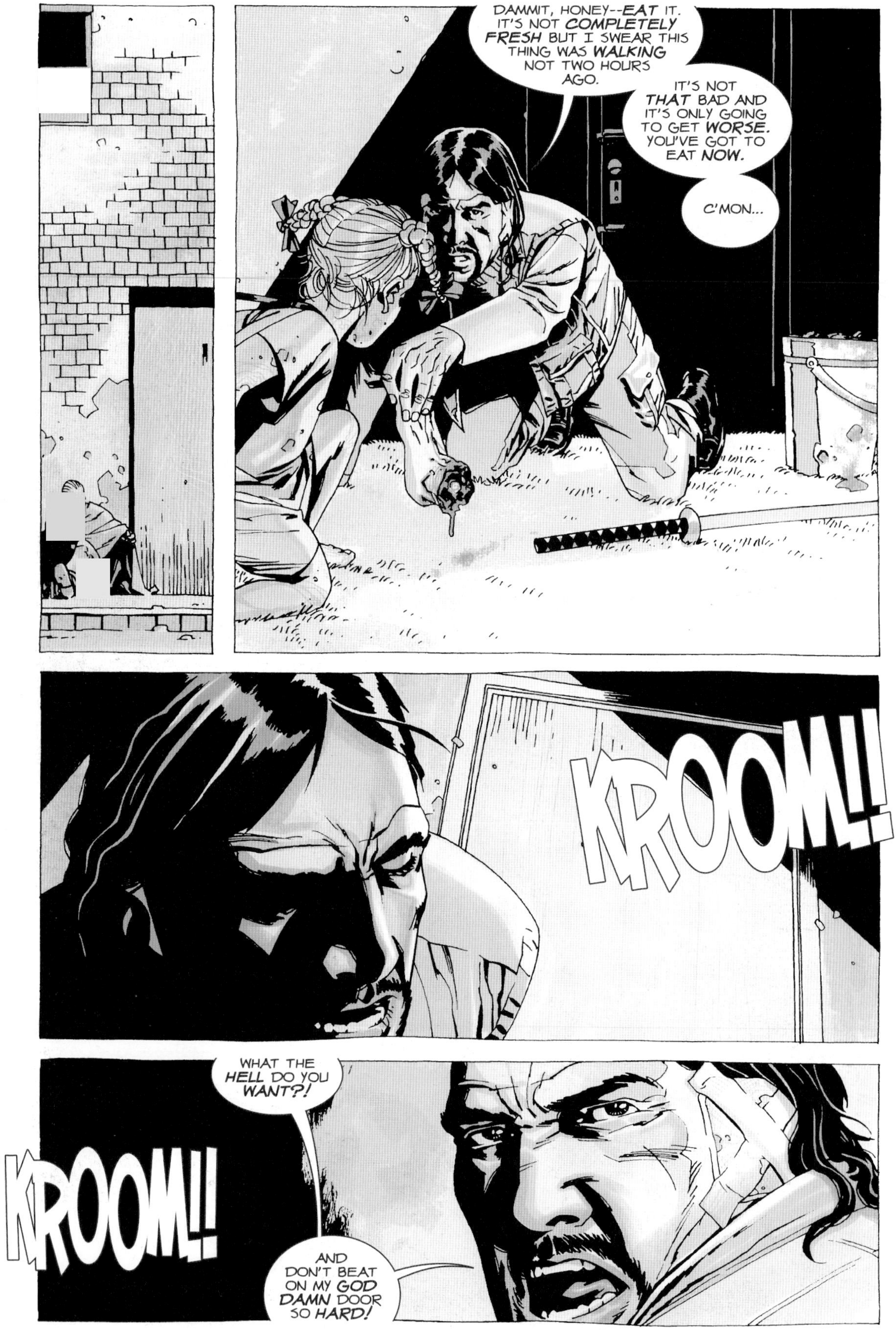
DAMMIT, HONEY--EAT IT. IT'S NOT COMPLETELY FRESH BUT I SWEAR THIS THING WAS WALKING NOT TWO HOURS AGO.
IT'S NOT THAT BAD AND IT'S ONLY GOING TO GET WORSE. YOU'VE GOT TO EAT NOW.
C'MON...
KROOM!!
KROOM!!
WHAT THE HELL DO YOU WANT?!
AND DON'T BEAT ON MY GOD DAMN DOOR SO HARD!

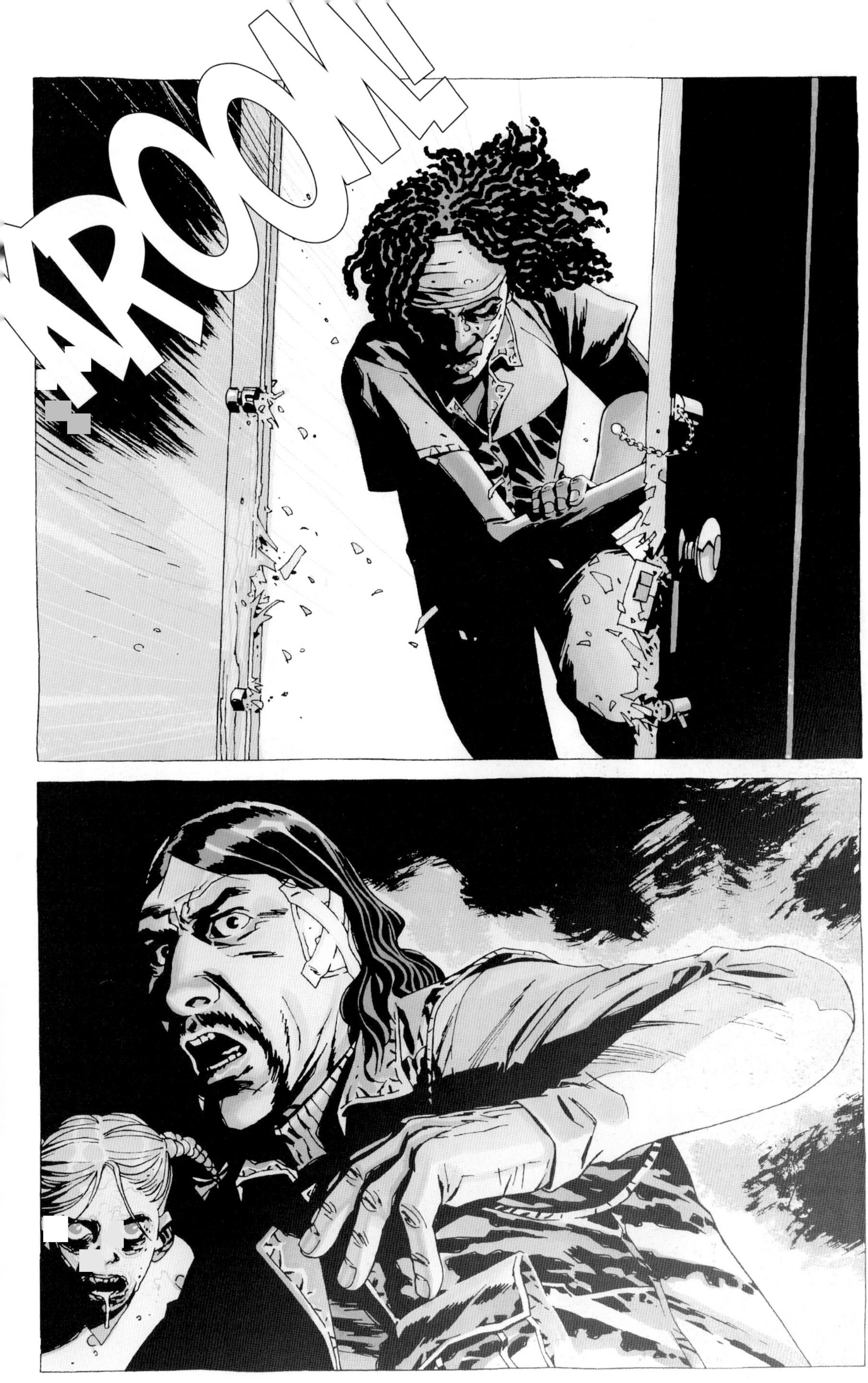
ROOM!

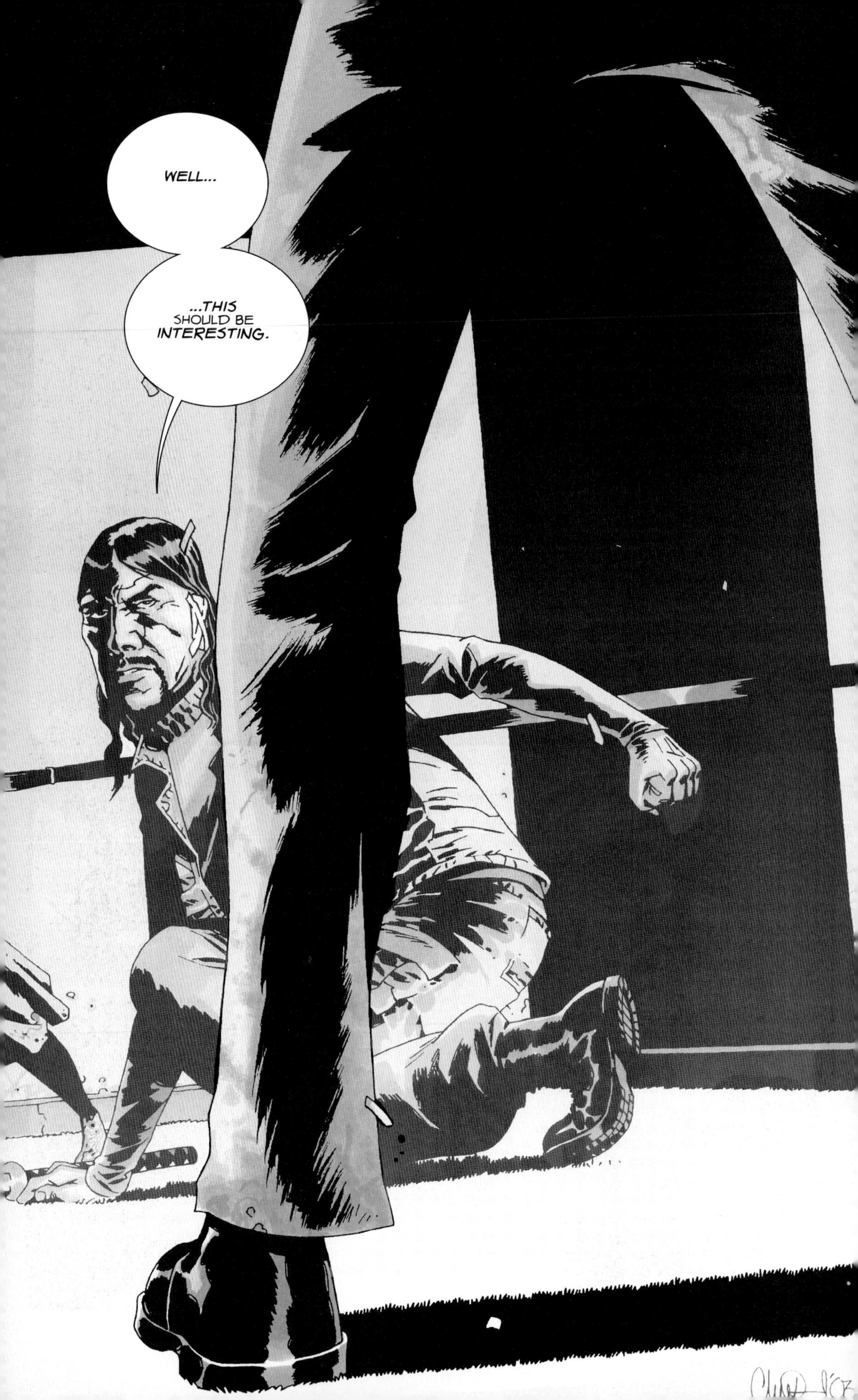
WELL...
...THIS SHOULD BE INTERESTING.

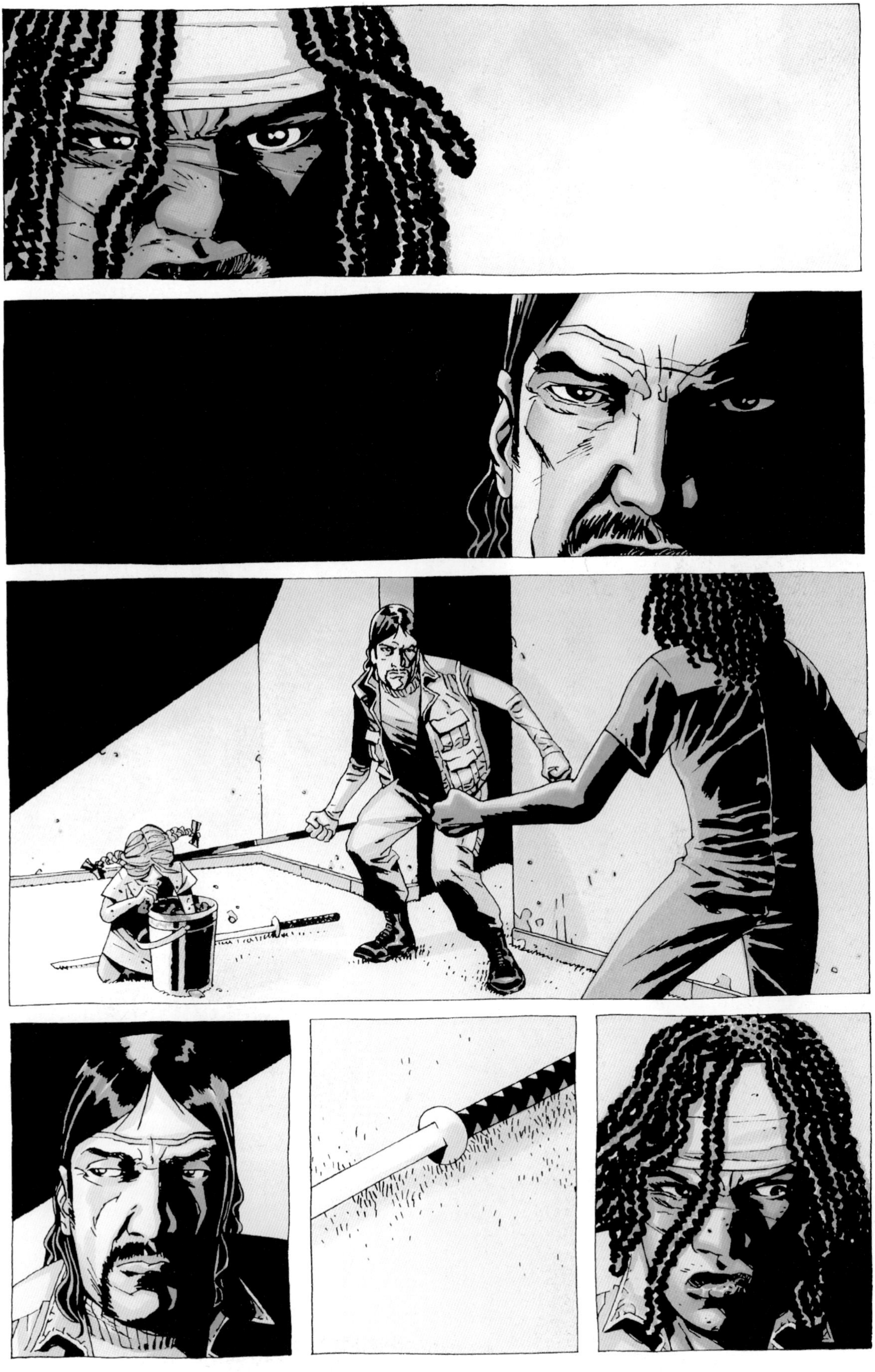

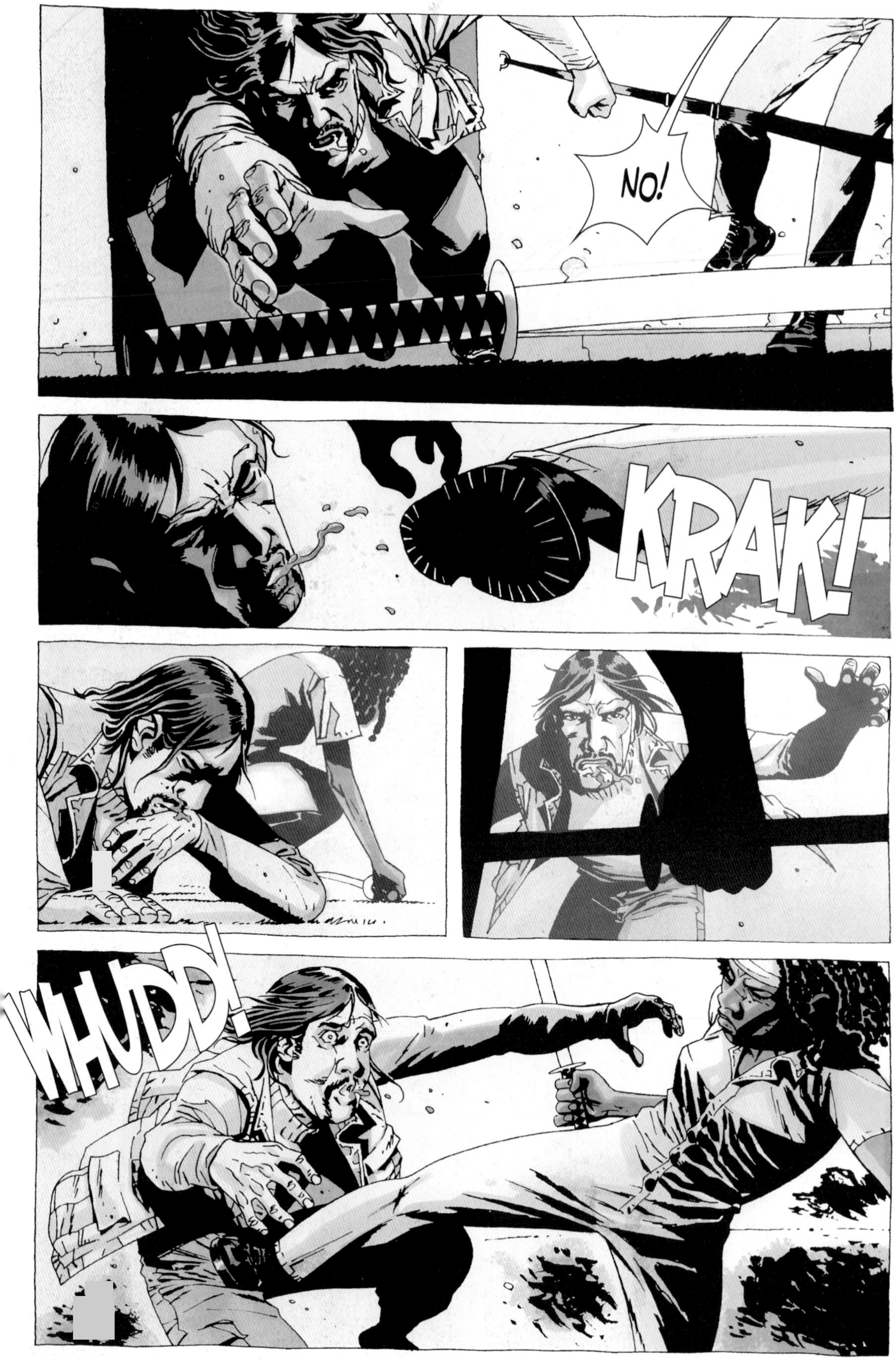
NO!
KRAK!
WHUDD!

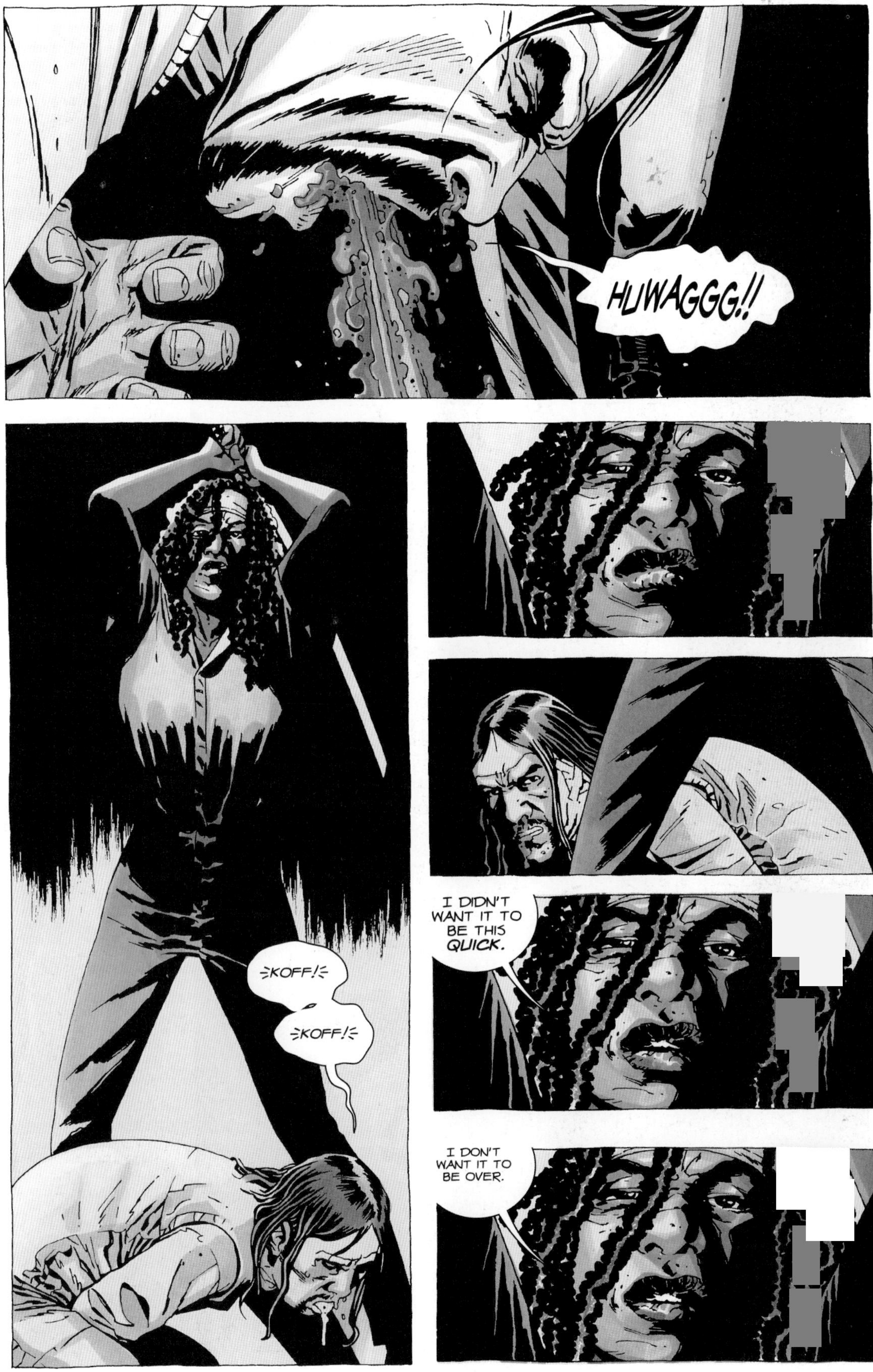
HUWAGGG!!
KOFF!
KOFF!
I DIDN'T WANT IT TO BE THIS QUICK.
I DON'T WANT IT TO BE OVER.

WHUMP!

WHUDD!

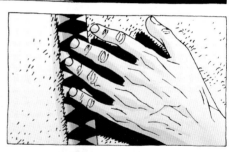

HRRKK!!

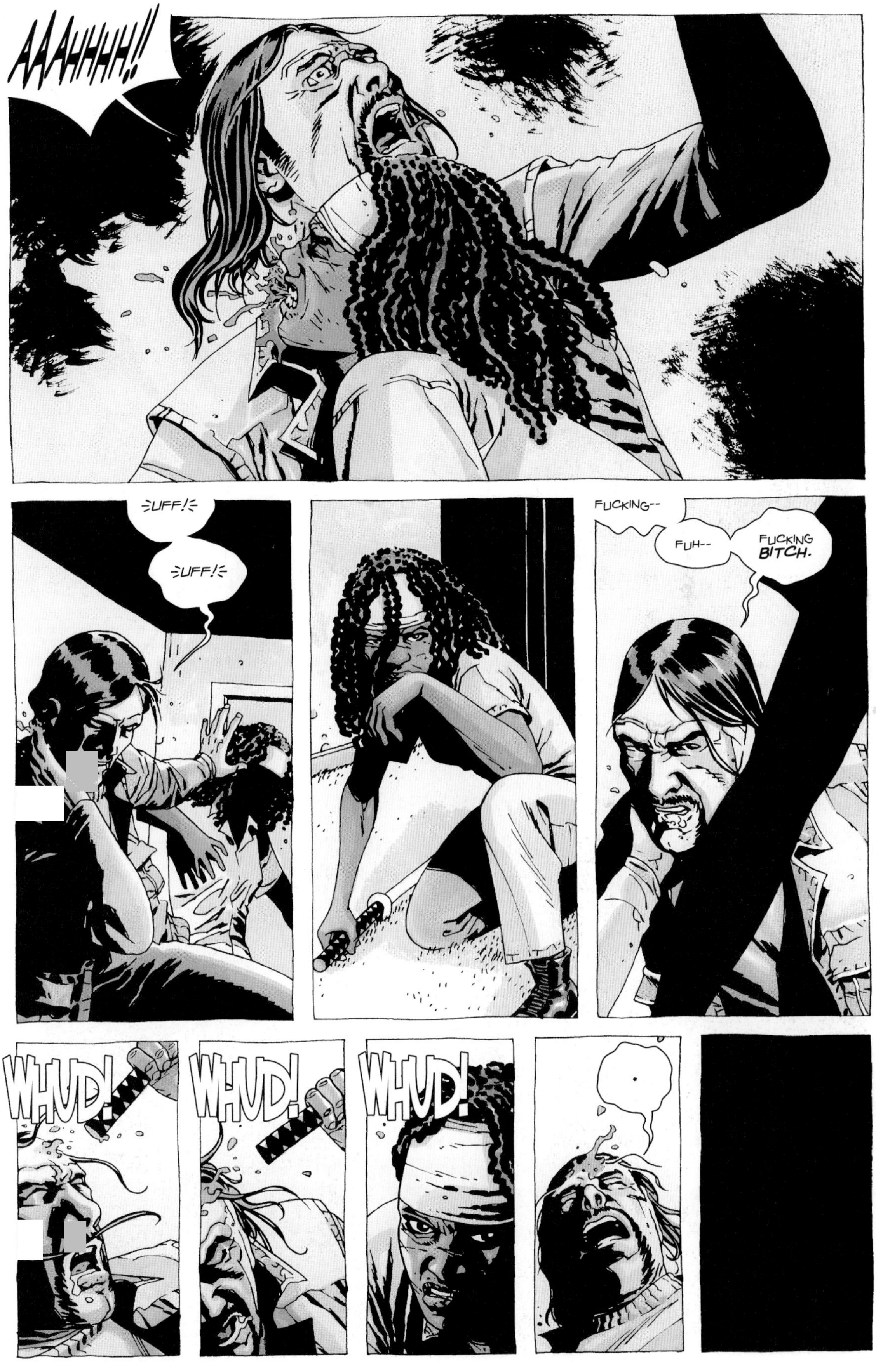
AAAHHHH!!
UFF!
UFF!
FUCKING--
FUH--
FUCKING BITCH.
WHUD!
WHUD!
WHUD!

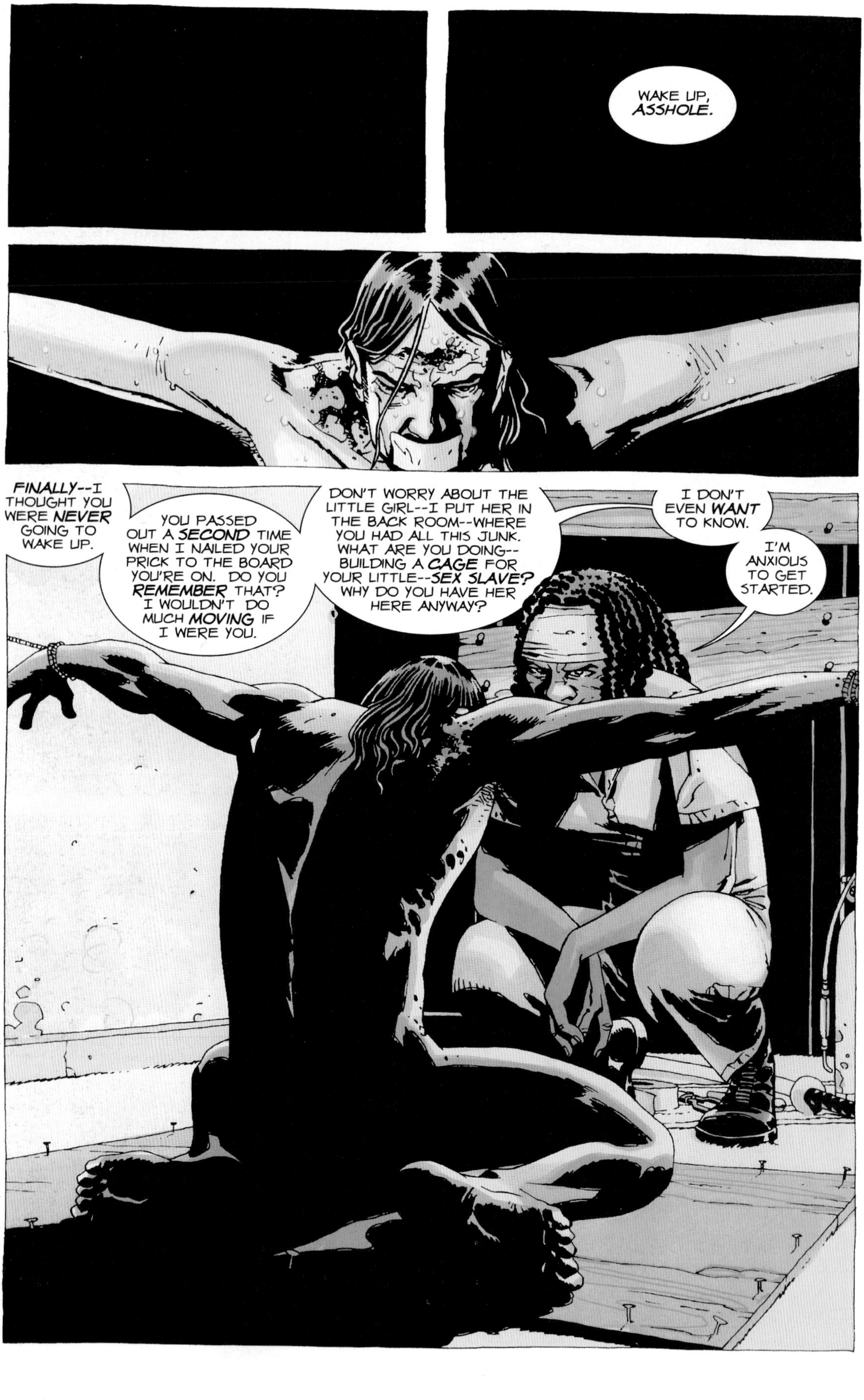
WAKE UP, ASSHOLE.
FINALLY--I THOUGHT YOU WERE NEVER GOING TO WAKE UP.
YOU PASSED OUT A SECOND TIME WHEN I NAILED YOUR PRICK TO THE BOARD YOU'RE ON. DO YOU REMEMBER THAT? I WOULDN'T DO MUCH MOVING IF I WERE YOU.
DON'T WORRY ABOUT THE LITTLE GIRL--I PUT HER IN THE BACK ROOM--WHERE YOU HAD ALL THIS JUNK. WHAT ARE YOU DOING--BUILDING A CAGE FOR YOUR LITTLE--SEX SLAVE? WHY DO YOU HAVE HER HERE ANYWAY?
I DON'T EVEN WANT TO KNOW.
I'M ANXIOUS TO GET STARTED.

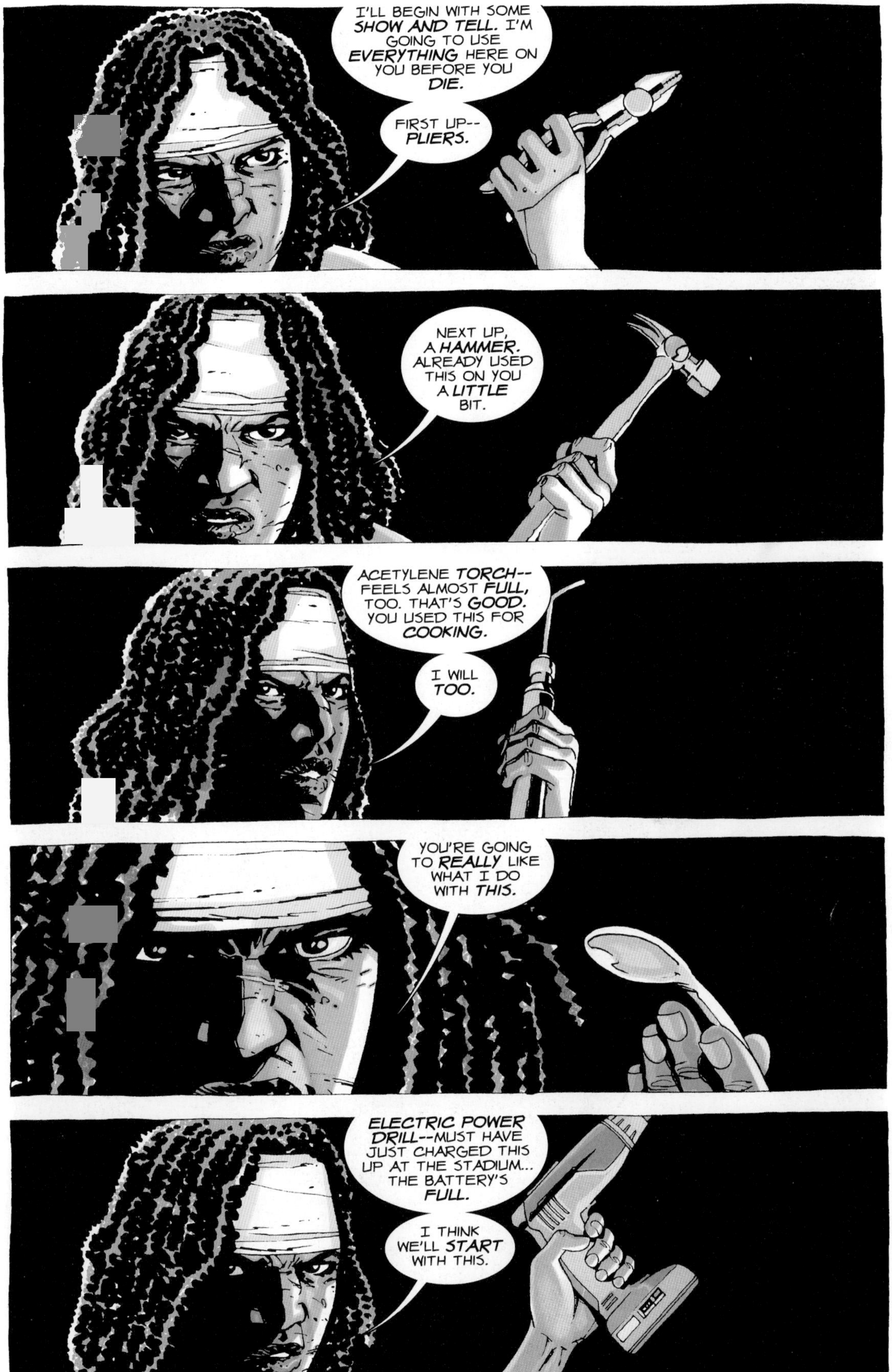
I'LL BEGIN WITH SOME SHOW AND TELL. I'M GOING TO USE EVERYTHING HERE ON YOU BEFORE YOU DIE.
FIRST UP-- PLIERS.
NEXT UP, A HAMMER. ALREADY USED THIS ON YOU A LITTLE BIT.
ACETYLENE TORCH-- FEELS ALMOST FULL, TOO. THAT'S GOOD. YOU USED THIS FOR COOKING.
I WILL TOO.
YOU'RE GOING TO REALLY LIKE WHAT I DO WITH THIS.
ELECTRIC POWER DRILL--MUST HAVE JUST CHARGED THIS UP AT THE STADIUM... THE BATTERY'S FULL.
I THINK WE'LL START WITH THIS.

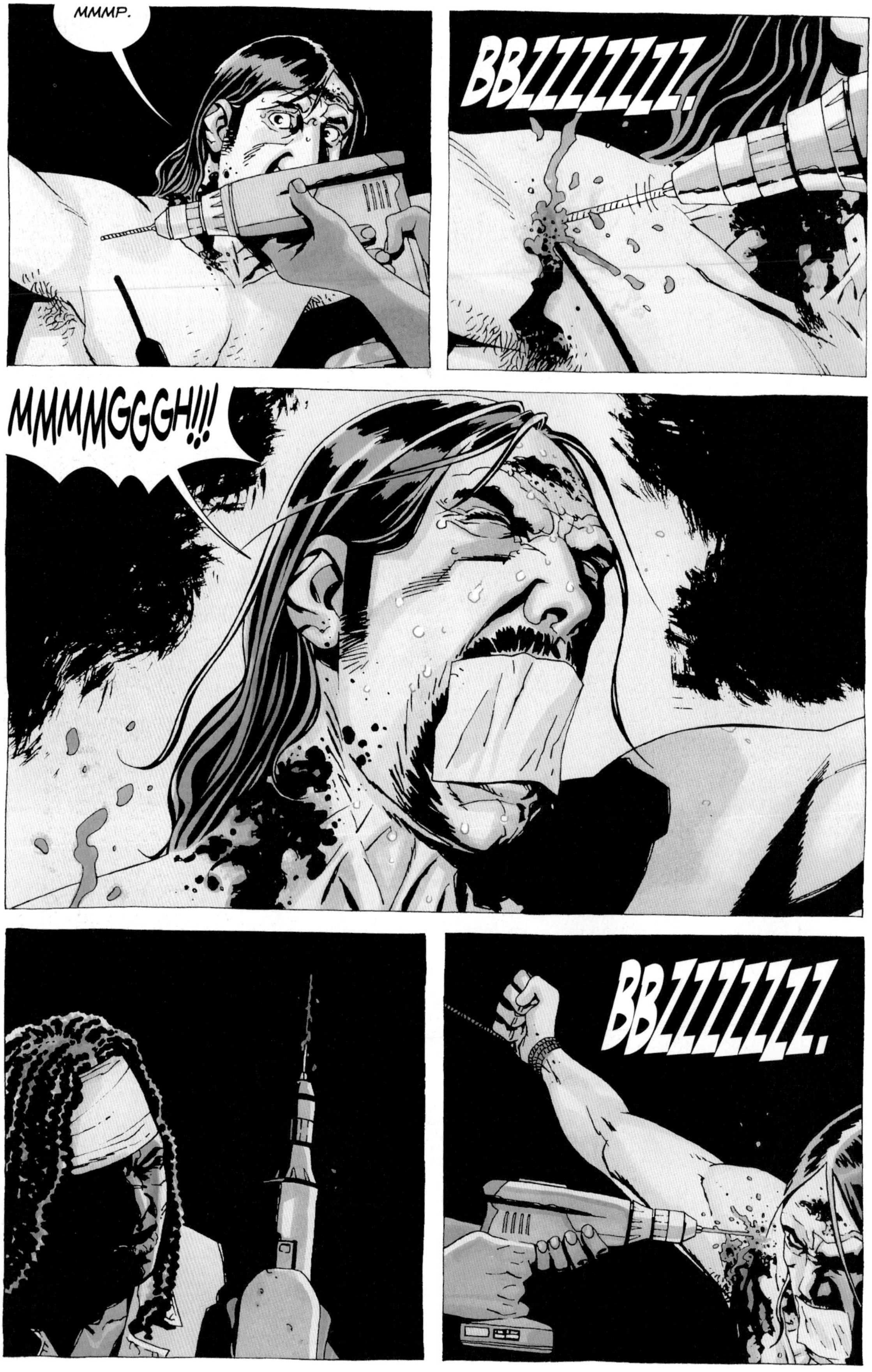
MMMP.
BBZZZZZZZZ.
MMMMGGGH!!!
BBZZZZZZZ.

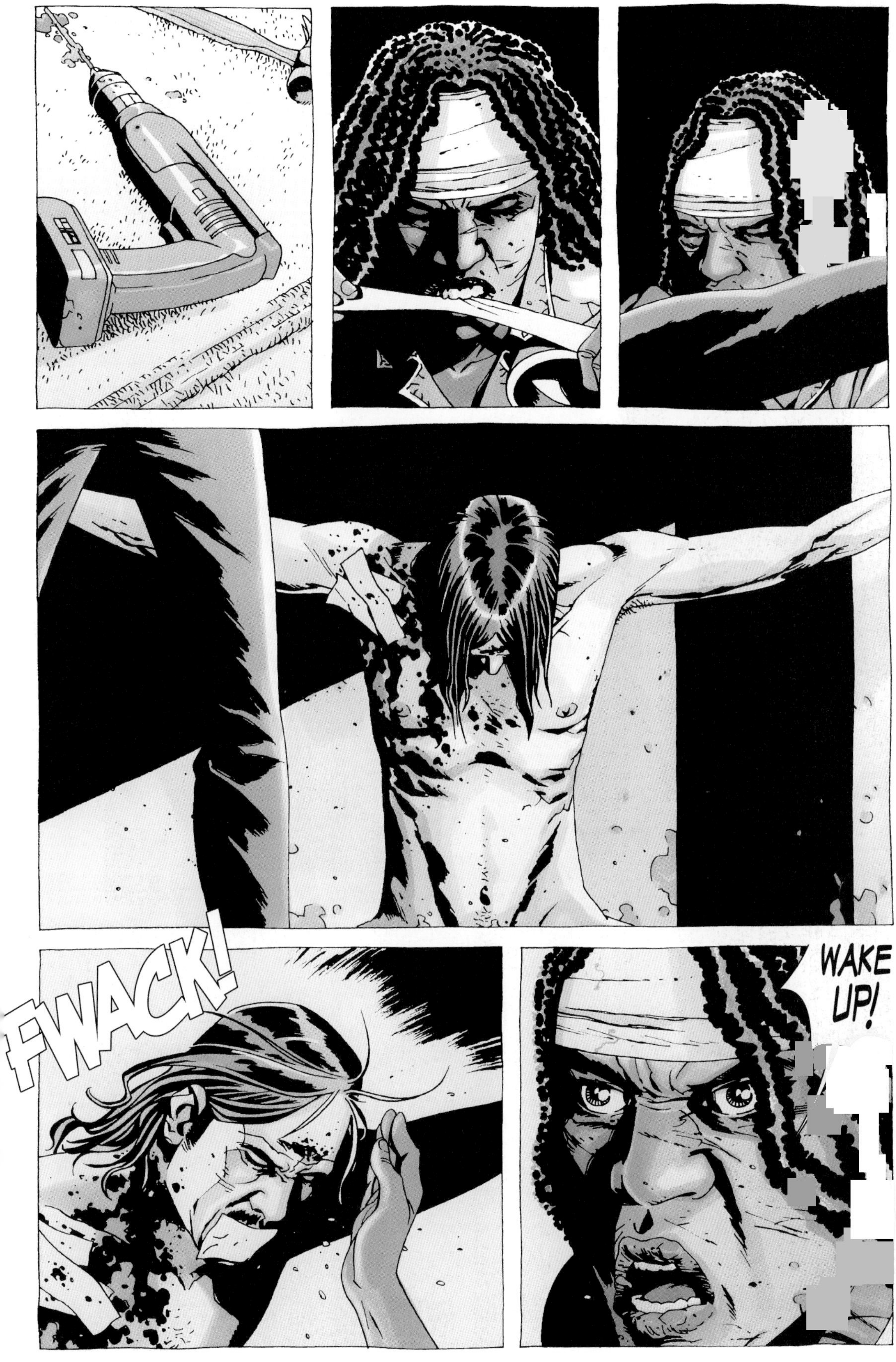
FWACK!
WAKE UP!

YOU'RE GOING TO LOVE THIS.

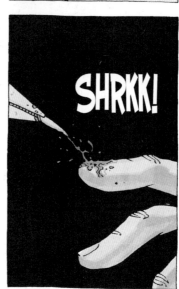

SHRKK!

MMUURGGH!

SKRRK!

MRRGH!

SHKK!

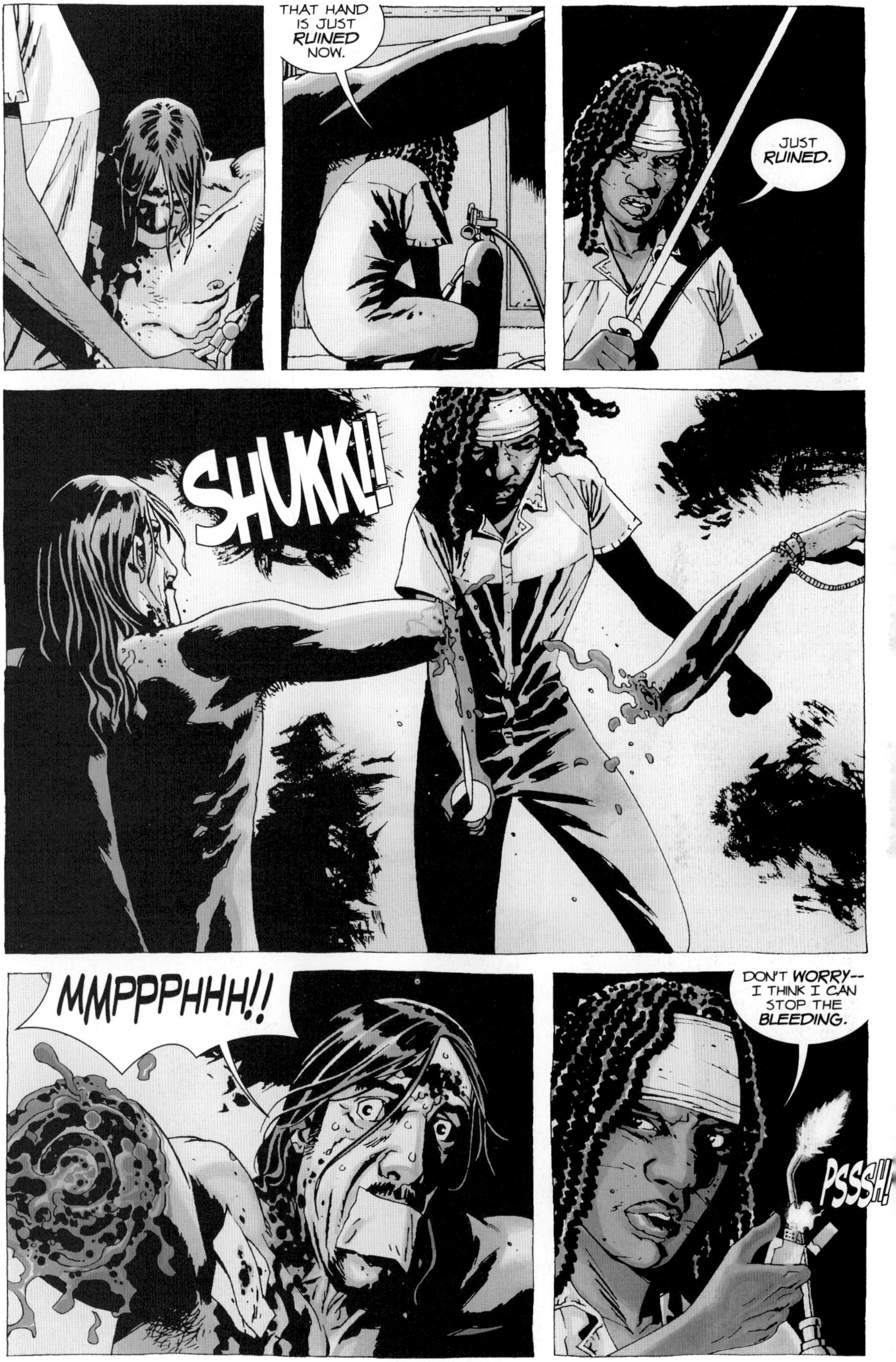
THAT HAND IS JUST RUINED NOW.
JUST RUINED.
SHUKK!!
MMPPPHHH!!
DON'T WORRY-- I THINK I CAN STOP THE BLEEDING.
PSSSH!

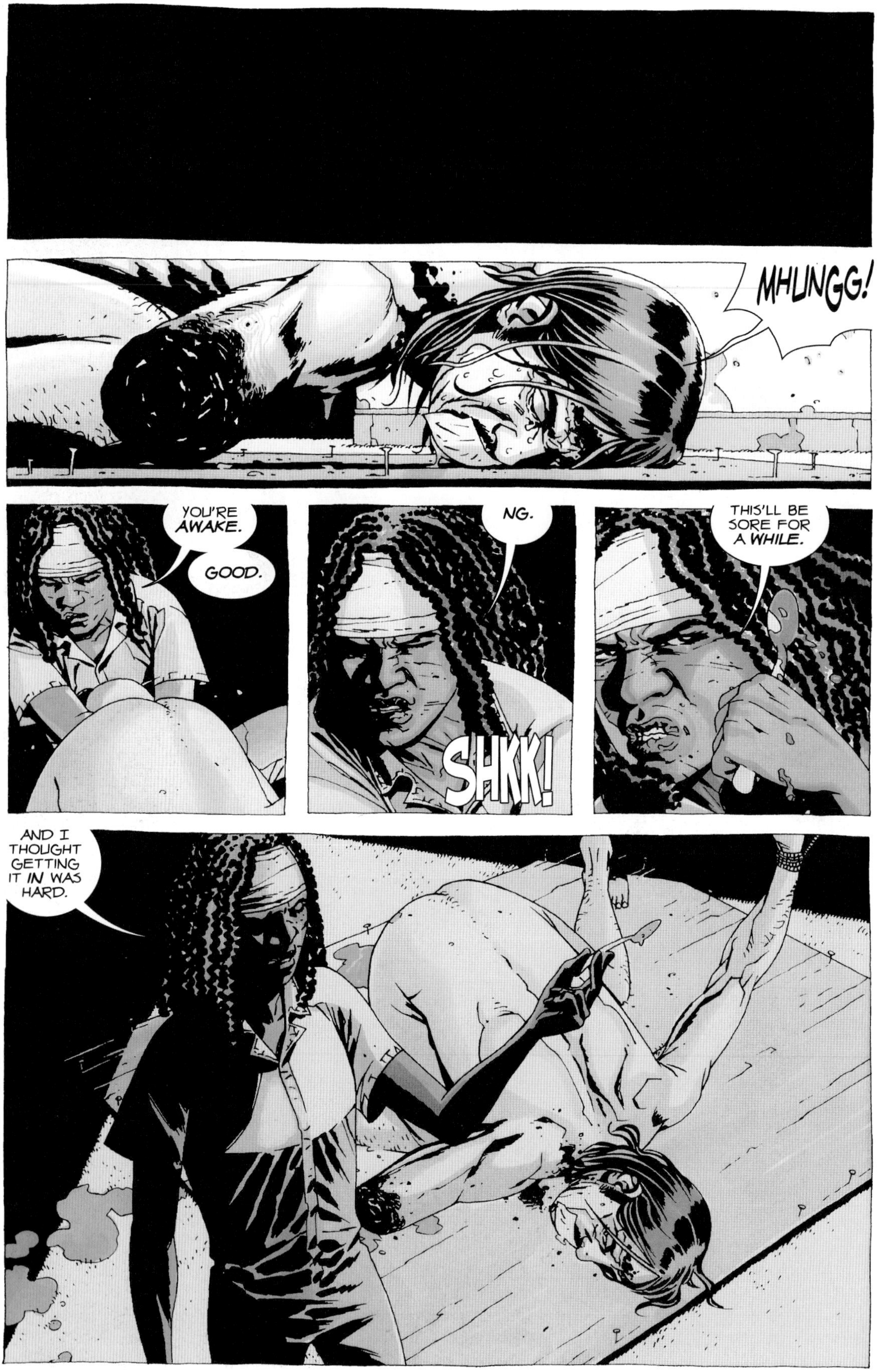
MHUNGG!
YOU'RE AWAKE.
GOOD.
NG.
SHKK!
THIS'LL BE SORE FOR A WHILE.
AND I THOUGHT GETTING IT IN WAS HARD.

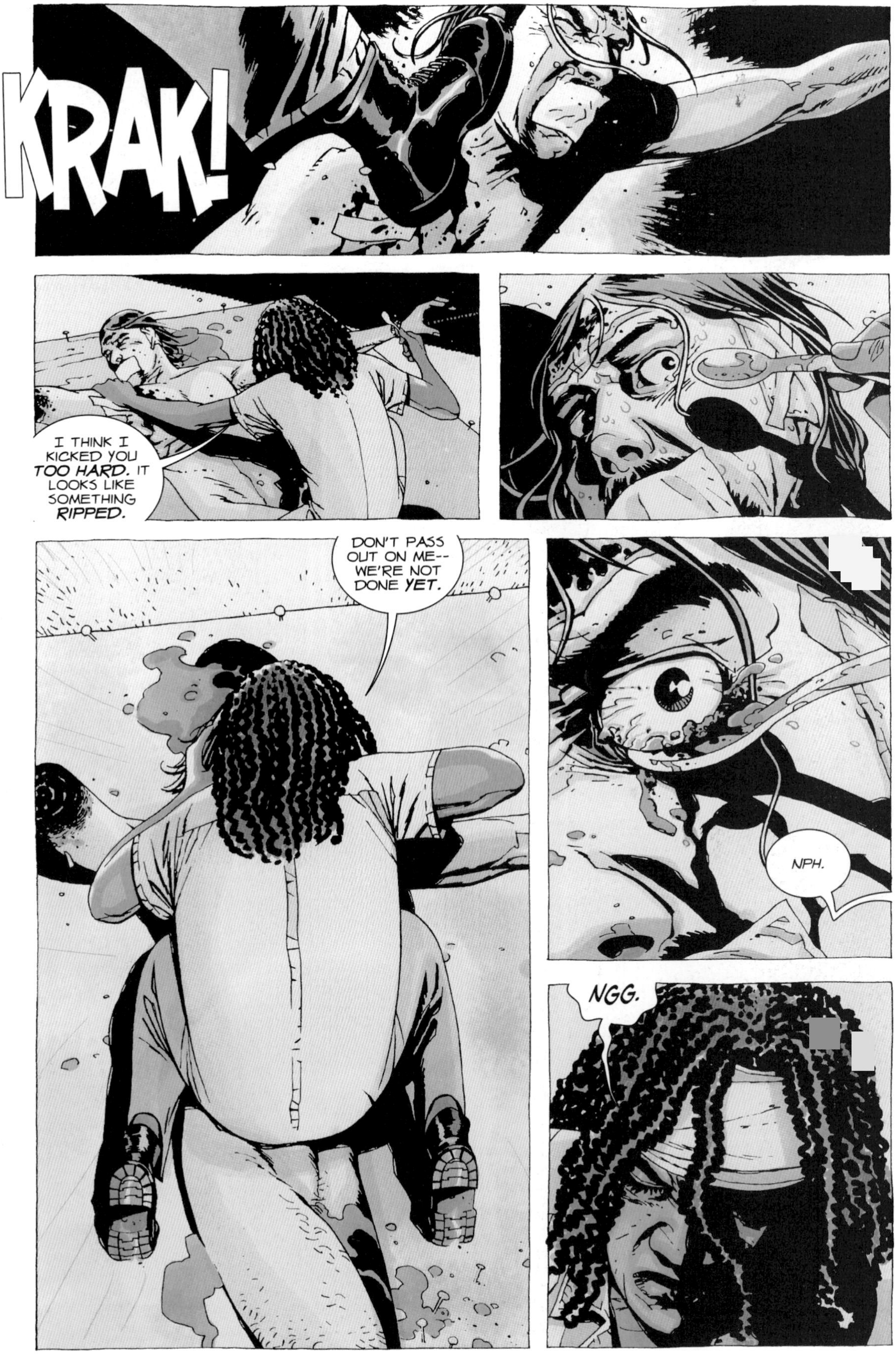
KRAK!
I THINK I KICKED YOU TOO HARD. IT LOOKS LIKE SOMETHING RIPPED.
DON'T PASS OUT ON ME-- WE'RE NOT DONE YET.
NPH.
NGG.

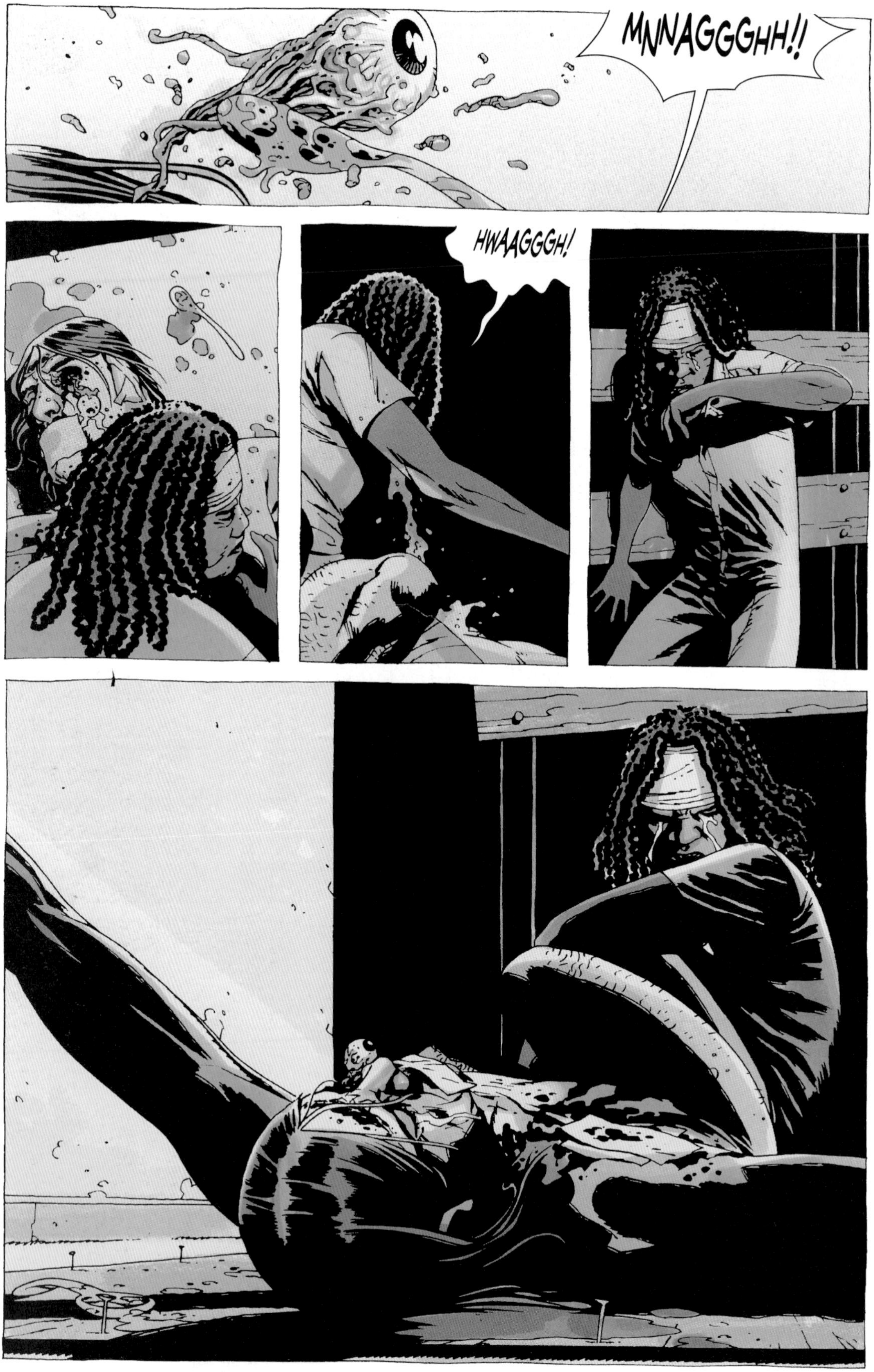
MNNAGGGHH!!
HWAAGGGH!

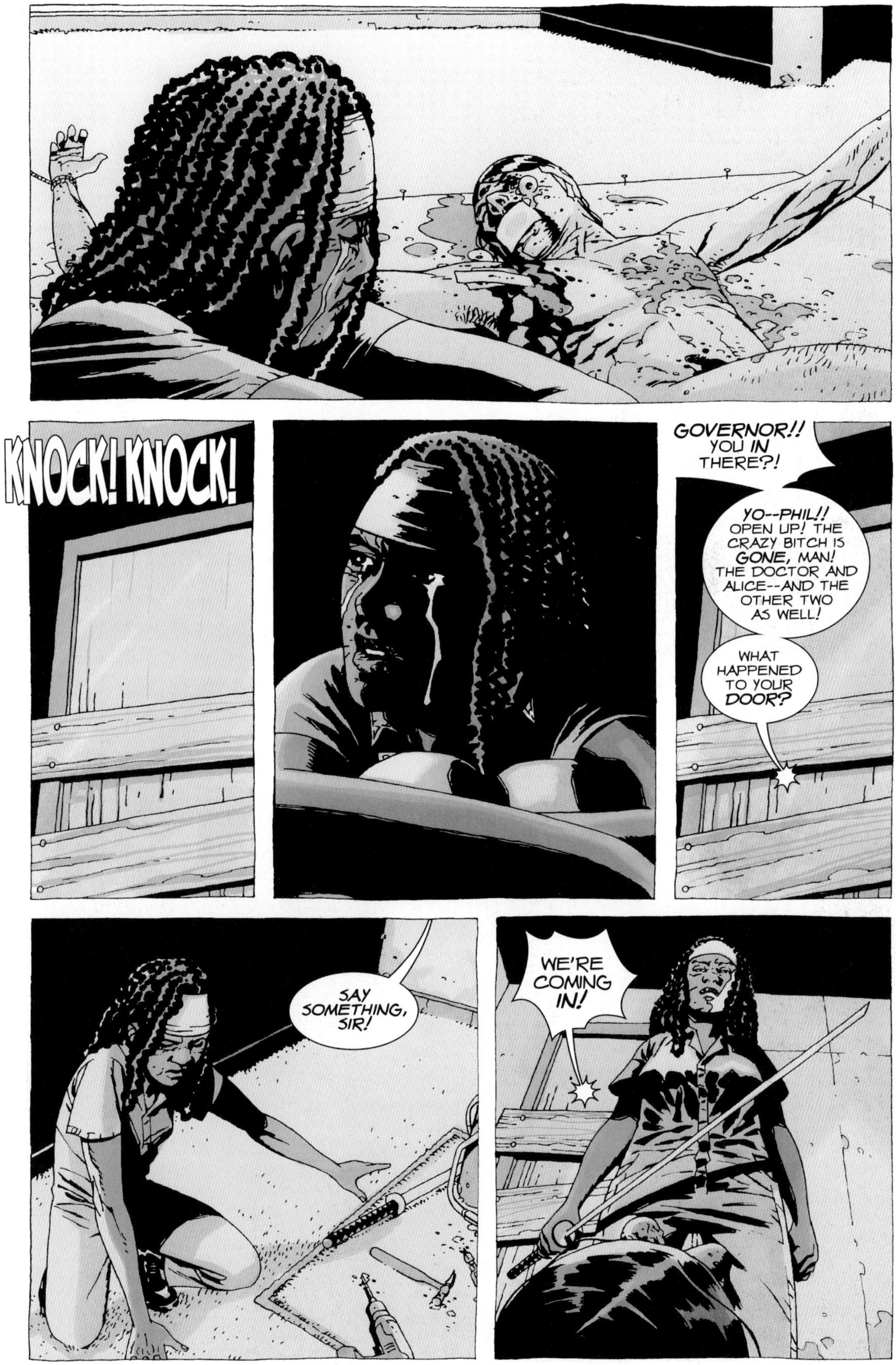
KNOCK! KNOCK!
GOVERNOR!! YOU IN THERE?!
YO--PHIL!! OPEN UP! THE CRAZY BITCH IS GONE, MAN! THE DOCTOR AND ALICE--AND THE OTHER TWO AS WELL!
WHAT HAPPENED TO YOUR DOOR?
SAY SOMETHING, SIR!
WE'RE COMING IN!

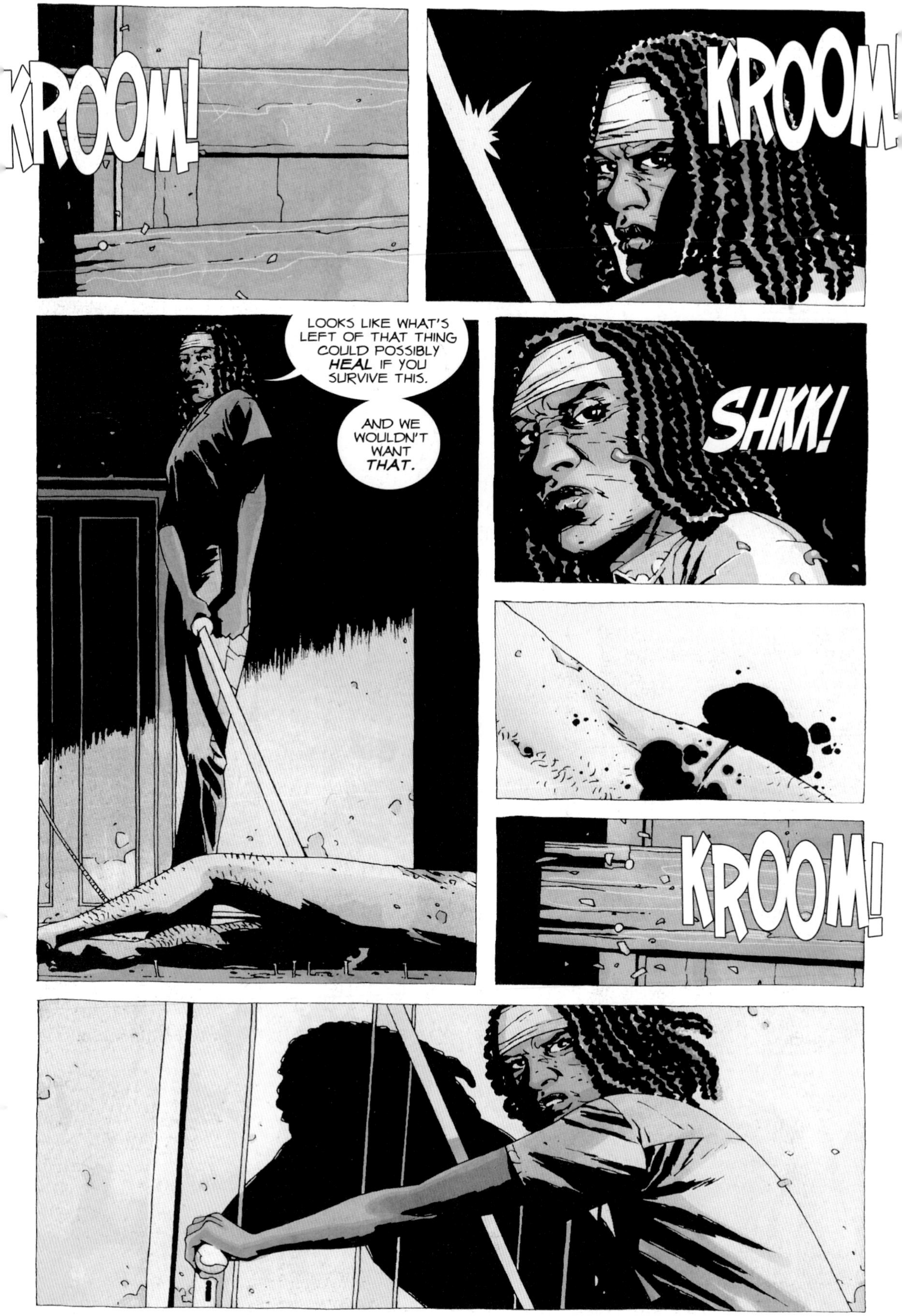
KROOM!
KROOM!
LOOKS LIKE WHAT'S LEFT OF THAT THING COULD POSSIBLY *HEAL* IF YOU SURVIVE THIS.
AND WE WOULDN'T WANT *THAT*.
SHKK!
KROOM!

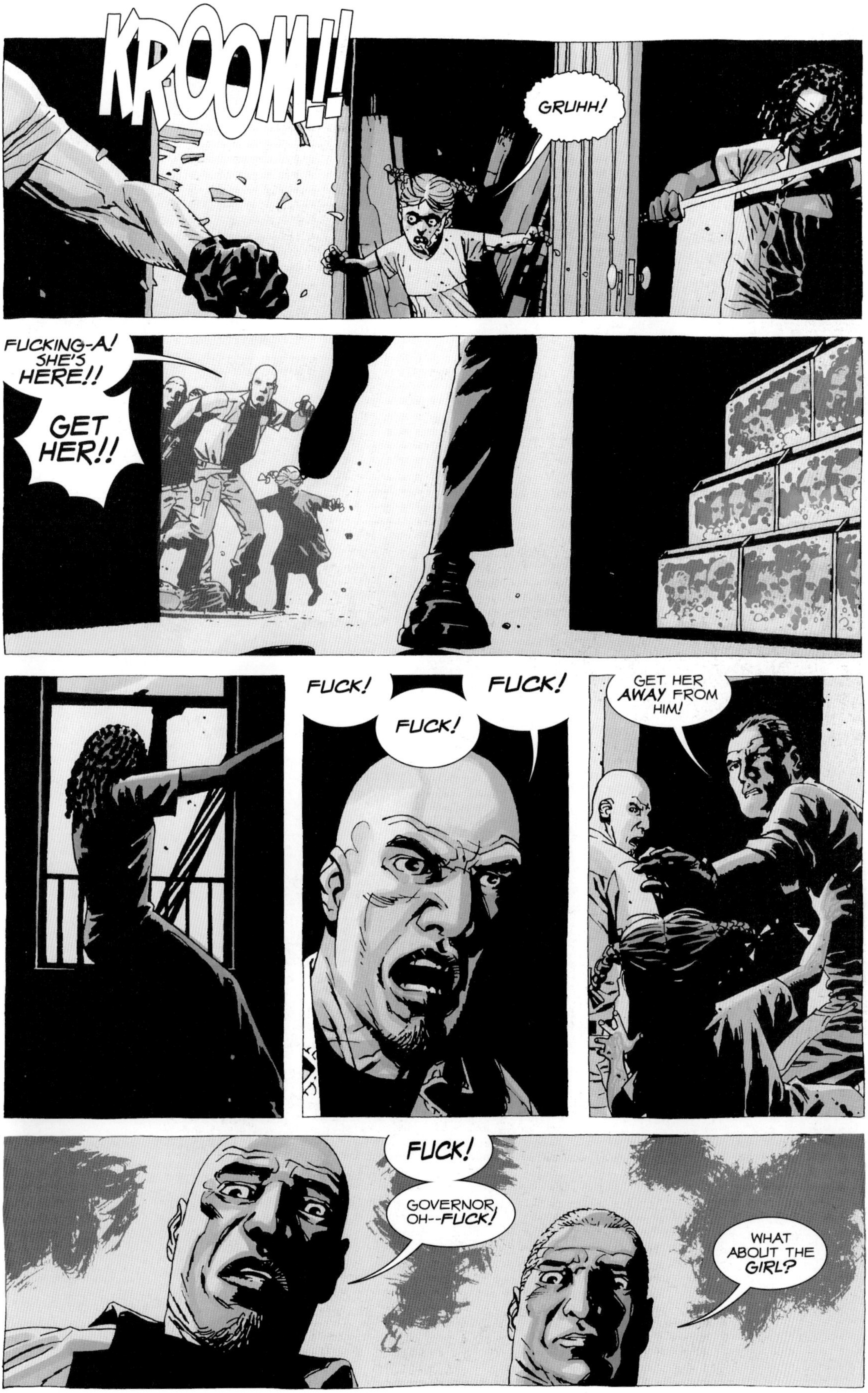
KROOM!!
GRUHH!
FUCKING-A! SHE'S HERE!!
GET HER!!
FUCK!
FUCK!
FUCK!
GET HER AWAY FROM HIM!
FUCK!
GOVERNOR, OH--FUCK!
WHAT ABOUT THE GIRL?

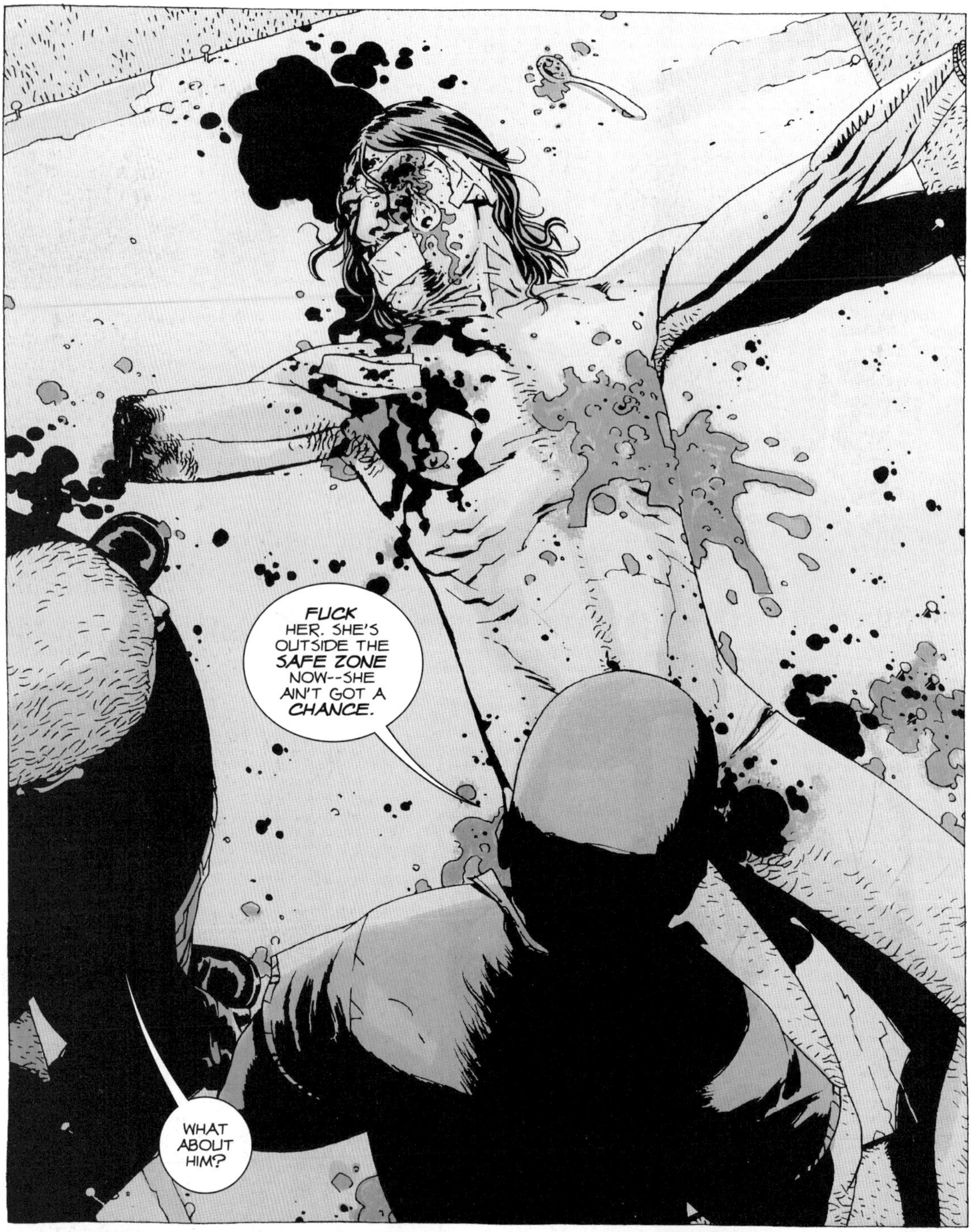
FUCK HER. SHE'S OUTSIDE THE SAFE ZONE NOW--SHE AIN'T GOT A CHANCE.
WHAT ABOUT HIM?

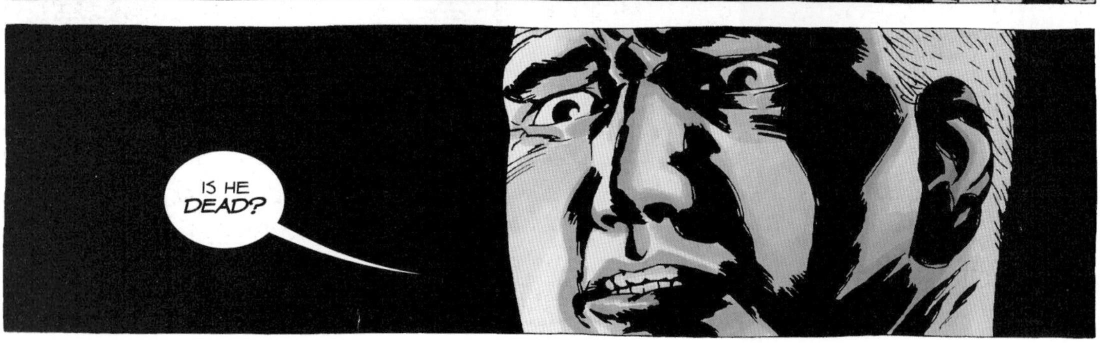
IS HE DEAD?

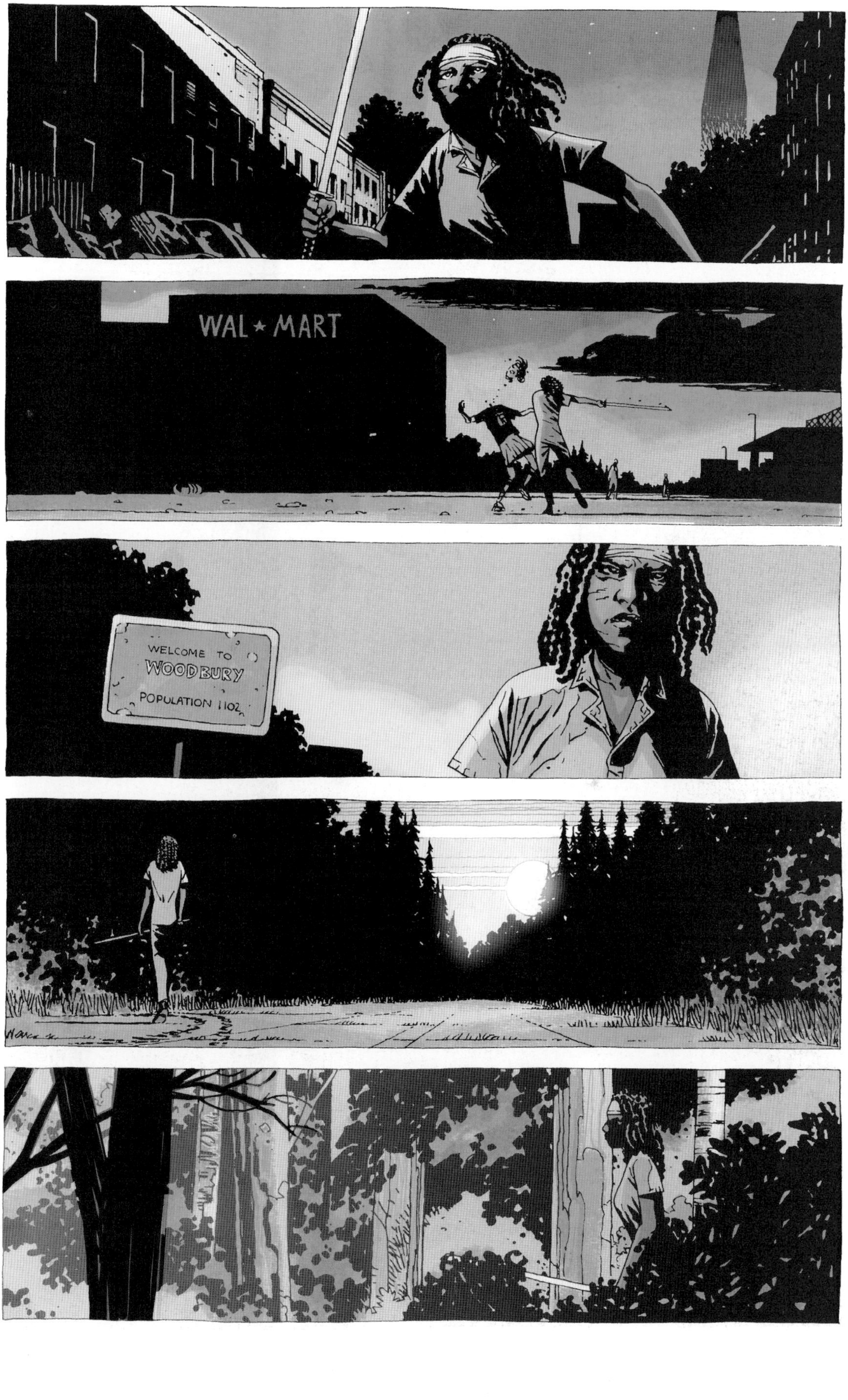
WAL ★ MART
WELCOME TO
WOODBURY
POPULATION 1102

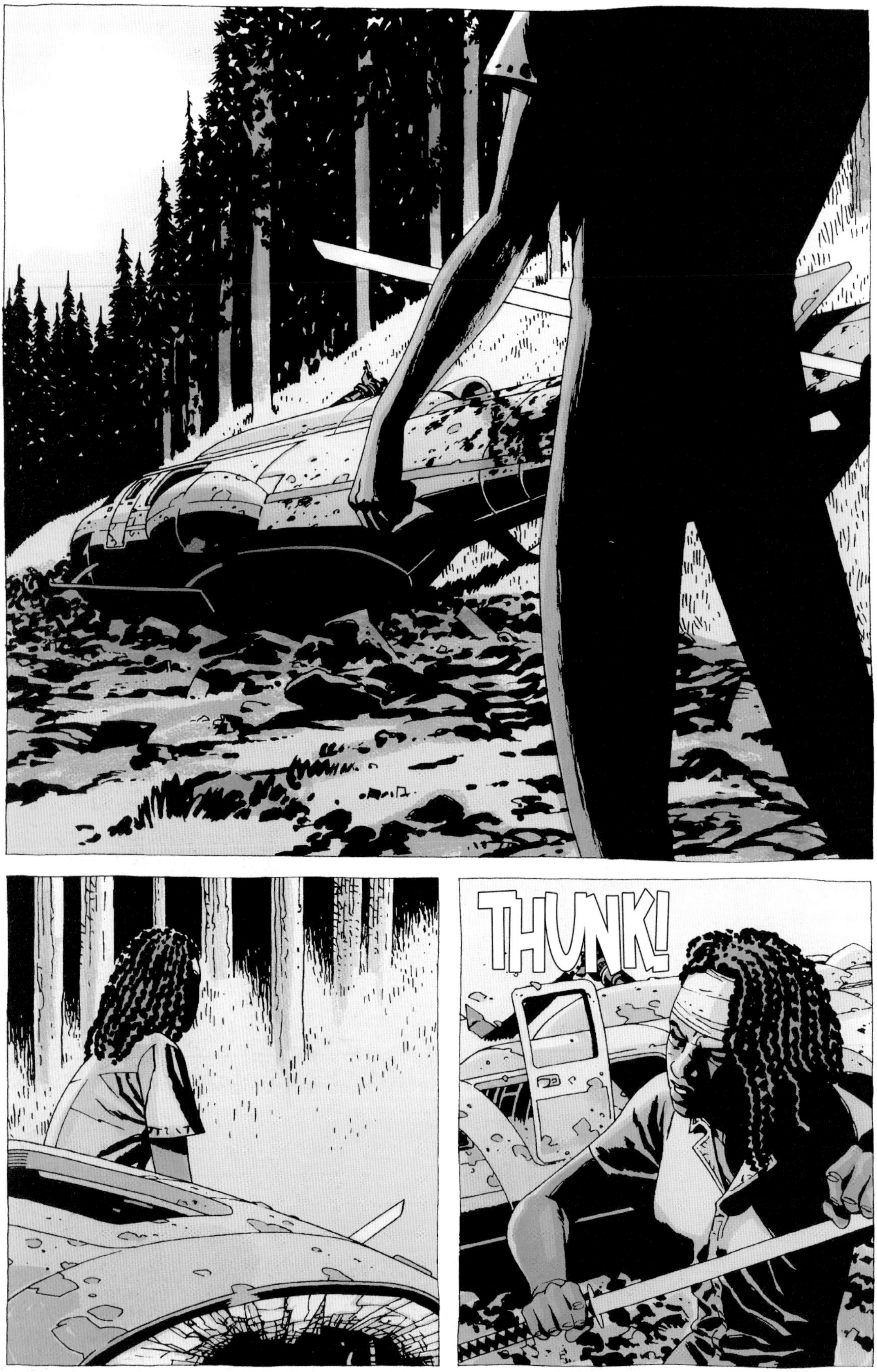
THUNK!

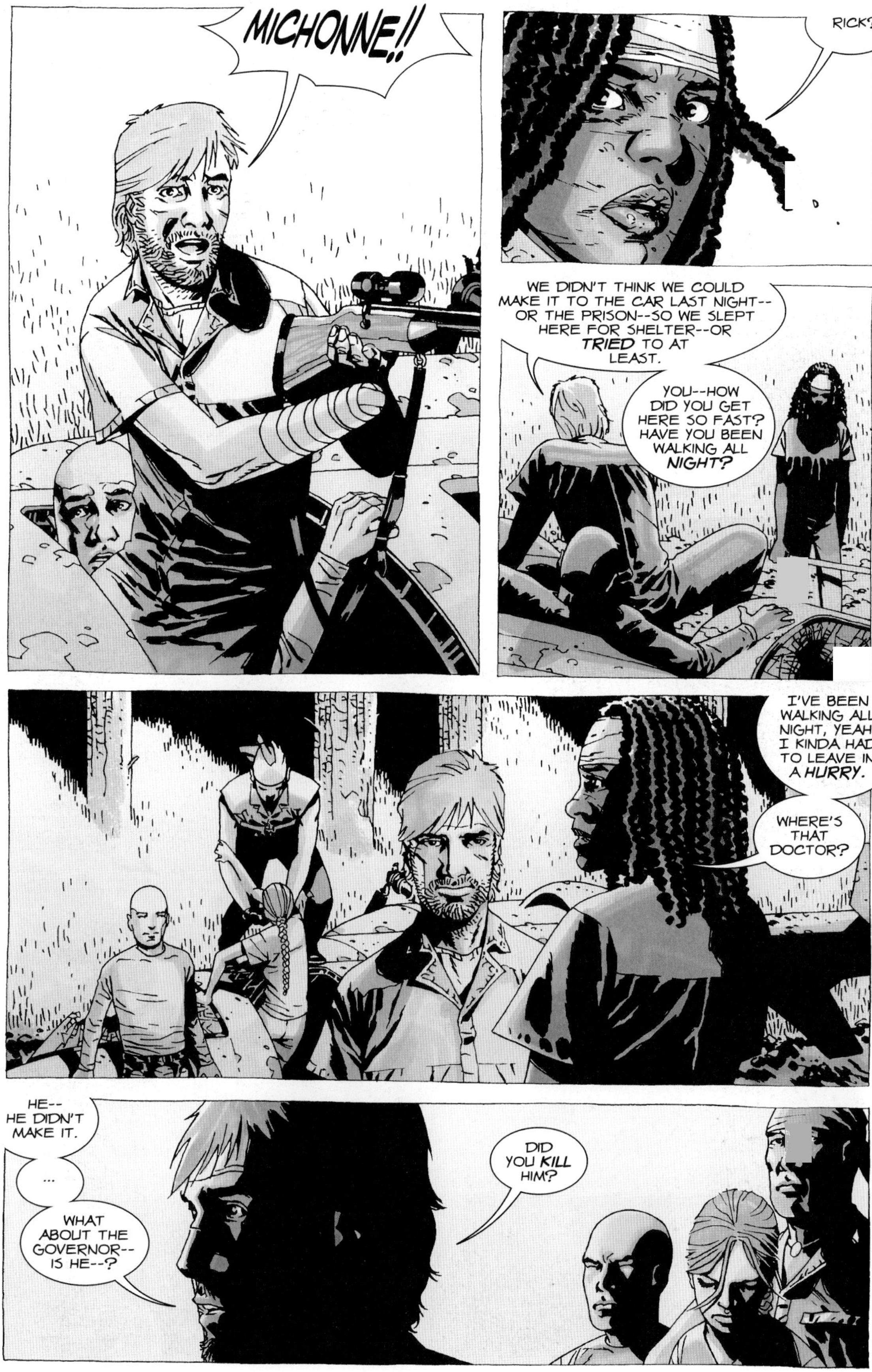
MICHONNE!!
RICK?
WE DIDN'T THINK WE COULD MAKE IT TO THE CAR LAST NIGHT-- OR THE PRISON--SO WE SLEPT HERE FOR SHELTER--OR TRIED TO AT LEAST.
YOU--HOW DID YOU GET HERE SO FAST? HAVE YOU BEEN WALKING ALL NIGHT?
I'VE BEEN WALKING ALL NIGHT, YEAH. I KINDA HAD TO LEAVE IN A HURRY.
WHERE'S THAT DOCTOR?
HE-- HE DIDN'T MAKE IT.
...
WHAT ABOUT THE GOVERNOR-- IS HE--?
DID YOU KILL HIM?

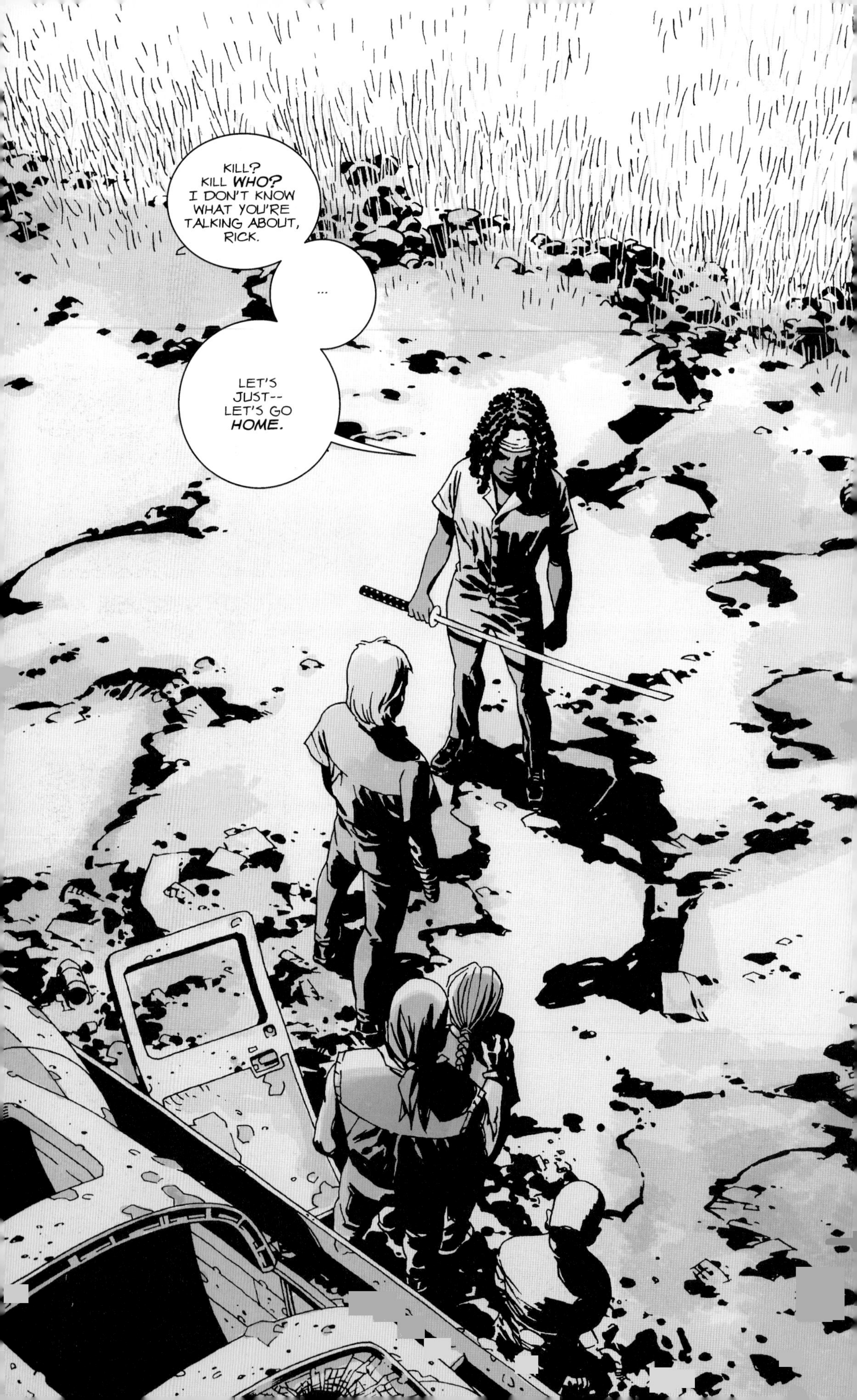
KILL? KILL WHO? I DON'T KNOW WHAT YOU'RE TALKING ABOUT, RICK.
...
LET'S JUST-- LET'S GO HOME.

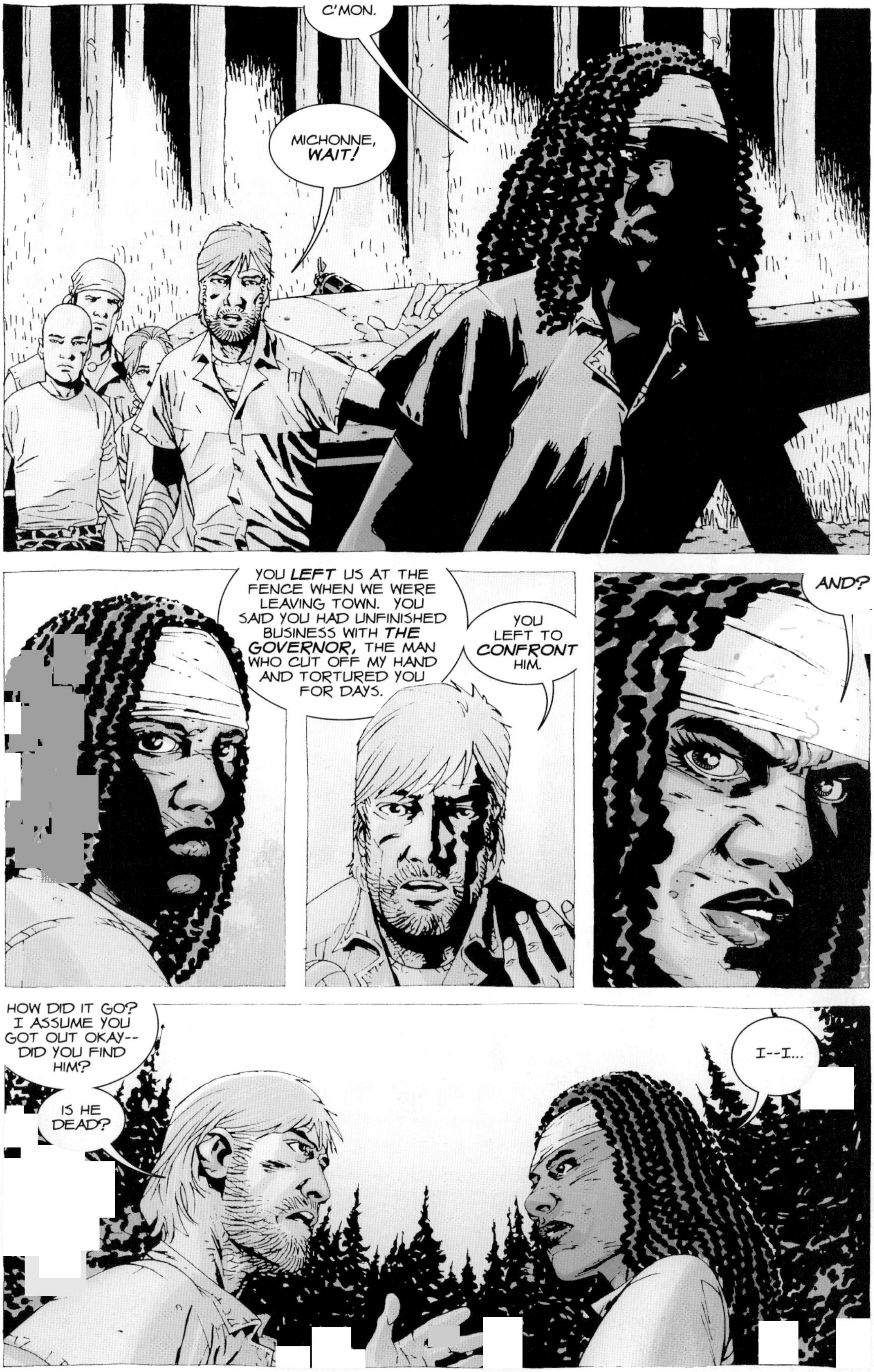
C'MON.
MICHONNE, WAIT!
YOU LEFT US AT THE FENCE WHEN WE WERE LEAVING TOWN. YOU SAID YOU HAD UNFINISHED BUSINESS WITH THE GOVERNOR, THE MAN WHO CUT OFF MY HAND AND TORTURED YOU FOR DAYS.
YOU LEFT TO CONFRONT HIM.
AND?
HOW DID IT GO? I ASSUME YOU GOT OUT OKAY-- DID YOU FIND HIM?
IS HE DEAD?
I--I...

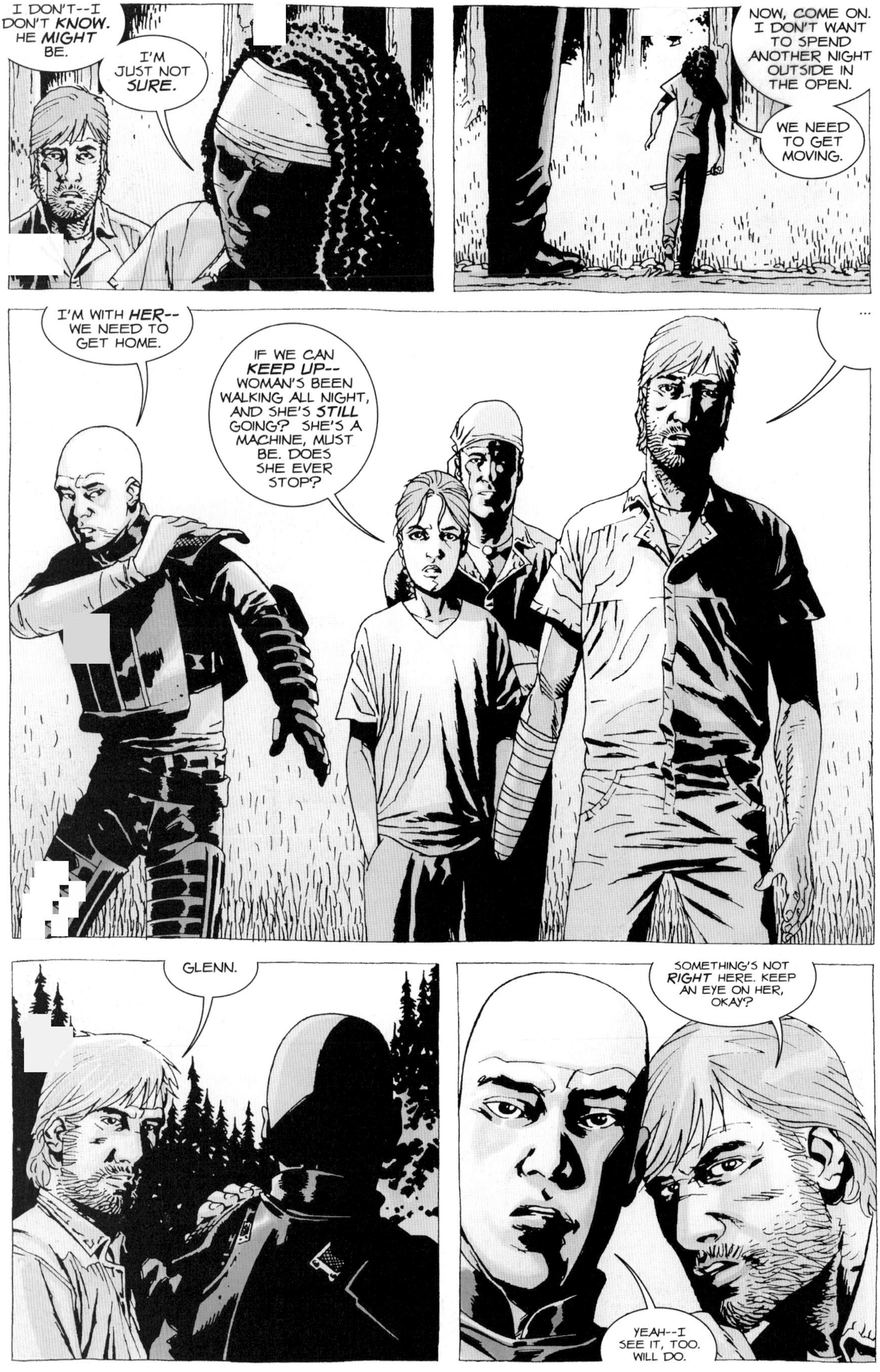
I DON'T--I DON'T KNOW. HE MIGHT BE.
I'M JUST NOT SURE.
NOW, COME ON. I DON'T WANT TO SPEND ANOTHER NIGHT OUTSIDE IN THE OPEN.
WE NEED TO GET MOVING.
I'M WITH HER-- WE NEED TO GET HOME.
IF WE CAN KEEP UP-- WOMAN'S BEEN WALKING ALL NIGHT, AND SHE'S STILL GOING? SHE'S A MACHINE, MUST BE. DOES SHE EVER STOP?
...
GLENN.
SOMETHING'S NOT RIGHT HERE. KEEP AN EYE ON HER, OKAY?
YEAH--I SEE IT, TOO. WILL DO.

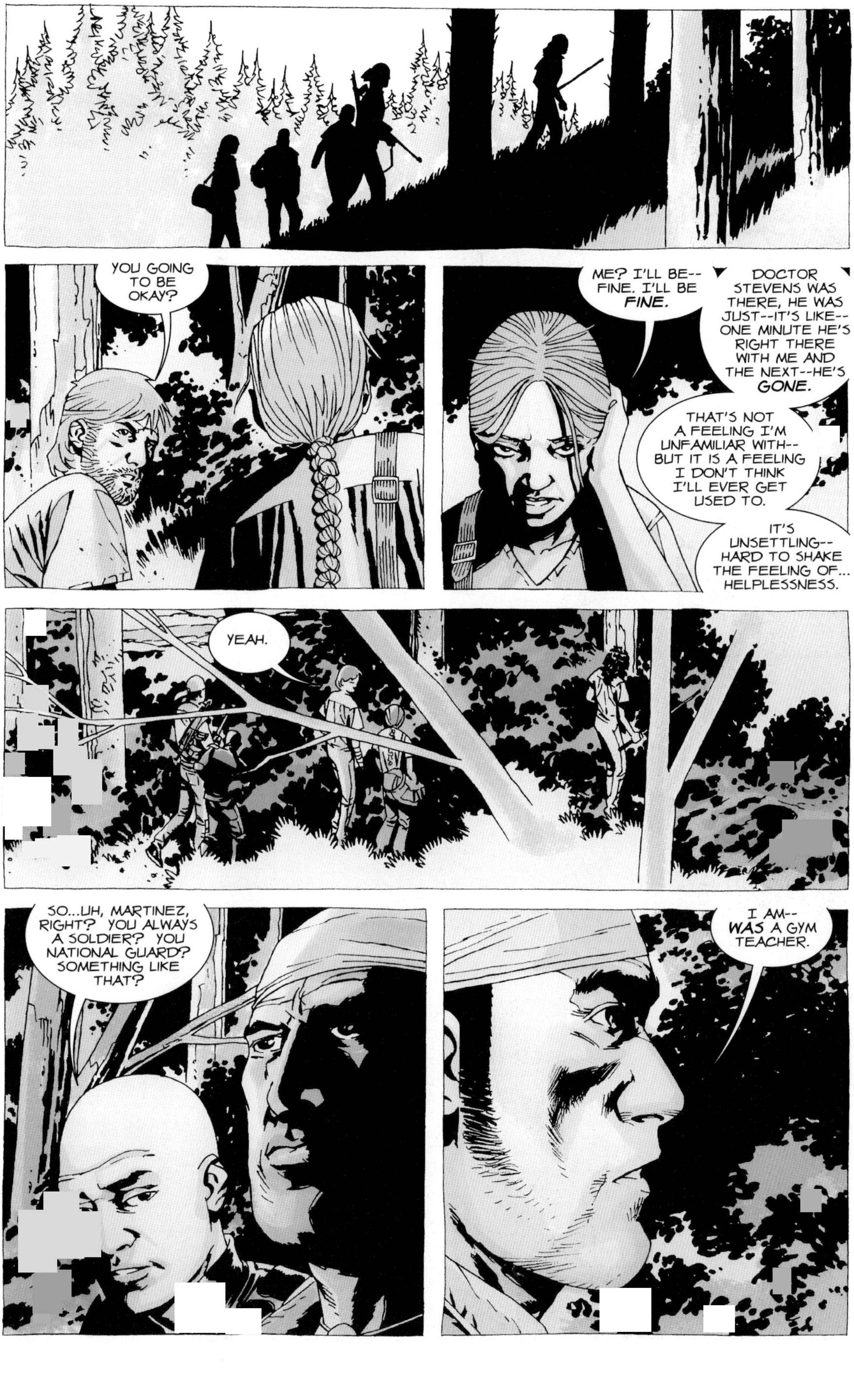
YOU GOING TO BE OKAY?
ME? I'LL BE-- FINE. I'LL BE *FINE.*
DOCTOR STEVENS WAS THERE, HE WAS JUST--IT'S LIKE-- ONE MINUTE HE'S RIGHT THERE WITH ME AND THE NEXT--HE'S *GONE.*
THAT'S NOT A FEELING I'M UNFAMILIAR WITH-- BUT IT IS A FEELING I DON'T THINK I'LL EVER GET USED TO.
IT'S UNSETTLING-- HARD TO SHAKE THE FEELING OF... HELPLESSNESS.
YEAH.
SO...UH, MARTINEZ, RIGHT? YOU ALWAYS A SOLDIER? YOU NATIONAL GUARD? SOMETHING LIKE THAT?
I AM-- *WAS* A GYM TEACHER.

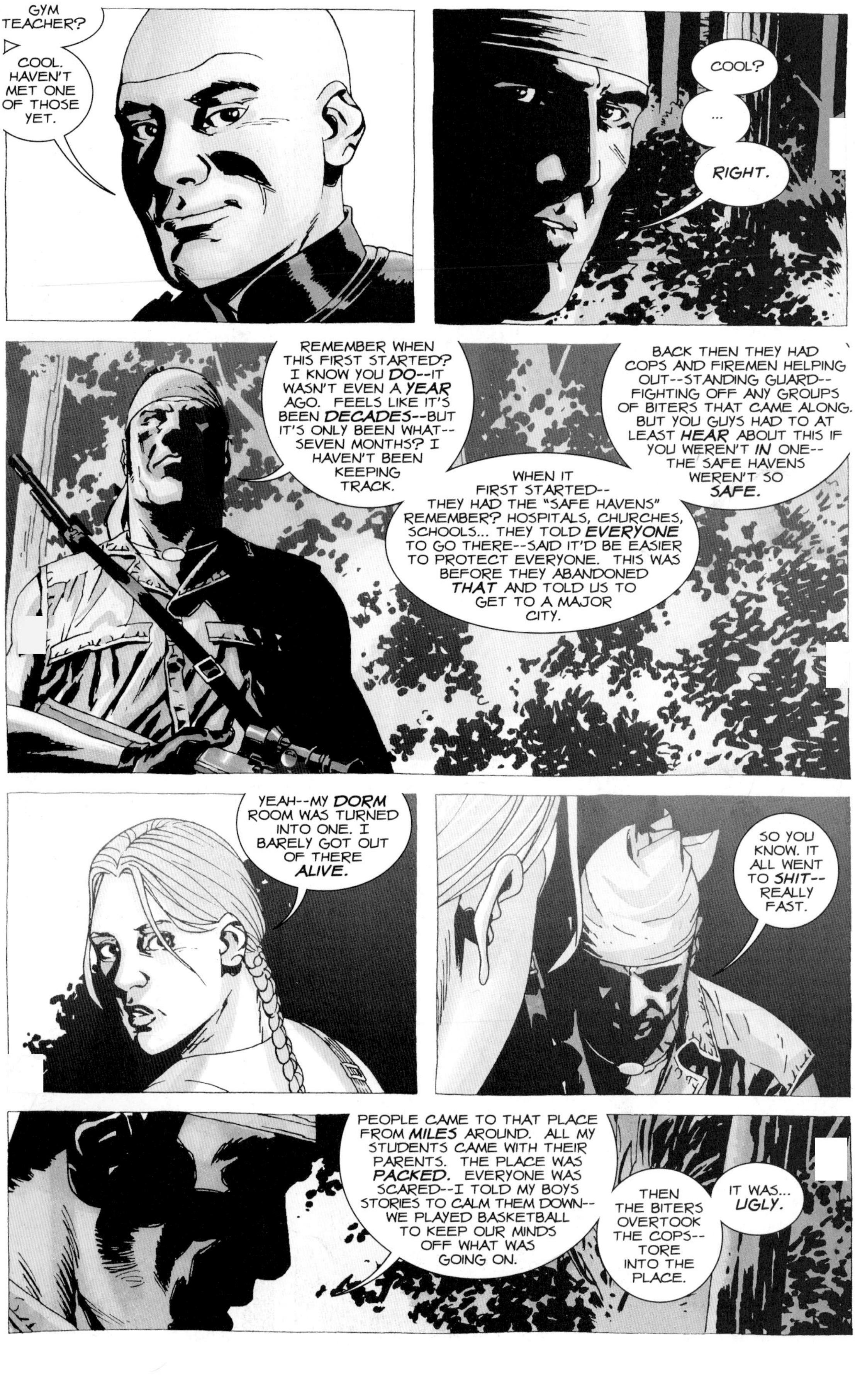
GYM TEACHER?
COOL. HAVEN'T MET ONE OF THOSE YET.
COOL?
...
RIGHT.
REMEMBER WHEN THIS FIRST STARTED? I KNOW YOU DO--IT WASN'T EVEN A YEAR AGO. FEELS LIKE IT'S BEEN DECADES--BUT IT'S ONLY BEEN WHAT--SEVEN MONTHS? I HAVEN'T BEEN KEEPING TRACK.
WHEN IT FIRST STARTED--THEY HAD THE "SAFE HAVENS" REMEMBER? HOSPITALS, CHURCHES, SCHOOLS... THEY TOLD EVERYONE TO GO THERE--SAID IT'D BE EASIER TO PROTECT EVERYONE. THIS WAS BEFORE THEY ABANDONED THAT AND TOLD US TO GET TO A MAJOR CITY.
BACK THEN THEY HAD COPS AND FIREMEN HELPING OUT--STANDING GUARD--FIGHTING OFF ANY GROUPS OF BITERS THAT CAME ALONG. BUT YOU GUYS HAD TO AT LEAST HEAR ABOUT THIS IF YOU WEREN'T IN ONE--THE SAFE HAVENS WEREN'T SO SAFE.
YEAH--MY DORM ROOM WAS TURNED INTO ONE. I BARELY GOT OUT OF THERE ALIVE.
SO YOU KNOW. IT ALL WENT TO SHIT--REALLY FAST.
PEOPLE CAME TO THAT PLACE FROM MILES AROUND. ALL MY STUDENTS CAME WITH THEIR PARENTS. THE PLACE WAS PACKED. EVERYONE WAS SCARED--I TOLD MY BOYS STORIES TO CALM THEM DOWN--WE PLAYED BASKETBALL TO KEEP OUR MINDS OFF WHAT WAS GOING ON.
THEN THE BITERS OVERTOOK THE COPS--TORE INTO THE PLACE.
IT WAS... UGLY.

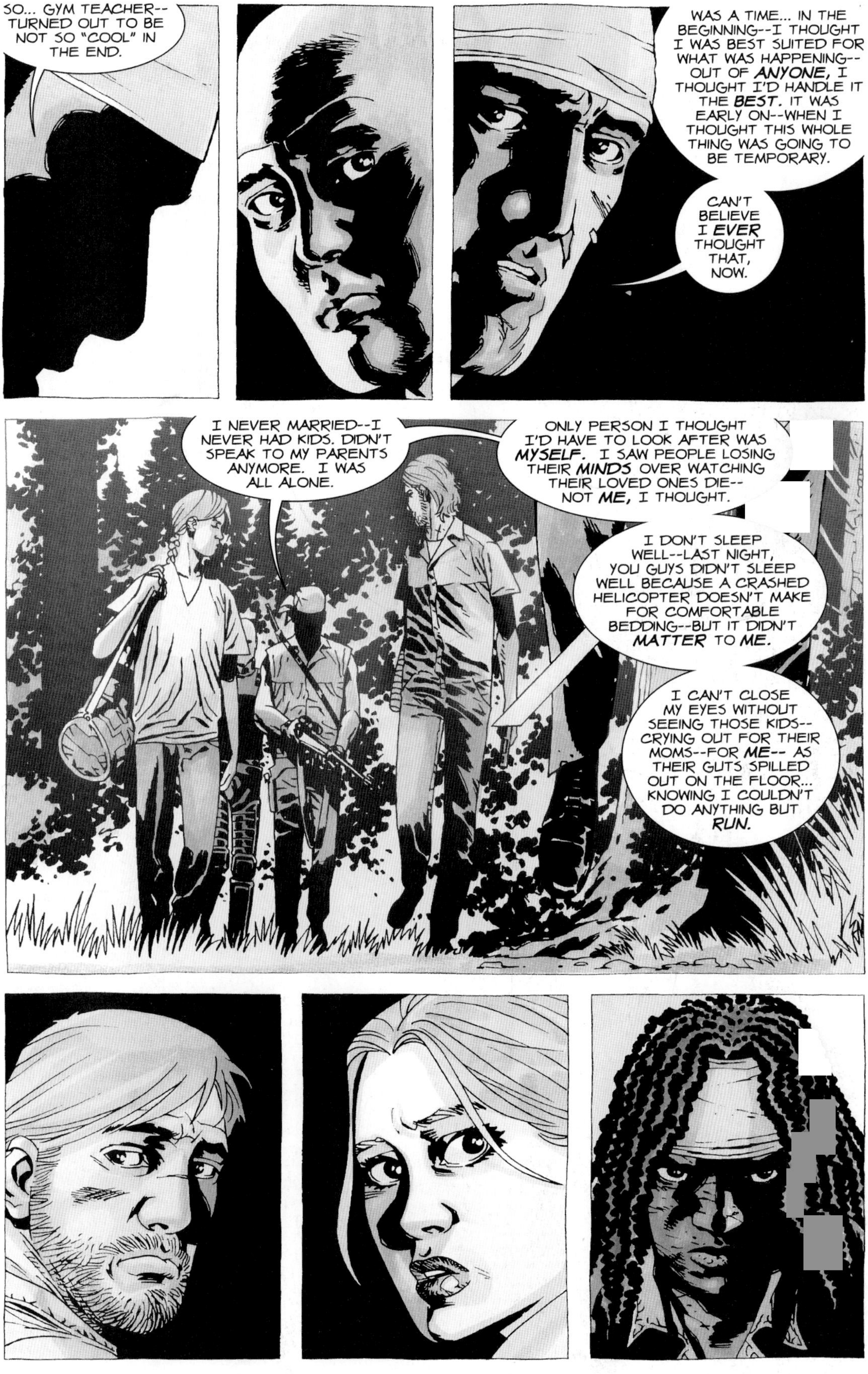
SO... GYM TEACHER--TURNED OUT TO BE NOT SO "COOL" IN THE END.
WAS A TIME... IN THE BEGINNING--I THOUGHT I WAS BEST SUITED FOR WHAT WAS HAPPENING--OUT OF ANYONE, I THOUGHT I'D HANDLE IT THE BEST. IT WAS EARLY ON--WHEN I THOUGHT THIS WHOLE THING WAS GOING TO BE TEMPORARY.
CAN'T BELIEVE I EVER THOUGHT THAT, NOW.
I NEVER MARRIED--I NEVER HAD KIDS. DIDN'T SPEAK TO MY PARENTS ANYMORE. I WAS ALL ALONE.
ONLY PERSON I THOUGHT I'D HAVE TO LOOK AFTER WAS MYSELF. I SAW PEOPLE LOSING THEIR MINDS OVER WATCHING THEIR LOVED ONES DIE--NOT ME, I THOUGHT.
I DON'T SLEEP WELL--LAST NIGHT, YOU GUYS DIDN'T SLEEP WELL BECAUSE A CRASHED HELICOPTER DOESN'T MAKE FOR COMFORTABLE BEDDING--BUT IT DIDN'T MATTER TO ME.
I CAN'T CLOSE MY EYES WITHOUT SEEING THOSE KIDS--CRYING OUT FOR THEIR MOMS--FOR ME-- AS THEIR GUTS SPILLED OUT ON THE FLOOR... KNOWING I COULDN'T DO ANYTHING BUT RUN.

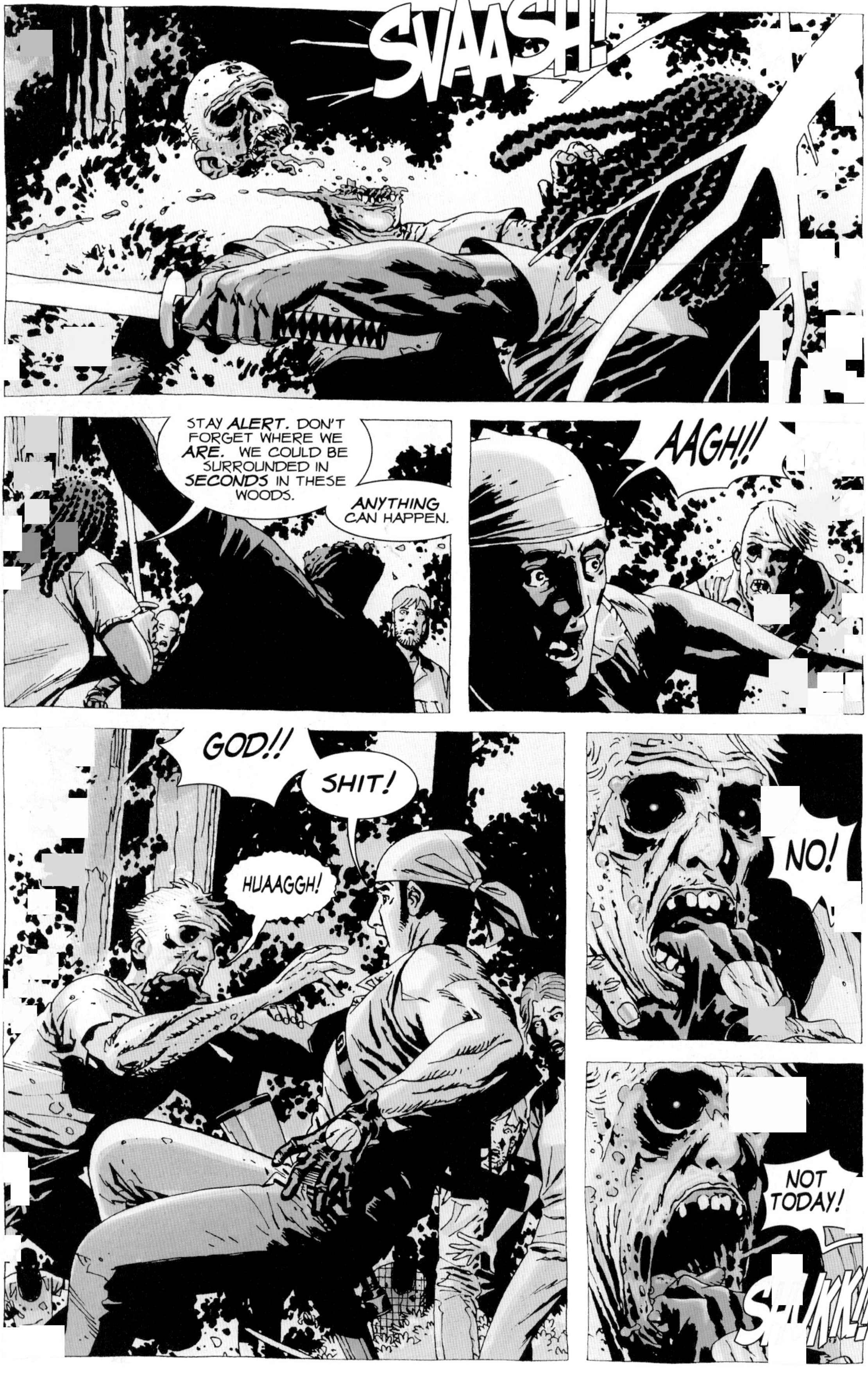
SVAASH!
STAY ALERT. DON'T FORGET WHERE WE ARE. WE COULD BE SURROUNDED IN SECONDS IN THESE WOODS.
ANYTHING CAN HAPPEN.
AAGH!!
GOD!!
SHIT!
HUAAGGH!
NO!
NOT TODAY!

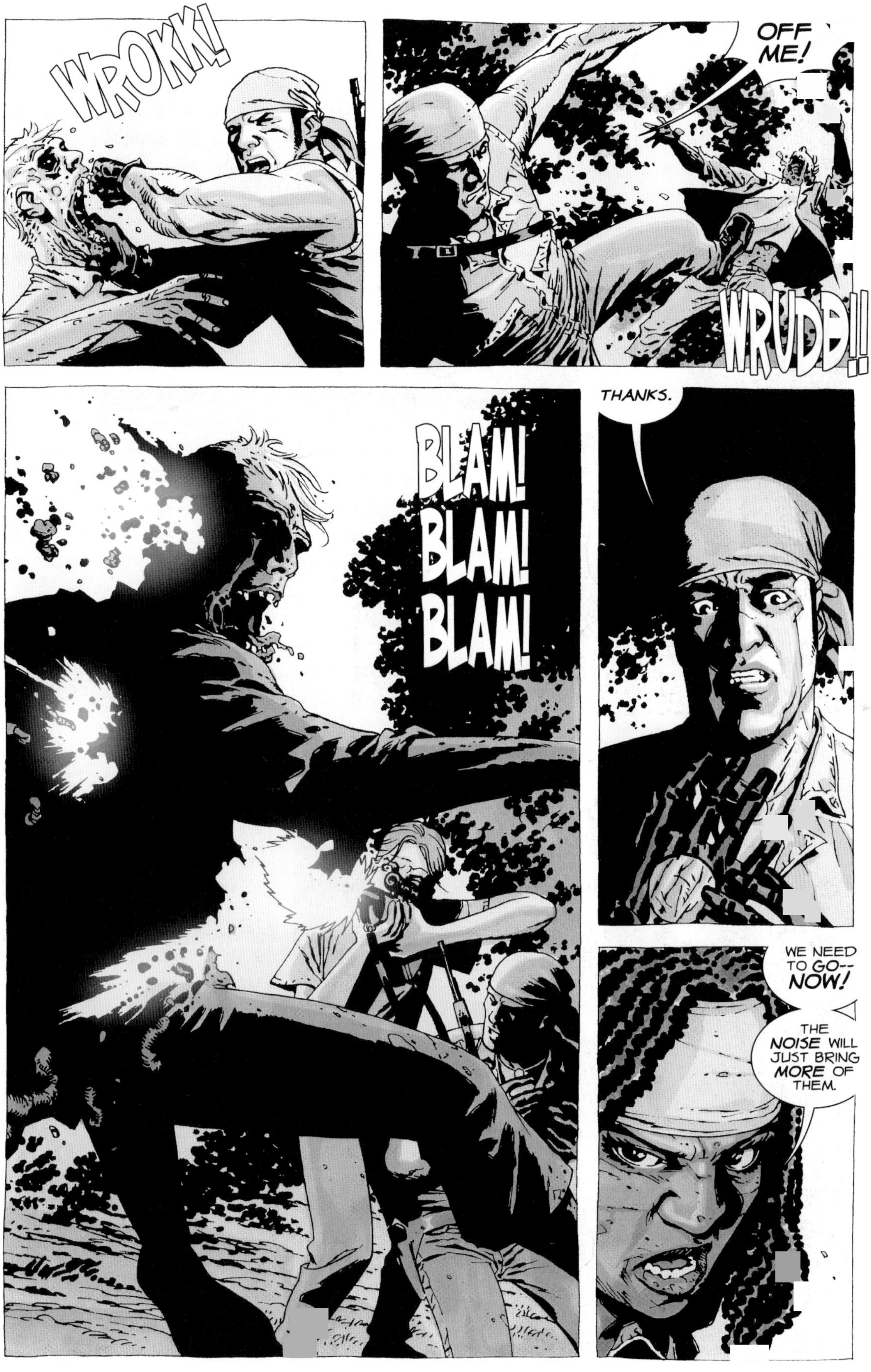

WROKK!
OFF ME!
WRUDD!!
BLAM! BLAM! BLAM!
THANKS.
WE NEED TO GO-- NOW!
THE NOISE WILL JUST BRING MORE OF THEM.

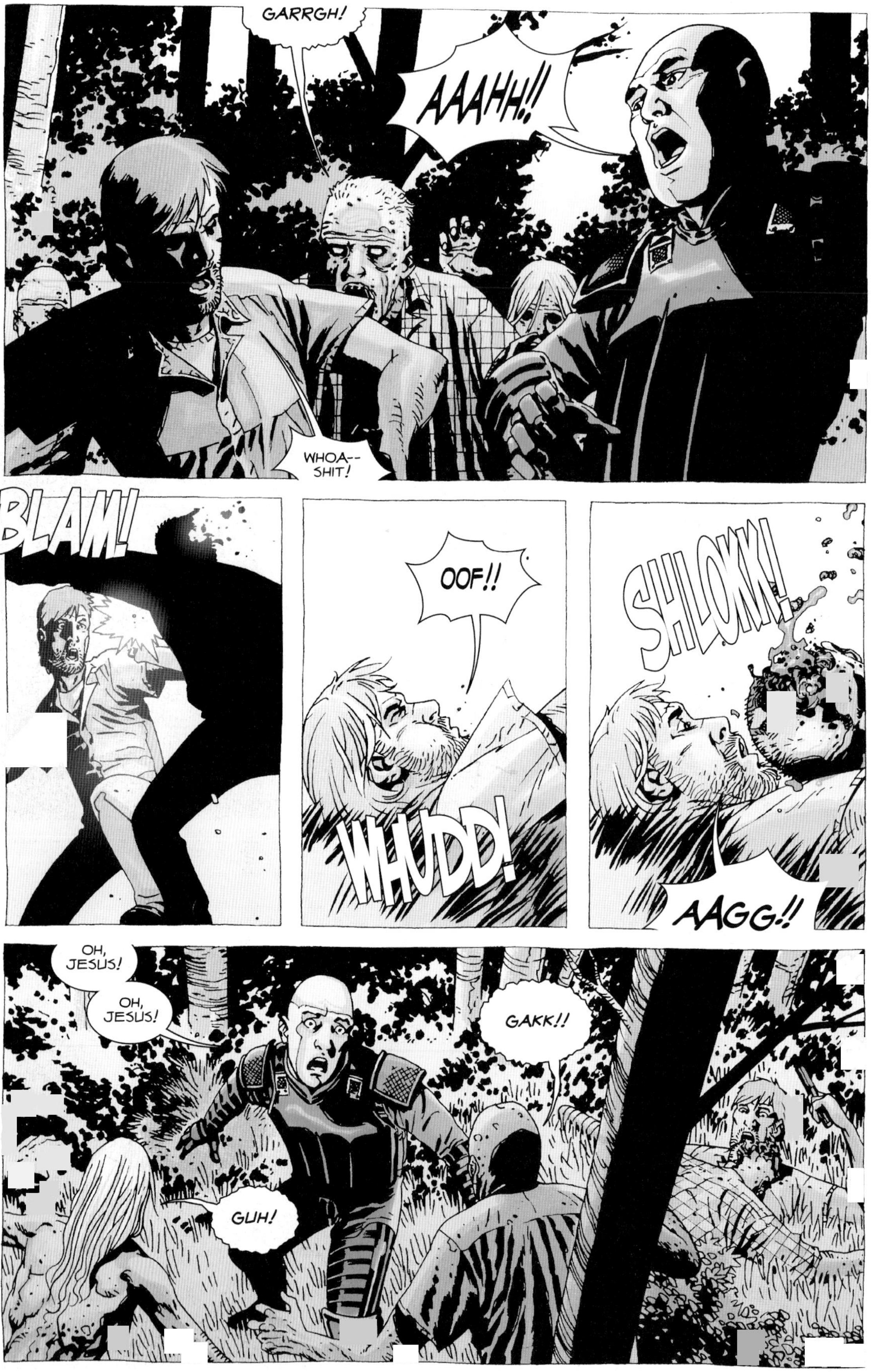
GARRGH!
AAAHH!!
WHOA--
SHIT!
BLAM!
OOF!!
WHUDD!
SHLOKK!
AAGG!!
OH,
JESUS!
OH,
JESUS!
GAKK!!
GUH!

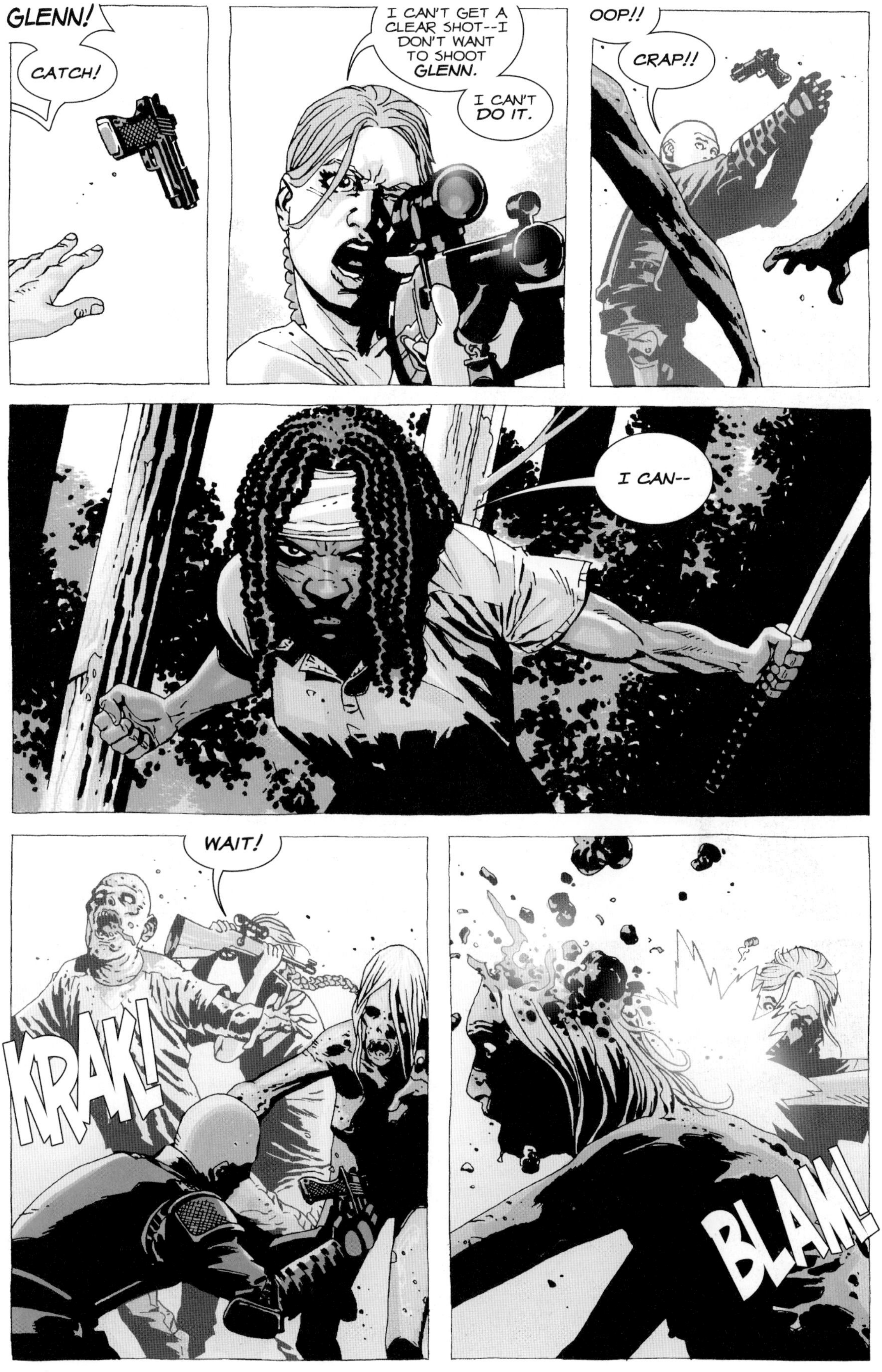
GLENN!
CATCH!
I CAN'T GET A CLEAR SHOT--I DON'T WANT TO SHOOT GLENN.
I CAN'T DO IT.
OOP!!
CRAP!!
I CAN--
WAIT!
KRAK!
BLAM!

WHUMP.

WHAT? YOU CAN STILL KILL *THAT* ONE. I ONLY KNOCKED HIM OVER.

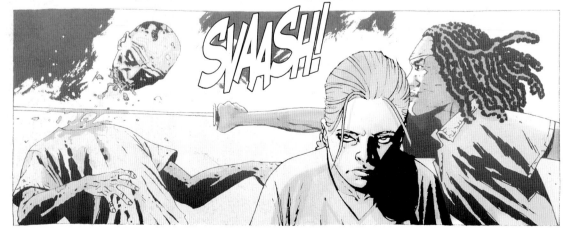

SVAASH!

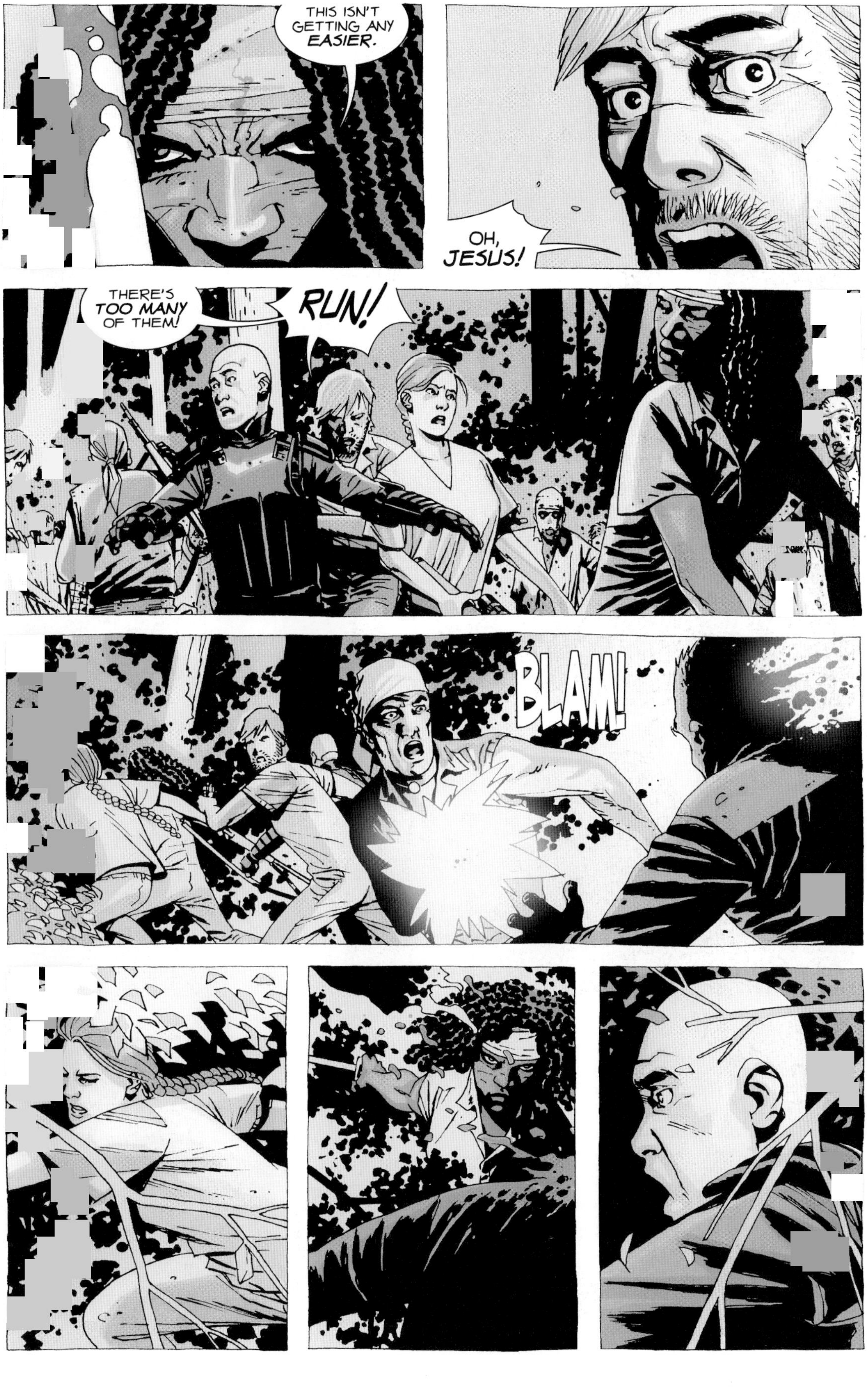
THIS ISN'T GETTING ANY EASIER.
OH, JESUS!
THERE'S TOO MANY OF THEM!
RUN!
BLAM!

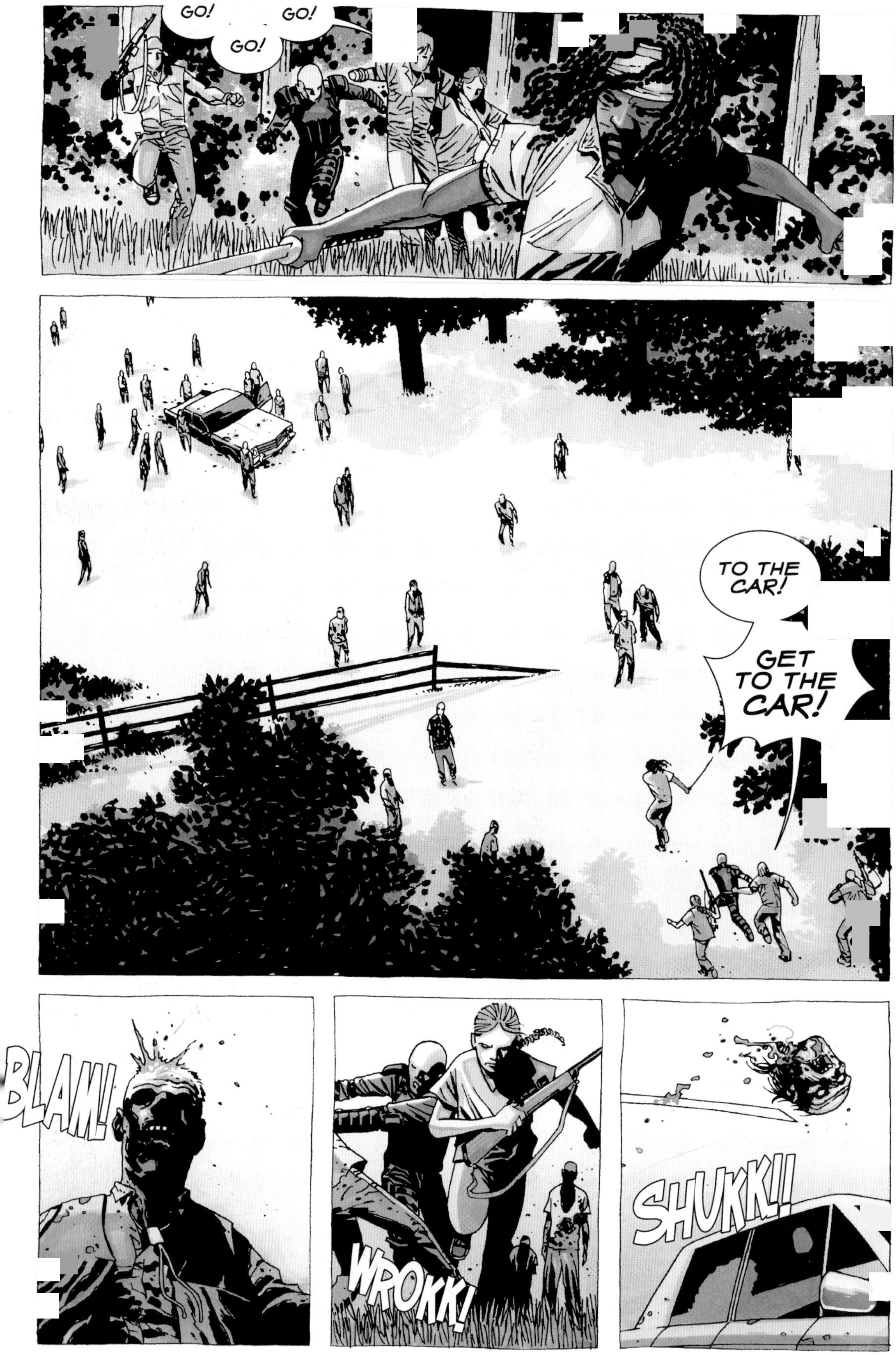
GO!
GO!
GO!
TO THE CAR!
GET TO THE CAR!
BLAM!
WROKK!
SHUKK!!

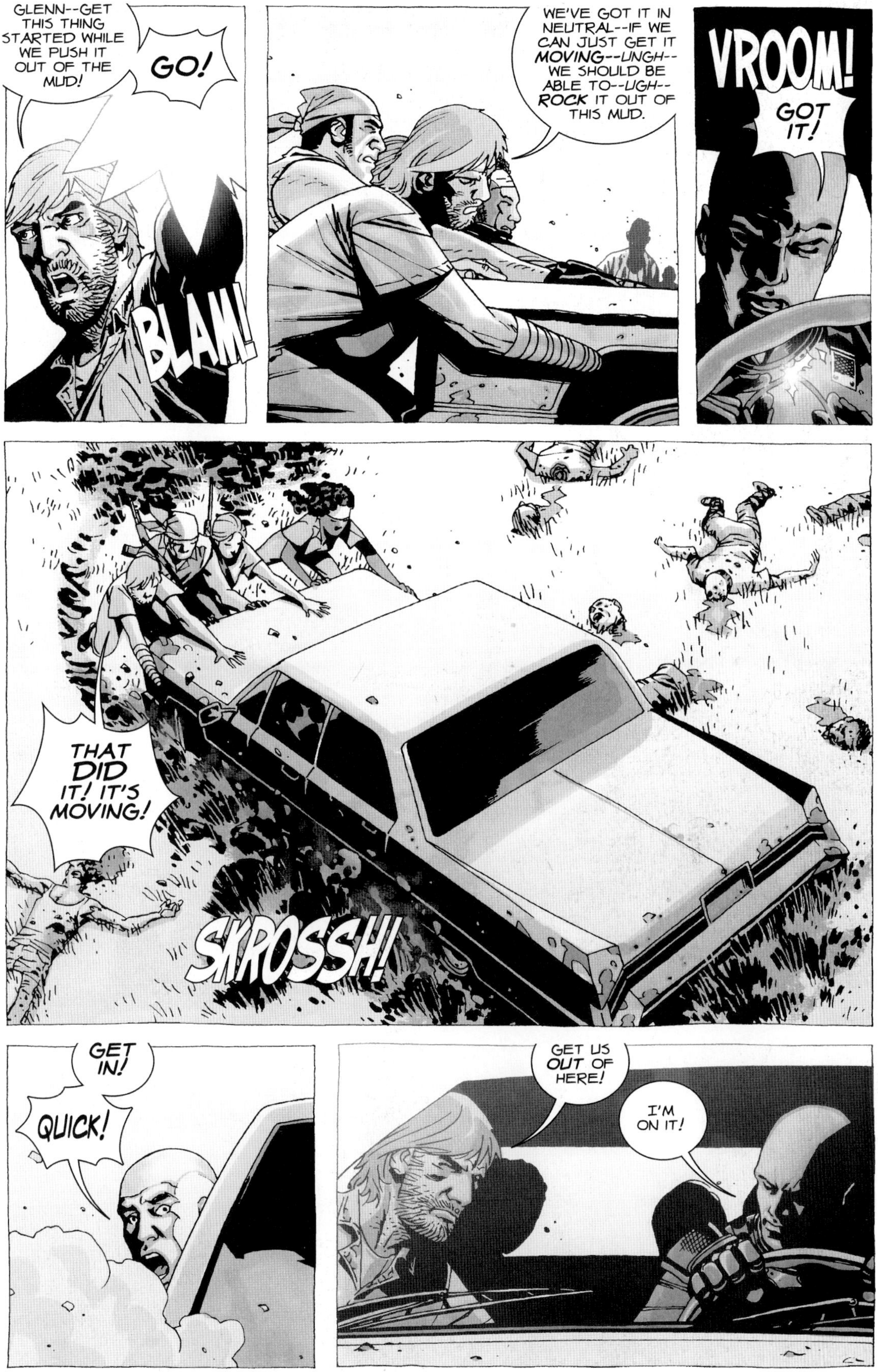

GLENN--GET THIS THING STARTED WHILE WE PUSH IT OUT OF THE MUD!
GO!
BLAM!
WE'VE GOT IT IN NEUTRAL--IF WE CAN JUST GET IT MOVING--UNGH--WE SHOULD BE ABLE TO--UGH--ROCK IT OUT OF THIS MUD.
VROOM!
GOT IT!
THAT DID IT! IT'S MOVING!
SKROSSH!
GET IN!
QUICK!
GET US OUT OF HERE!
I'M ON IT!

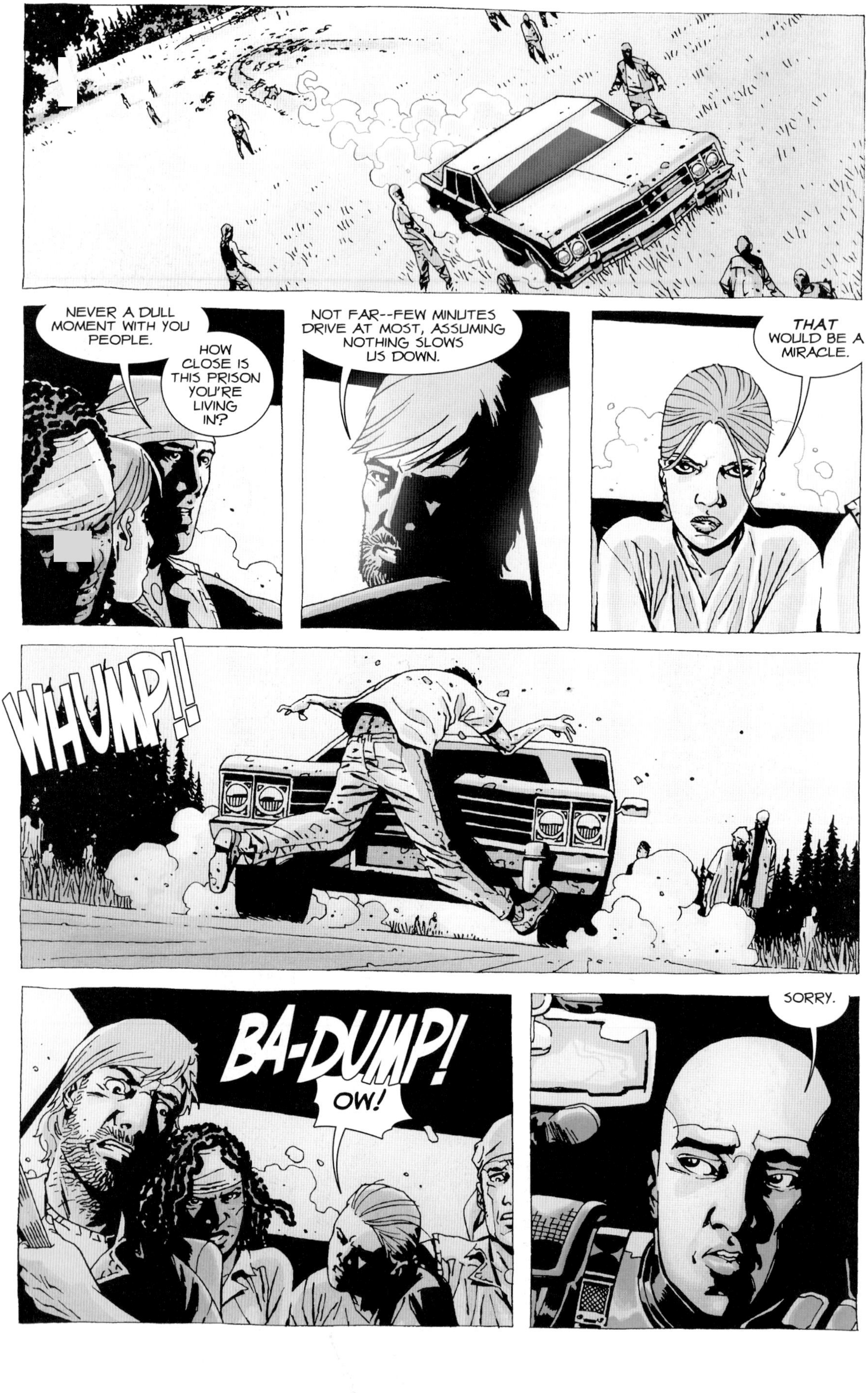
NEVER A DULL MOMENT WITH YOU PEOPLE.
HOW CLOSE IS THIS PRISON YOU'RE LIVING IN?
NOT FAR--FEW MINUTES DRIVE AT MOST, ASSUMING NOTHING SLOWS US DOWN.
THAT WOULD BE A MIRACLE.
WHUMP!!
BA-DUMP!
OW!
SORRY.

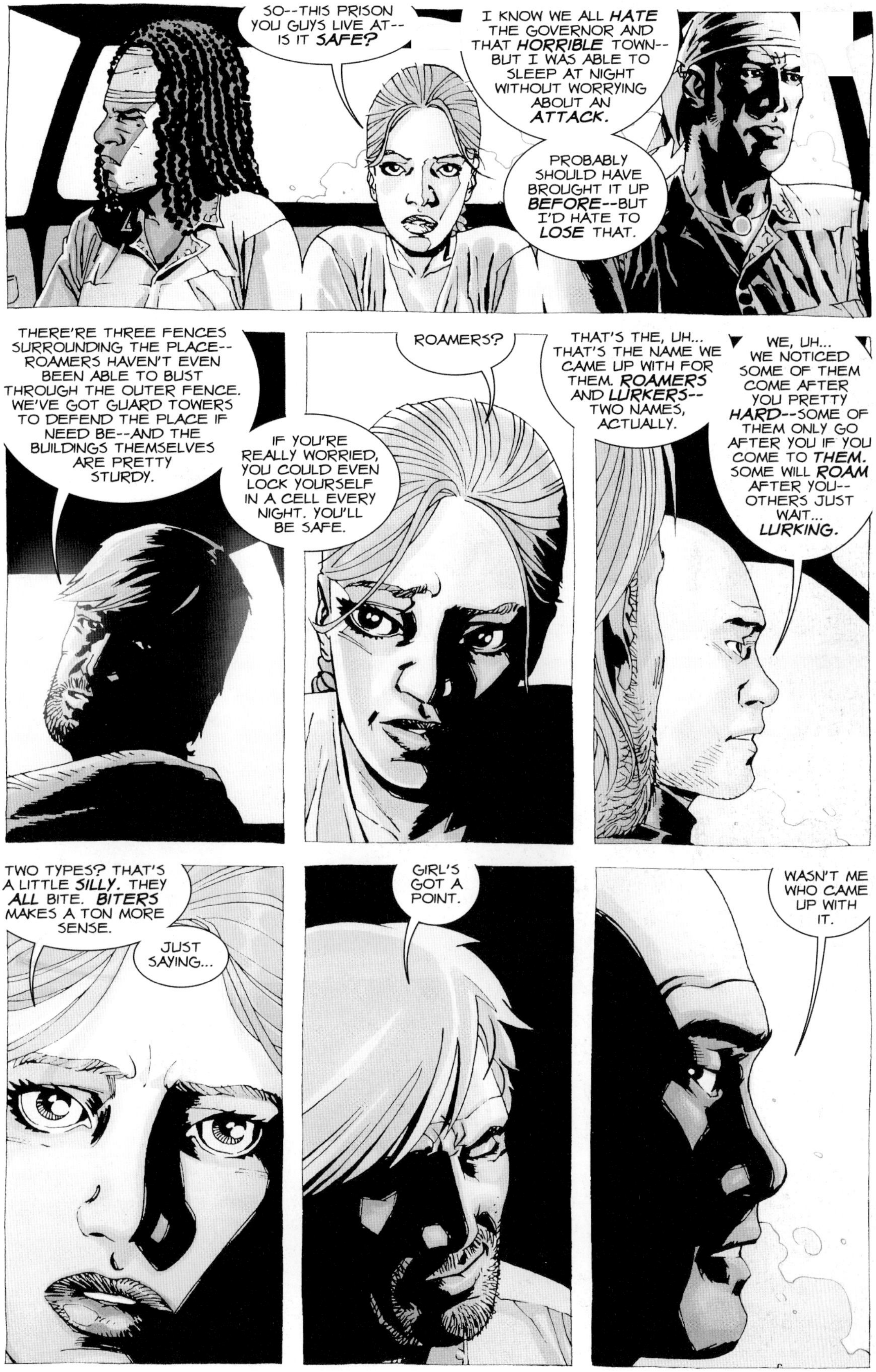
SO--THIS PRISON YOU GUYS LIVE AT-- IS IT SAFE?
I KNOW WE ALL HATE THE GOVERNOR AND THAT HORRIBLE TOWN-- BUT I WAS ABLE TO SLEEP AT NIGHT WITHOUT WORRYING ABOUT AN ATTACK.
PROBABLY SHOULD HAVE BROUGHT IT UP BEFORE--BUT I'D HATE TO LOSE THAT.
THERE'RE THREE FENCES SURROUNDING THE PLACE-- ROAMERS HAVEN'T EVEN BEEN ABLE TO BUST THROUGH THE OUTER FENCE. WE'VE GOT GUARD TOWERS TO DEFEND THE PLACE IF NEED BE--AND THE BUILDINGS THEMSELVES ARE PRETTY STURDY.
IF YOU'RE REALLY WORRIED, YOU COULD EVEN LOCK YOURSELF IN A CELL EVERY NIGHT. YOU'LL BE SAFE.
ROAMERS?
THAT'S THE, UH... THAT'S THE NAME WE CAME UP WITH FOR THEM. ROAMERS AND LURKERS-- TWO NAMES, ACTUALLY.
WE, UH... WE NOTICED SOME OF THEM COME AFTER YOU PRETTY HARD--SOME OF THEM ONLY GO AFTER YOU IF YOU COME TO THEM. SOME WILL ROAM AFTER YOU-- OTHERS JUST WAIT... LURKING.
TWO TYPES? THAT'S A LITTLE SILLY. THEY ALL BITE. BITERS MAKES A TON MORE SENSE.
JUST SAYING...
GIRL'S GOT A POINT.
WASN'T ME WHO CAME UP WITH IT.

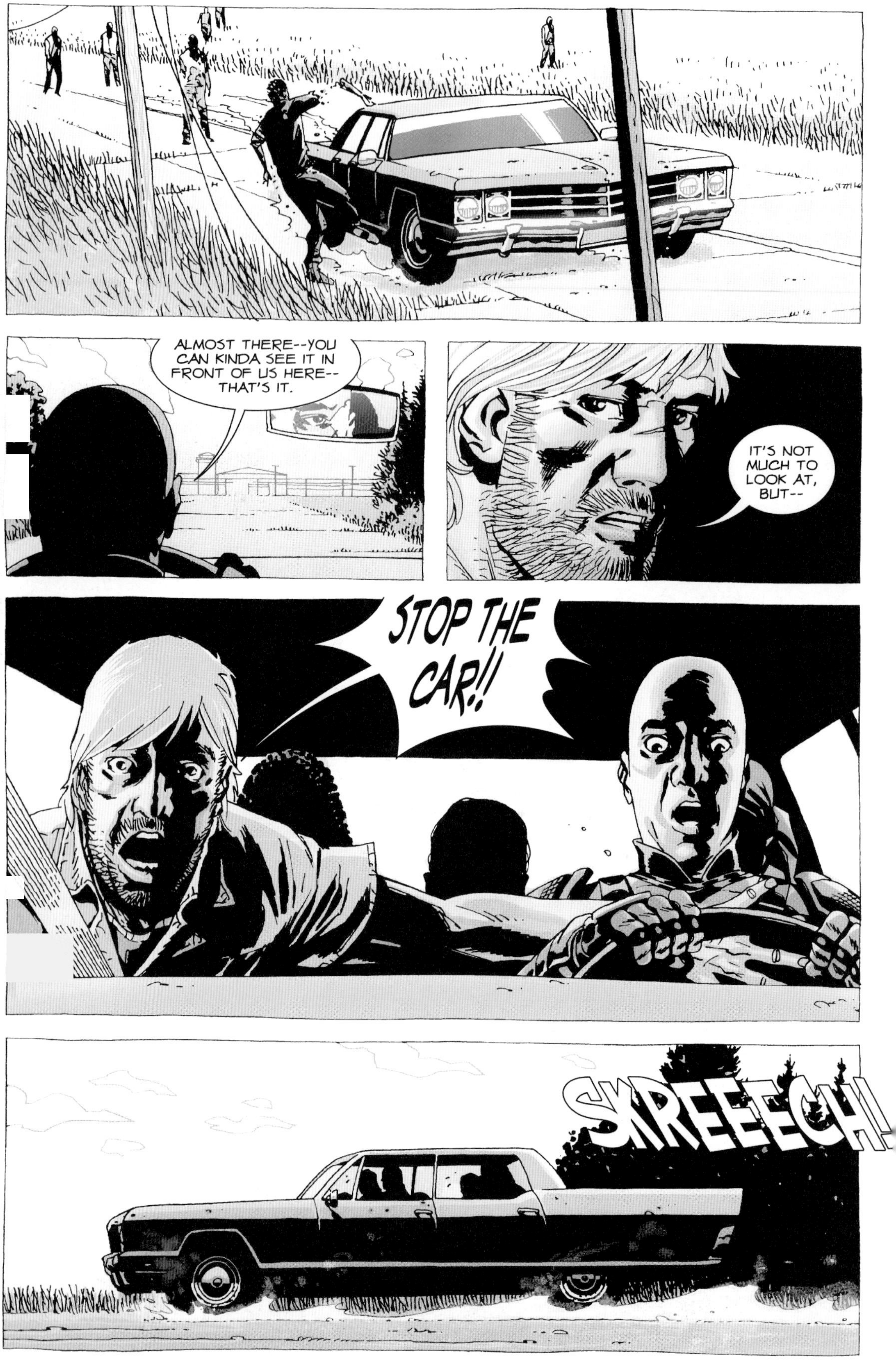
ALMOST THERE--YOU CAN KINDA SEE IT IN FRONT OF US HERE-- THAT'S IT.
IT'S NOT MUCH TO LOOK AT, BUT--
STOP THE CAR!!
SKREEEECH!

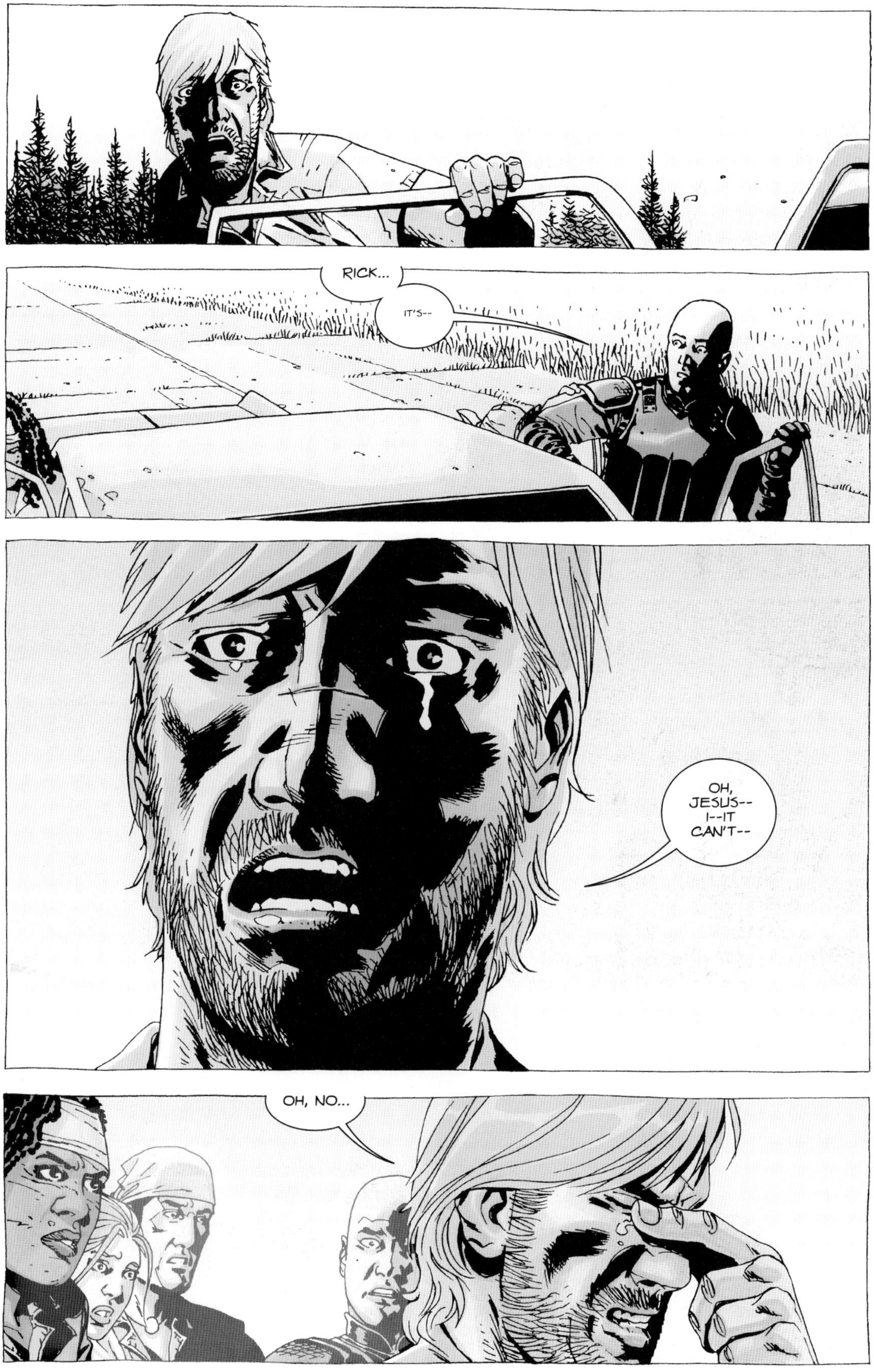
RICK...
IT'S--
OH, JESUS-- I--IT CAN'T--
OH, NO...

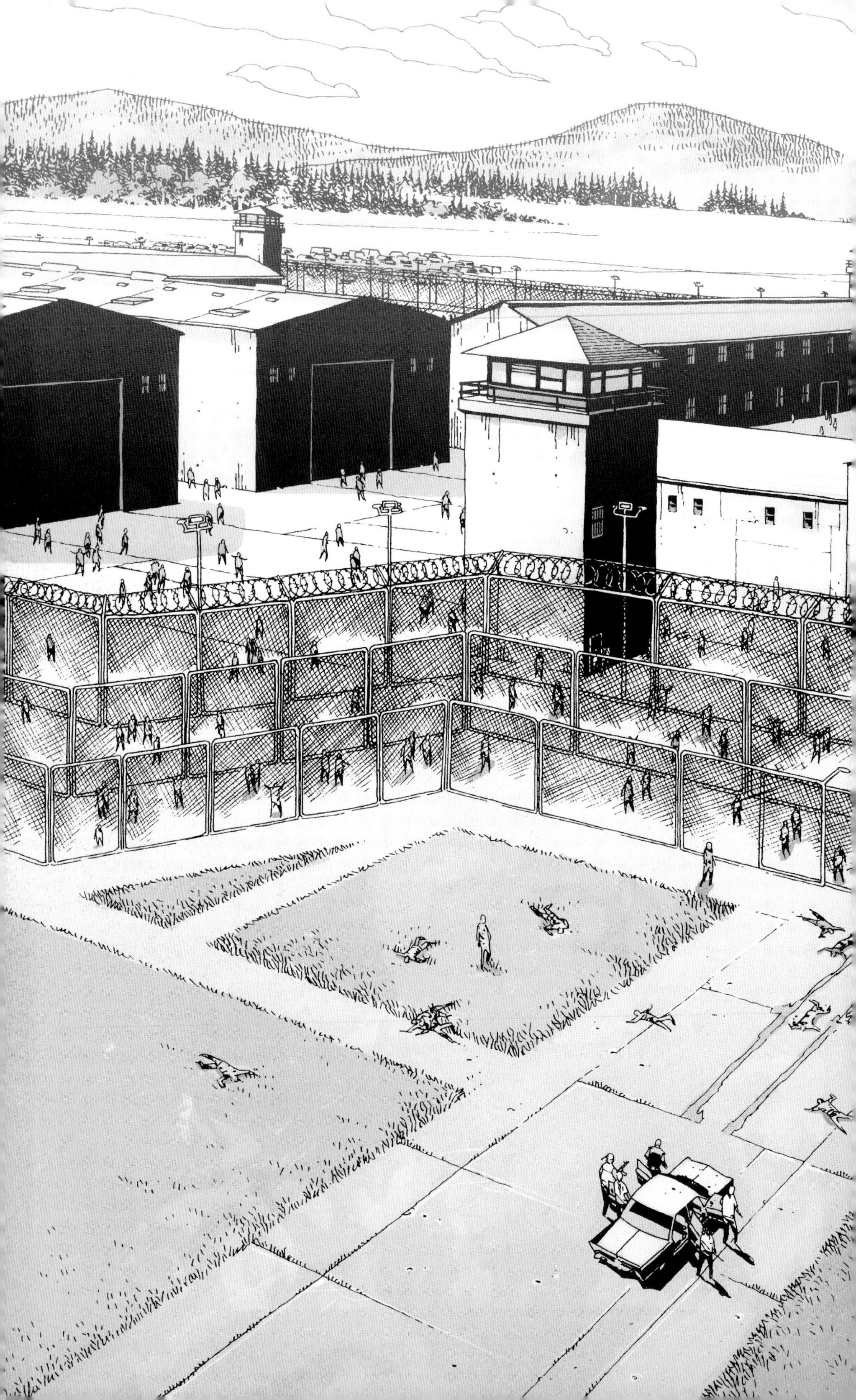

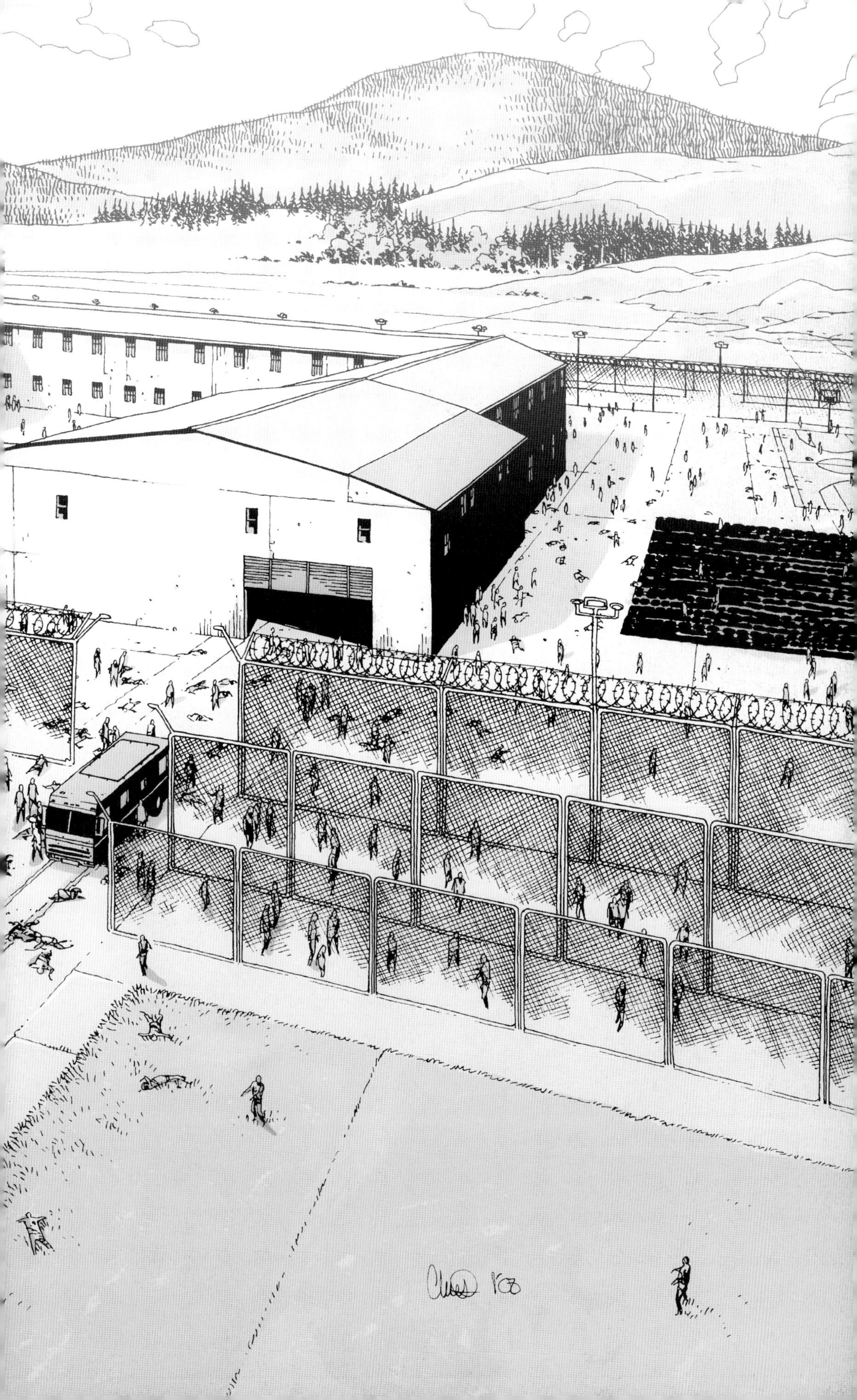

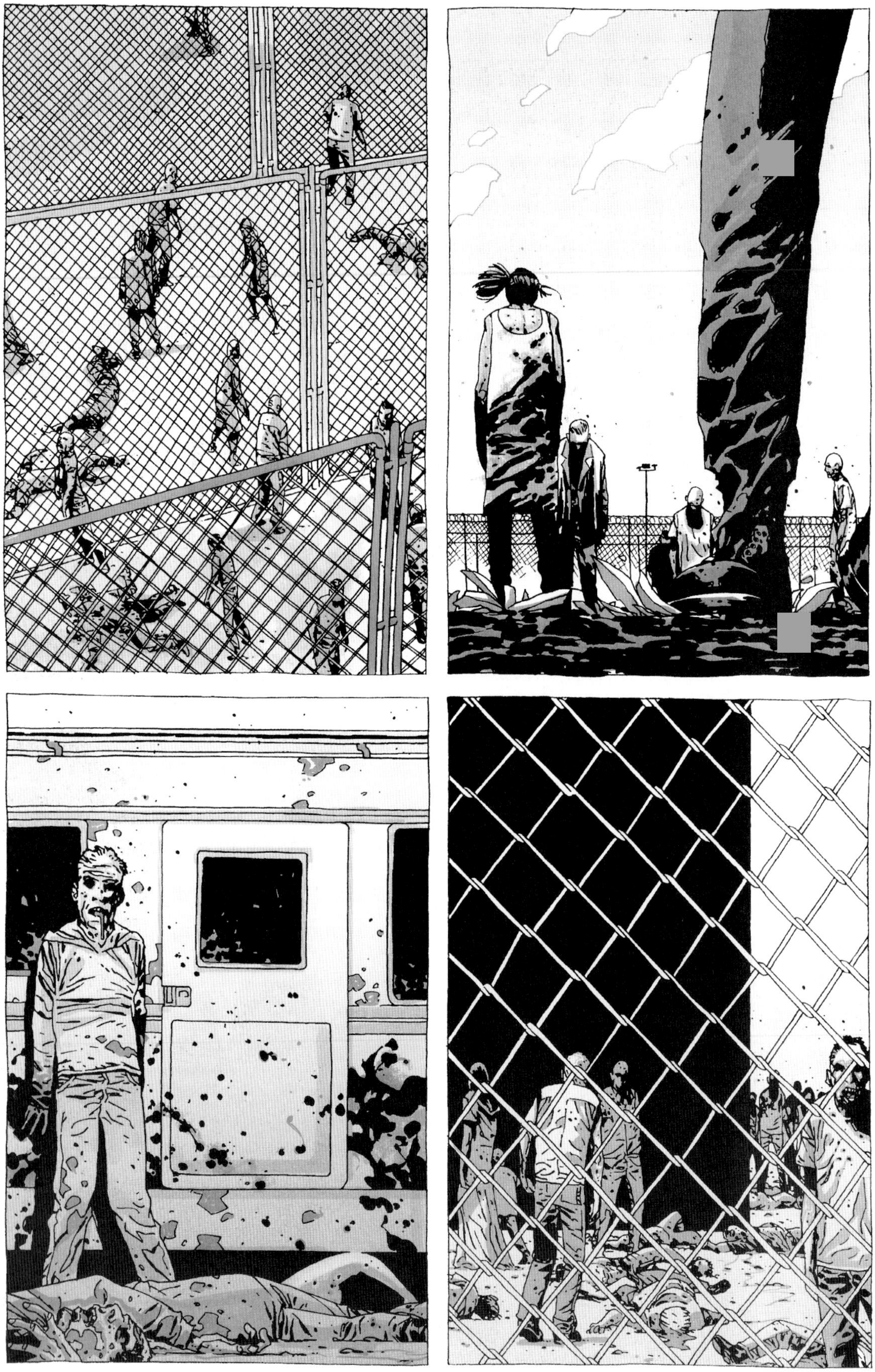

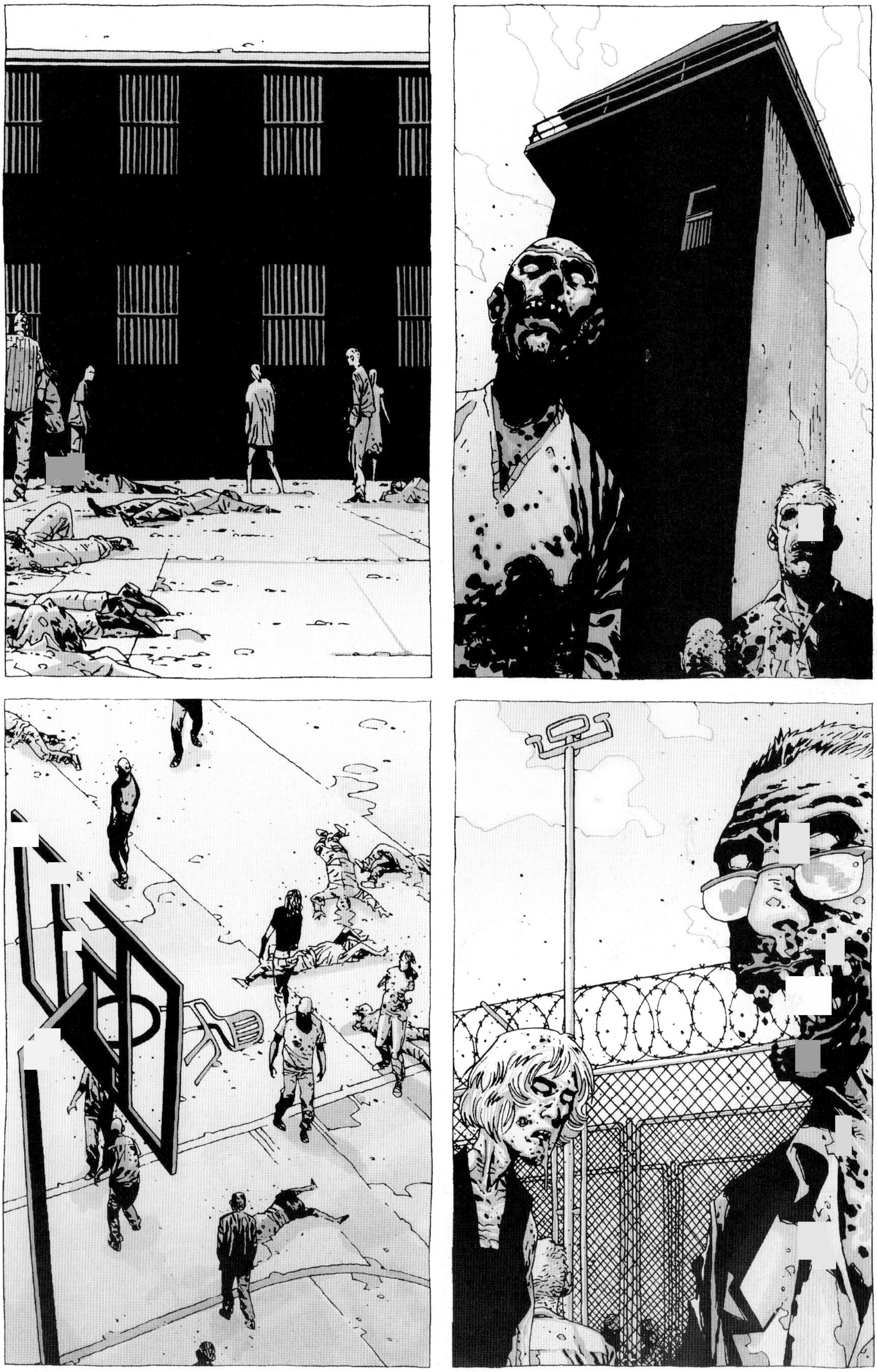

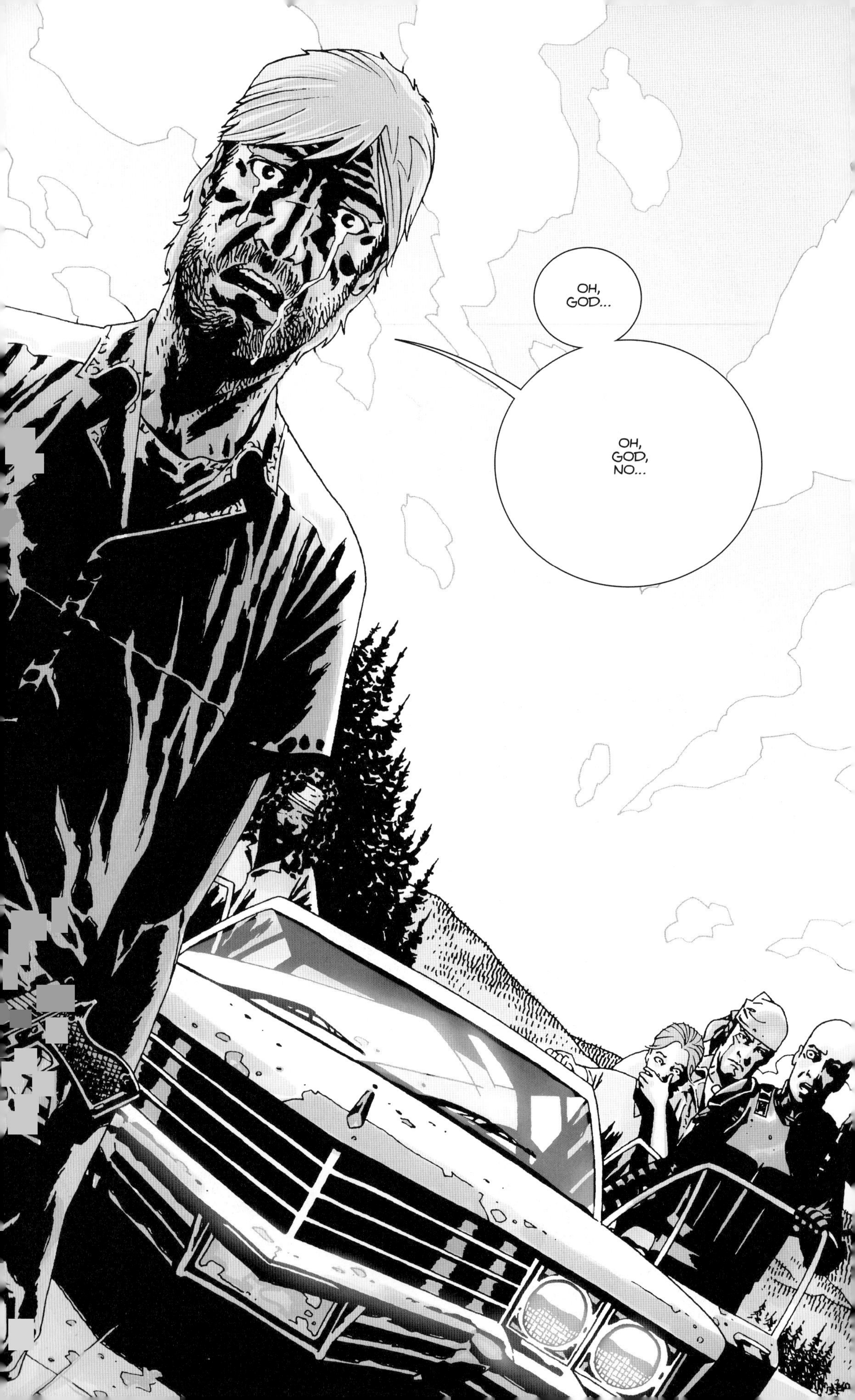
OH, GOD...
OH, GOD, NO...

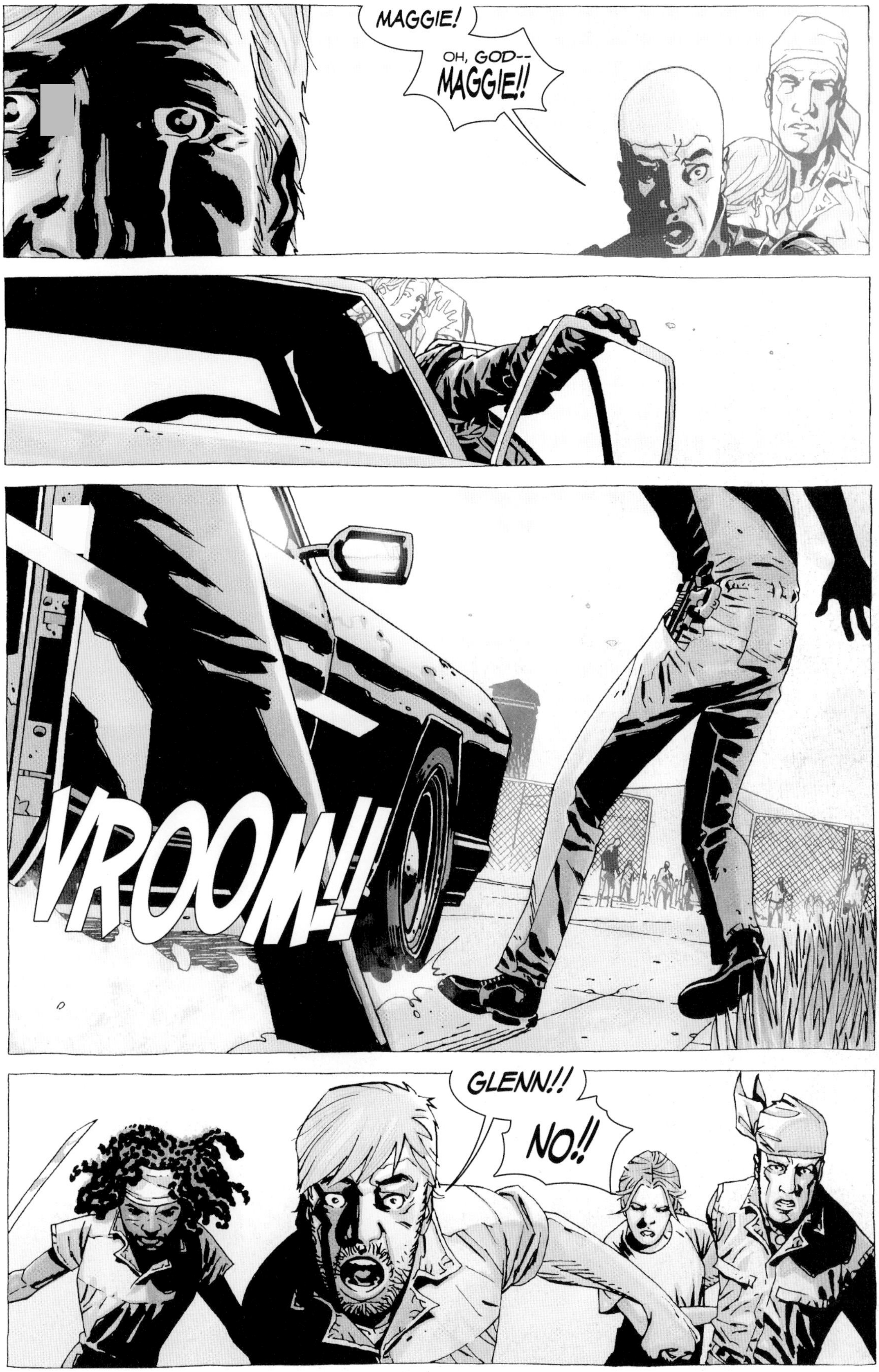
MAGGIE!
OH, GOD-- MAGGIE!!
VROOM!!
GLENN!!
NO!!

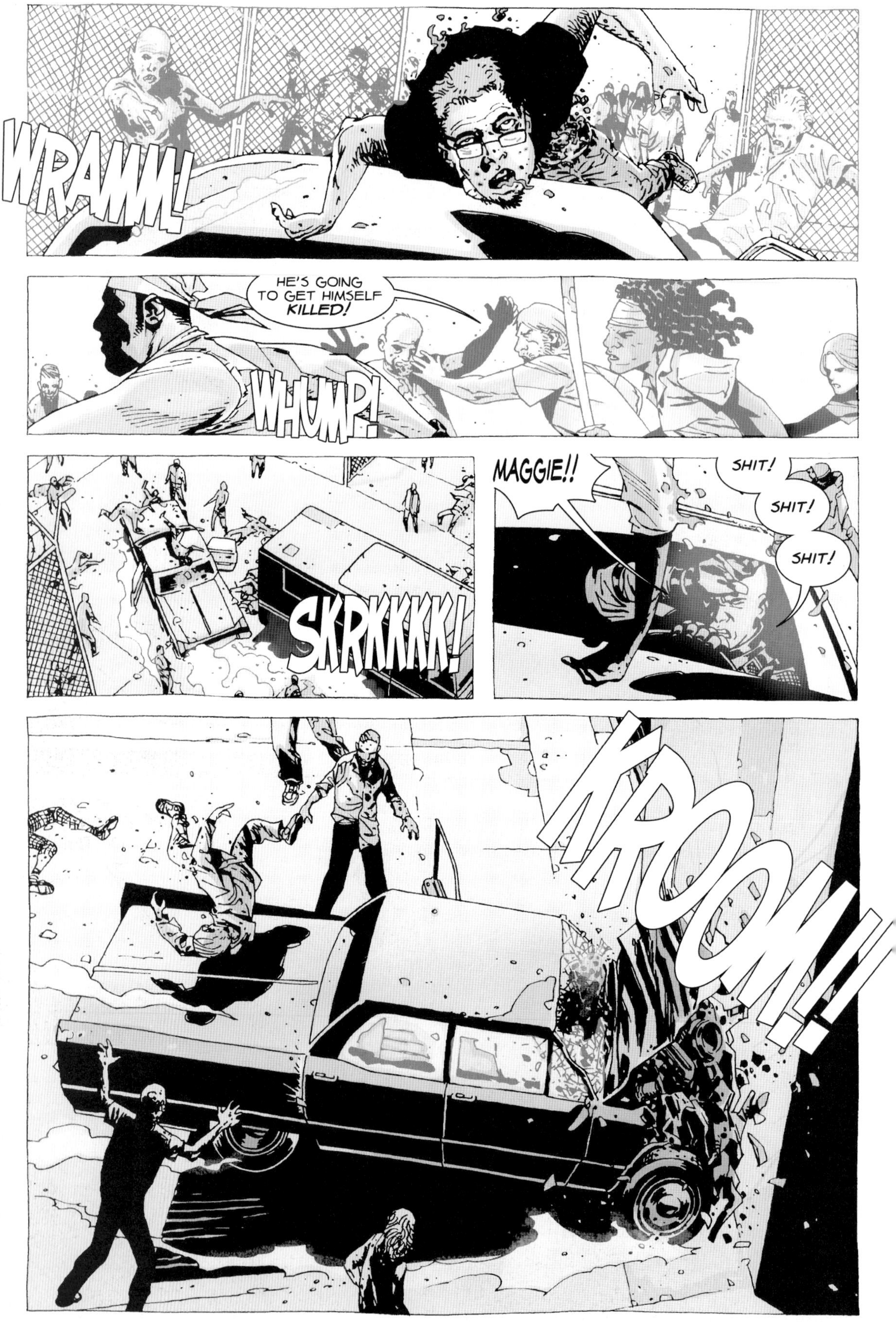
WRAMM!
HE'S GOING TO GET HIMSELF KILLED!
WHUMP!
SKRKKKK!
MAGGIE!!
SHIT!
SHIT!
SHIT!
KROOM!!!

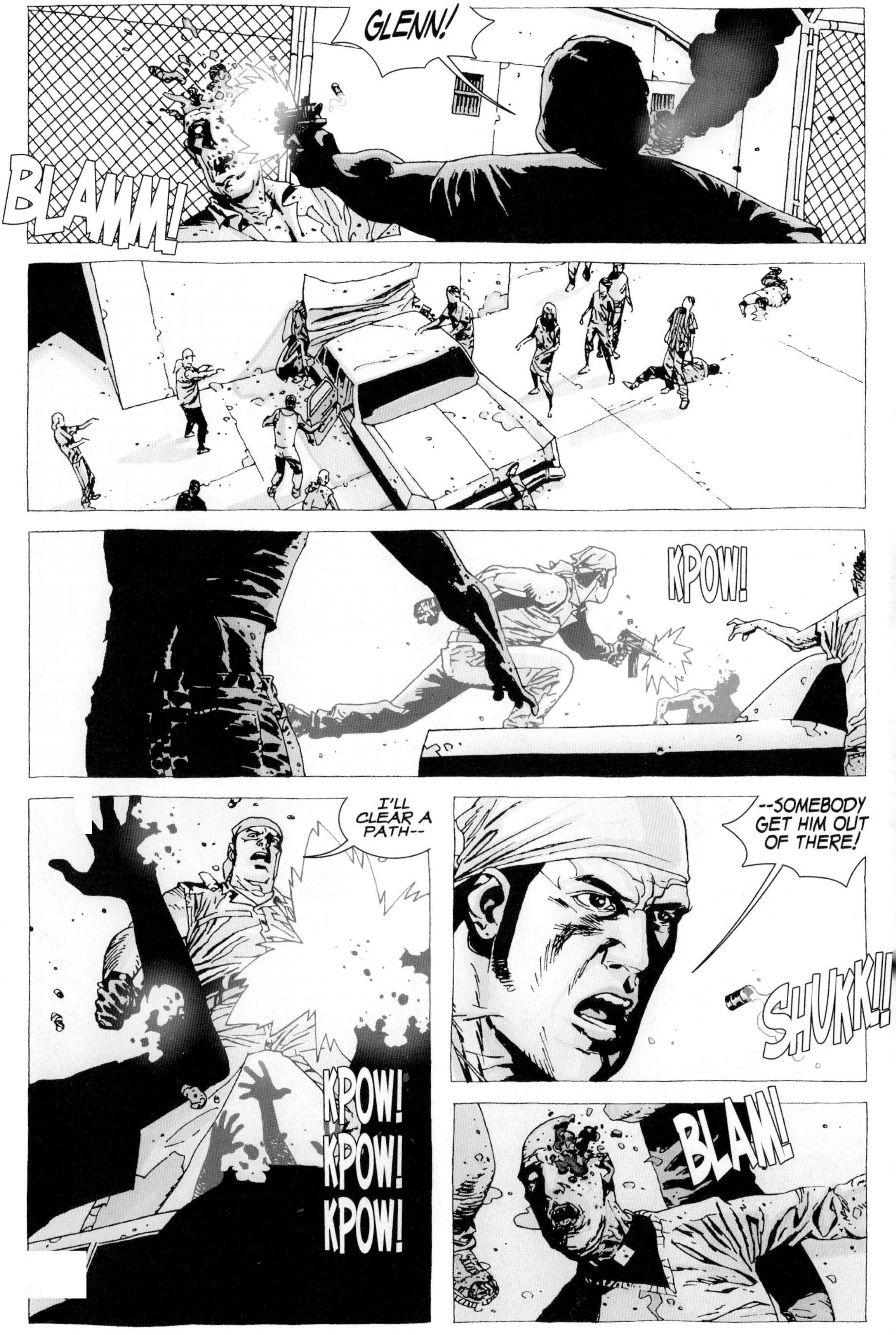
GLENN!
BLAMM!
KPOW!
I'LL CLEAR A PATH--
KPOW!
KPOW!
KPOW!
--SOMEBODY GET HIM OUT OF THERE!
SHUKK!!
BLAM!

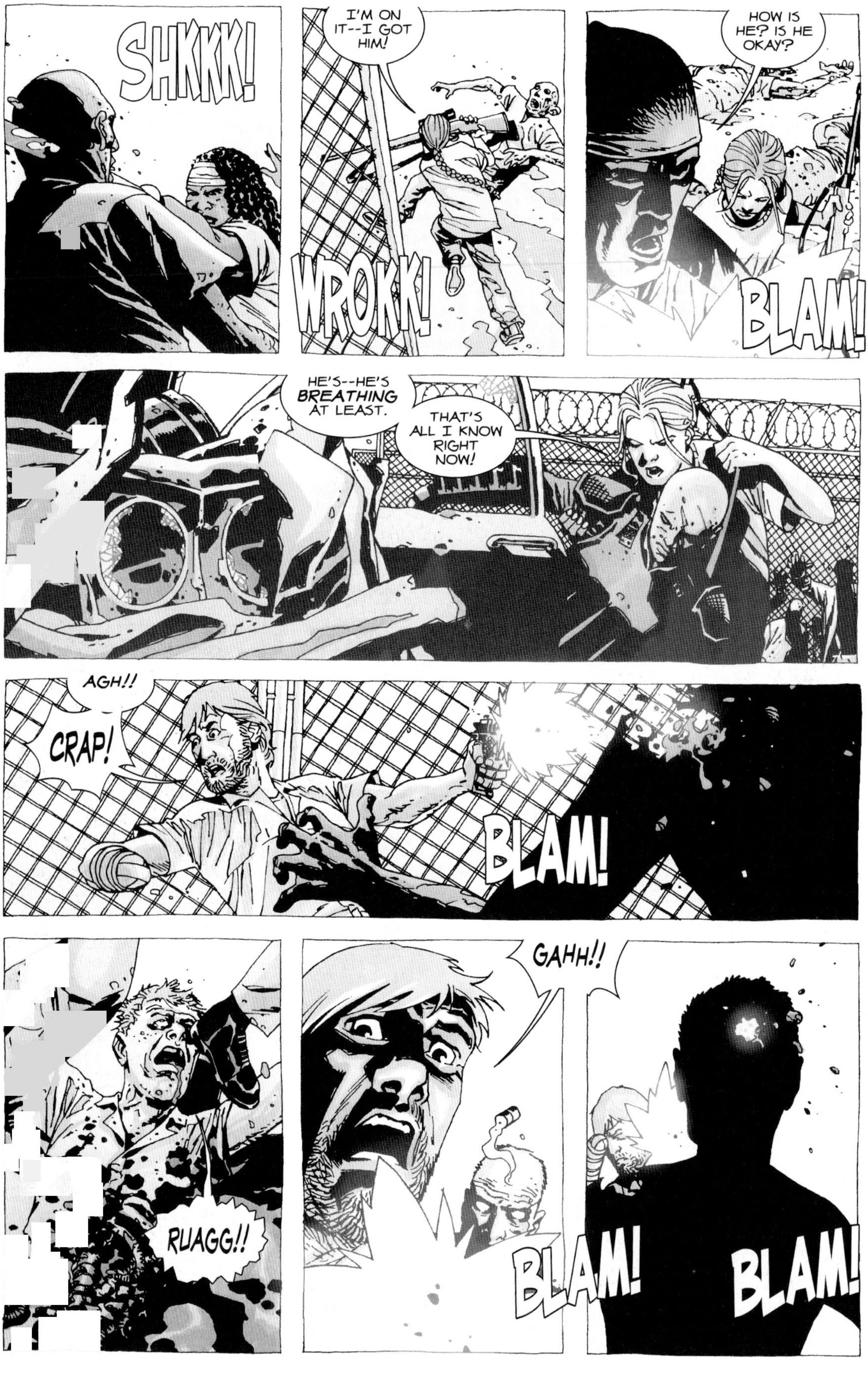
SHKKK!
I'M ON IT--I GOT HIM!
WROKK!
HOW IS HE? IS HE OKAY?
BLAM!
HE'S--HE'S *BREATHING* AT LEAST.
THAT'S ALL I KNOW RIGHT NOW!
AGH!!
CRAP!
BLAM!
RUAGG!!
GAHH!!
BLAM!
BLAM!

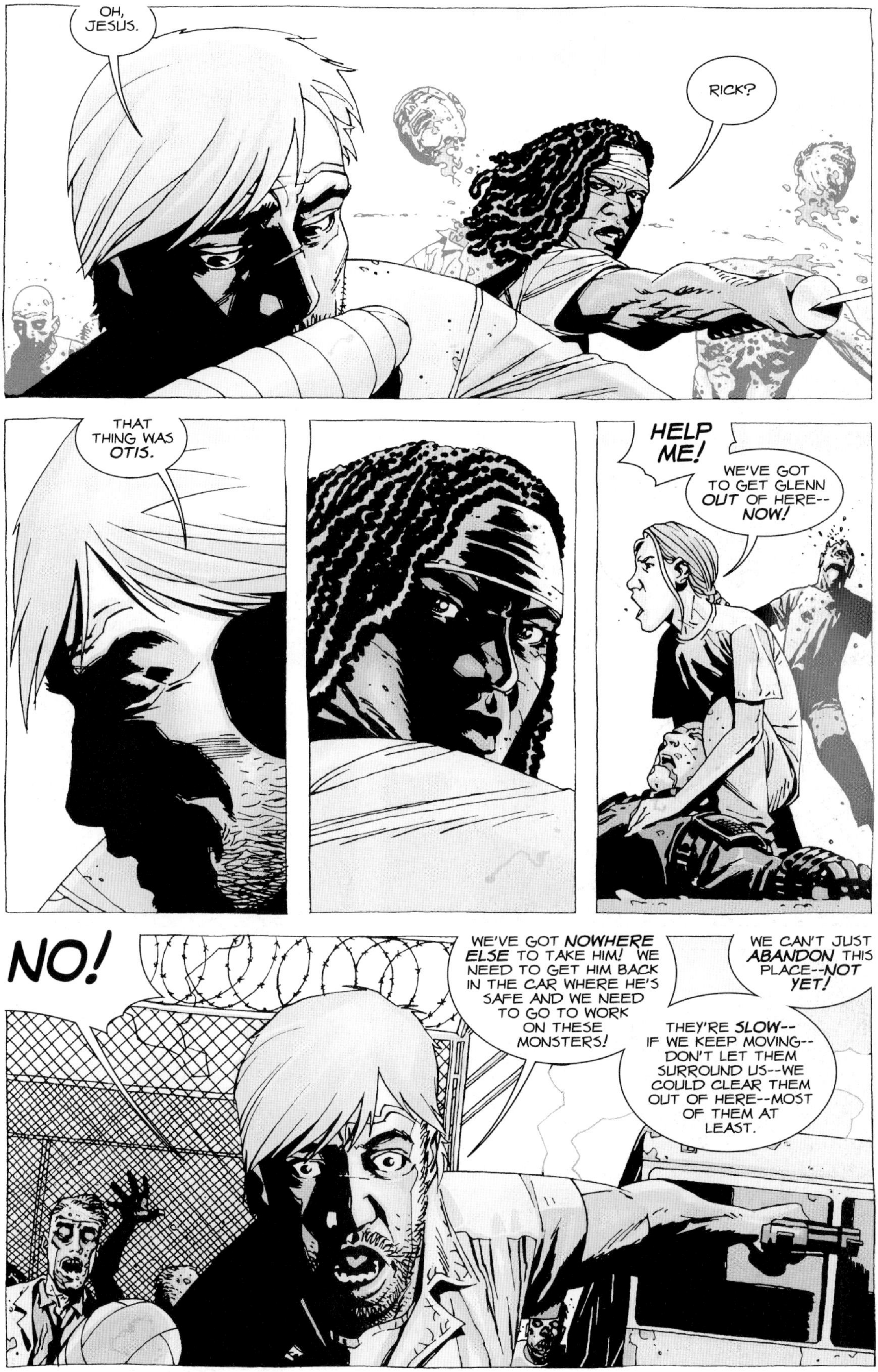
OH, JESUS.
RICK?
THAT THING WAS OTIS.
HELP ME!
WE'VE GOT TO GET GLENN OUT OF HERE--NOW!
NO!
WE'VE GOT NOWHERE ELSE TO TAKE HIM! WE NEED TO GET HIM BACK IN THE CAR WHERE HE'S SAFE AND WE NEED TO GO TO WORK ON THESE MONSTERS!
WE CAN'T JUST ABANDON THIS PLACE--NOT YET!
THEY'RE SLOW--IF WE KEEP MOVING--DON'T LET THEM SURROUND US--WE COULD CLEAR THEM OUT OF HERE--MOST OF THEM AT LEAST.

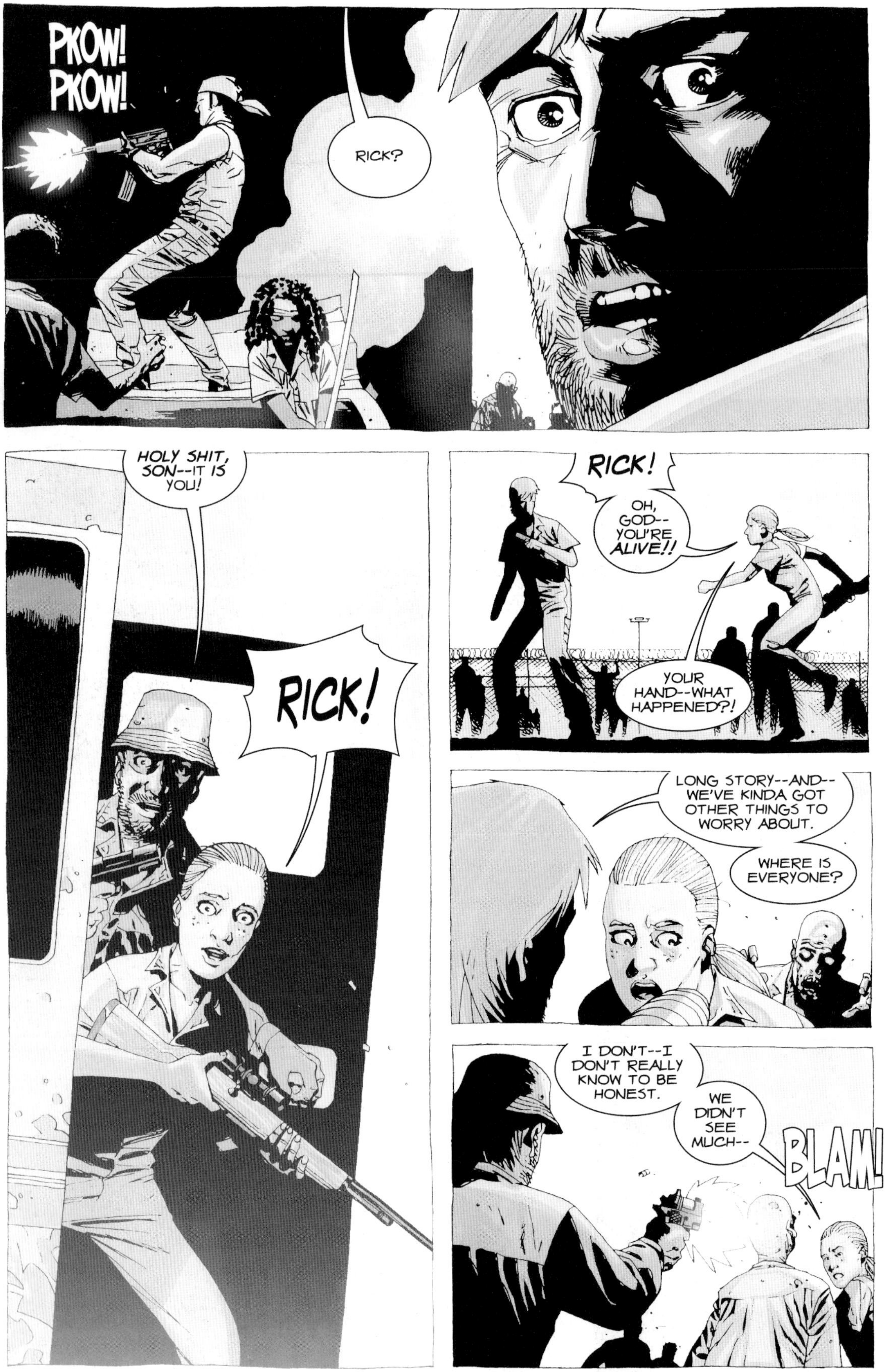
PKOW! PKOW!
RICK?
HOLY SHIT, SON--IT IS YOU!
RICK!
RICK!
OH, GOD-- YOU'RE ALIVE!!
YOUR HAND--WHAT HAPPENED?!
LONG STORY--AND-- WE'VE KINDA GOT OTHER THINGS TO WORRY ABOUT.
WHERE IS EVERYONE?
I DON'T--I DON'T REALLY KNOW TO BE HONEST.
WE DIDN'T SEE MUCH--
BLAM!

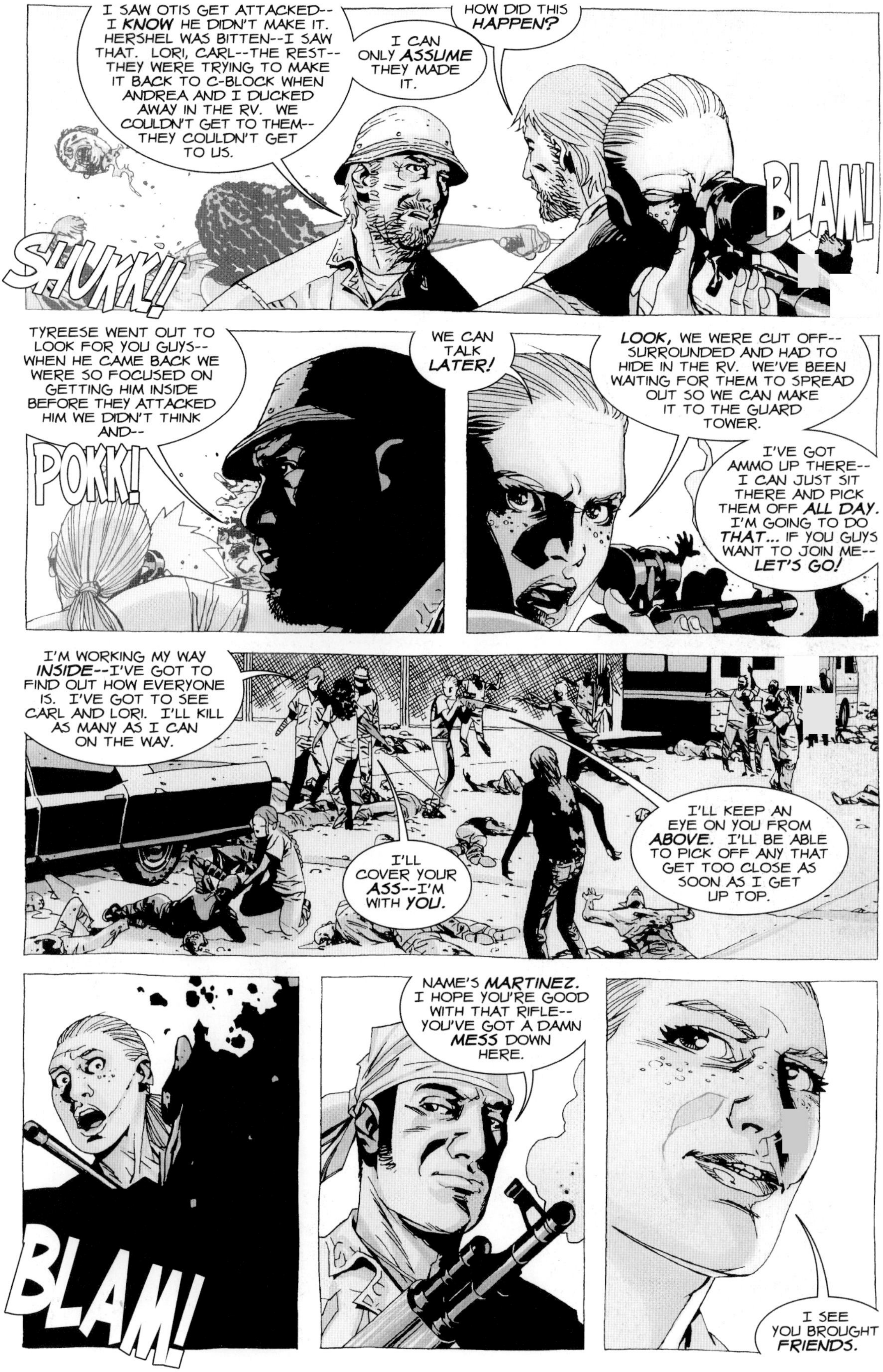

HOW DID THIS HAPPEN?
I SAW OTIS GET ATTACKED-- I KNOW HE DIDN'T MAKE IT. HERSHEL WAS BITTEN--I SAW THAT. LORI, CARL--THE REST-- THEY WERE TRYING TO MAKE IT BACK TO C-BLOCK WHEN ANDREA AND I DUCKED AWAY IN THE RV. WE COULDN'T GET TO THEM-- THEY COULDN'T GET TO US.
I CAN ONLY ASSUME THEY MADE IT.
SHUKK!!
BLAM!
TYREESE WENT OUT TO LOOK FOR YOU GUYS-- WHEN HE CAME BACK WE WERE SO FOCUSED ON GETTING HIM INSIDE BEFORE THEY ATTACKED HIM WE DIDN'T THINK AND--
POKK!
WE CAN TALK LATER!
LOOK, WE WERE CUT OFF-- SURROUNDED AND HAD TO HIDE IN THE RV. WE'VE BEEN WAITING FOR THEM TO SPREAD OUT SO WE CAN MAKE IT TO THE GUARD TOWER.
I'VE GOT AMMO UP THERE-- I CAN JUST SIT THERE AND PICK THEM OFF ALL DAY. I'M GOING TO DO THAT... IF YOU GUYS WANT TO JOIN ME-- LET'S GO!
I'M WORKING MY WAY INSIDE--I'VE GOT TO FIND OUT HOW EVERYONE IS. I'VE GOT TO SEE CARL AND LORI. I'LL KILL AS MANY AS I CAN ON THE WAY.
I'LL COVER YOUR ASS--I'M WITH YOU.
I'LL KEEP AN EYE ON YOU FROM ABOVE. I'LL BE ABLE TO PICK OFF ANY THAT GET TOO CLOSE AS SOON AS I GET UP TOP.
BLAM!
NAME'S MARTINEZ. I HOPE YOU'RE GOOD WITH THAT RIFLE-- YOU'VE GOT A DAMN MESS DOWN HERE.
I SEE YOU BROUGHT FRIENDS.

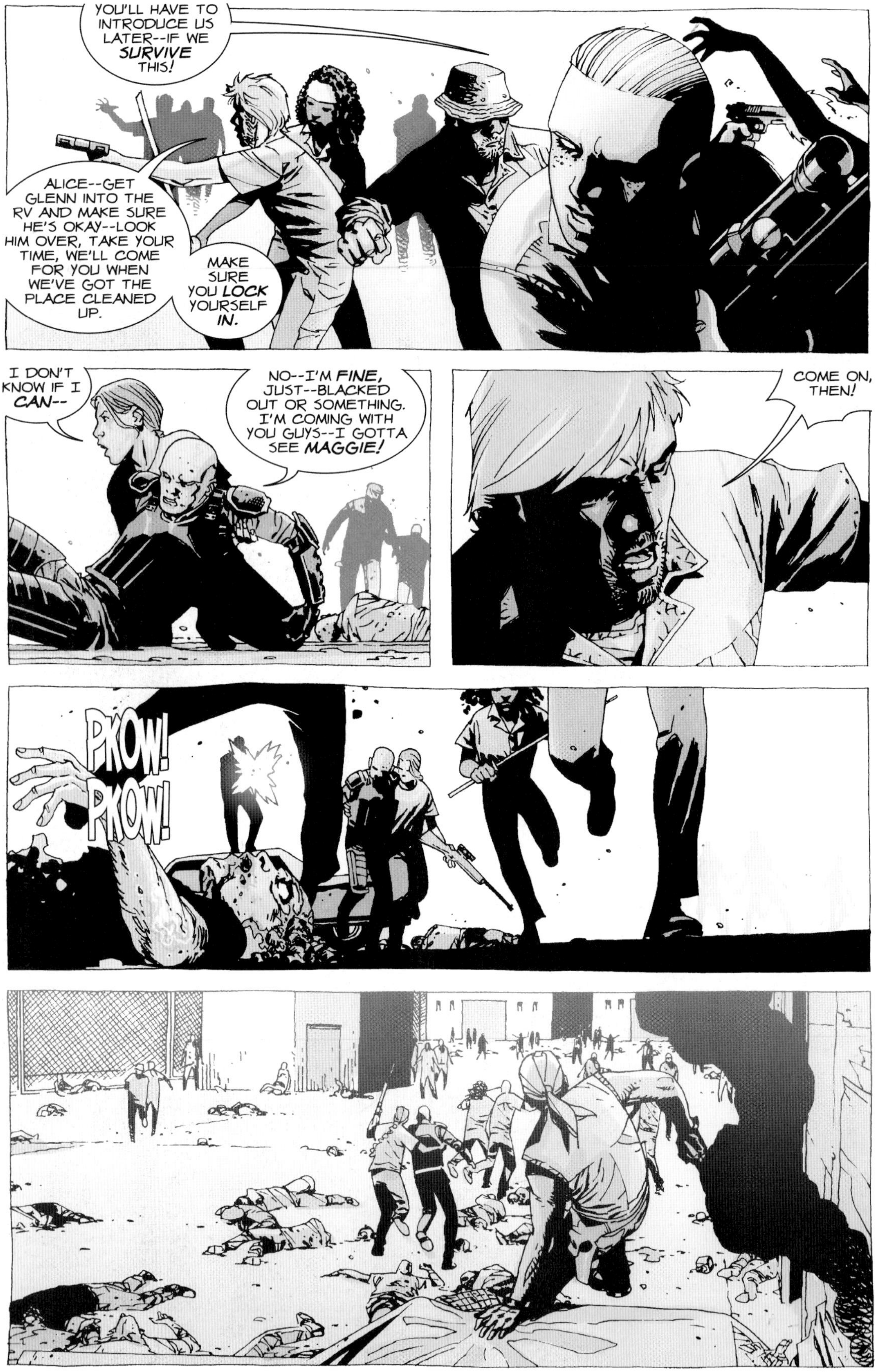
YOU'LL HAVE TO INTRODUCE US LATER--IF WE SURVIVE THIS!
ALICE--GET GLENN INTO THE RV AND MAKE SURE HE'S OKAY--LOOK HIM OVER, TAKE YOUR TIME, WE'LL COME FOR YOU WHEN WE'VE GOT THE PLACE CLEANED UP.
MAKE SURE YOU LOCK YOURSELF IN.
I DON'T KNOW IF I CAN--
NO--I'M FINE, JUST--BLACKED OUT OR SOMETHING. I'M COMING WITH YOU GUYS--I GOTTA SEE MAGGIE!
COME ON, THEN!
PKOW!
PKOW!

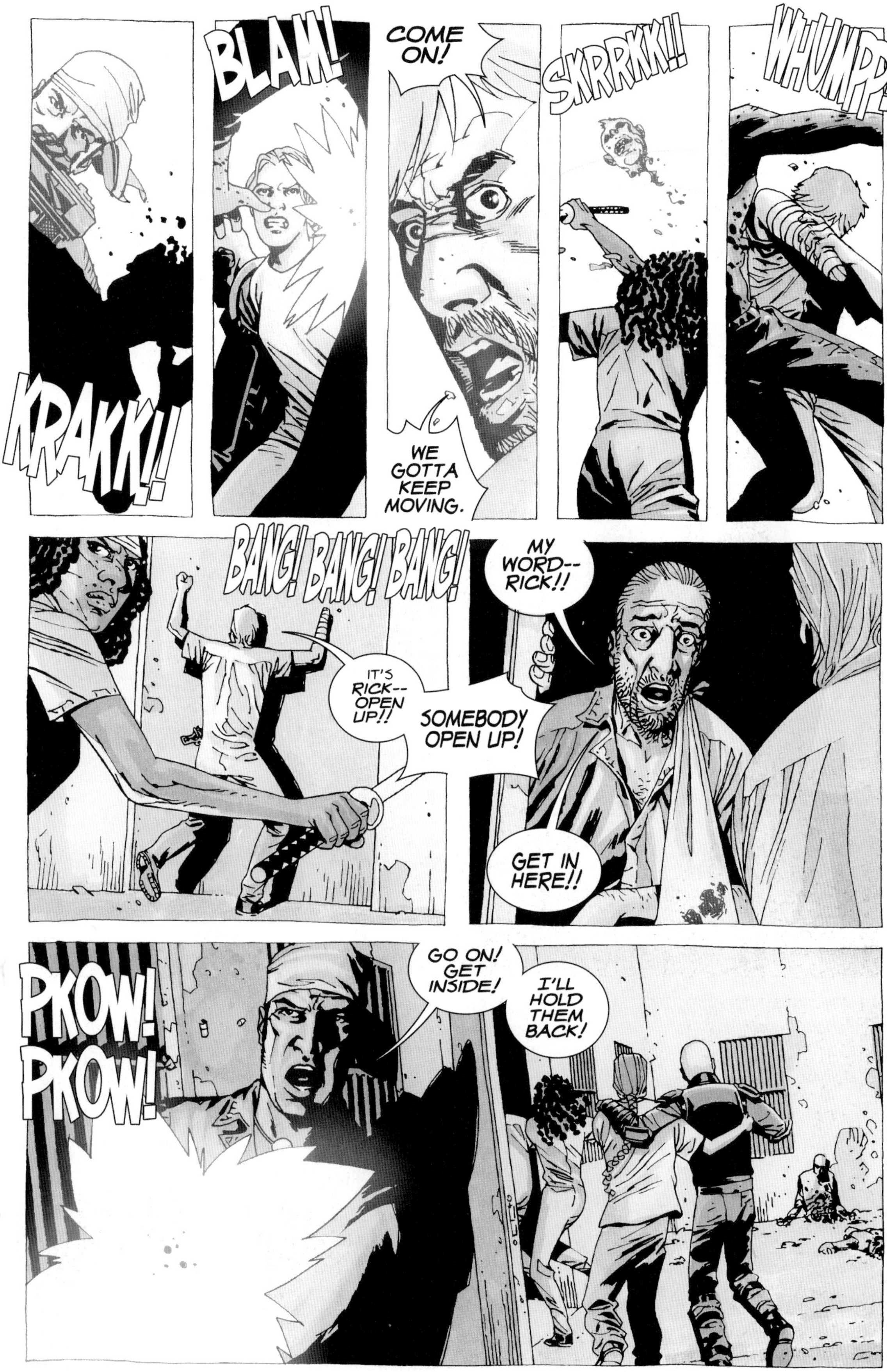
KRAKK!!
BLAM!
COME ON!
WE GOTTA KEEP MOVING.
SKRRKK!!
WHUMPP!
BANG! BANG! BANG!
IT'S RICK-- OPEN UP!!
SOMEBODY OPEN UP!
MY WORD-- RICK!!
GET IN HERE!!
PKOW! PKOW!
GO ON! GET INSIDE!
I'LL HOLD THEM BACK!

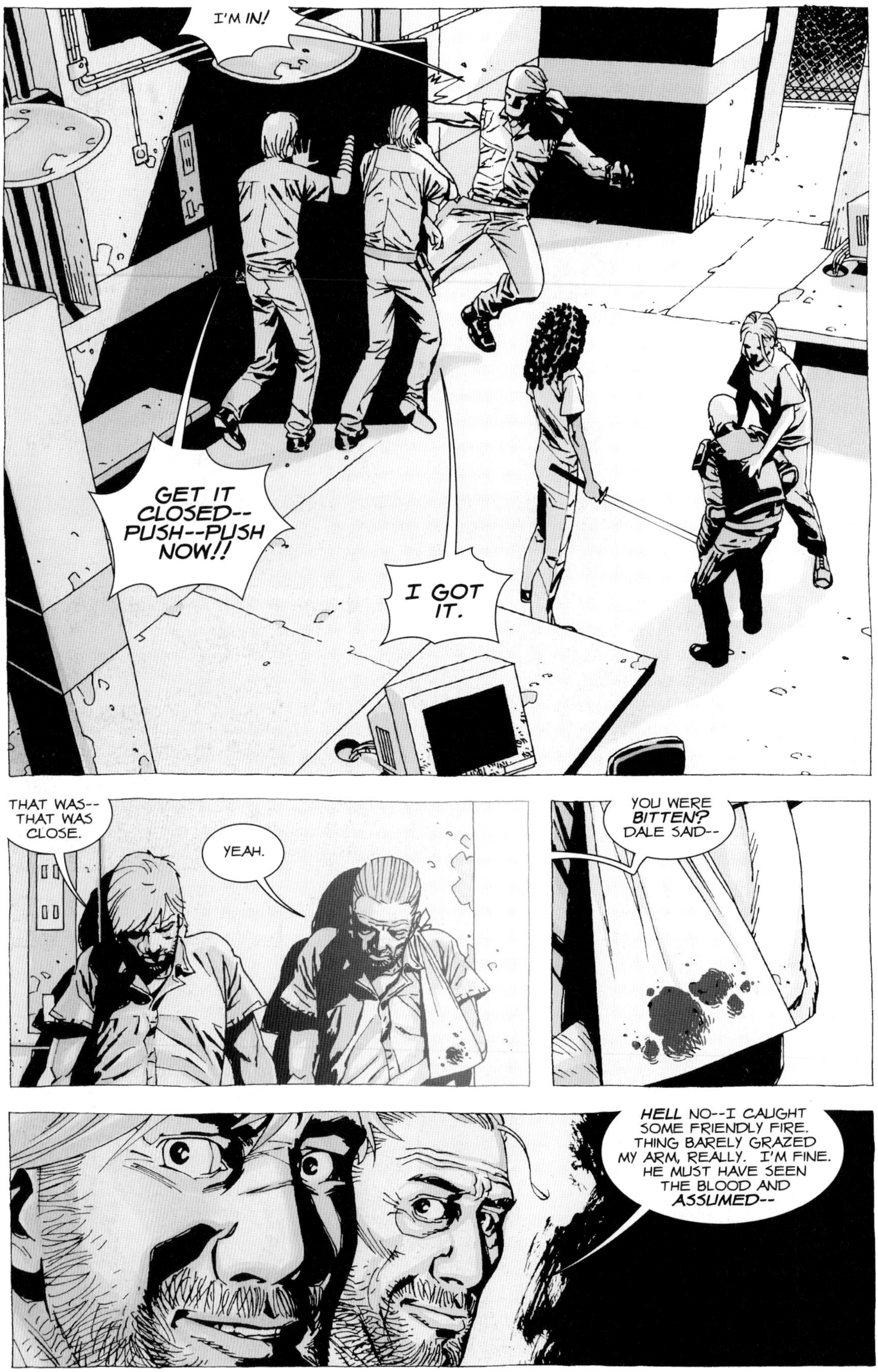
I'M IN!
GET IT CLOSED--PUSH--PUSH NOW!!
I GOT IT.
THAT WAS--THAT WAS CLOSE.
YEAH.
YOU WERE BITTEN? DALE SAID--
HELL NO--I CAUGHT SOME FRIENDLY FIRE. THING BARELY GRAZED MY ARM, REALLY. I'M FINE. HE MUST HAVE SEEN THE BLOOD AND ASSUMED--

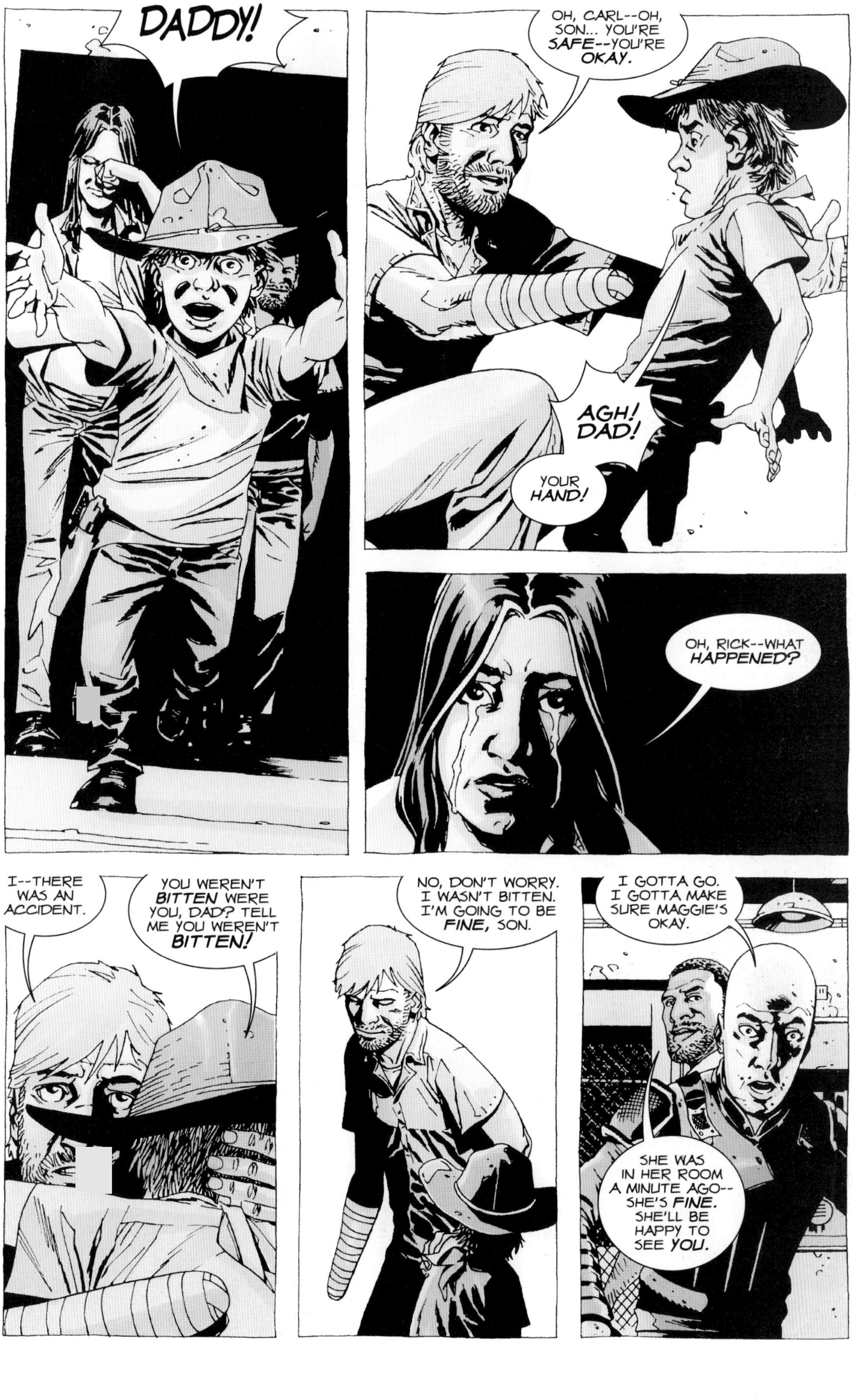
DADDY!
OH, CARL--OH, SON... YOU'RE SAFE--YOU'RE OKAY.
AGH! DAD!
YOUR HAND!
OH, RICK--WHAT HAPPENED?
I--THERE WAS AN ACCIDENT.
YOU WEREN'T BITTEN WERE YOU, DAD? TELL ME YOU WEREN'T BITTEN!
NO, DON'T WORRY. I WASN'T BITTEN. I'M GOING TO BE FINE, SON.
I GOTTA GO. I GOTTA MAKE SURE MAGGIE'S OKAY.
SHE WAS IN HER ROOM A MINUTE AGO--SHE'S FINE. SHE'LL BE HAPPY TO SEE YOU.

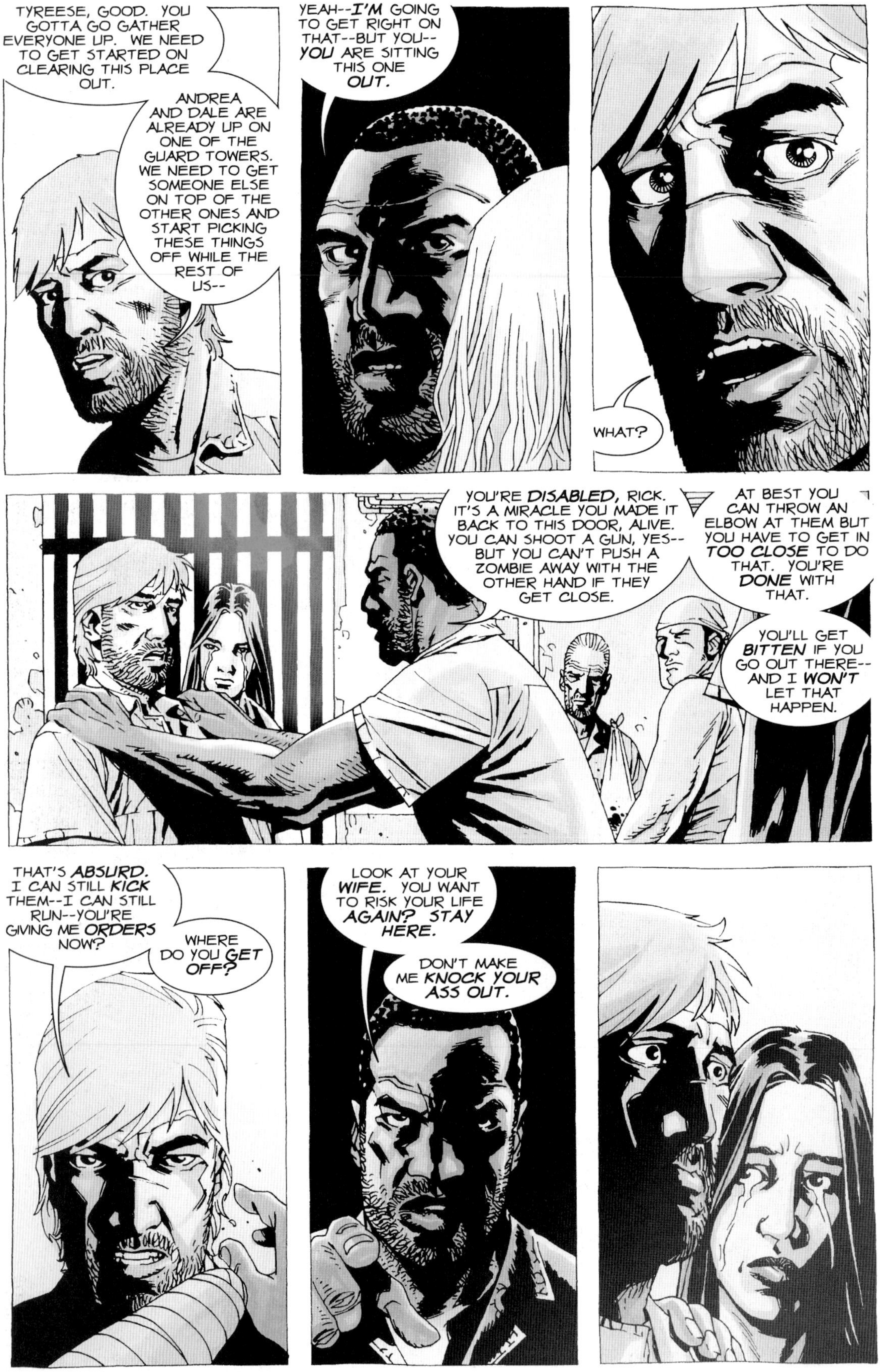
TYREESE, GOOD. YOU GOTTA GO GATHER EVERYONE UP. WE NEED TO GET STARTED ON CLEARING THIS PLACE OUT.
ANDREA AND DALE ARE ALREADY UP ON ONE OF THE GUARD TOWERS. WE NEED TO GET SOMEONE ELSE ON TOP OF THE OTHER ONES AND START PICKING THESE THINGS OFF WHILE THE REST OF US--
YEAH--I'M GOING TO GET RIGHT ON THAT--BUT YOU--YOU ARE SITTING THIS ONE OUT.
WHAT?
YOU'RE DISABLED, RICK. IT'S A MIRACLE YOU MADE IT BACK TO THIS DOOR, ALIVE. YOU CAN SHOOT A GUN, YES--BUT YOU CAN'T PUSH A ZOMBIE AWAY WITH THE OTHER HAND IF THEY GET CLOSE.
AT BEST YOU CAN THROW AN ELBOW AT THEM BUT YOU HAVE TO GET IN TOO CLOSE TO DO THAT. YOU'RE DONE WITH THAT.
YOU'LL GET BITTEN IF YOU GO OUT THERE--AND I WON'T LET THAT HAPPEN.
THAT'S ABSURD. I CAN STILL KICK THEM--I CAN STILL RUN--YOU'RE GIVING ME ORDERS NOW?
WHERE DO YOU GET OFF?
LOOK AT YOUR WIFE. YOU WANT TO RISK YOUR LIFE AGAIN? STAY HERE.
DON'T MAKE ME KNOCK YOUR ASS OUT.

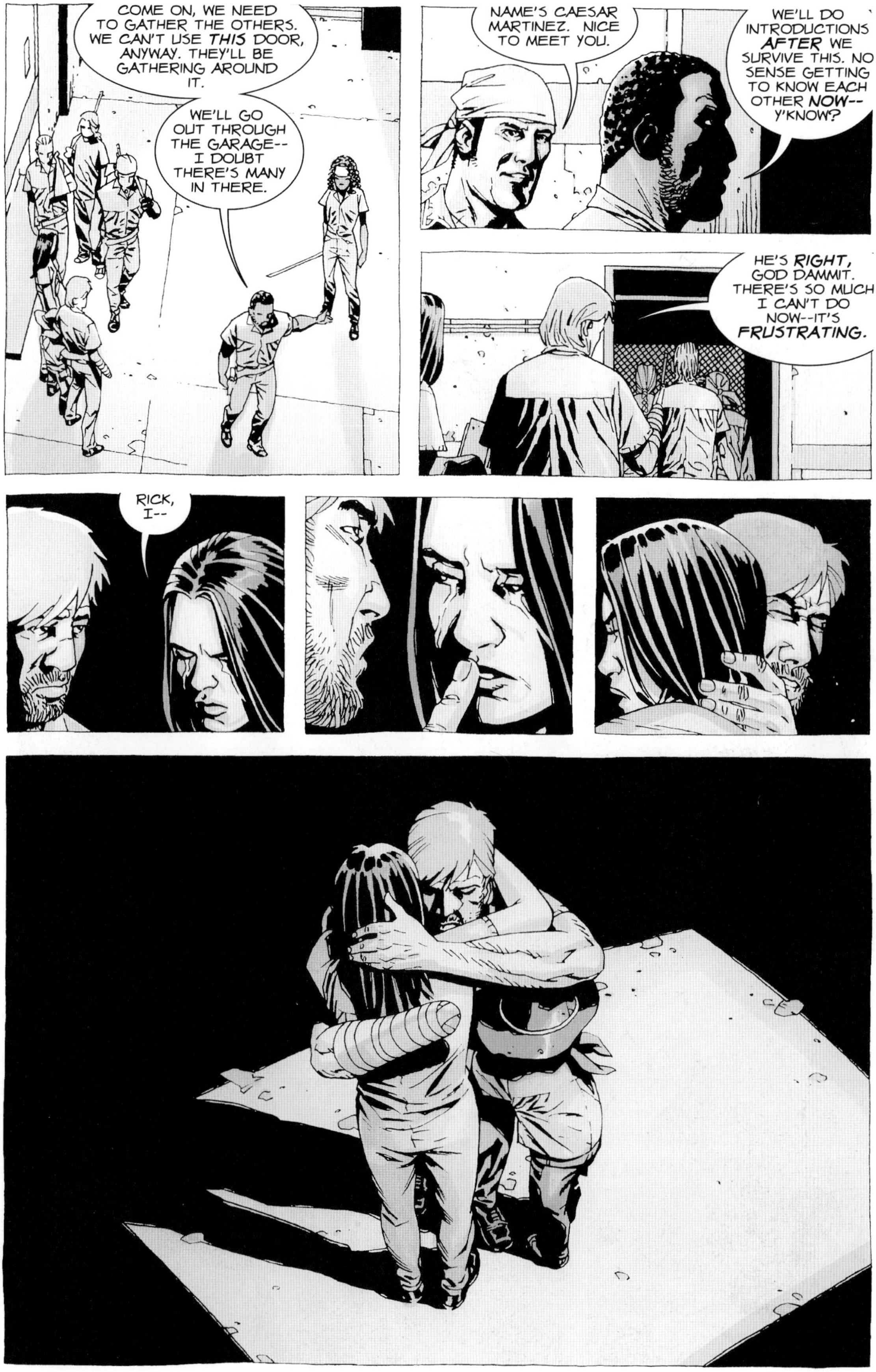
COME ON, WE NEED TO GATHER THE OTHERS. WE CAN'T USE THIS DOOR, ANYWAY. THEY'LL BE GATHERING AROUND IT.
WE'LL GO OUT THROUGH THE GARAGE-- I DOUBT THERE'S MANY IN THERE.
NAME'S CAESAR MARTINEZ. NICE TO MEET YOU.
WE'LL DO INTRODUCTIONS AFTER WE SURVIVE THIS. NO SENSE GETTING TO KNOW EACH OTHER NOW-- Y'KNOW?
HE'S RIGHT, GOD DAMMIT. THERE'S SO MUCH I CAN'T DO NOW--IT'S FRUSTRATING.
RICK, I--

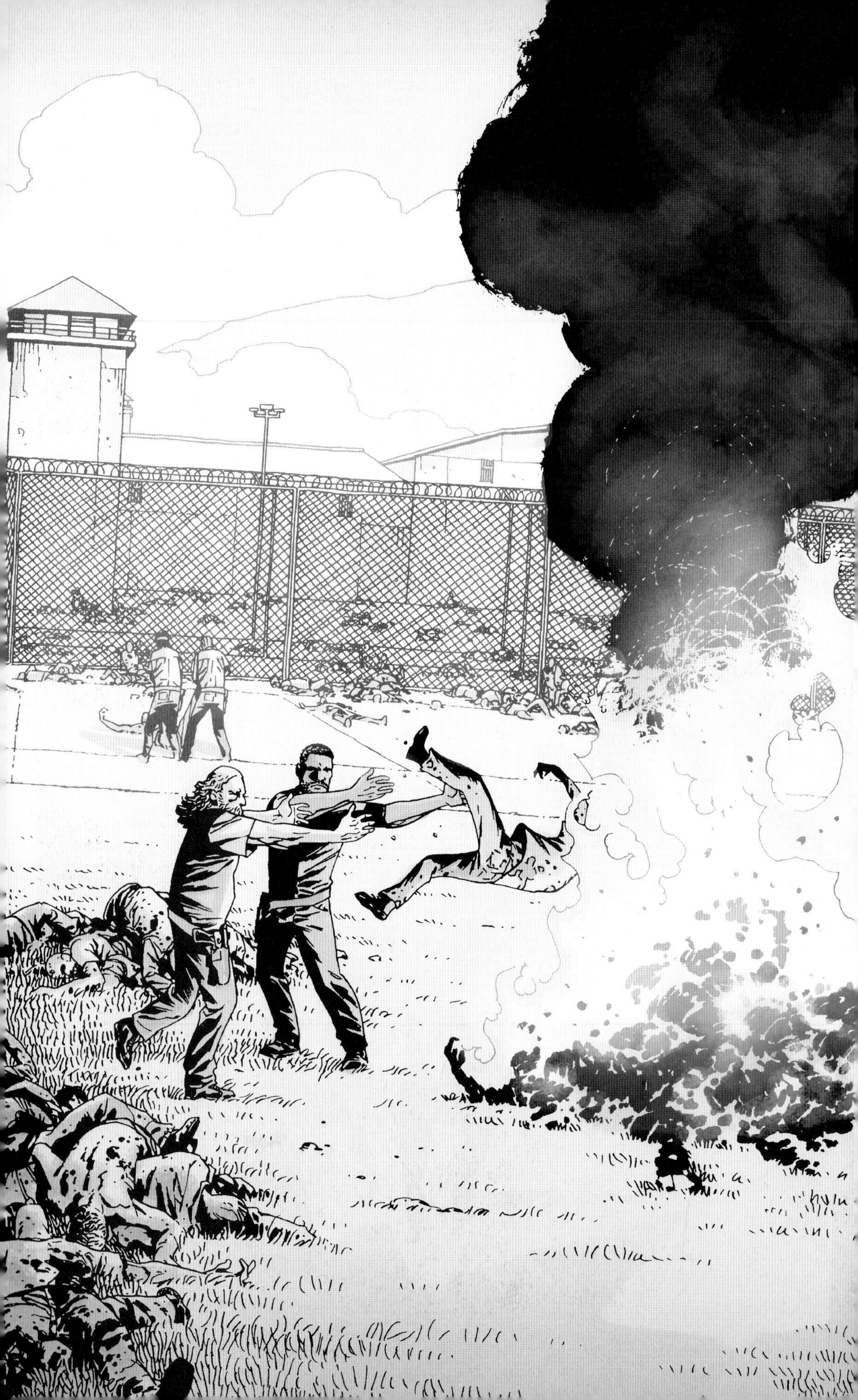

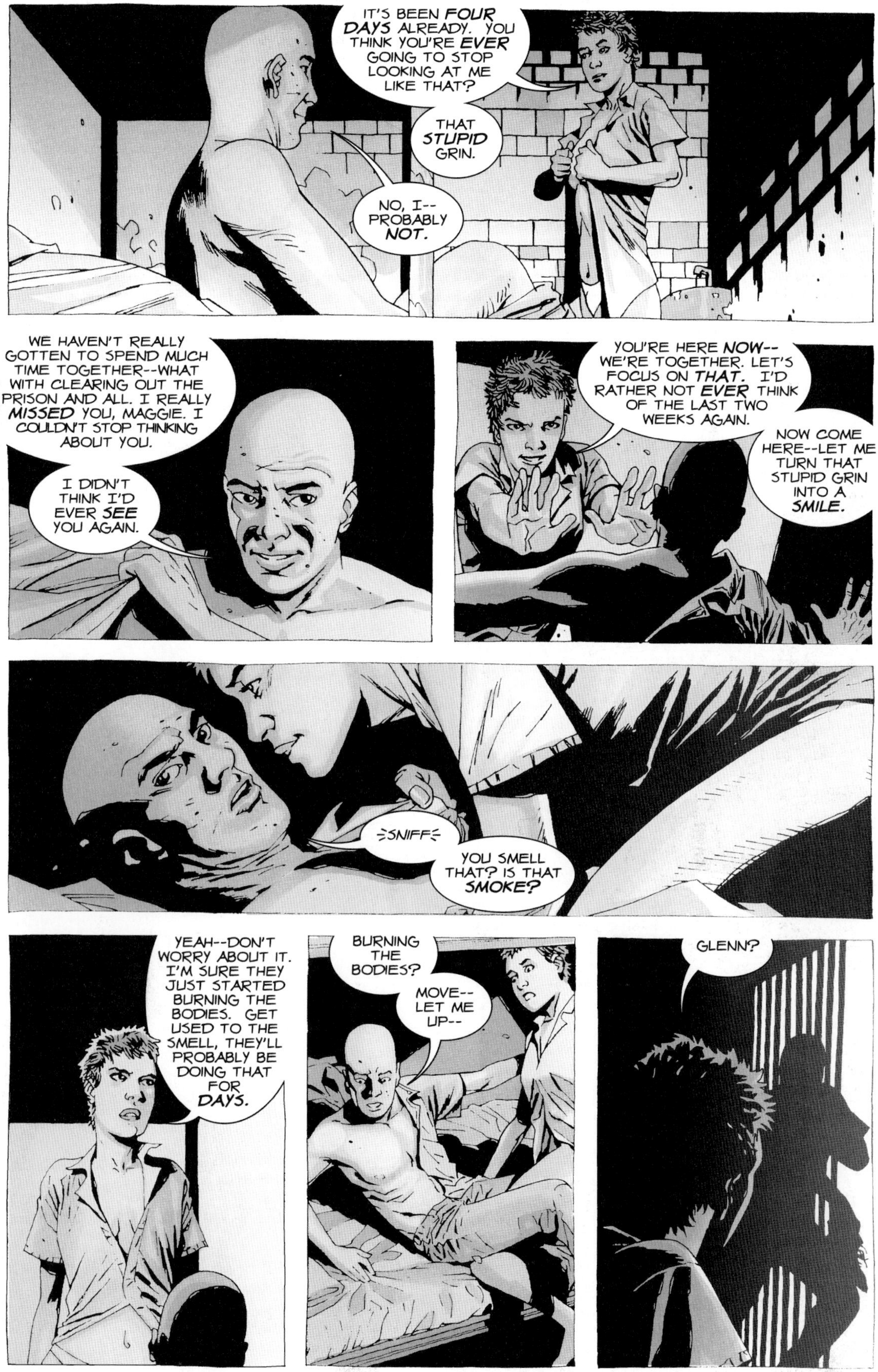
IT'S BEEN FOUR DAYS ALREADY. YOU THINK YOU'RE EVER GOING TO STOP LOOKING AT ME LIKE THAT?
THAT STUPID GRIN.
NO, I-- PROBABLY NOT.
WE HAVEN'T REALLY GOTTEN TO SPEND MUCH TIME TOGETHER--WHAT WITH CLEARING OUT THE PRISON AND ALL. I REALLY MISSED YOU, MAGGIE. I COULDN'T STOP THINKING ABOUT YOU.
I DIDN'T THINK I'D EVER SEE YOU AGAIN.
YOU'RE HERE NOW-- WE'RE TOGETHER. LET'S FOCUS ON THAT. I'D RATHER NOT EVER THINK OF THE LAST TWO WEEKS AGAIN.
NOW COME HERE--LET ME TURN THAT STUPID GRIN INTO A SMILE.
SNIFF
YOU SMELL THAT? IS THAT SMOKE?
YEAH--DON'T WORRY ABOUT IT. I'M SURE THEY JUST STARTED BURNING THE BODIES. GET USED TO THE SMELL, THEY'LL PROBABLY BE DOING THAT FOR DAYS.
BURNING THE BODIES?
MOVE-- LET ME UP--
GLENN?

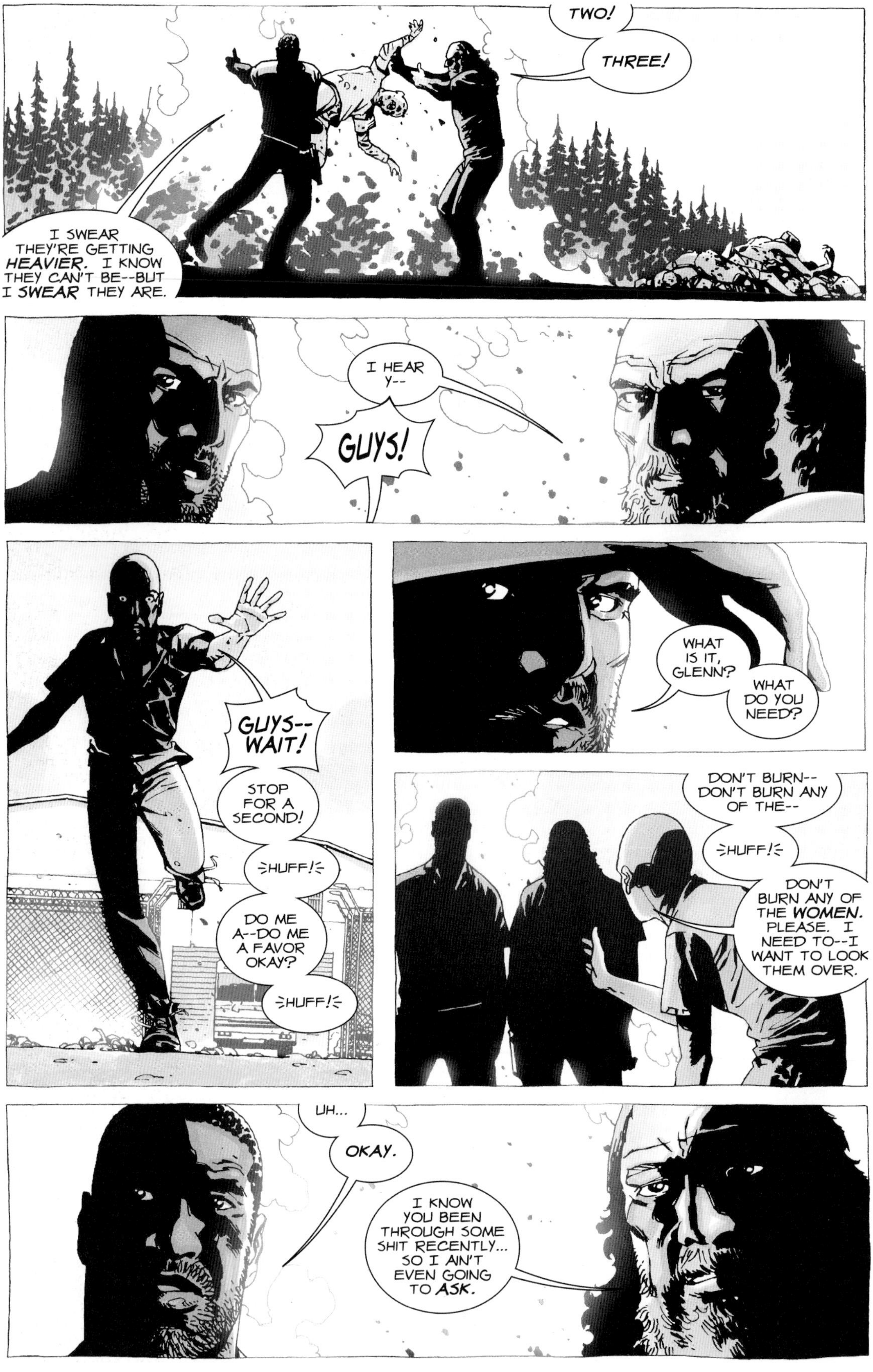
TWO!
THREE!
I SWEAR THEY'RE GETTING HEAVIER. I KNOW THEY CAN'T BE--BUT I SWEAR THEY ARE.
I HEAR Y--
GUYS!
GUYS--WAIT!
STOP FOR A SECOND!
HUFF!
DO ME A--DO ME A FAVOR OKAY?
HUFF!
WHAT IS IT, GLENN?
WHAT DO YOU NEED?
DON'T BURN--DON'T BURN ANY OF THE--
HUFF!
DON'T BURN ANY OF THE WOMEN. PLEASE. I NEED TO--I WANT TO LOOK THEM OVER.
UH...
OKAY.
I KNOW YOU BEEN THROUGH SOME SHIT RECENTLY... SO I AIN'T EVEN GOING TO ASK.

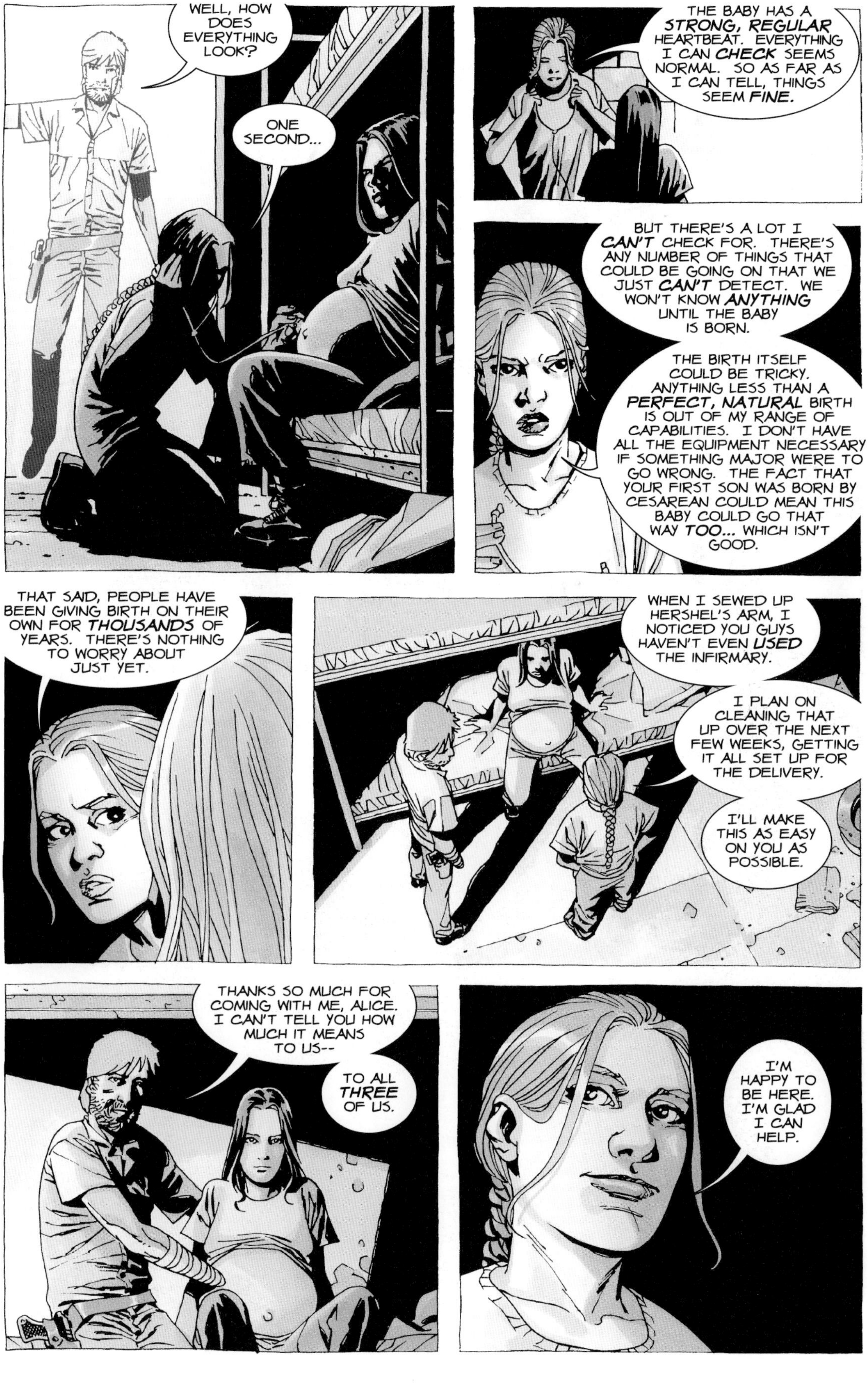
WELL, HOW DOES EVERYTHING LOOK?
ONE SECOND...
THE BABY HAS A STRONG, REGULAR HEARTBEAT. EVERYTHING I CAN CHECK SEEMS NORMAL. SO AS FAR AS I CAN TELL, THINGS SEEM FINE.
BUT THERE'S A LOT I CAN'T CHECK FOR. THERE'S ANY NUMBER OF THINGS THAT COULD BE GOING ON THAT WE JUST CAN'T DETECT. WE WON'T KNOW ANYTHING UNTIL THE BABY IS BORN.
THE BIRTH ITSELF COULD BE TRICKY. ANYTHING LESS THAN A PERFECT, NATURAL BIRTH IS OUT OF MY RANGE OF CAPABILITIES. I DON'T HAVE ALL THE EQUIPMENT NECESSARY IF SOMETHING MAJOR WERE TO GO WRONG. THE FACT THAT YOUR FIRST SON WAS BORN BY CESAREAN COULD MEAN THIS BABY COULD GO THAT WAY TOO... WHICH ISN'T GOOD.
THAT SAID, PEOPLE HAVE BEEN GIVING BIRTH ON THEIR OWN FOR THOUSANDS OF YEARS. THERE'S NOTHING TO WORRY ABOUT JUST YET.
WHEN I SEWED UP HERSHEL'S ARM, I NOTICED YOU GUYS HAVEN'T EVEN USED THE INFIRMARY.
I PLAN ON CLEANING THAT UP OVER THE NEXT FEW WEEKS, GETTING IT ALL SET UP FOR THE DELIVERY.
I'LL MAKE THIS AS EASY ON YOU AS POSSIBLE.
THANKS SO MUCH FOR COMING WITH ME, ALICE. I CAN'T TELL YOU HOW MUCH IT MEANS TO US--
TO ALL THREE OF US.
I'M HAPPY TO BE HERE. I'M GLAD I CAN HELP.

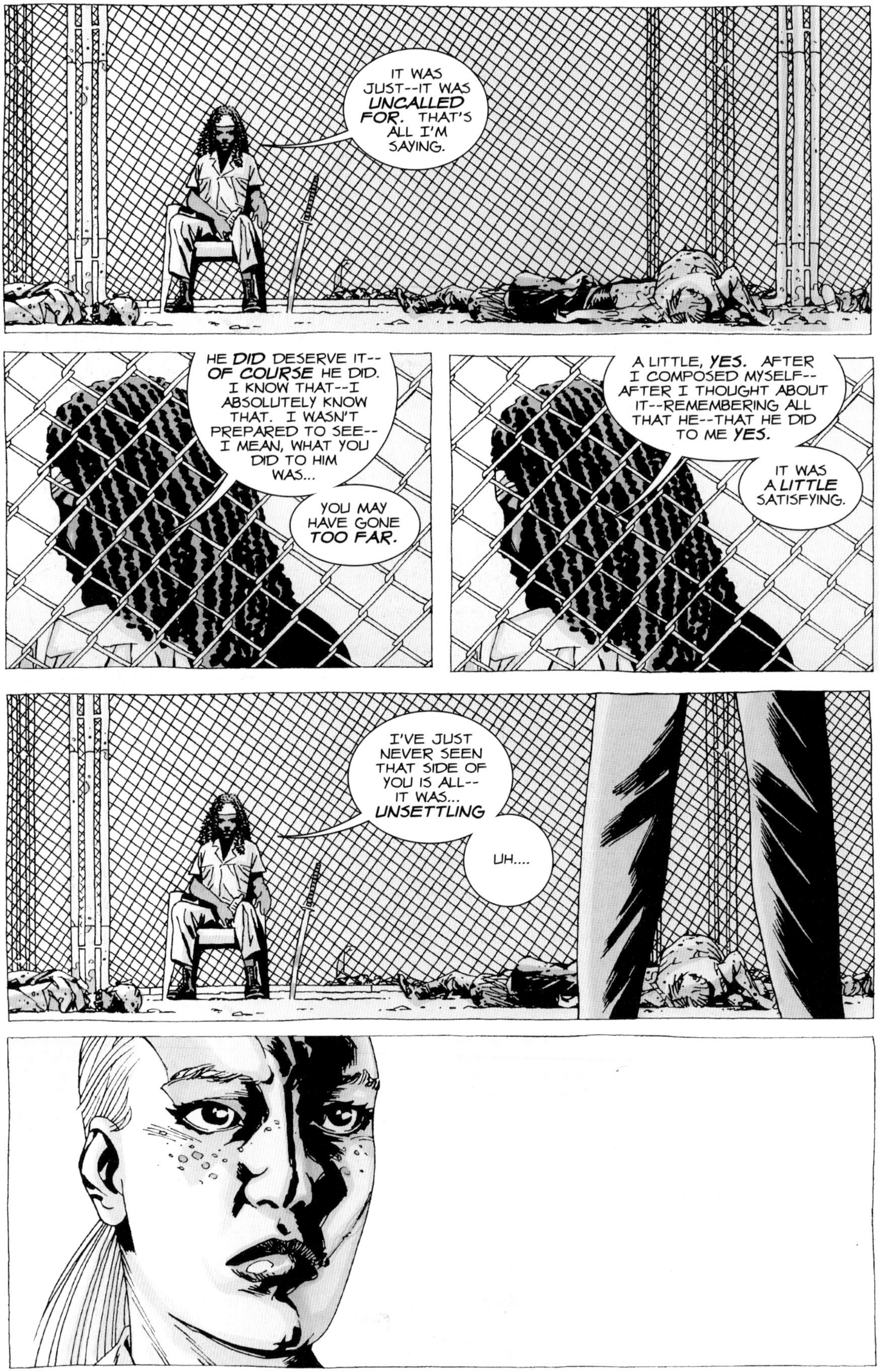

IT WAS JUST--IT WAS UNCALLED FOR. THAT'S ALL I'M SAYING.
HE DID DESERVE IT--OF COURSE HE DID. I KNOW THAT--I ABSOLUTELY KNOW THAT. I WASN'T PREPARED TO SEE--I MEAN, WHAT YOU DID TO HIM WAS...
YOU MAY HAVE GONE TOO FAR.
A LITTLE, YES. AFTER I COMPOSED MYSELF--AFTER I THOUGHT ABOUT IT--REMEMBERING ALL THAT HE--THAT HE DID TO ME YES.
IT WAS A LITTLE SATISFYING.
I'VE JUST NEVER SEEN THAT SIDE OF YOU IS ALL--IT WAS... UNSETTLING
UH....

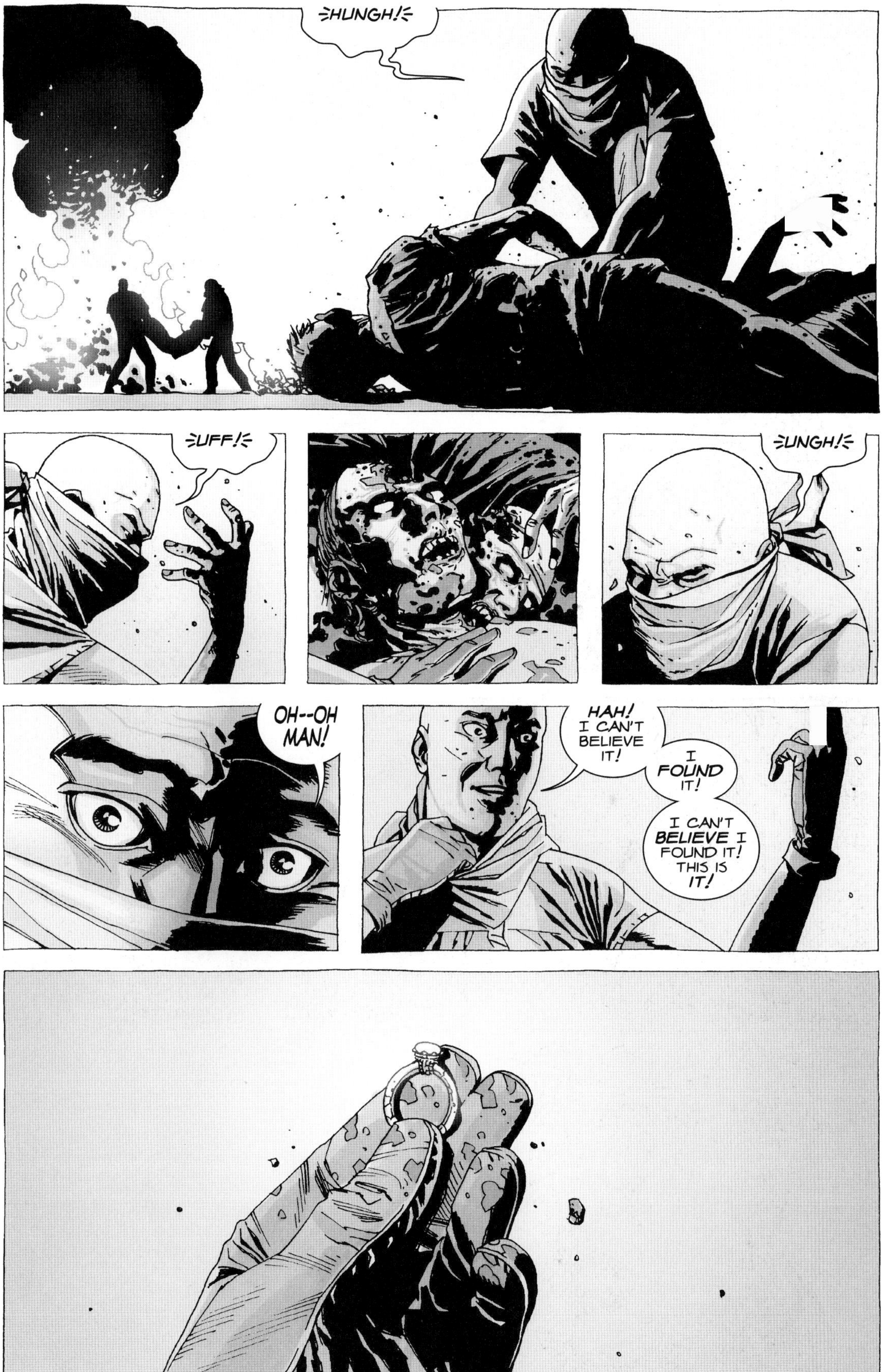
HUNGH!
UFF!
UNGH!
OH--OH MAN!
HAH! I CAN'T BELIEVE IT!
I FOUND IT!
I CAN'T BELIEVE I FOUND IT! THIS IS IT!

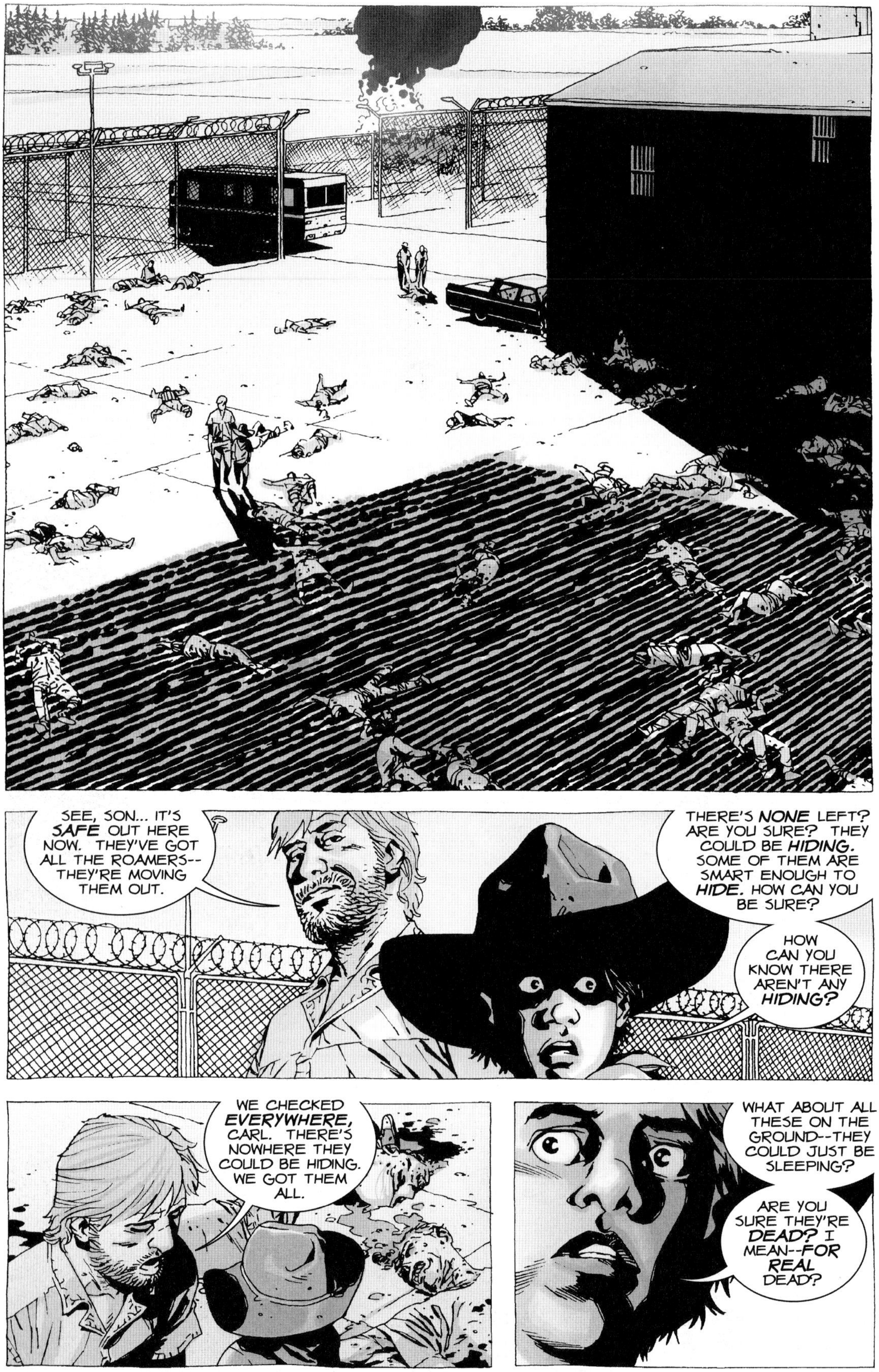
SEE, SON... IT'S SAFE OUT HERE NOW. THEY'VE GOT ALL THE ROAMERS-- THEY'RE MOVING THEM OUT.
THERE'S NONE LEFT? ARE YOU SURE? THEY COULD BE HIDING. SOME OF THEM ARE SMART ENOUGH TO HIDE. HOW CAN YOU BE SURE?
HOW CAN YOU KNOW THERE AREN'T ANY HIDING?
WE CHECKED EVERYWHERE, CARL. THERE'S NOWHERE THEY COULD BE HIDING. WE GOT THEM ALL.
WHAT ABOUT ALL THESE ON THE GROUND--THEY COULD JUST BE SLEEPING?
ARE YOU SURE THEY'RE DEAD? I MEAN--FOR REAL DEAD?

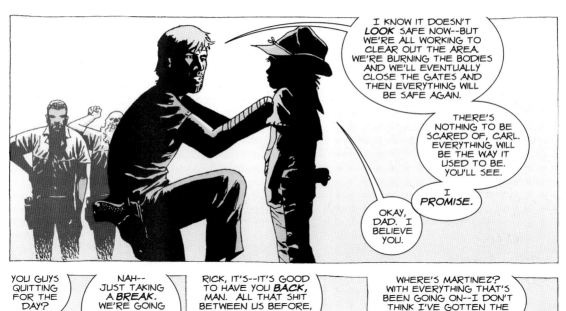

I KNOW IT DOESN'T *LOOK* SAFE NOW--BUT WE'RE ALL WORKING TO CLEAR OUT THE AREA. WE'RE BURNING THE BODIES AND WE'LL EVENTUALLY CLOSE THE GATES AND THEN EVERYTHING WILL BE SAFE AGAIN.

THERE'S NOTHING TO BE SCARED OF, CARL. EVERYTHING WILL BE THE WAY IT USED TO BE. YOU'LL SEE.

I *PROMISE.*

OKAY, DAD. I BELIEVE YOU.

YOU GUYS QUITTING FOR THE DAY?

NAH-- JUST TAKING A *BREAK.* WE'RE GOING TO GET SOME WATER BEFORE WE *PASS OUT.*

RICK, IT'S--IT'S GOOD TO HAVE YOU *BACK,* MAN. ALL THAT SHIT BETWEEN US BEFORE, I JUST WANTED TO SAY--I'M DONE WITH IT IF *YOU* ARE.

YEAH, TYREESE-- *ABSOLUTELY.* THAT MEANS A LOT TO ME.

WHERE'S MARTINEZ? WITH EVERYTHING THAT'S BEEN GOING ON--I DON'T THINK I'VE GOTTEN THE CHANCE TO INTRODUCE HIM TO *CARL.*

MARTINEZ? THAT TOUGH GUY YOU BROUGHT BACK WITH YOU? HE'S A MONSTER RICK--HE WAS DRAGGING THOSE BODIES AROUND ALL BY HIMSELF EARLIER... BUT I THINK HE WENT *INSIDE.*

I HAVEN'T SEEN HIM FOR *HOURS.*

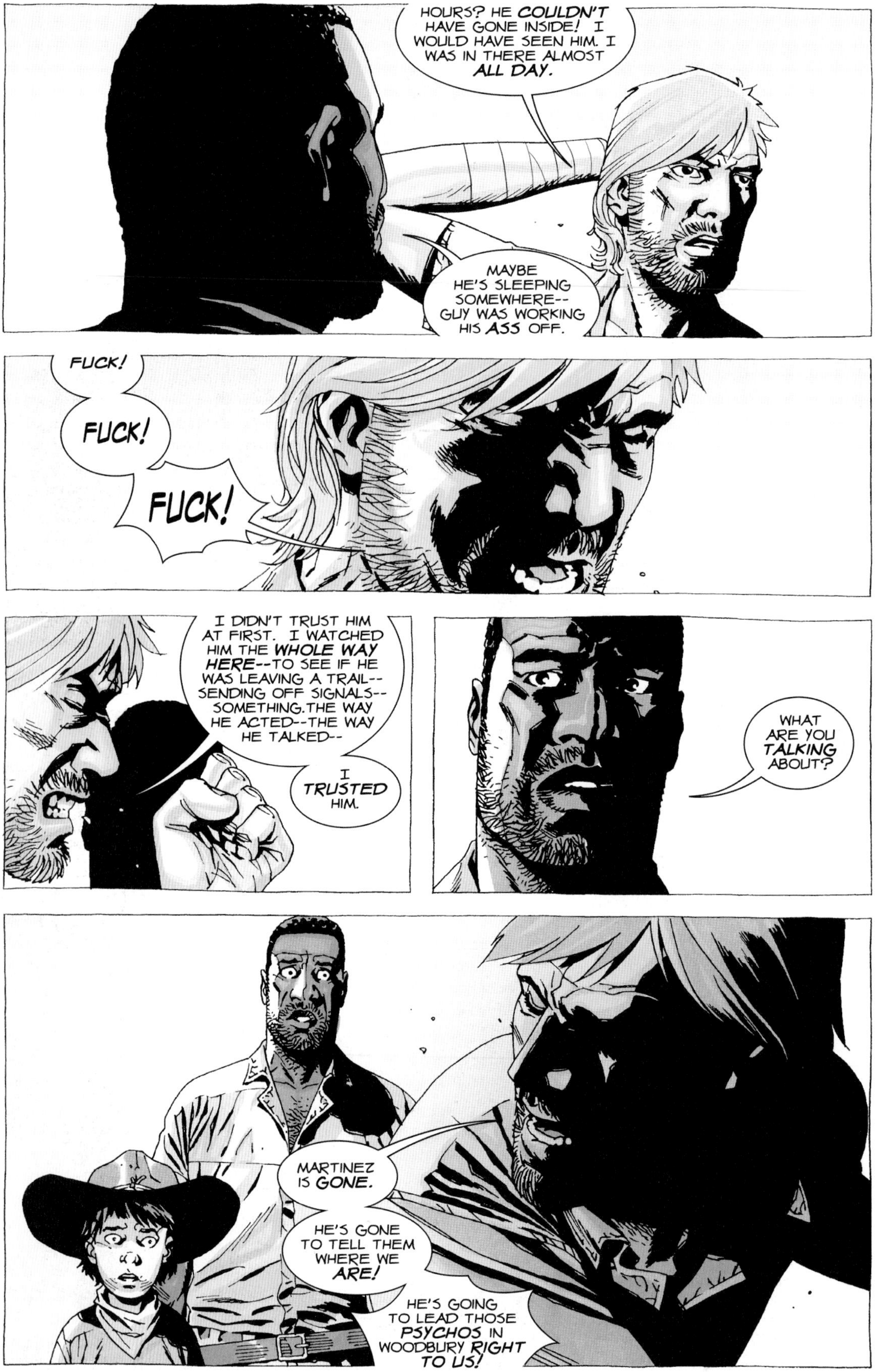
HOURS? HE COULDN'T HAVE GONE INSIDE! I WOULD HAVE SEEN HIM. I WAS IN THERE ALMOST ALL DAY.
MAYBE HE'S SLEEPING SOMEWHERE-- GUY WAS WORKING HIS ASS OFF.
FUCK!
FUCK!
FUCK!
I DIDN'T TRUST HIM AT FIRST. I WATCHED HIM THE WHOLE WAY HERE--TO SEE IF HE WAS LEAVING A TRAIL-- SENDING OFF SIGNALS-- SOMETHING. THE WAY HE ACTED--THE WAY HE TALKED--
I TRUSTED HIM.
WHAT ARE YOU TALKING ABOUT?
MARTINEZ IS GONE.
HE'S GONE TO TELL THEM WHERE WE ARE!
HE'S GOING TO LEAD THOSE PSYCHOS IN WOODBURY RIGHT TO US!

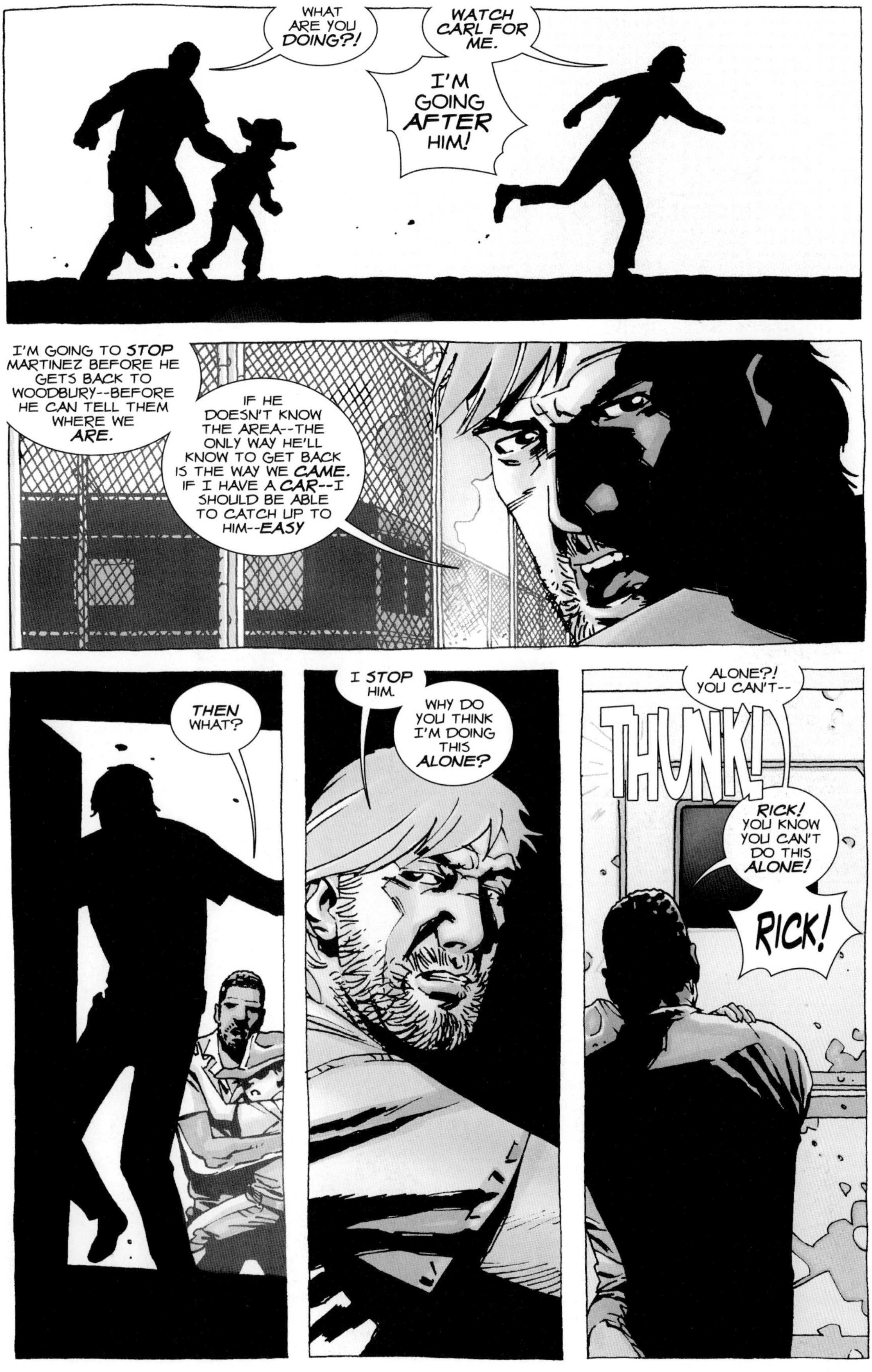
WHAT ARE YOU DOING?!
WATCH CARL FOR ME.
I'M GOING AFTER HIM!
I'M GOING TO STOP MARTINEZ BEFORE HE GETS BACK TO WOODBURY--BEFORE HE CAN TELL THEM WHERE WE ARE.
IF HE DOESN'T KNOW THE AREA--THE ONLY WAY HE'LL KNOW TO GET BACK IS THE WAY WE CAME. IF I HAVE A CAR--I SHOULD BE ABLE TO CATCH UP TO HIM--EASY
THEN WHAT?
I STOP HIM.
WHY DO YOU THINK I'M DOING THIS ALONE?
ALONE?! YOU CAN'T--
THUNK!
RICK! YOU KNOW YOU CAN'T DO THIS ALONE!
RICK!

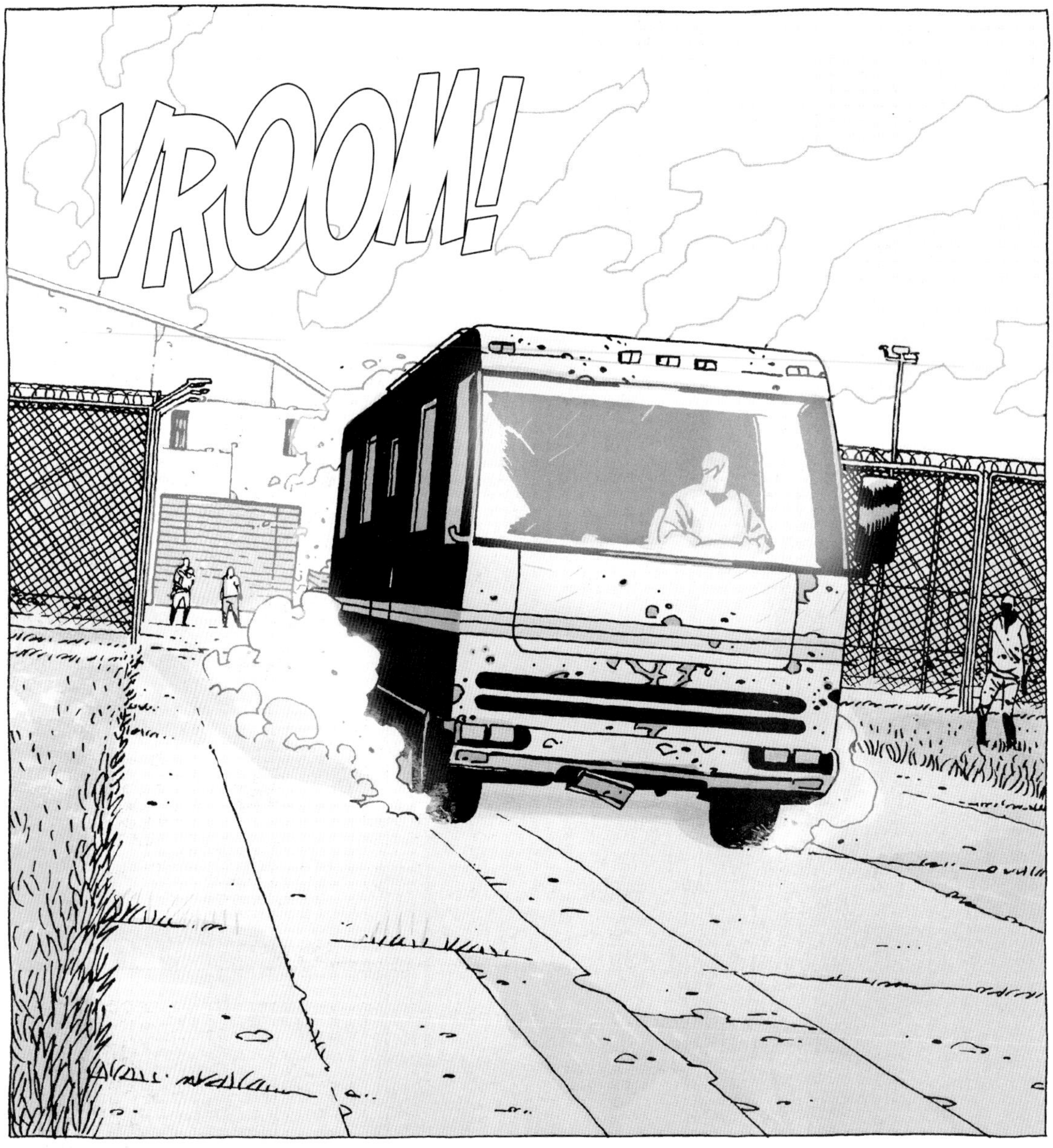
VROOM!

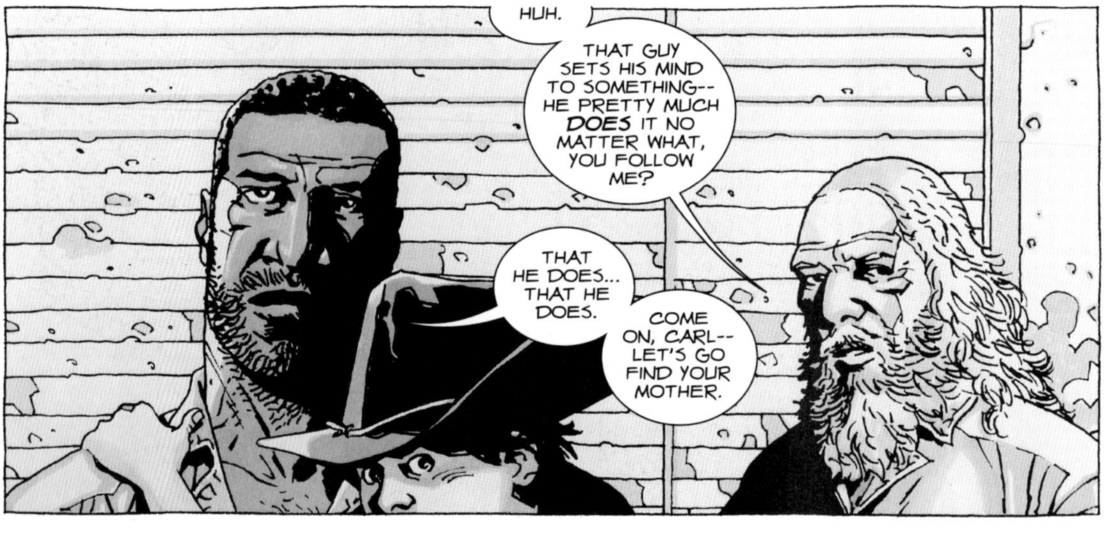
HUH.
THAT GUY SETS HIS MIND TO SOMETHING-- HE PRETTY MUCH *DOES* IT NO MATTER WHAT, YOU FOLLOW ME?
THAT HE DOES... THAT HE DOES.
COME ON, CARL-- LET'S GO FIND YOUR MOTHER.

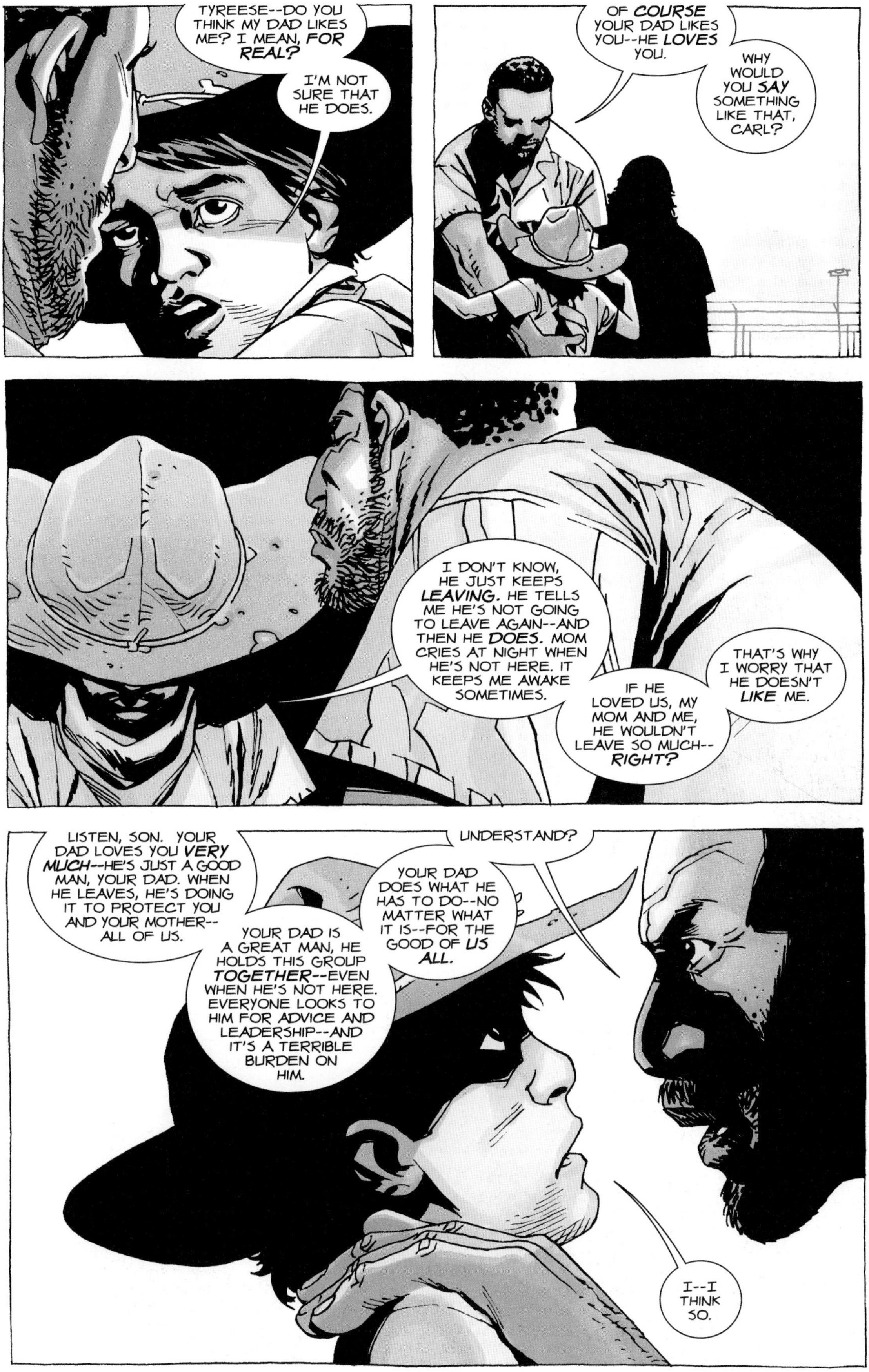
TYREESE--DO YOU THINK MY DAD LIKES ME? I MEAN, FOR REAL?
I'M NOT SURE THAT HE DOES.
OF COURSE YOUR DAD LIKES YOU--HE LOVES YOU.
WHY WOULD YOU SAY SOMETHING LIKE THAT, CARL?
I DON'T KNOW, HE JUST KEEPS LEAVING. HE TELLS ME HE'S NOT GOING TO LEAVE AGAIN--AND THEN HE DOES. MOM CRIES AT NIGHT WHEN HE'S NOT HERE. IT KEEPS ME AWAKE SOMETIMES.
IF HE LOVED US, MY MOM AND ME, HE WOULDN'T LEAVE SO MUCH--RIGHT?
THAT'S WHY I WORRY THAT HE DOESN'T LIKE ME.
LISTEN, SON. YOUR DAD LOVES YOU VERY MUCH--HE'S JUST A GOOD MAN, YOUR DAD. WHEN HE LEAVES, HE'S DOING IT TO PROTECT YOU AND YOUR MOTHER--ALL OF US.
YOUR DAD IS A GREAT MAN, HE HOLDS THIS GROUP TOGETHER--EVEN WHEN HE'S NOT HERE. EVERYONE LOOKS TO HIM FOR ADVICE AND LEADERSHIP--AND IT'S A TERRIBLE BURDEN ON HIM.
YOUR DAD DOES WHAT HE HAS TO DO--NO MATTER WHAT IT IS--FOR THE GOOD OF US ALL.
UNDERSTAND?
I--I THINK SO.

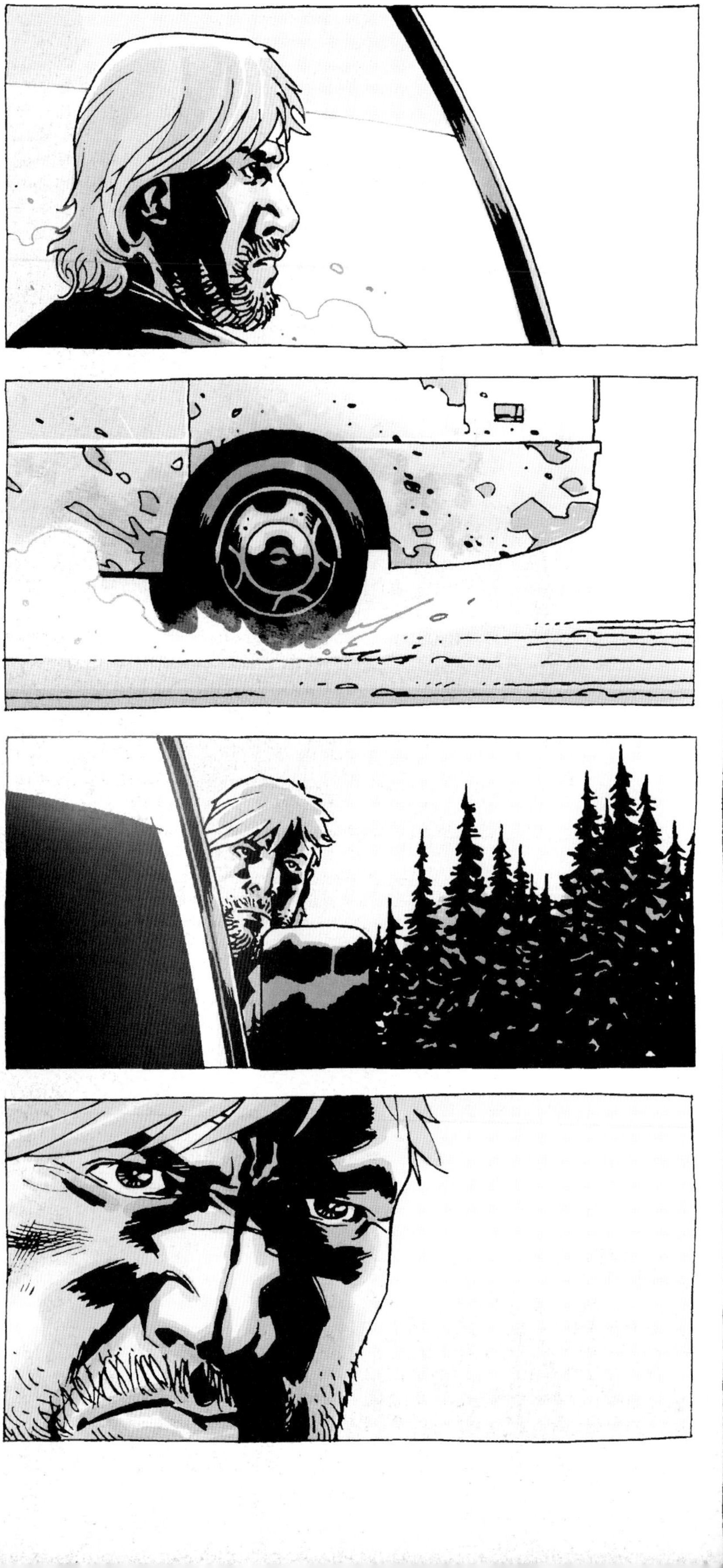
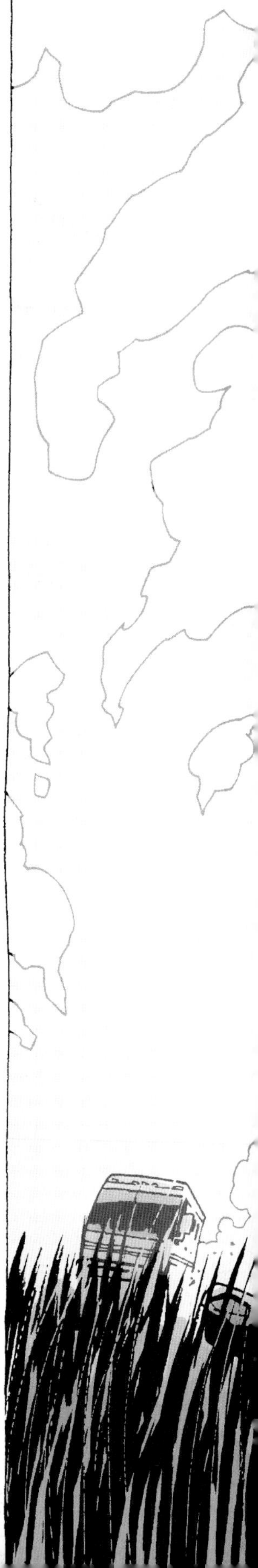

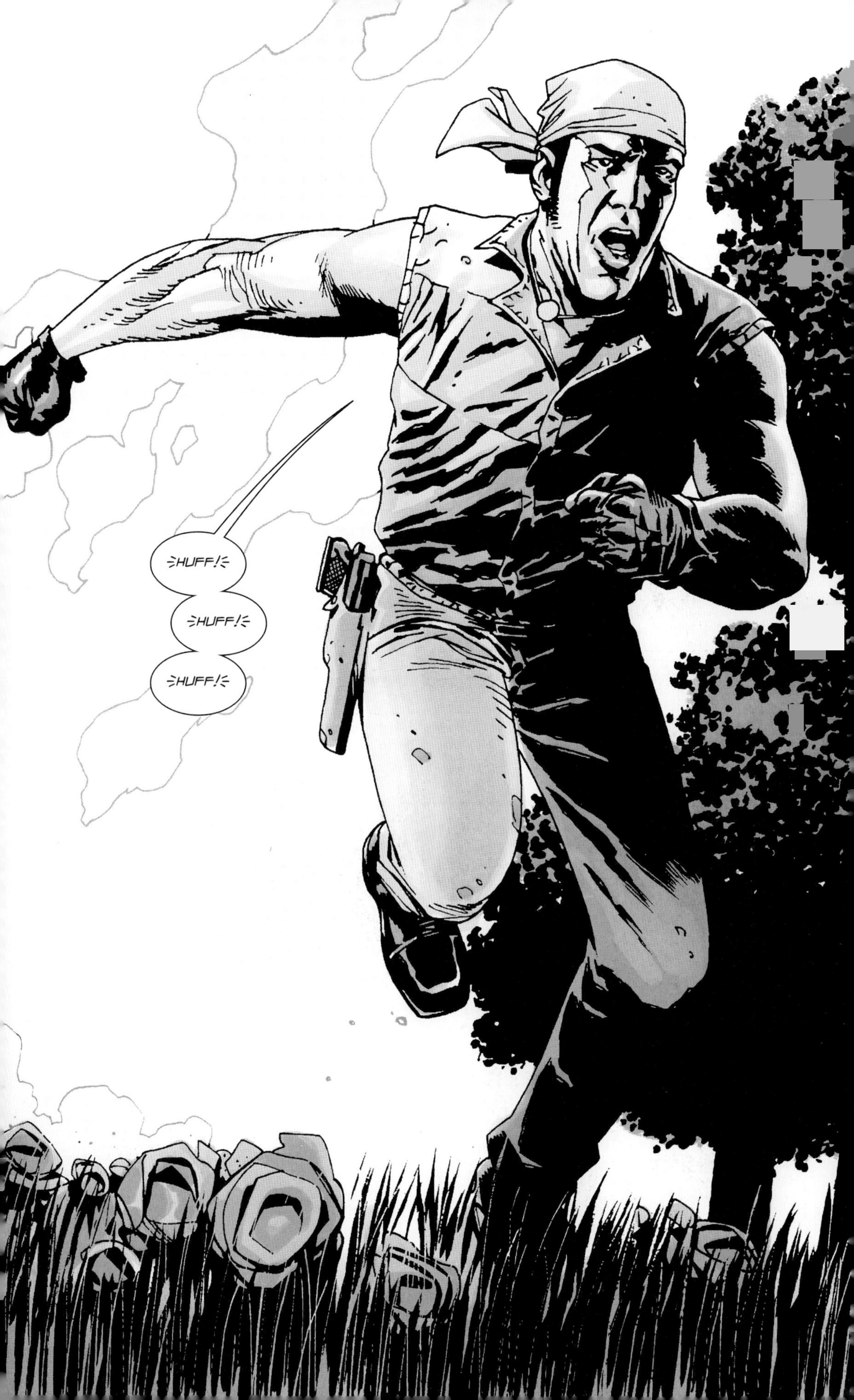
HUFF!
HUFF!
HUFF!

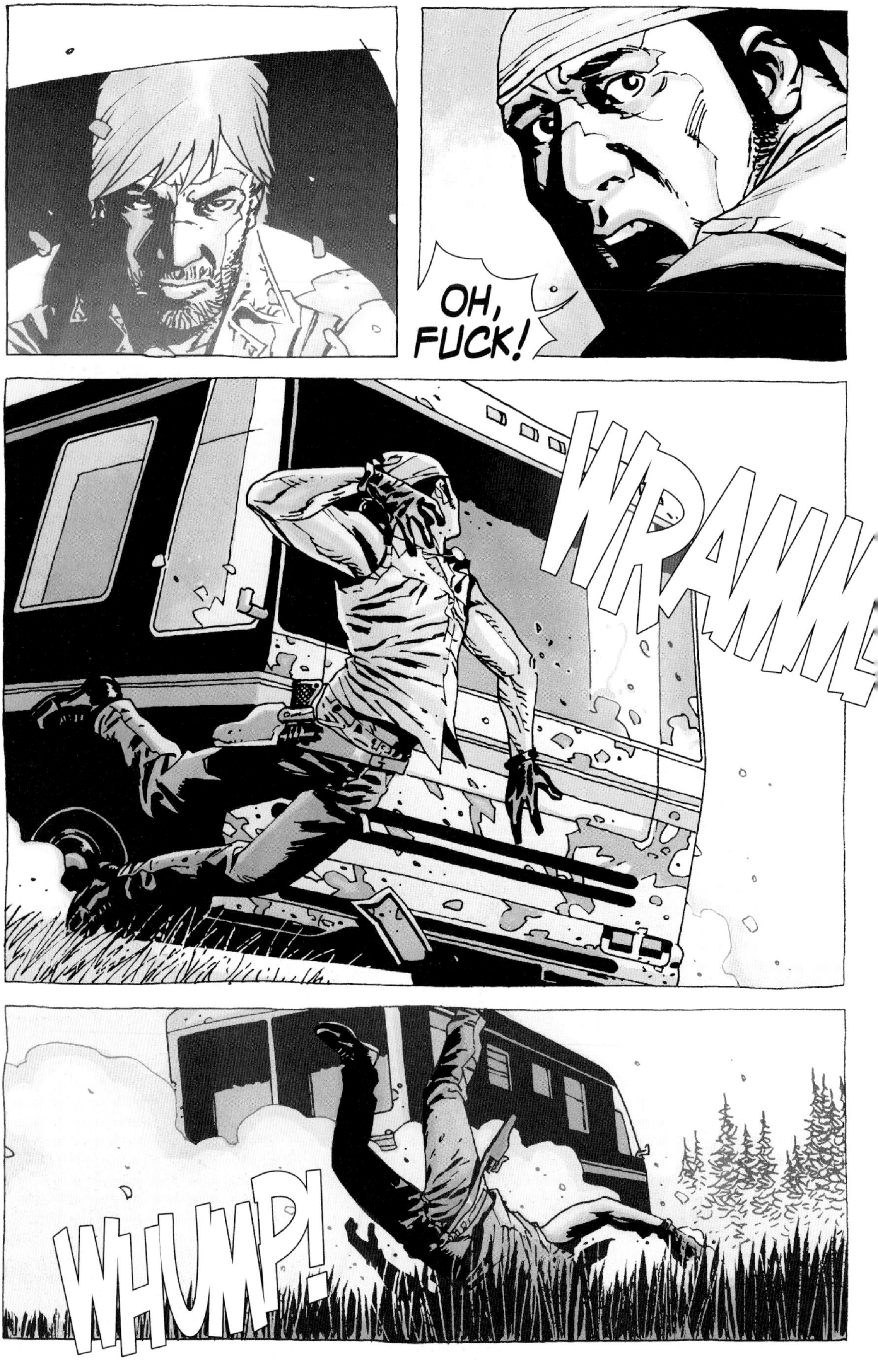
OH, FUCK!
WRAMM
WHUMP!

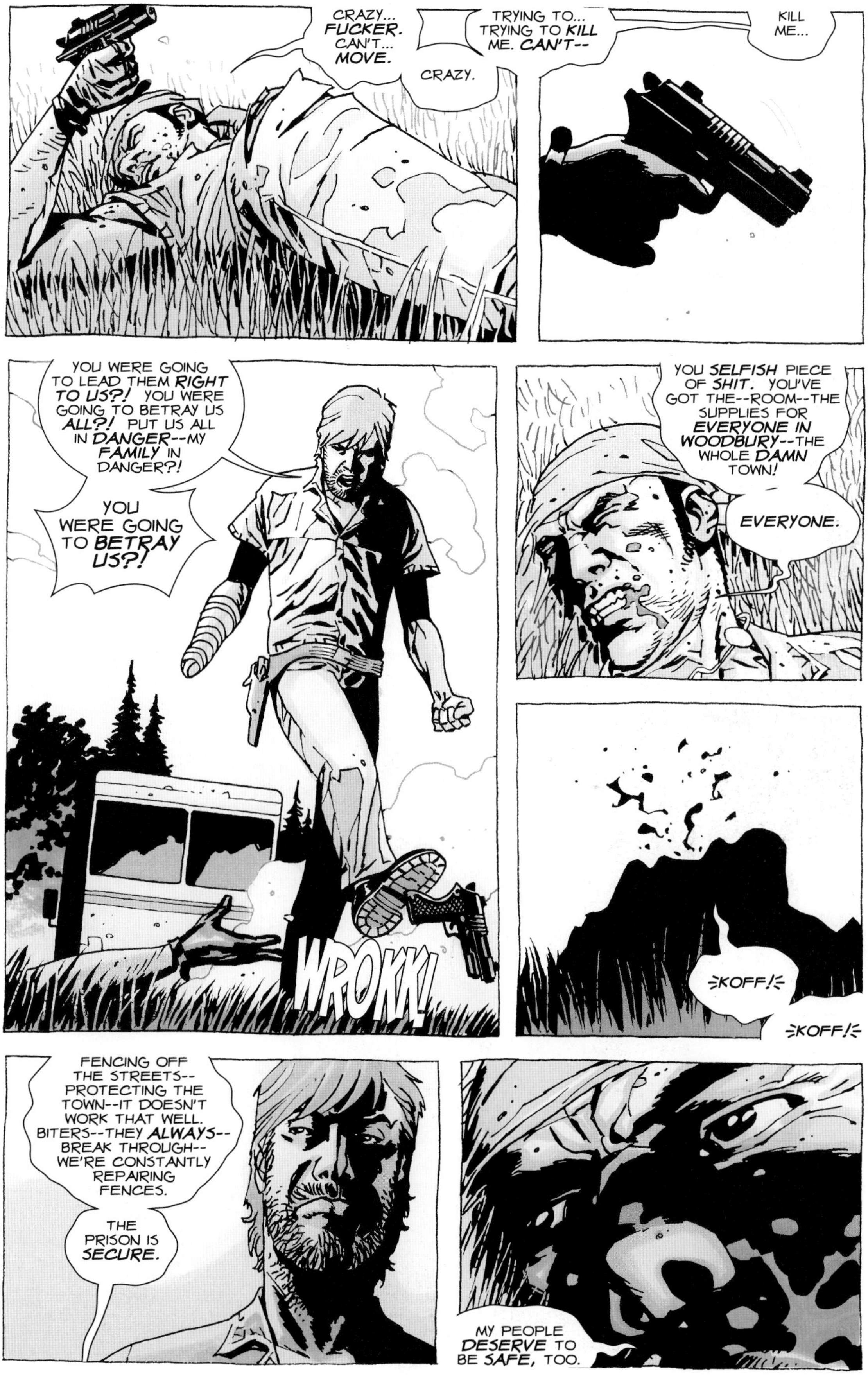

CRAZY... FUCKER. CAN'T... MOVE.
CRAZY.
TRYING TO... TRYING TO KILL ME. CAN'T--
KILL ME...
YOU WERE GOING TO LEAD THEM RIGHT TO US?! YOU WERE GOING TO BETRAY US ALL?! PUT US ALL IN DANGER--MY FAMILY IN DANGER?!
YOU WERE GOING TO BETRAY US?!
WROKK!
YOU SELFISH PIECE OF SHIT. YOU'VE GOT THE--ROOM--THE SUPPLIES FOR EVERYONE IN WOODBURY--THE WHOLE DAMN TOWN!
EVERYONE.
KOFF!
KOFF!
FENCING OFF THE STREETS--PROTECTING THE TOWN--IT DOESN'T WORK THAT WELL. BITERS--THEY ALWAYS--BREAK THROUGH--WE'RE CONSTANTLY REPAIRING FENCES.
THE PRISON IS SECURE.
MY PEOPLE DESERVE TO BE SAFE, TOO.

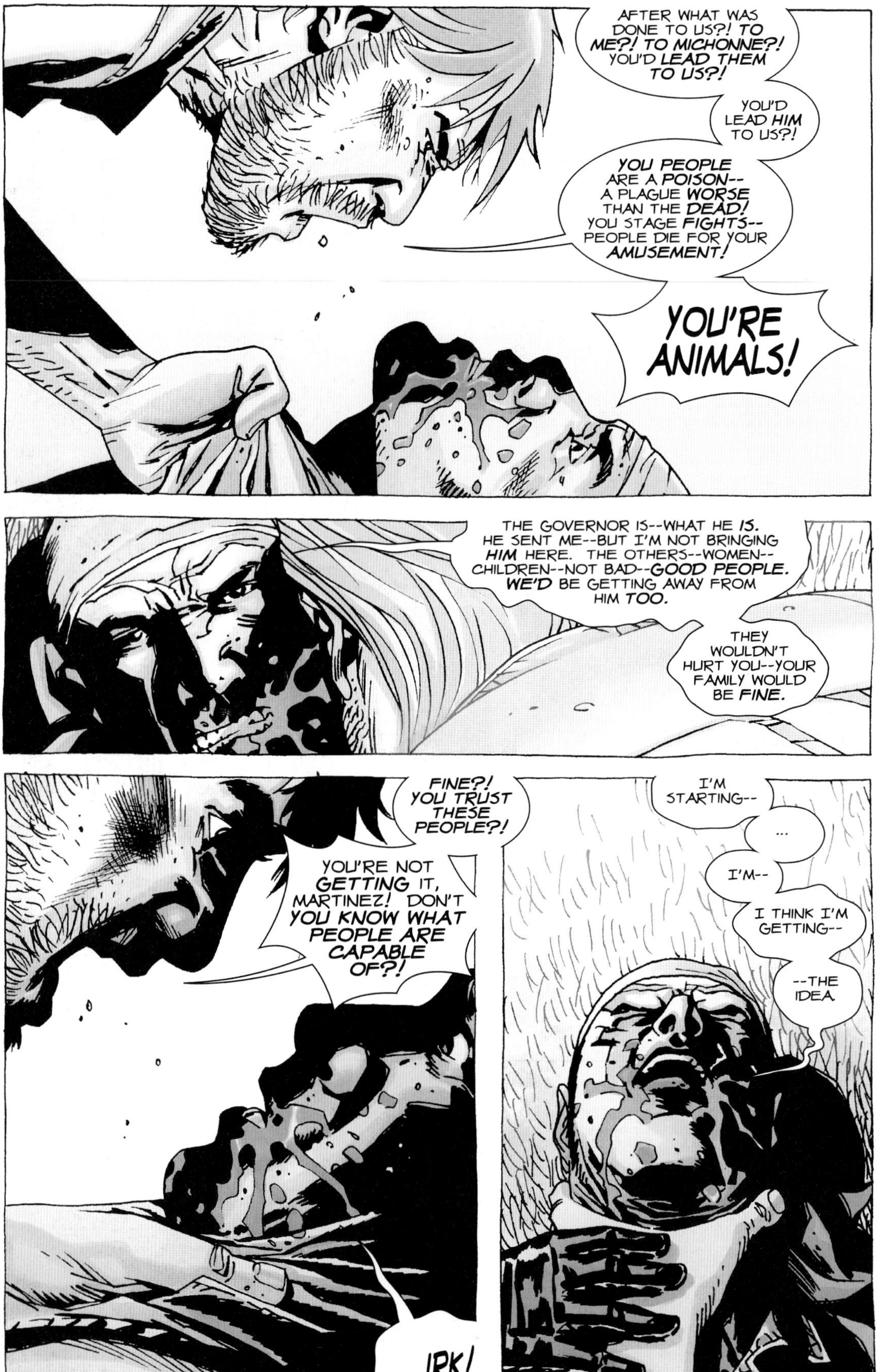
AFTER WHAT WAS DONE TO US?! TO ME?! TO MICHONNE?! YOU'D LEAD THEM TO US?!
YOU'D LEAD HIM TO US?!
YOU PEOPLE ARE A POISON-- A PLAGUE WORSE THAN THE DEAD! YOU STAGE FIGHTS-- PEOPLE DIE FOR YOUR AMUSEMENT!
YOU'RE ANIMALS!
THE GOVERNOR IS--WHAT HE IS. HE SENT ME--BUT I'M NOT BRINGING HIM HERE. THE OTHERS--WOMEN--CHILDREN--NOT BAD--GOOD PEOPLE. WE'D BE GETTING AWAY FROM HIM TOO.
THEY WOULDN'T HURT YOU--YOUR FAMILY WOULD BE FINE.
FINE?! YOU TRUST THESE PEOPLE?!
YOU'RE NOT GETTING IT, MARTINEZ! DON'T YOU KNOW WHAT PEOPLE ARE CAPABLE OF?!
IRK!
I'M STARTING--
...
I'M--
I THINK I'M GETTING--
--THE IDEA

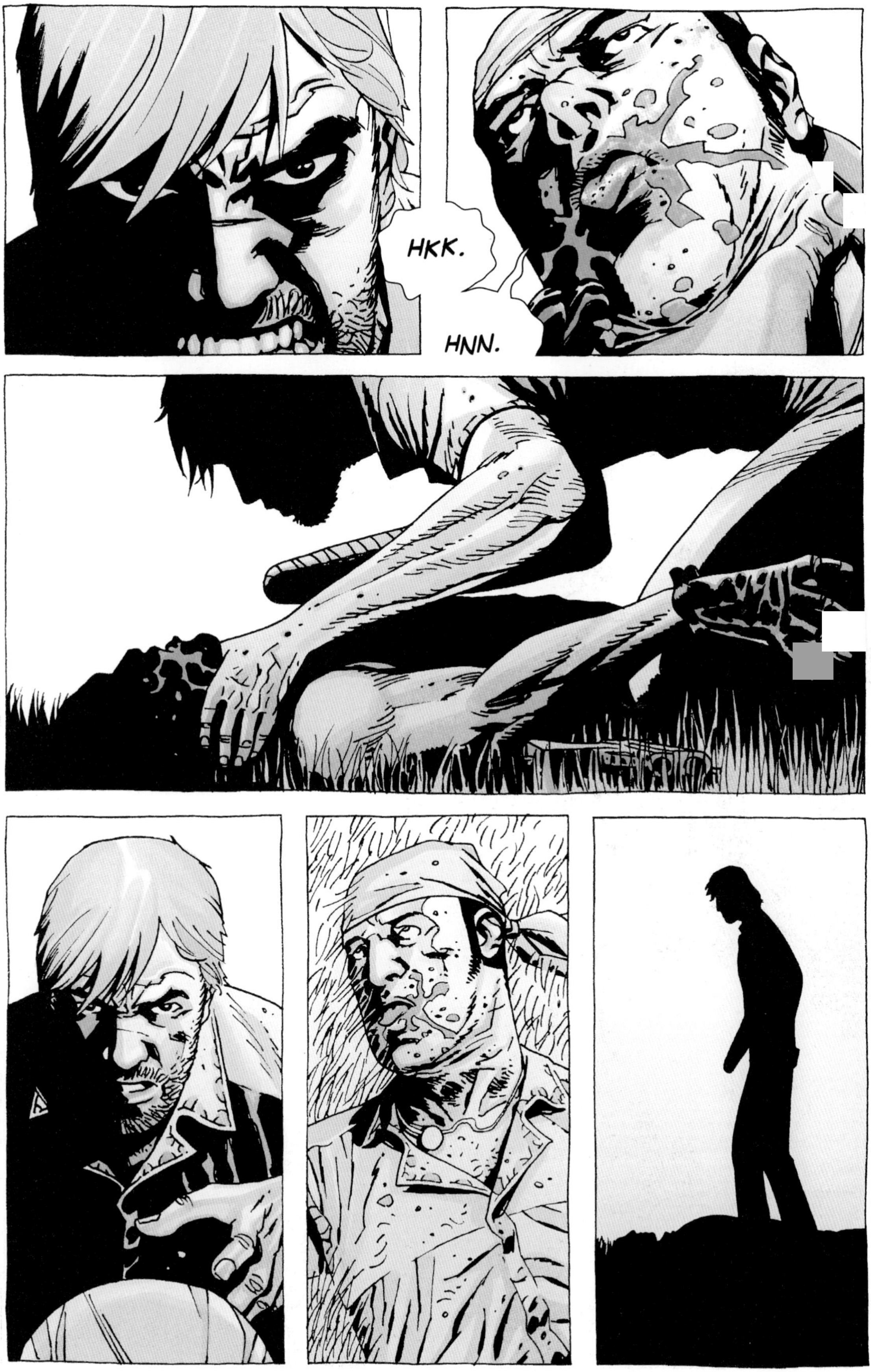
HKK.
HNN.

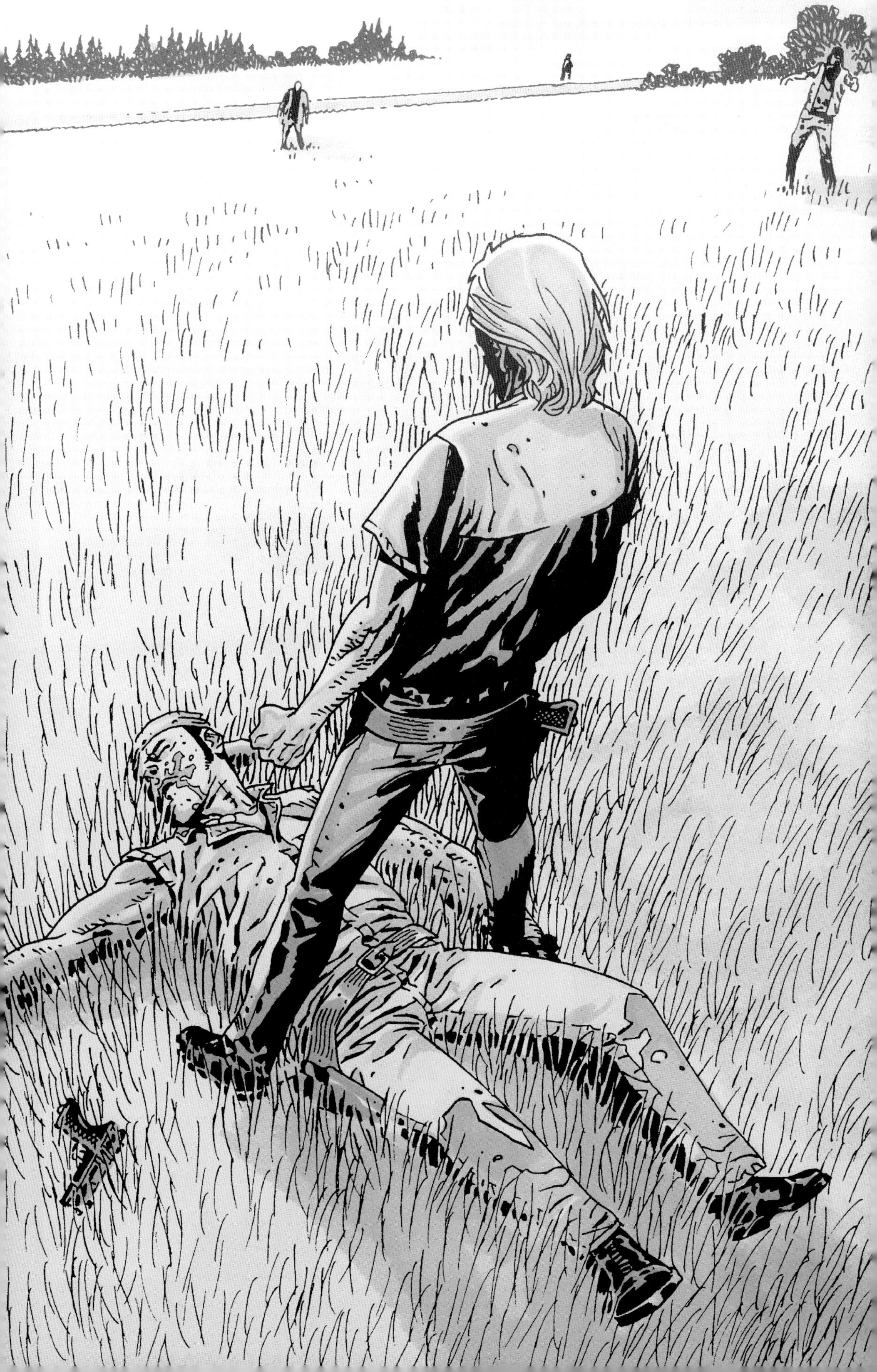

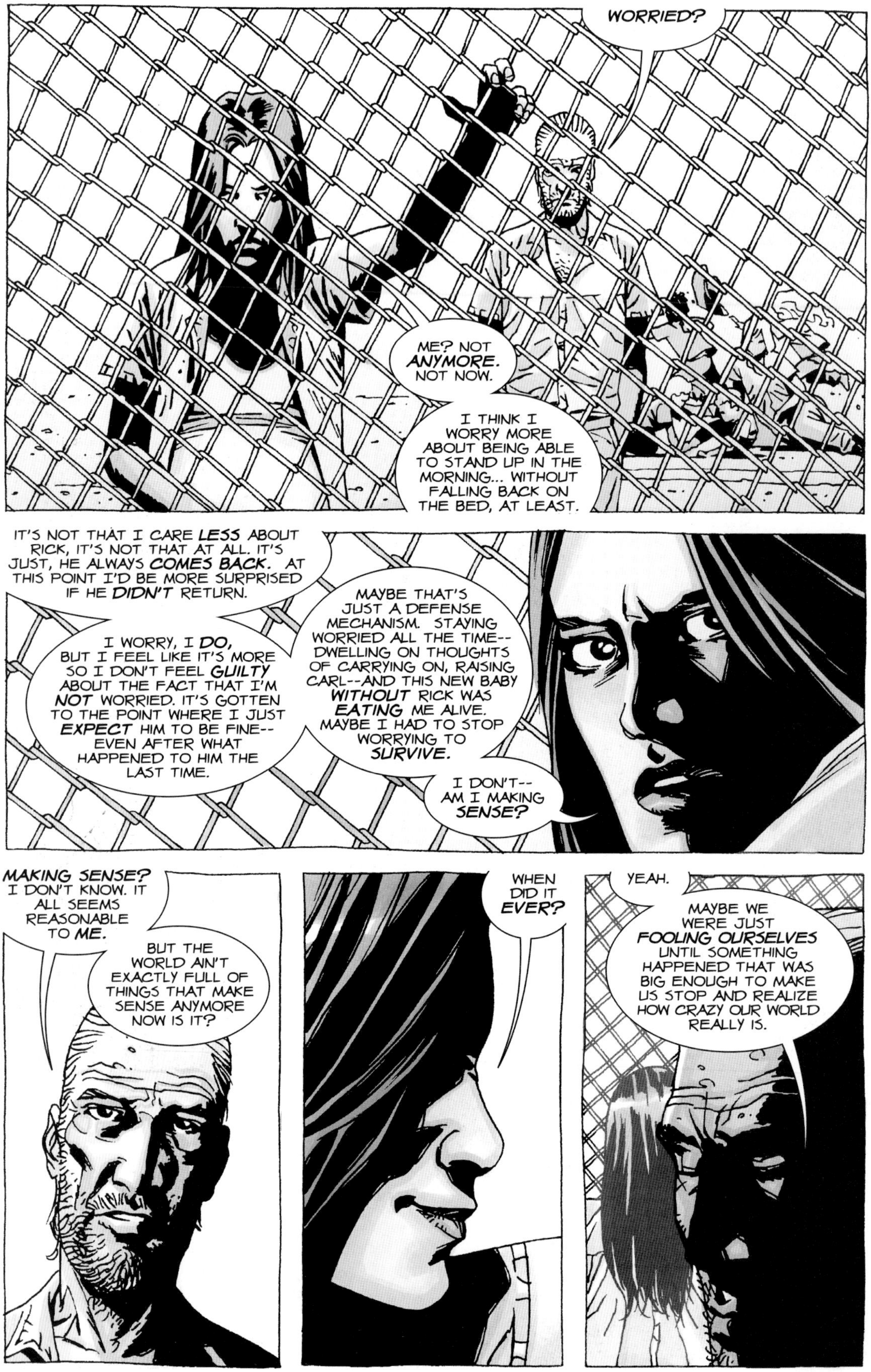
WORRIED?
ME? NOT ANYMORE. NOT NOW.
I THINK I WORRY MORE ABOUT BEING ABLE TO STAND UP IN THE MORNING... WITHOUT FALLING BACK ON THE BED, AT LEAST.
IT'S NOT THAT I CARE LESS ABOUT RICK, IT'S NOT THAT AT ALL. IT'S JUST, HE ALWAYS COMES BACK. AT THIS POINT I'D BE MORE SURPRISED IF HE DIDN'T RETURN.
I WORRY, I DO, BUT I FEEL LIKE IT'S MORE SO I DON'T FEEL GUILTY ABOUT THE FACT THAT I'M NOT WORRIED. IT'S GOTTEN TO THE POINT WHERE I JUST EXPECT HIM TO BE FINE-- EVEN AFTER WHAT HAPPENED TO HIM THE LAST TIME.
MAYBE THAT'S JUST A DEFENSE MECHANISM. STAYING WORRIED ALL THE TIME-- DWELLING ON THOUGHTS OF CARRYING ON, RAISING CARL--AND THIS NEW BABY WITHOUT RICK WAS EATING ME ALIVE. MAYBE I HAD TO STOP WORRYING TO SURVIVE.
I DON'T-- AM I MAKING SENSE?
MAKING SENSE? I DON'T KNOW. IT ALL SEEMS REASONABLE TO ME.
BUT THE WORLD AIN'T EXACTLY FULL OF THINGS THAT MAKE SENSE ANYMORE NOW IS IT?
WHEN DID IT EVER?
YEAH.
MAYBE WE WERE JUST FOOLING OURSELVES UNTIL SOMETHING HAPPENED THAT WAS BIG ENOUGH TO MAKE US STOP AND REALIZE HOW CRAZY OUR WORLD REALLY IS.

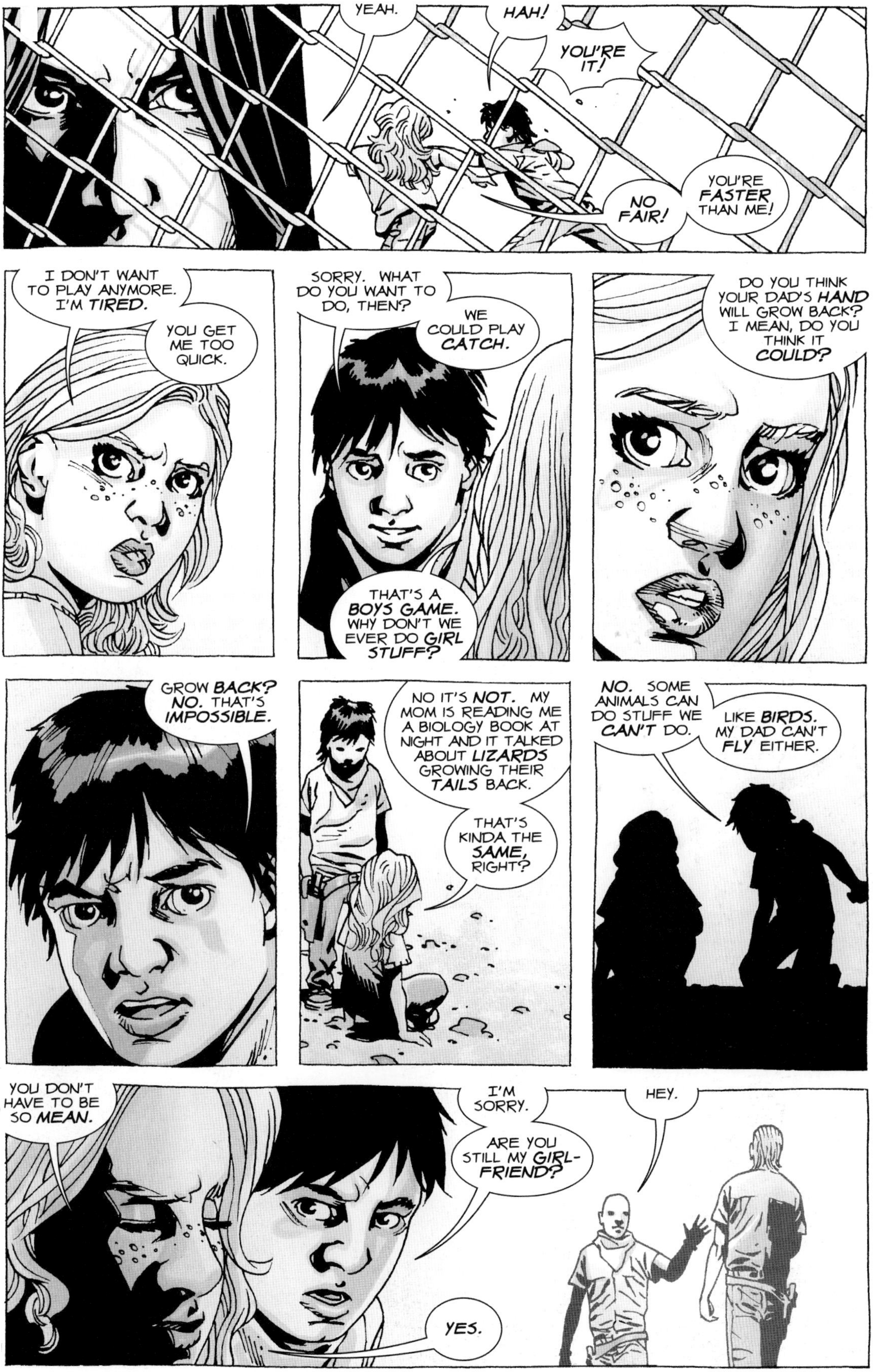
YEAH.
HAH!
YOU'RE IT!
NO FAIR!
YOU'RE FASTER THAN ME!
I DON'T WANT TO PLAY ANYMORE. I'M TIRED.
YOU GET ME TOO QUICK.
SORRY. WHAT DO YOU WANT TO DO, THEN?
WE COULD PLAY CATCH.
THAT'S A BOYS GAME. WHY DON'T WE EVER DO GIRL STUFF?
DO YOU THINK YOUR DAD'S HAND WILL GROW BACK? I MEAN, DO YOU THINK IT COULD?
GROW BACK? NO. THAT'S IMPOSSIBLE.
NO IT'S NOT. MY MOM IS READING ME A BIOLOGY BOOK AT NIGHT AND IT TALKED ABOUT LIZARDS GROWING THEIR TAILS BACK.
THAT'S KINDA THE SAME, RIGHT?
NO. SOME ANIMALS CAN DO STUFF WE CAN'T DO.
LIKE BIRDS. MY DAD CAN'T FLY EITHER.
YOU DON'T HAVE TO BE SO MEAN.
I'M SORRY.
ARE YOU STILL MY GIRL-FRIEND?
YES.
HEY.

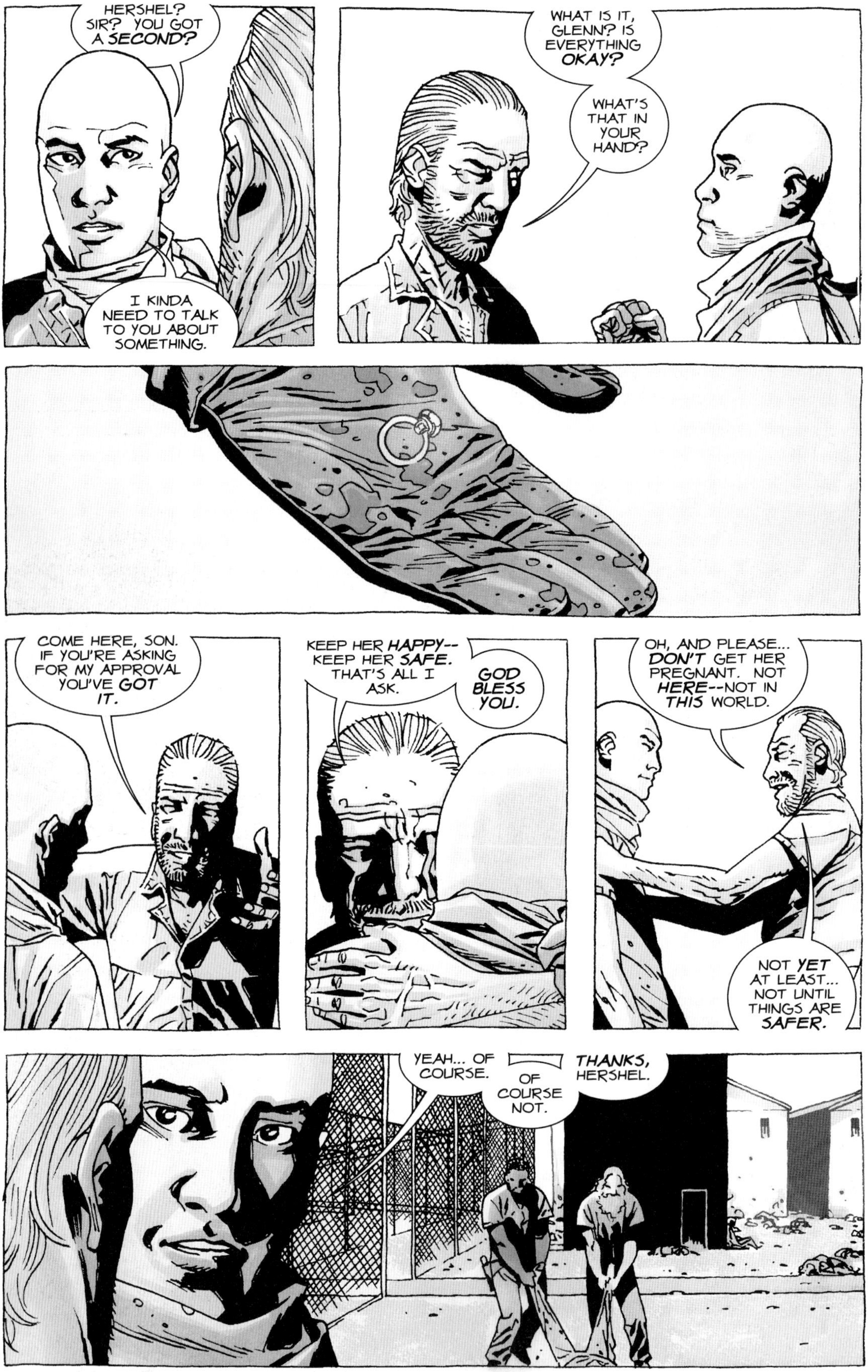
HERSHEL? SIR? YOU GOT A SECOND?
I KINDA NEED TO TALK TO YOU ABOUT SOMETHING.
WHAT IS IT, GLENN? IS EVERYTHING OKAY?
WHAT'S THAT IN YOUR HAND?
COME HERE, SON. IF YOU'RE ASKING FOR MY APPROVAL YOU'VE GOT IT.
KEEP HER HAPPY-- KEEP HER SAFE. THAT'S ALL I ASK.
GOD BLESS YOU.
OH, AND PLEASE... DON'T GET HER PREGNANT. NOT HERE--NOT IN THIS WORLD.
NOT YET AT LEAST... NOT UNTIL THINGS ARE SAFER.
YEAH... OF COURSE.
OF COURSE NOT.
THANKS, HERSHEL.

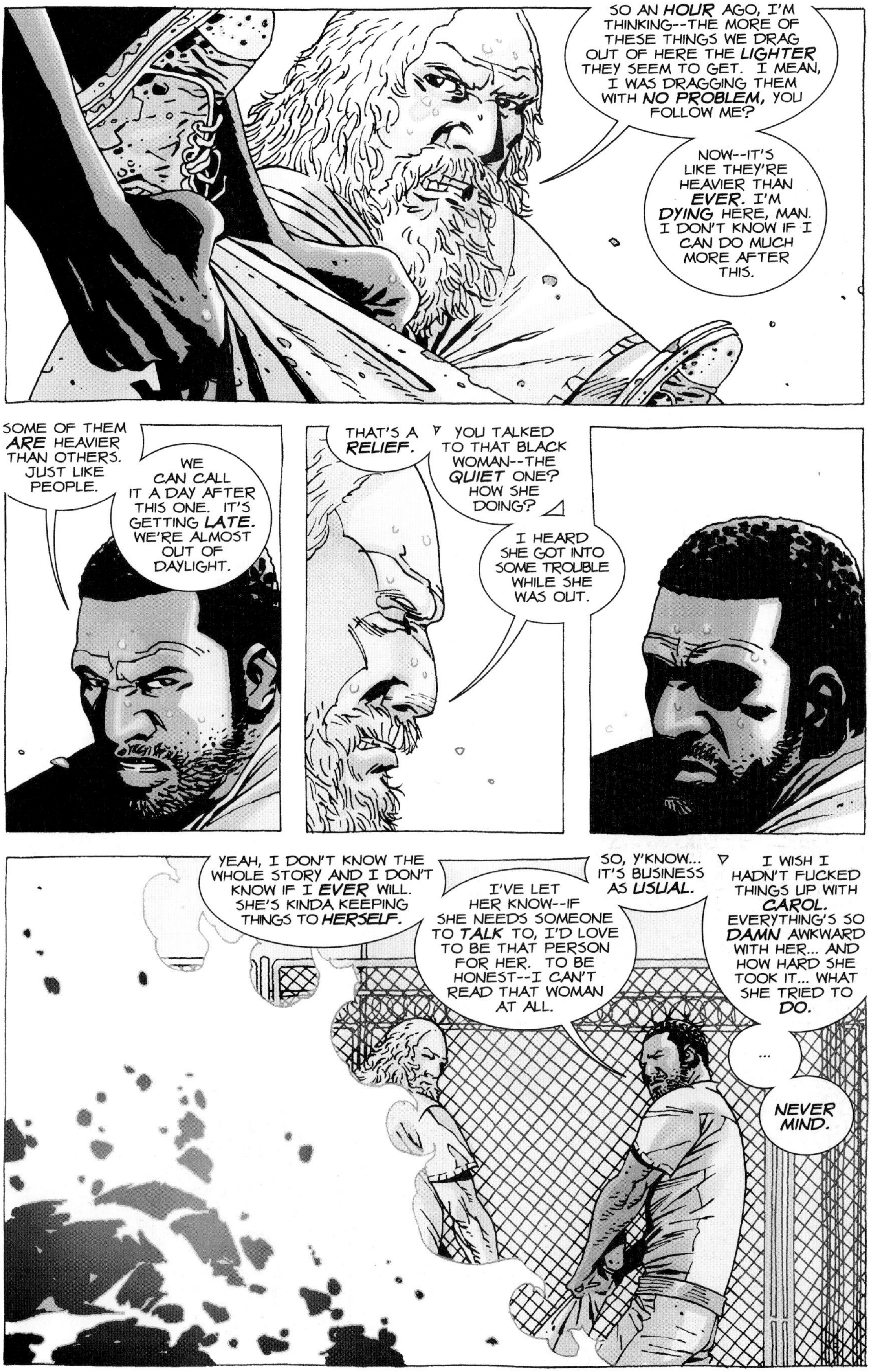
SO AN HOUR AGO, I'M THINKING--THE MORE OF THESE THINGS WE DRAG OUT OF HERE THE LIGHTER THEY SEEM TO GET. I MEAN, I WAS DRAGGING THEM WITH NO PROBLEM, YOU FOLLOW ME?
NOW--IT'S LIKE THEY'RE HEAVIER THAN EVER. I'M DYING HERE, MAN. I DON'T KNOW IF I CAN DO MUCH MORE AFTER THIS.
SOME OF THEM ARE HEAVIER THAN OTHERS. JUST LIKE PEOPLE.
WE CAN CALL IT A DAY AFTER THIS ONE. IT'S GETTING LATE. WE'RE ALMOST OUT OF DAYLIGHT.
THAT'S A RELIEF.
YOU TALKED TO THAT BLACK WOMAN--THE QUIET ONE? HOW SHE DOING?
I HEARD SHE GOT INTO SOME TROUBLE WHILE SHE WAS OUT.
YEAH, I DON'T KNOW THE WHOLE STORY AND I DON'T KNOW IF I EVER WILL. SHE'S KINDA KEEPING THINGS TO HERSELF.
I'VE LET HER KNOW--IF SHE NEEDS SOMEONE TO TALK TO, I'D LOVE TO BE THAT PERSON FOR HER. TO BE HONEST--I CAN'T READ THAT WOMAN AT ALL.
SO, Y'KNOW... IT'S BUSINESS AS USUAL.
I WISH I HADN'T FUCKED THINGS UP WITH CAROL. EVERYTHING'S SO DAMN AWKWARD WITH HER... AND HOW HARD SHE TOOK IT... WHAT SHE TRIED TO DO.
...
NEVER MIND.

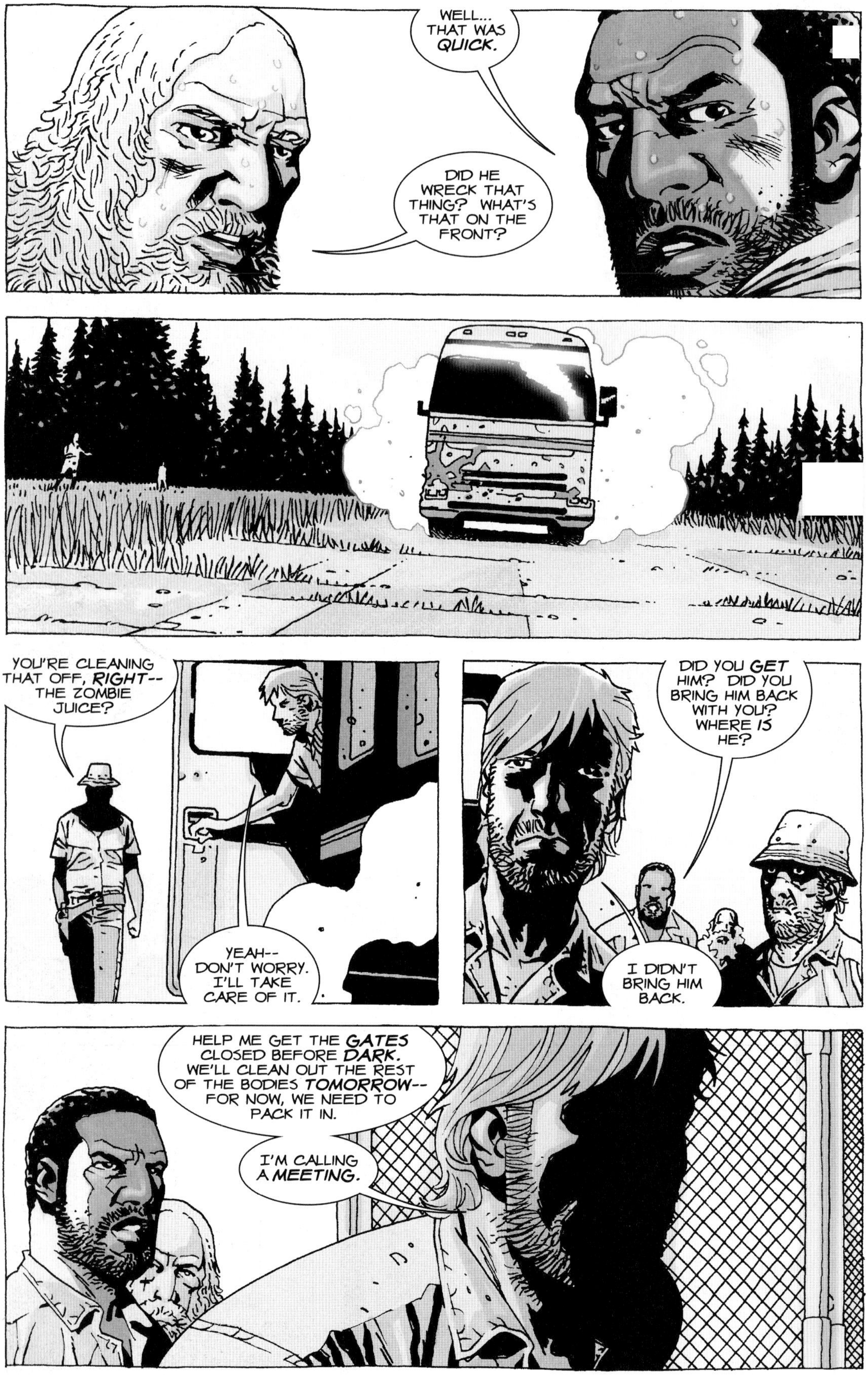
WELL... THAT WAS QUICK.
DID HE WRECK THAT THING? WHAT'S THAT ON THE FRONT?
YOU'RE CLEANING THAT OFF, RIGHT-- THE ZOMBIE JUICE?
YEAH-- DON'T WORRY. I'LL TAKE CARE OF IT.
DID YOU GET HIM? DID YOU BRING HIM BACK WITH YOU? WHERE IS HE?
I DIDN'T BRING HIM BACK.
HELP ME GET THE GATES CLOSED BEFORE DARK. WE'LL CLEAN OUT THE REST OF THE BODIES TOMORROW-- FOR NOW, WE NEED TO PACK IT IN.
I'M CALLING A MEETING.

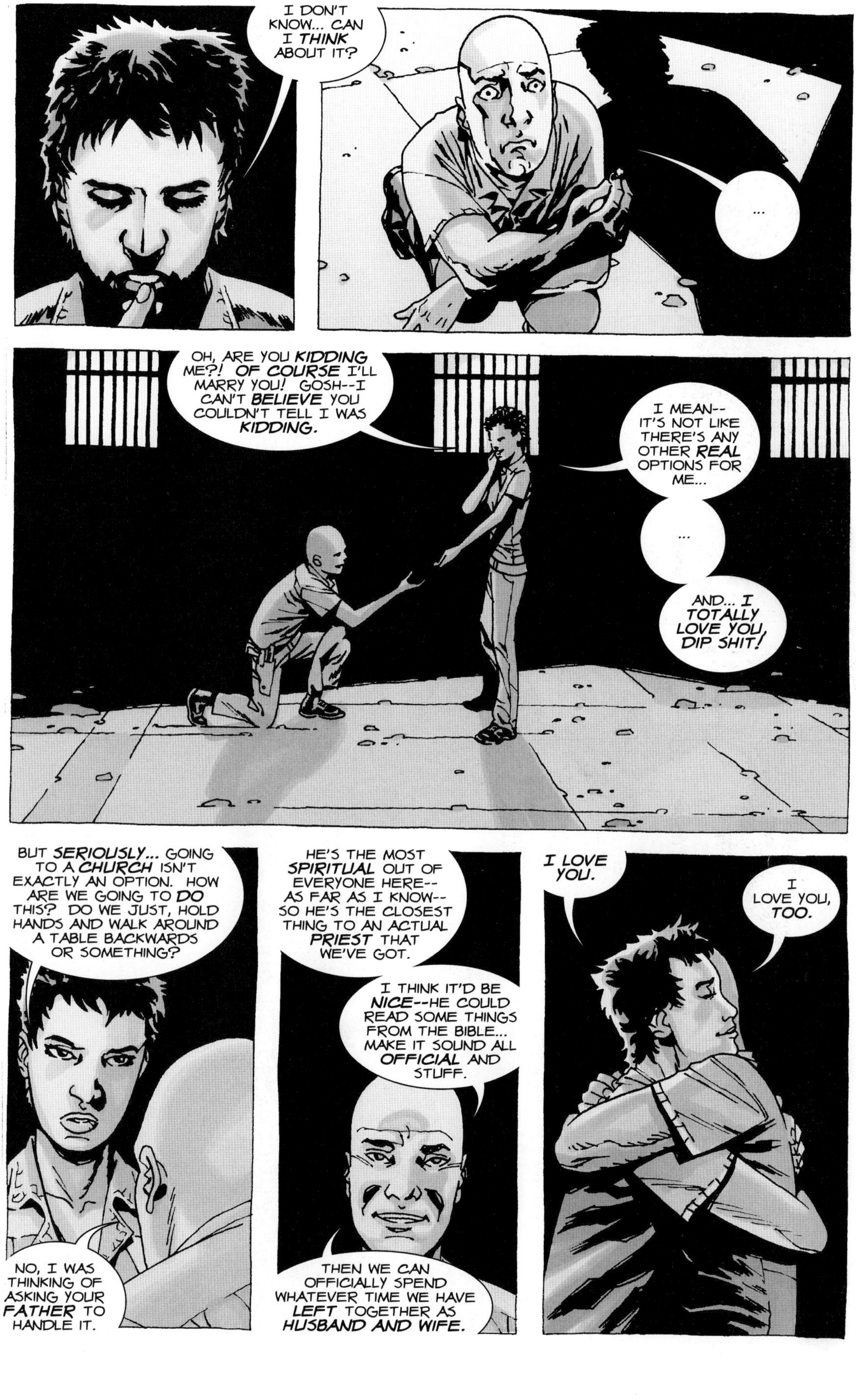
I DON'T KNOW... CAN I THINK ABOUT IT?
...
OH, ARE YOU KIDDING ME?! OF COURSE I'LL MARRY YOU! GOSH--I CAN'T BELIEVE YOU COULDN'T TELL I WAS KIDDING.
I MEAN-- IT'S NOT LIKE THERE'S ANY OTHER REAL OPTIONS FOR ME...
...
AND... I TOTALLY LOVE YOU, DIP SHIT!
BUT SERIOUSLY... GOING TO A CHURCH ISN'T EXACTLY AN OPTION. HOW ARE WE GOING TO DO THIS? DO WE JUST, HOLD HANDS AND WALK AROUND A TABLE BACKWARDS OR SOMETHING?
NO, I WAS THINKING OF ASKING YOUR FATHER TO HANDLE IT.
HE'S THE MOST SPIRITUAL OUT OF EVERYONE HERE-- AS FAR AS I KNOW-- SO HE'S THE CLOSEST THING TO AN ACTUAL PRIEST THAT WE'VE GOT.
I THINK IT'D BE NICE--HE COULD READ SOME THINGS FROM THE BIBLE... MAKE IT SOUND ALL OFFICIAL AND STUFF.
THEN WE CAN OFFICIALLY SPEND WHATEVER TIME WE HAVE LEFT TOGETHER AS HUSBAND AND WIFE.
I LOVE YOU.
I LOVE YOU, TOO.

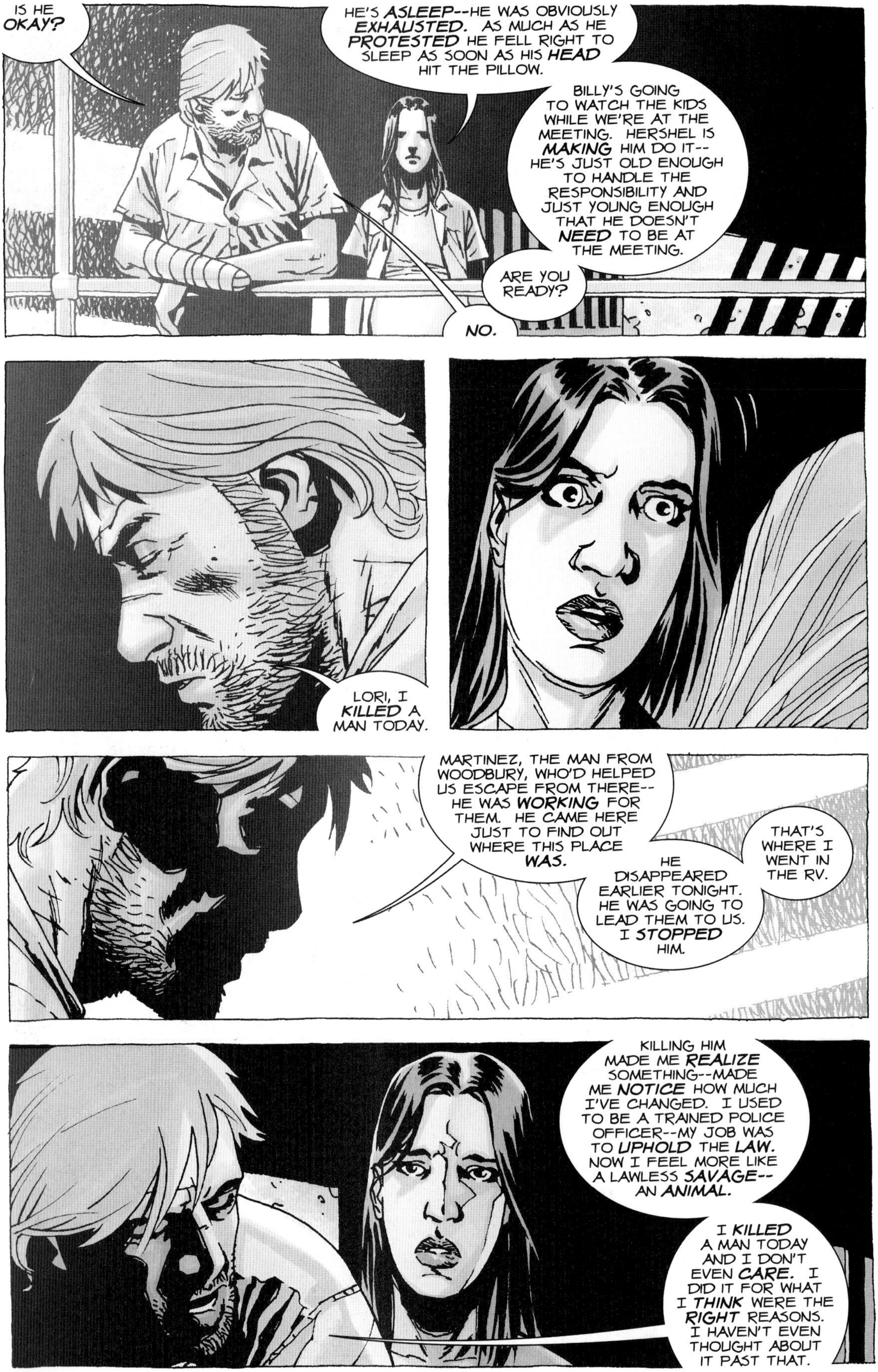
IS HE OKAY?
HE'S ASLEEP--HE WAS OBVIOUSLY EXHAUSTED. AS MUCH AS HE PROTESTED HE FELL RIGHT TO SLEEP AS SOON AS HIS HEAD HIT THE PILLOW.
BILLY'S GOING TO WATCH THE KIDS WHILE WE'RE AT THE MEETING. HERSHEL IS MAKING HIM DO IT-- HE'S JUST OLD ENOUGH TO HANDLE THE RESPONSIBILITY AND JUST YOUNG ENOUGH THAT HE DOESN'T NEED TO BE AT THE MEETING.
ARE YOU READY?
NO.
LORI, I KILLED A MAN TODAY.
MARTINEZ, THE MAN FROM WOODBURY, WHO'D HELPED US ESCAPE FROM THERE-- HE WAS WORKING FOR THEM. HE CAME HERE JUST TO FIND OUT WHERE THIS PLACE WAS.
HE DISAPPEARED EARLIER TONIGHT. HE WAS GOING TO LEAD THEM TO US. I STOPPED HIM.
THAT'S WHERE I WENT IN THE RV.
KILLING HIM MADE ME REALIZE SOMETHING--MADE ME NOTICE HOW MUCH I'VE CHANGED. I USED TO BE A TRAINED POLICE OFFICER--MY JOB WAS TO UPHOLD THE LAW. NOW I FEEL MORE LIKE A LAWLESS SAVAGE-- AN ANIMAL.
I KILLED A MAN TODAY AND I DON'T EVEN CARE. I DID IT FOR WHAT I THINK WERE THE RIGHT REASONS. I HAVEN'T EVEN THOUGHT ABOUT IT PAST THAT.

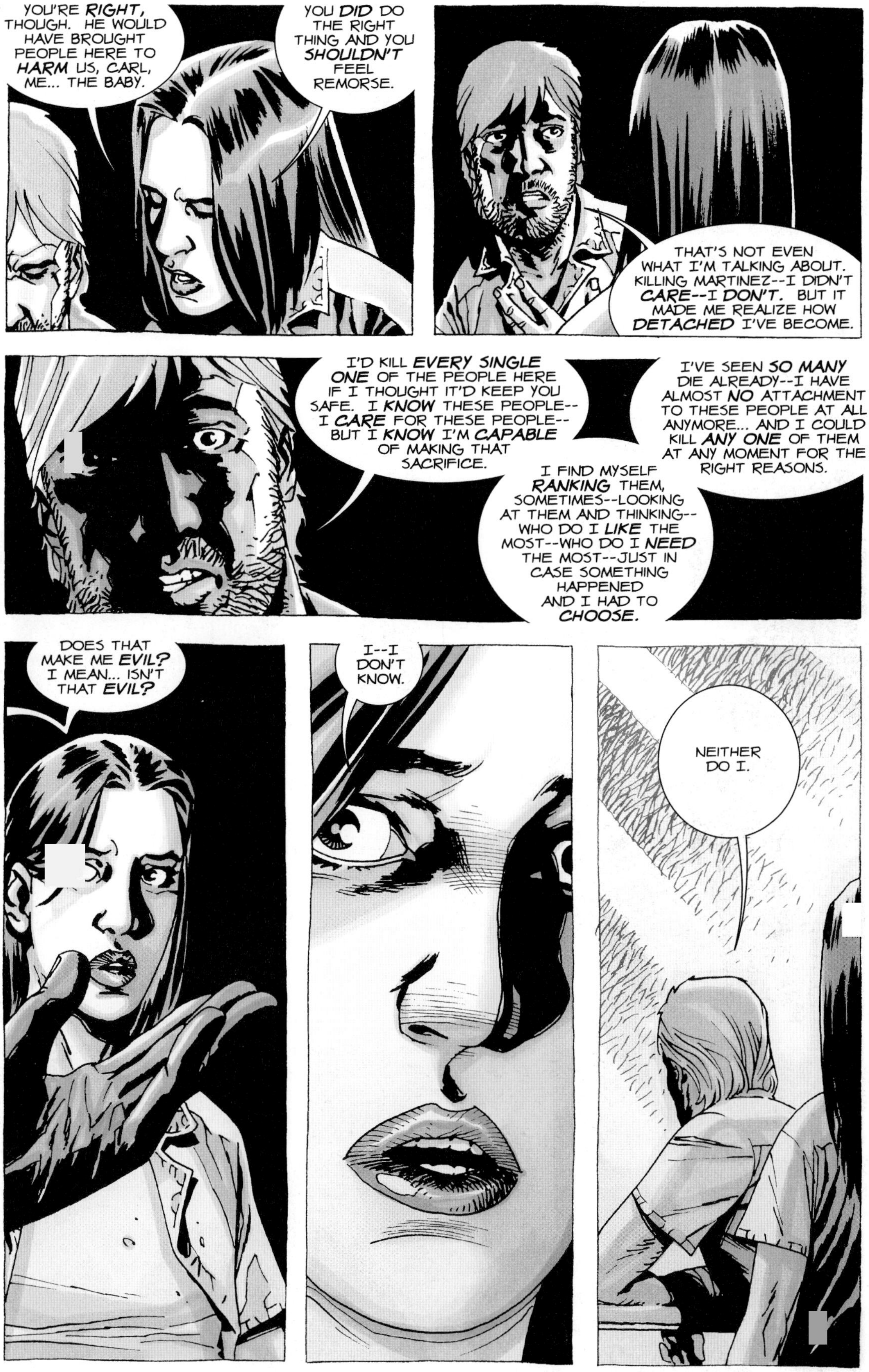
YOU'RE RIGHT, THOUGH. HE WOULD HAVE BROUGHT PEOPLE HERE TO HARM US, CARL, ME... THE BABY.
YOU DID DO THE RIGHT THING AND YOU SHOULDN'T FEEL REMORSE.
THAT'S NOT EVEN WHAT I'M TALKING ABOUT. KILLING MARTINEZ--I DIDN'T CARE--I DON'T. BUT IT MADE ME REALIZE HOW DETACHED I'VE BECOME.
I'D KILL EVERY SINGLE ONE OF THE PEOPLE HERE IF I THOUGHT IT'D KEEP YOU SAFE. I KNOW THESE PEOPLE-- I CARE FOR THESE PEOPLE-- BUT I KNOW I'M CAPABLE OF MAKING THAT SACRIFICE.
I'VE SEEN SO MANY DIE ALREADY--I HAVE ALMOST NO ATTACHMENT TO THESE PEOPLE AT ALL ANYMORE... AND I COULD KILL ANY ONE OF THEM AT ANY MOMENT FOR THE RIGHT REASONS.
I FIND MYSELF RANKING THEM, SOMETIMES--LOOKING AT THEM AND THINKING-- WHO DO I LIKE THE MOST--WHO DO I NEED THE MOST--JUST IN CASE SOMETHING HAPPENED AND I HAD TO CHOOSE.
DOES THAT MAKE ME EVIL? I MEAN... ISN'T THAT EVIL?
I--I DON'T KNOW.
NEITHER DO I.

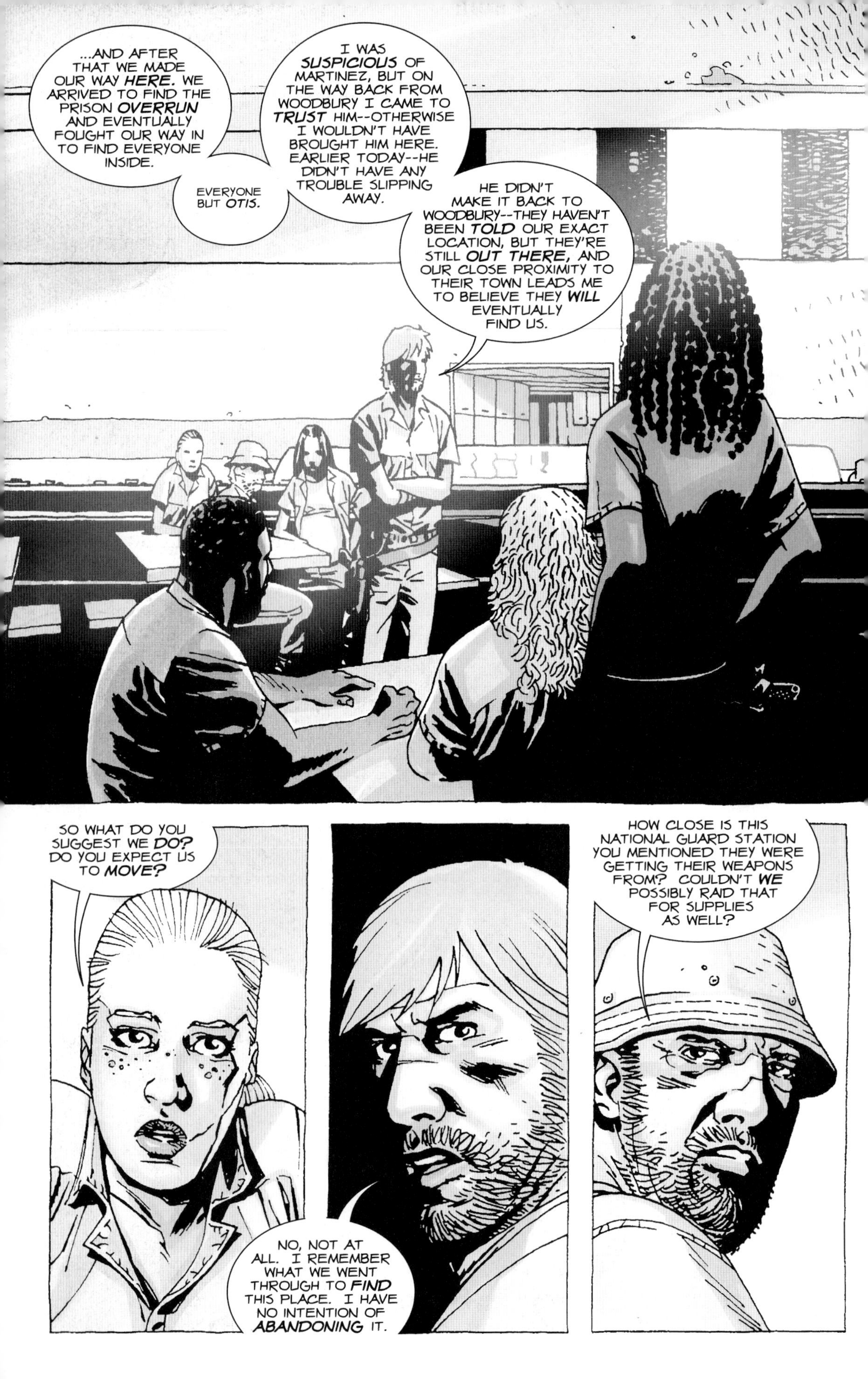
...AND AFTER THAT WE MADE OUR WAY HERE. WE ARRIVED TO FIND THE PRISON OVERRUN AND EVENTUALLY FOUGHT OUR WAY IN TO FIND EVERYONE INSIDE.
EVERYONE BUT OTIS.
I WAS SUSPICIOUS OF MARTINEZ, BUT ON THE WAY BACK FROM WOODBURY I CAME TO TRUST HIM--OTHERWISE I WOULDN'T HAVE BROUGHT HIM HERE. EARLIER TODAY--HE DIDN'T HAVE ANY TROUBLE SLIPPING AWAY.
HE DIDN'T MAKE IT BACK TO WOODBURY--THEY HAVEN'T BEEN TOLD OUR EXACT LOCATION, BUT THEY'RE STILL OUT THERE, AND OUR CLOSE PROXIMITY TO THEIR TOWN LEADS ME TO BELIEVE THEY WILL EVENTUALLY FIND US.
SO WHAT DO YOU SUGGEST WE DO? DO YOU EXPECT US TO MOVE?
NO, NOT AT ALL. I REMEMBER WHAT WE WENT THROUGH TO FIND THIS PLACE. I HAVE NO INTENTION OF ABANDONING IT.
HOW CLOSE IS THIS NATIONAL GUARD STATION YOU MENTIONED THEY WERE GETTING THEIR WEAPONS FROM? COULDN'T WE POSSIBLY RAID THAT FOR SUPPLIES AS WELL?

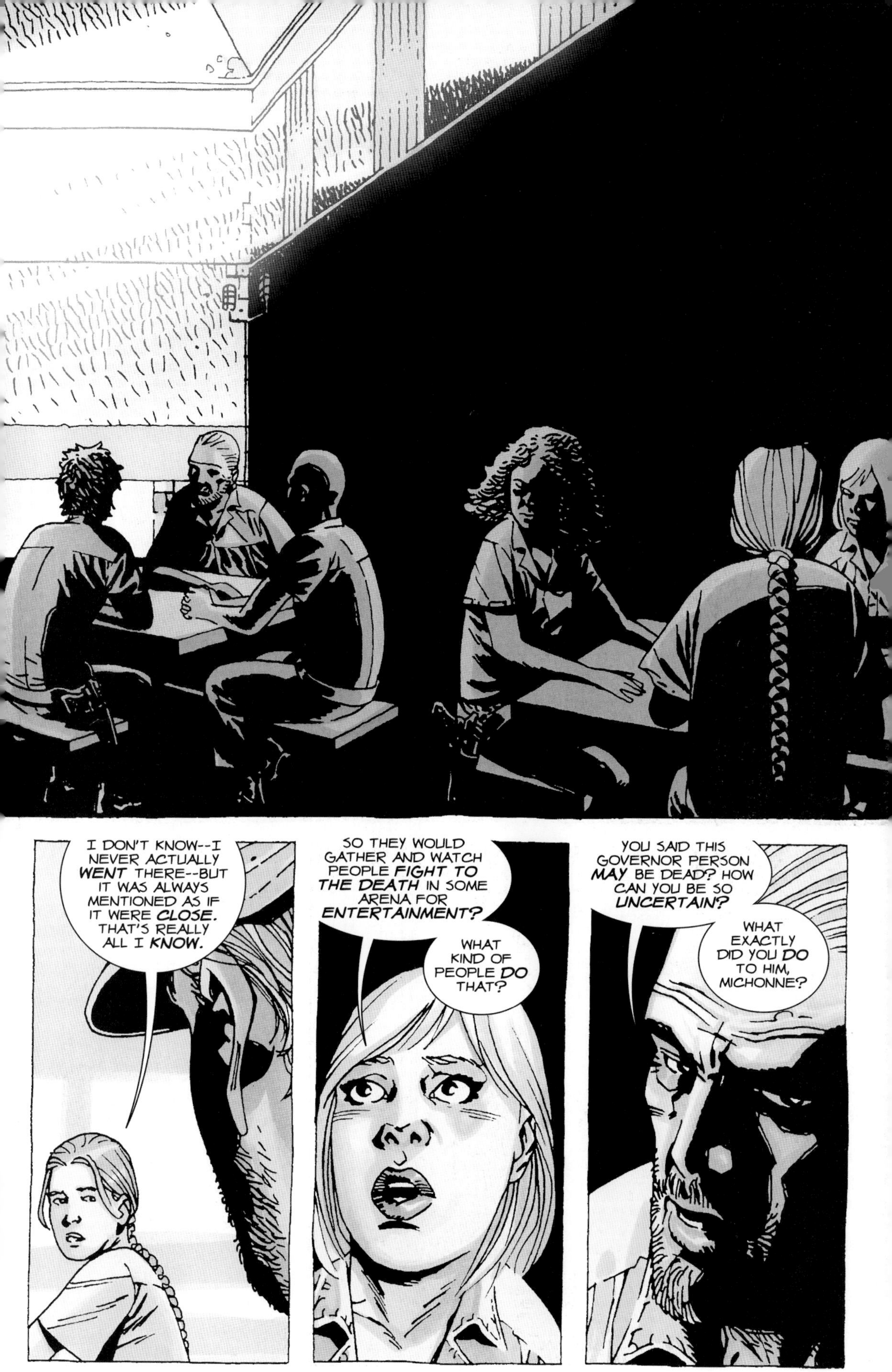

I DON'T KNOW--I NEVER ACTUALLY WENT THERE--BUT IT WAS ALWAYS MENTIONED AS IF IT WERE CLOSE. THAT'S REALLY ALL I KNOW.
SO THEY WOULD GATHER AND WATCH PEOPLE FIGHT TO THE DEATH IN SOME ARENA FOR ENTERTAINMENT?
WHAT KIND OF PEOPLE DO THAT?
YOU SAID THIS GOVERNOR PERSON MAY BE DEAD? HOW CAN YOU BE SO UNCERTAIN?
WHAT EXACTLY DID YOU DO TO HIM, MICHONNE?

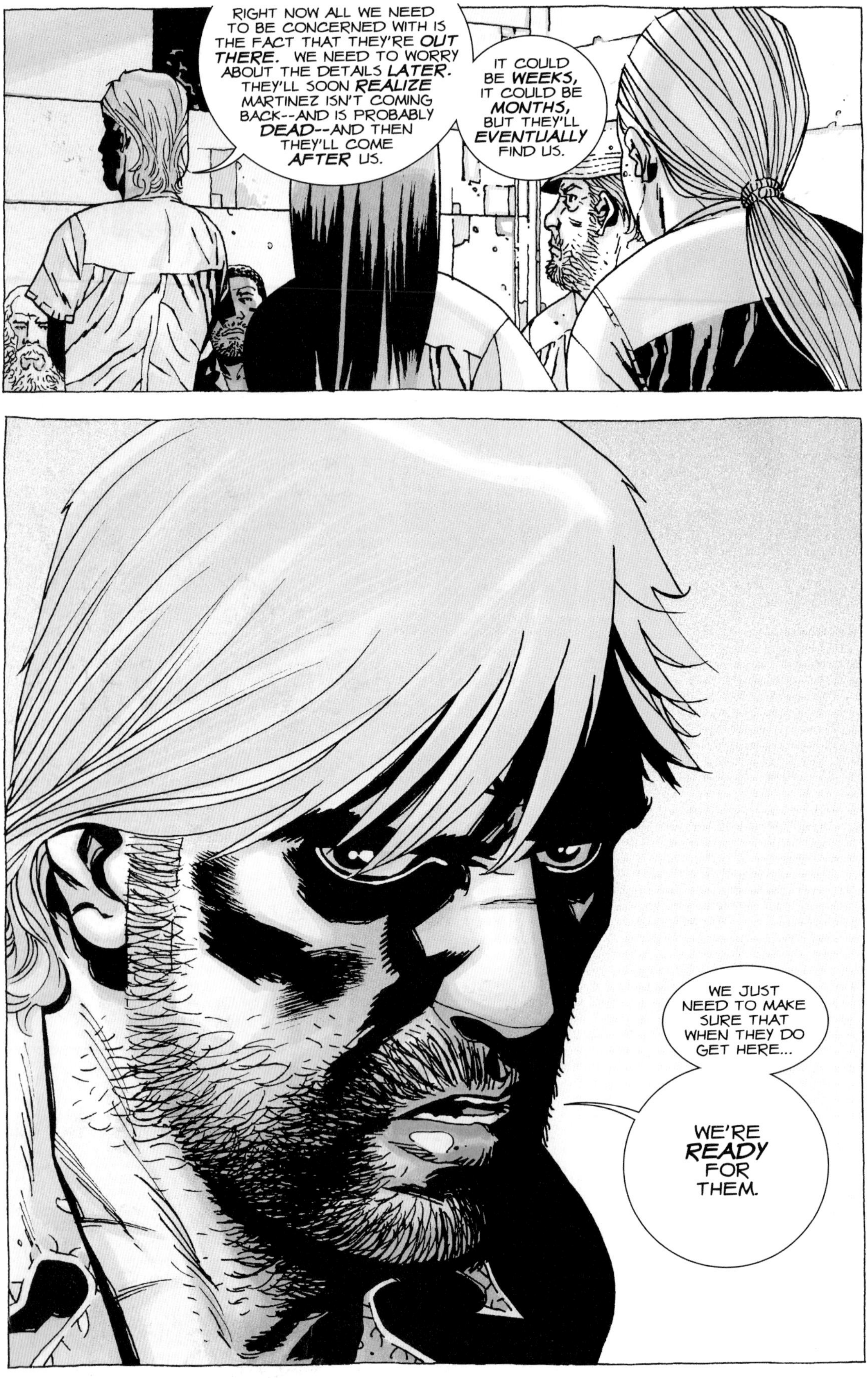
RIGHT NOW ALL WE NEED TO BE CONCERNED WITH IS THE FACT THAT THEY'RE OUT THERE. WE NEED TO WORRY ABOUT THE DETAILS LATER. THEY'LL SOON REALIZE MARTINEZ ISN'T COMING BACK--AND IS PROBABLY DEAD--AND THEN THEY'LL COME AFTER US.
IT COULD BE WEEKS, IT COULD BE MONTHS, BUT THEY'LL EVENTUALLY FIND US.
WE JUST NEED TO MAKE SURE THAT WHEN THEY DO GET HERE...
WE'RE READY FOR THEM.

TO BE CONTINUED...

MORE GREAT BOOKS FROM ROBERT KIRKMAN & IMAGE COMICS!

THE ASTOUNDING WOLF-MAN
VOL. 1 TP
ISBN: 978-1-58240-862-0
$14.99
VOL. 2 TP
ISBN: 978-1-60706-007-9
$14.99
VOL. 3 TP
ISBN: 978-1-60706-111-3
$16.99
VOL. 4 TP
ISBN: 978-1-60706-249-3
$16.99

BATTLE POPE
VOL. 1: GENESIS TP
ISBN: 978-1-58240-572-8
$14.99
VOL. 2: MAYHEM TP
ISBN: 978-1-58240-529-2
$12.99
VOL. 3: PILLOW TALK TP
ISBN: 978-1-58240-677-0
$12.99
VOL. 4: WRATH OF GOD TP
ISBN: 978-1-58240-751-7
$9.99

BRIT
VOL. 1: OLD SOLDIER TP
ISBN: 978-1-58240-678-7
$14.99
VOL. 2: AWOL
ISBN: 978-1-58240-864-4
$14.99
VOL. 3: FUBAR
ISBN: 978-1-60706-061-1
$16.99

CAPES
VOL. 1: PUNCHING THE CLOCK TP
ISBN: 978-1-58240-756-2
$17.99

HAUNT
VOL. 1 TP
ISBN: 978-1-60706-154-0
$9.99
VOL. 2 TP
ISBN: 978-1-60706-229-5
$16.99

THE INFINITE
VOL. 1 TP
ISBN: 978-1-60706-475-6
$9.99

INVINCIBLE
VOL. 1: FAMILY MATTERS TP
ISBN: 978-1-58240-711-1
$12.99
VOL. 2: EIGHT IS ENOUGH TP
ISBN: 978-1-58240-347-2
$12.99

VOL. 3: PERFECT STRANGERS TP
ISBN: 978-1-58240-793-7
$12.99
VOL. 4: HEAD OF THE CLASS TP
ISBN: 978-1-58240-440-2
$14.95
VOL. 5: THE FACTS OF LIFE TP
ISBN: 978-1-58240-554-4
$14.99
VOL. 6: A DIFFERENT WORLD TP
ISBN: 978-1-58240-579-7
$14.99
VOL. 7: THREE'S COMPANY TP
ISBN: 978-1-58240-656-5
$14.99
VOL. 8: MY FAVORITE MARTIAN TP
ISBN: 978-1-58240-683-1
$14.99
VOL. 9: OUT OF THIS WORLD TP
ISBN: 978-1-58240-827-9
$14.99
VOL. 10: WHO'S THE BOSS TP
ISBN: 978-1-60706-013-0
$16.99
VOL. 11: HAPPY DAYS TP
ISBN: 978-1-60706-062-8
$16.99
VOL. 12: STILL STANDING TP
ISBN: 978-1-60706-166-3
$16.99
VOL. 13: GROWING PAINS TP
ISBN: 978-1-60706-251-6
$16.99
VOL. 14: THE VILTRUMITE WAR TP
ISBN: 978-1-60706-367-4
$19.99
VOL. 15: GET SMART TP
ISBN: 978-1-60706-498-5
$16.99
ULTIMATE COLLECTION, VOL. 1 HC
ISBN 978-1-58240-500-1
$34.95
ULTIMATE COLLECTION, VOL. 2 HC
ISBN: 978-1-58240-594-0
$34.99
ULTIMATE COLLECTION, VOL. 3 HC
ISBN: 978-1-58240-763-0
$34.99
ULTIMATE COLLECTION, VOL. 4 HC
ISBN: 978-1-58240-989-4
$34.99
ULTIMATE COLLECTION, VOL. 5 HC
ISBN: 978-1-60706-116-8
$34.99
ULTIMATE COLLECTION, VOL. 6 HC
ISBN: 978-1-60706-360-5
$34.99
ULTIMATE COLLECTION, VOL. 7 HC
ISBN: 978-1-60706-509-8
$39.99
THE OFFICIAL HANDBOOK OF THE INVINCIBLE UNIVERSE TP
ISBN: 978-1-58240-831-6
$12.99

INVINCIBLE PRESENTS,
VOL. 1: ATOM EVE & REX SPLODE TP
ISBN: 978-1-60706-255-4
$14.99
THE COMPLETE INVINCIBLE LIBRARY,
VOL. 2 HC
ISBN: 978-1-60706-112-0
$125.00
THE COMPLETE INVINCIBLE LIBRARY,
VOL. 3 HC
ISBN: 978-1-60706-421-3
$125.00
INVINCIBLE COMPENDIUM VOL. 1
ISBN: 978-1-60706-411-4
$64.99

THE WALKING DEAD
VOL. 1: DAYS GONE BYE TP
ISBN: 978-1-58240-672-5
$9.99
VOL. 2: MILES BEHIND US TP
ISBN: 978-1-58240-775-3
$14.99
VOL. 3: SAFETY BEHIND BARS TP
ISBN: 978-1-58240-805-7
$14.99
VOL. 4: THE HEART'S DESIRE TP
ISBN: 978-1-58240-530-8
$14.99
VOL. 5: THE BEST DEFENSE TP
ISBN: 978-1-58240-612-1
$14.99
VOL. 6: THIS SORROWFUL LIFE TP
ISBN: 978-1-58240-684-8
$14.99
VOL. 7: THE CALM BEFORE TP
ISBN: 978-1-58240-828-6
$14.99
VOL. 8: MADE TO SUFFER TP
ISBN: 978-1-58240-883-5
$14.99
VOL. 9: HERE WE REMAIN TP
ISBN: 978-1-60706-022-2
$14.99
VOL. 10: WHAT WE BECOME TP
ISBN: 978-1-60706-075-8
$14.99
VOL. 11: FEAR THE HUNTERS TP
ISBN: 978-1-60706-181-6
$14.99
VOL. 12: LIFE AMONG THEM TP
ISBN: 978-1-60706-254-7
$14.99
VOL. 13: TOO FAR GONE TP
ISBN: 978-1-60706-329-2
$14.99
VOL. 14: NO WAY OUT TP
ISBN: 978-1-60706-392-8
$14.99
VOL. 15: WE FIND OURSELVES TP
ISBN: 978-1-60706-392-6
$14.99
BOOK ONE HC
ISBN: 978-1-58240-619-0
$34.99

BOOK TWO HC
ISBN: 978-1-58240-698-5
$34.99
BOOK THREE HC
ISBN: 978-1-58240-825-5
$34.99
BOOK FOUR HC
ISBN: 978-1-60706-000-0
$34.99
BOOK FIVE HC
ISBN: 978-1-60706-171-7
$34.99
BOOK SIX HC
ISBN: 978-1-60706-327-8
$34.99
BOOK SEVEN HC
ISBN: 978-1-60706-439-8
$34.99
DELUXE HARDCOVER, VOL. 1
ISBN: 978-1-58240-619-0
$100.00
DELUXE HARDCOVER, VOL. 2
ISBN: 978-1-60706-029-7
$100.00
DELUXE HARDCOVER, VOL. 3
ISBN: 978-1-60706-330-8
$100.00
THE WALKING DEAD: THE COVERS,
VOL. 1 HC
ISBN: 978-1-60706-002-4
$24.99
THE WALKING DEAD SURVIVORS' GUIDE
ISBN: 978-1-60706-458-9
$12.99

REAPER
GRAPHIC NOVEL
ISBN: 978-1-58240-354-2
$6.95

SUPER DINOSAUR
VOL. 1
ISBN: 978-1-60706-420-6
$9.99
DELUXE COLORING BOOK
ISBN: 978-1-60706-481-7
$4.99

SUPERPATRIOT
AMERICA'S FIGHTING FORCE
ISBN: 978-1-58240-355-1
$14.99

TALES OF THE REALM
HARDCOVER
ISBN: 978-1-58240-426-0
$34.95
TRADE PAPERBACK
ISBN: 978-1-58240-394-6
$14.95

TECH JACKET
VOL. 1: THE BOY FROM EARTH TP
ISBN: 978-1-58240-771-5
$14.99

TO FIND YOUR NEAREST COMIC BOOK STORE, CALL: 1-888-COMIC-BOOK